DANYA

DANYA

A WOMAN
OF ANCIENT
GALILEE

ANNE MCGIVERN

RESOURCE *Publications* · Eugene, Oregon

Resource Publications
An Imprint of Wipf and Stock Publishers
199 W. 8th Ave., Suite 3
Eugene, OR 97401

www.wipfandstock.com

PAPERBACK ISBN: 978-1-5326-5279-0
HARDCOVER ISBN: 978-1-5326-5280-6
EBOOK ISBN: 978-1-5326-5281-3

Manufactured in the U.S.A.   03/13/18

CONTENTS

PART III: 13 TO 16 CE

Characters in this novel who are mentioned in historical accounts of the period or in Scripture include:

Judah ben Hezekiah, Simon of Perea, and Anthronges the Shepherd—leaders of rebel movements in ancient Palestine circa 4 BCE

Herod Archelaus—a son of Herod the Great. Appointed by Rome to govern the Roman territories of Judea, Idumea, and Samaria

Herod Antipas—also a son of Herod the Great. Appointed by Rome to govern the territories of Perea and Galilee

Chuza—Chief Steward of Herod Antipas

Joanna, Chuza's wife—one of the early followers of Yeshua of Nazareth

Quintilius Varus—Roman legate of the province of Syria

Saddok the Pharisee—leader of a census rebellion circa 6 CE

Hanina ben Dosa—Jewish sage and miracle worker

Miryam, Yosef, Yaakov, Joses, Yeshua, Simon, Judas—members of a family from Nazareth

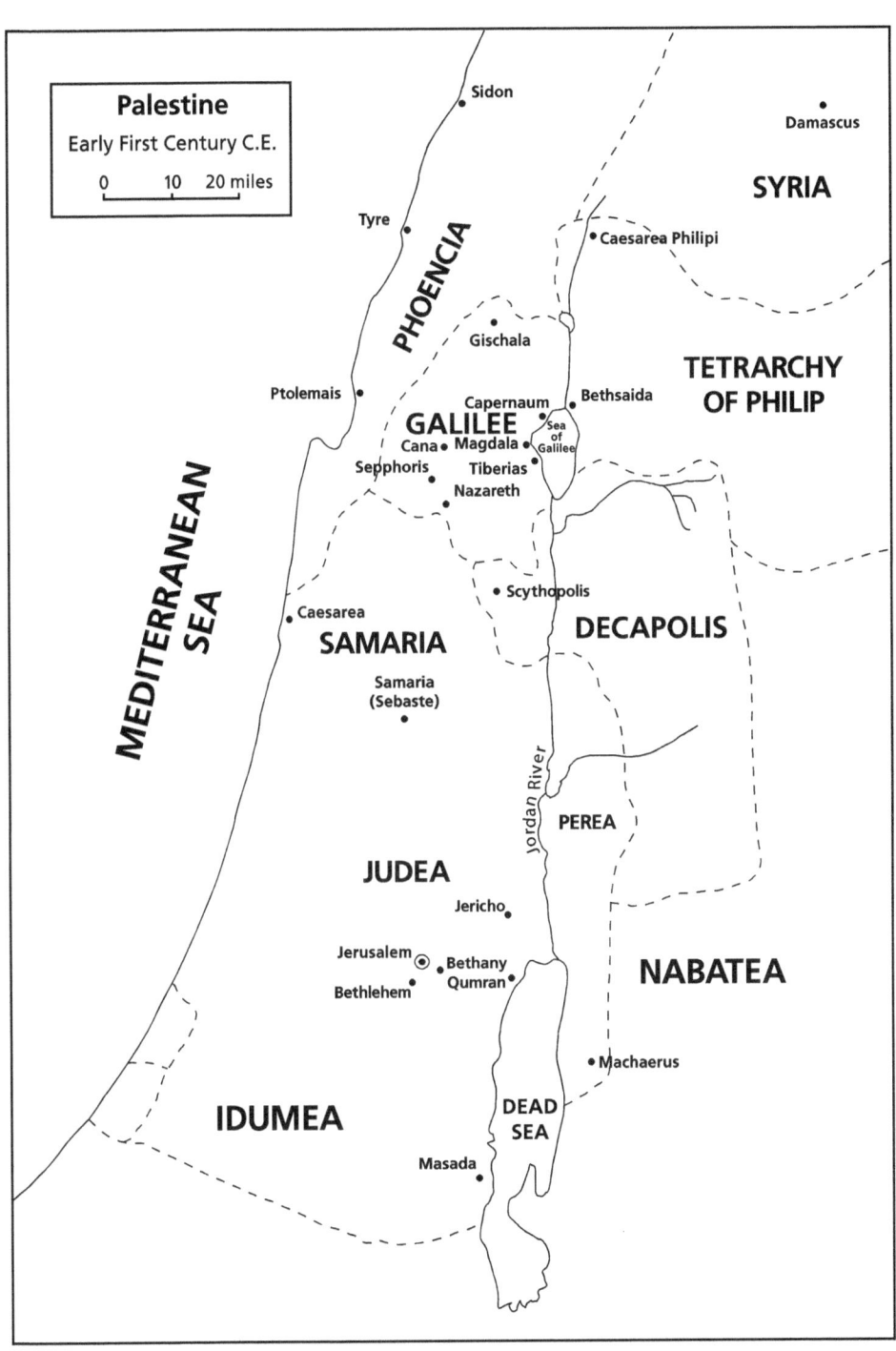

PART 1:
4 TO 3 BCE

THE RAID

My first sensation upon awakening that night was an unusual silence, the absence of my brother Lev's restless sleep-breathing. His empty mat signaled that the moment had finally arrived: the raid on Sepphoris, the Roman capital city of Galilee, would take place tonight. But Lev had snuck off to join the rebels without me! I tightened the combs in my braided hair and donned the clothing I'd hidden under my mat. Disguised in the head covering and tunic of a young man, I crept by my father, sleeping in the other room, and slipped out the door. I was a swift runner; I would catch up to Lev and participate in this holy adventure with him.

The village was quiet; all of Nazareth was holding its breath. The only sound was the slap of my sandaled feet against the hardened dirt of the footpath leading up the hill and away from the village. The full moon's light illuminated each rock and twisted root along my way, so I moved quickly without harm. I thought that the brightness was a good omen; a sign that this truly was The Holy One's plan for me. That like my heroine Esther, who also had lost her mother at an early age, I, too, had been chosen to save our people from the enemy. Just last week, Lev had sworn me to silence, then revealed the plans for the upcoming raid to me. When I'd begged to participate in it, he rebuked me harshly. "Danya, you're a thirteen-year-old girl! You can't come with me!" But I would follow my brother until, as usual, he would give in.

As I climbed, I imagined myself infiltrating the Roman enemy's armory in Sepphoris. I could almost feel the sting of the gladius' blade when I would test its point with my fingertip. I flexed my wrist, gauging its strength, and determined it would be strong enough to hoist a javelin onto my shoulder. We would spurn the cumbersome Roman shields and breastplates since they didn't suit our style of fighting. After the armory we would steal our way on to the treasury. I conjured up the hushed chill of the imperial vault and the clinking of gold coins dropping into my sack. This money would fuel the fires of revolution and incite the land of Judah to rebel against Roman domination. I dared to envision myself crowned with an olive wreath by my people, like my other heroine, Judith. I, too, would be bold enough to go down a mountain and cross a valley to the camp of Israel's enemy in order to save our people.

I reached the top of the ridge bordering our village. From this vantage point, I hoped to spot the raiding party stealing its way across the Netopha valley and run fast enough to catch up to them. People always said that Lev and I looked alike. We were close in height and had heavy eyebrows. Our noses were straight as styluses. And since my tunic easily concealed my small breasts, I might yet be able to slip unnoticed into the ranks of these young men.

But nothing stirred in the vineyards below me, or in the olive groves below them, or in the grain fields of the valley. No smoke or fire spewed from the city on the hill. Sepphoris appeared as calm and haughty as always. It was possible that Lev and his band had decided not to attack tonight and had instead gone out into the countryside to train. I'd have to wait on this overlook until I could discern their whereabouts.

Suddenly, from the valley below, a small dust cloud spiraled up from the dry bed of the Nahal Zippori River. I squinted and watched hungrily as another dust cloud arose, then another, and another, and another. These swirling towers appeared to stretch from the floor of the valley all the way up to the heavens. Sand and grit springing up from the flying footsteps of the revolutionaries must have created them. A sign of the coming of the Lord's Kingdom! The moment to advance and triumph had finally arrived!

I pulled my head covering tightly around my face, leaving only my eyes exposed, and started running down the hill to join the freedom fighters, then stopped in the vineyard halfway down the hill and narrowed my eyes to examine the clouds more closely. The dust towers billowed and drifted into one another, forming an arch that floated over and across the valley. But the arch was sweeping *away* from the marble and lime-stone buildings of the city on the hill—rolling *away* from Sepphoris—not towards it.

My stomach pitched as I realized that the dust clouds were blowing towards me because the footsteps creating it were heading east. The assault on Sepphoris had already taken place. The insurgents were flee-ing with their spoils. Jewish revolutionaries had plundered the Roman capital of Galilee—and I had been left behind!

Struck with a sudden, violent dizziness, I had to sit down and lower my head between my knees. Why was my brother Lev chosen, but not me? Like him, I burned with the desire to please Adonai. I was as strong and as clever as he was. I could recite even more of the Torah than he could. Then I cried, "Just like a girl," as the village boys would have taunted.

Dawn seeped in as the rebel troop headed straight towards my hill-side. I dried my face with my sleeve. There would be other raids in other places. Maybe I could still join them. I squatted among the vines to conceal myself and watch their approach. No one pursued them. The spies must've been right: most of the city's Roman auxiliary had left for Jerusalem to help maintain order during the upcoming Passover celebra-tions. The few guards left behind would have been no match for these dedicated revolutionaries.

The band followed their leader into the olive grove below me. Individual shapes emerged as the dust clouds settled. I tried to spot my brother, thin-shouldered, his gait a prowl, but many of the young men looked like him. Silent except for some coughing as they caught their breaths, the rebels slumped against the olive trees. Their sacks of weap-ons and coins clunked onto the ground.

I'd never before seen their leader, Judah ben Hezekiah, though I'd heard much about him. He was a Galilean from a village north of ours. It was said that, as a boy, Judah had witnessed his father's beheading by King Herod's soldiers, and that he had vowed then to carry on his father's work. Some called him an Anointed One or a resistance chieftain; others said he was merely a thief. Though Judah ben Hezekiah appeared to be not much older than Lev, he had a powerful build, far more muscular than my brother's. Bloodstains, rust-colored like his hair, spattered his tunic.

I crawled down through more rows of vines and got myself very close to the group. A tremor of hushed exhilaration rippled through their ranks. They had looted a treasury and an armory of the Emperor Augustus. Tiny Galilee had hurled its sling at the Roman giant. The weapons amassed to subjugate our people would now liberate us. A whoop of triumph, Lev's voice, shot up from the olive grove.

"Shut up," Judah snarled.

I spotted my brother when his leader kicked him in the stomach. Lev's startled moan echoed in my throat.

"No celebrating until we get to the caves of Arbel!" Judah rasped. "Get up! We have many miles to go to reach safety." He paced back and forth among the reclining men. "Stand! Fall into formation!" he commanded. When a few resisted, he taunted them, calling them "women."

Judah's stony eyes scanned the hillside for intruders. I squeezed myself under a staked vine, trying to make myself invisible. Leaves scraped my forehead. I held my breath and waited for the blow of Judah's foot. How could I shield myself from Judah's censure since even my brother had been unable to? Though I assumed that Roman generals treated their soldiers cruelly, I had not expected a Jewish leader to brutalize his own fighters.

The rebels, grumbling, stood, shouldered their sacks, and set out. Peering out through the greenery, I saw Judah draw his sword and raise it over his head like an army's standard. Its blade reflected the rays of the rising sun. "No master but God!" he proclaimed.

The ragged column set off, heading northeast, with Judah in the lead. Lev fell in at the rear. He was hunched over, trying to keep up, with one hand dragging his sack of plunder and the other clutching his stomach. Immobilized by fear, I could not run after him. But I like to think he looked up and caught a glimpse of me—or knew I'd be on the hillside—because he removed his hand from his stomach and threw a kiss in my direction.

I scrambled back to the top of the ridge and balanced atop its two highest rocks. A wind whipped up, sealing the freedom fighters into their dust cloud while I watched the whirl of sacred purpose move on without me.

PREPARATIONS FOR FLIGHT

Returning to the village quivering with rage at myself, at Lev, even at The Holy One, I stubbed my toes on the very rocks and roots I'd avoided earlier. I'd been left behind, certainly by Lev and perhaps by The Holy One as well. Did I lack the courage to answer His call? Or had I not been chosen because I was a girl? But The Holy One knew that I was different from the other girls. I was smarter, faster, and stronger. I wasn't meant for the small life of a village woman. I was capable of so much more!

Nazareth was still asleep as I ran through it. Pressing my ear to the door covering of our two-room house, I listened with relief to the sound of Father's fitful snoring. I tiptoed to my mat in the back room, lay down, and curled myself around my newly hatched resentment, as if it were an eaglet fallen from the nest and needed my protection to stay alive.

Father's habit was to rise before me for prayer and study and then to rouse me to prepare our breakfast. But this morning, as I was still pretending to sleep, loud voices in the courtyard outside our doorway disturbed us both.

"Wake up, Micah!"

"We are in grave danger."

"You're the rosh ha-knesset. You must do something."

"It's time for action, not reflection!"

Father hated to be pulled away from his studies. I heard him sigh loudly, and the parchment scrolls crinkle as he rolled them up. The shouting outside grew more insistent. Quickly, I put on my own tunic and folded up my mat. As I emerged from my room, Father was plodding to the doorway to face five agitated men.

"What's all this shouting about?" he said distractedly. He rubbed at the ache that resided in his hip.

Aaron, one of Father's pupils, spoke first. "Some shepherds have just awakened the whole village with their shouting about a band of fifty men they saw fleeing from Sepphoris. These men lugged heavy sacks, though what those sacks contained or who the men were, the shepherds couldn't say. But they were sure that Judah ben Hezekiah led them."

"Judah ben Hezekiah?" Father smoothed his long, unruly beard with his ink-stained fingers. "They're certain it was he?"

"They said they would swear so on the Torah," said Aaron.

Father straightened up and spoke with uncharacteristic force. "Gather all the information you can. Speak to everyone. The whole village must assemble. This very evening."

After the men left, Father asked me where Lev was. I shrugged and busied myself with the breakfast preparations, practicing the lie—not really a lie—that I would tell if he or anyone asked me about the raid. "I'm only a girl. How could I know anything?"

And why would I know anything? After all, girls learned only domestic skills, and these were taught by women. Most boys hardly spoke to their sisters, unless it was to order them around. But my brother was different. Our mother had died when we were very young; Lev was four and I was two. With our older half-brother Chuza living in Jerusalem, and our father often absorbed by his teaching and the village's knesset affairs, Lev and I were frequently left to ourselves as we grew up. My brother taught me the lessons boys learned: how to throw a sling, pin a wrestling opponent, debate the lessons of the Torah, and keep an accounting of money. He shared with me the knowledge of the world beyond our little village that he was able to gather. As long as I had finished my chores, Father allowed me to observe when he instructed Lev and the other boys in reading and writing; but it was Lev, in private, who showed me how to form the letters on a wax tablet and to read the words of the Torah from the scrolls. We had always kept each other's secrets. I loved him fiercely.

As it turned out, I wasn't called upon to lie. A ripe apricot lasted longer than a secret in our village. By late afternoon, everyone knew the names of the three young men from Nazareth who had joined Judah's band. Also the six from the town of Japha, the two from Gaba, and the three from Besara. Everyone had also learned that Judah and his followers had looted Sepphoris's treasury and arsenal and killed five of its guards during the raid.

In the evening, we gathered in the village's common area around the olive and wine presses, the same place where we met twice a week to pray, trade, and conduct village business. Our knesset had twelve elected leaders, including Father. Usually our assembly was a happy time, but today fear and anger furrowed the faces of my people. The men, smelling of freshly tilled earth and the sheep and goats they tended, clustered in the center. The women clumped silently on the fringes, clutching their young children tightly and ordering their older ones to stay near them.

Father and the other knesset leaders stood on an elevated stone platform in the middle of the knot of men. Father looked tall and distinguished up there. On level ground, he was a handbreadth shorter than Lev and me. The assembly opened with the shema', *"Hear, O Israel, the Lord our God, the Lord is one; and you shall love the Lord your God with all your heart, and with all your soul, and with all your might."* Conversation faded as the prayers continued. *"Graciously favor us, our Father, with understanding from Thee, and discernment and insight out of Thy Torah. Blessed art Thou, O Lord, gracious bestower of understanding. Behold our afflictions—"*

"Our afflictions," shouted tiny Samuel, who was perched atop the olive press. "We're here to discuss our afflictions."

Namir screamed and shook his fist at the knesset leaders. "Yes, get to the point—the afflictions Rome will send our way when they find their capital city has been looted!"

Ze'ev, Samuel's father, rattled his walking stick at my father. "This is your fault, Micah." His voice quavered with age and fury. "You incited your son and those boys with your Lord's Kingdom blather!"

Aaron's father stood up on the bench where Ze'ev sat. "You even taught your girl to read, you fool. You're supposed to teach Torah, not revolution!"

A stone landed near Father. Several women standing near me backed away. More accusations were flung at Father, and the space between the women and me widened. I stared at them and turned up my nose, but a little voice within me cried, "Mama, Papa." My fear of losing Father, buried in a cave deep within my heart, sprang out from its confinement. But at that moment, my friends Naomi and Miryam and their mothers pushed through the cold circle enlarging around me and grasped my hands.

Father held up his arms and shouted, "*Enough!*" The strength of his voice surprised me. His eyes burned with intensity. "I have never counseled violence. You know that I oppose it."

The denouncements faded. Though Lev often complained that Father's scholarship was useless, most of the villagers respected him for it. Father's learning, which he had brought with him from Jerusalem many years ago, gave him power in our little world.

The men then turned on each other and argued about the attack. Our neighbor Amos raised his arms in praise of it. "Away with the Roman infidels and their Jewish allies!" he declared.

"The Romans steal our land; they tax us into poverty; they worship false gods," cried Oron. "It's time we drove them out. These brave rebels are showing us the way."

Another leader of the knesset quoted the prophet Isaiah. "*I will contend with those who contend with you, and I will save your children.*"

"*Silence.*" Father's voice rose above all the others. "We haven't assembled to debate the wisdom of this attack. It has happened, and, though we don't know when or in what way, there will be retaliation. We must decide how to protect our people and property from Roman vengeance."

The assembly dragged on into the night, but after much wrangling, decisions were made. Most people agreed that it was best to flee and seek safety elsewhere, taking their valuables and animals with them. Since it was so close to the harvest, some people insisted on staying behind to bring it in. They would store or sell the flax, barley, and wheat and then they, too, would flee. In the meantime, the Jebel Qafzeh caves south of the village would be provisioned as hiding places for them.

Back in our house after the meeting, Father fell asleep sitting upright on our dining bench. I laid a barley loaf, olives, and dates on the table and kissed the shock of thick white hair that crowned his head. "Supper is ready, Father."

At mealtimes, Father was usually quiet and distracted by his own thoughts. "What mysteries is he unraveling, what truths is he formulating?" Lev would whisper, and then make me laugh by imitating Father's faraway gaze and his laborious chewing of food.

But tonight Father fixed his eyes on me throughout our meal, studying me as if I were a difficult text. His attentiveness made me anxious. I worried that he might know of my attempt to follow Lev and that I would be punished for it.

When we finished eating, Father said, "I'm going to take you to Jerusalem, Danya. You'll stay there with your brother Chuza until it's safe for you to return to Nazareth."

Father rarely spoke the name of his son Chuza, the only child of his first marriage. Five lonely years after the death of his first wife, Chuza's mother, Father married Nahara, the woman who became the mother of Lev and me. My half-brother Chuza had gone off to Jerusalem when I was very young, so I hardly knew him.

Lev had the courage to fight for our people. I must be brave enough to tell Father I wanted to do the same. With my eyes down, but my voice firm, I said, "No. Not to Chuza's. I want to go with Lev. To join his group."

"That's no place for you, daughter."

Heat flamed up my neck and onto my face. "It may be The Holy One's will for me. These men are heroes, Papa. They will free our people. I want to do that, too."

He tugged at his beard. "They're not heroes. And armed revolt won't liberate us."

"If I can't go to Lev, I'll wait here for him. He'll come back for me."

Father stood and walked over to the doorway. He pushed back its covering and stared out at the darkness. "It breaks my heart that your brother has joined this violent movement. Lev may never come back; I may have lost another son."

I blinked hard to keep my tears from spilling over. "He will come back someday, Papa. I know it."

Father left the doorway and sat next to me. Gently, he lifted my chin until my eyes met his gaze. "And if he does, I will be here to shelter him. I'm needed here. I plan to return to Nazareth once you're settled in Jerusalem. You'll see Lev when it's safe for both of you here."

I knew my father was being kind and protective. But scalding tears erupted from my eyes at the prospect of having to live in a strange city with a half-brother I barely knew. I slammed my wooden plate on the table and broke it in two. "Chuza is a Roman collaborator, and you know it. That's why we don't see him anymore, isn't it?"

Father enclosed my work-roughened hands in his. "Chuza is an important man in Jerusalem. He can protect you, and that's what matters now. I can't risk losing you, too, my little light."

I bit the insides of my cheeks until I tasted blood. "I never get my way, Papa."

Father kissed my right palm and then my left. His tenderness drained the heat from me. "This is your way, Danya. You don't see it now, but you will. If you are searching for the Holy One's will, the first step is to stay alive."

Quickly, our villagers began to scatter like mustard seeds, flying with the wind from Galilee to wherever they had family or the possibility of work. Some went to other regions of the land of Judah, like Judea or Idumea. Others set out for Phoenicia or Syria or cities like Scythopolis that had large Jewish communities. Father planned that we would make the five-day journey to Jerusalem with a group of thirteen others from our village. Most of us hoped to return to Nazareth someday, but we had no idea when that would be.

The handful that chose to stay in the village believed they would prosper by harvesting their own fields and those of their absent neighbors. Our neighbor Amos and his wife elected to do this. Amos was already deeply in debt, as were many other men, and he feared losing his land if he were not there to bring in this harvest. I overheard Father and Amos speaking in low voices in the courtyard at night.

"I'll manage your orchard and garden, Micah," said Amos. "But I must ask a favor of you in return."

"Certainly."

"Take my daughter, Naomi, to Jerusalem with you."

My father was silent a long time. "My son Chuza will be under no obligation to support her, so I can't promise I will be able to find a good situation for her there."

"I know you'll do what you can. But, if necessary—"Amos stopped to blow his nose. "She can be sold. Better my daughter be a slave in Jerusalem than raped or murdered by Roman soldiers here."

I bit on my tunic to keep from crying out. Slaves in Jewish households served for seven years unless bought back by their relatives. Though Naomi's parents were vigorous, hard-working people, they had little chance of gathering up enough money to buy her back from slavery. Naomi might have to stay in Jerusalem for seven years!

Our friend Miryam was fleeing to Egypt with her parents, her husband Yosef, their new baby Yeshua, and Yosef's two sons from his first marriage. People tried to convince Yosef not to go so far, but he believed his family would not be safe anywhere in the land of Judah. Though there were jobs for talented carpenters in our own country, Yosef remained resolute about going to Egypt, insisting that he had had a dream instructing him to go there.

During that week following the raid on Sepphoris, Miryam, Naomi, and I spent many backbreaking hours at the grindstone milling the grain we'd need for our journeys. Our families had shared this grindstone, and the courtyard it sat in, all our lives. None of us had sisters, so we often eased the tedium of our grinding, spinning, and weaving chores by working together. Miryam was the older sister I wished I had; Naomi the younger one I rejoiced I didn't.

Being the smallest and youngest, Naomi had only to feed the kernels of grain into the mill and pour the ground meal into sacks. Miryam and I performed the actual grinding. Together we trudged in a circle, our arms straining against the weight of the heavy topstone as we pushed against the handle bolted to it. It was like wading through ankle-deep mud.

"Look at me. My hands are shaking," said Naomi. "I'm spilling the grain all over. Do you know I may have to be a servant in some stranger's house? Can you imagine that? My father says I may have to stay in Jerusalem for a long time. That it may not be safe here for me for several years. I could be an old woman before I see Nazareth again!" She bent over and hobbled around like some of the crones who congregated around the village well, then she tripped and fell down. She laughed at herself, her giggle fluttering around in her throat, then escaping and flickering about like a hummingbird. Annoying as her chatter was, her laughter lightened our hearts.

As Miryam and I continued pushing the grinding stone, Naomi continued babbling. "But at least I'm going to Jerusalem, not Egypt. Miryam, where did Yosef get such an idea? Egypt may be safe, but it's foreign. Are there any Jews there? You won't know the language. Who will you talk to?"

"Maybe Miryam won't be able to talk all the time," I said. "You should try it yourself sometime." Miryam gave the back of my leg a little kick, and I turned around to her and rolled my eyes.

Naomi didn't stop to take a breath. "I always thought Miryam should've married Lev. He's sooo good-looking. Those eyes of his: they burn right through you. And those full, pouty lips: dreamy. He was in love with you, Miryam, I'm sure of it. But after all, maybe you are better off. Having a bandit for a husband would be worse than having one who drags you off to Egypt."

"And you'll be lucky to find a husband who doesn't divorce you in a day," I said.

"So you're complimenting me on my husband?" Miryam asked. "Why, thank you!" Her wit sweetened, rather than stung like mine did.

"Yes. No," said Naomi. "I mean, yes, it's good you married Yosef after all, I guess. Is that what I mean?"

I squeezed the bar harder. "Do you ever know what you're saying, Naomi? You should have to listen to yourself, so you'd know how annoying you are. And, by the way, Lev is not a bandit!"

"Then what is he? Look at all the trouble he and his friends have caused us. My mother says . . ."

"I don't care what your mother says!" Naomi's dark bushy hair was two times the size of her tiny face. It looked like the top of a terebinth tree. I had an urge to pull it and dropped my hands from the grindstone handle to do just that.

Miryam grunted with the sudden burden of having to push the heavy stone herself. "Ouch! Danya, you need to tell me when you're going to stop." She rubbed the fingers of her right hand with her left, and her high forehead creased in pain.

"Sorry, Miryam." I placed my callused hands back on the grindstone's handle. Pulling Naomi's hair would be a waste of time, anyway. It wouldn't shut her mouth.

Miryam picked up the thread of our conversation. "Our family will be all right in Egypt. Yosef will find work there. And I'll be occupied with our three little boys to tend."

Miryam's absence would be a great loss to me. She was the gentle yet strong friend I'd always relied on. "How I wish I could go to Egypt with you, Miryam! I'm afraid of living in Jerusalem."

"What are you afraid of?" asked Miryam.

"Afraid that Chuza and his wife Joanna won't like me. Afraid that I'll be useless there. They already have servants. What will I do all day?" I wished I could have voiced my deeper fears. Not what would I do in Jerusalem, but what was my purpose anywhere? Was there something wrong with me that The Holy One hadn't chosen me for the task I'd thought was mine?

"If you don't have to work, you'll get to read," Miryam pointed out. "You're so blessed, Danya. The only girl in Nazareth who can read and write and now you'll have time to do both. And you'll see some strange and wonderful people and things in Jerusalem. When we're old women, sitting in this courtyard on warm evenings, you'll entertain us with fabulous stories of your days in Jerusalem."

"Oh, the Temple! The Temple! I have always wanted to see the Temple," interrupted Naomi. "To see if it's as beautiful as people say. And I'm dying to see your brother Chuza. Is he handsome like Lev?"

Miryam gave me a little kick to remind me to be patient.

"I forget what he looks like. He left Nazareth when I was four years old." I remembered very little about Chuza except that he would argue bitterly with Father. How strange memory is: though I couldn't remember Chuza's face, I recalled the hoarse timbre of his voice and the image of a scab on his clenched fist.

"I wonder what Chuza's wife is like? You told me that Joanna is a silk merchant's daughter, so she must have gorgeous clothes. Please don't read all day, Danya. Go to the shops with me."

I sighed loudly, vainly hoping Naomi would realize it was time to stop talking. "We won't have money to shop, Naomi."

"But we still can look. I hear there are stalls selling things from all over the world! Jewels and spices and leathers and linen and silk. Oh, maybe Joanna's father would give us a really good price on some silk."

"Stop it, stop it, stop it!" I said. "You've given me a headache."

"Fortunately, we've finished," said Miryam, giving the grindstone handle one last shove. "We have more than enough barley for our journeys." Miryam frowned in pain as she rubbed her aching palms.

I remembered what Lev had said once about Miryam as he was trying to talk himself out of his love for her. "She has red, rough hands and looks very ordinary, like any other girl in this village. Her front teeth are crooked, and her hair has hardly any curl. And yet, when she smiles and laughs, her eyes shine. And she is just so beautiful!"

At that moment Miryam turned her smile on Naomi and me. "I have something to give you before we're separated. Come this way." She led us up the same path I had run along in the quiet moonlight only a few nights before, up to the top of the Nazareth ridge. Today the hillsides were full of our villagers who were hastily picking any ripened fruit from their orchards and vines to carry away with them. Goats bleated, children cried, and people called to one another. We climbed up to the ridge's highest point, the same spot where I'd so recently experienced such bitter disappointment.

"I want to tell you a story," Miryam said, sitting down and wedging us together between two tall rocks. "Remember last year when my parents wanted me to marry Yosef? I'd seen him only once and I hadn't even met his two little boys. Deep down, I was anxious and confused about everything. Should I follow my parents' wishes and marry Yosef? But what if I never came to love him? Could I be a good mother to his children? What does The Holy One want me to do? What is my place in His plan?"

Naomi said, "I never worry about things like that."

"Of course not," I snapped.

"Why should I?" Naomi challenged.

"Stop, you two," Miryam said, and continued her story. "One wet, dark afternoon I came up here. I sat right where we are now. I prayed. I cried. I begged Adonai to give me a sign, to tell me what I should do. Then I stopped crying and just waited for an answer. Suddenly, the most amazing thing happened: a strong light broke through the clouds right over the valley below. It began moving quickly towards me."

Like my dust towers, I thought.

"Were you scared?" said Naomi. "I would've run away!"

"I was afraid so I hid behind these rocks. Then the light swept right to here . . . and stopped. It seemed to be waiting for me to say or do something."

Naomi interrupted, "I definitely would've run away at that point. Did you?"

"No. Although I didn't know what it wanted, I trusted it. It waited. It shimmered. It grew brighter and lovelier. It seemed to be inviting me in, pulling me into itself. It was so beautiful! I have no words to explain how it drew me to it. After some time—I can't say how long—I stepped into it. I said 'Yes.' That was all: just 'Yes.' Then it filled me with its brightness, and I felt myself glowing."

We were all silent until Naomi whispered, "Maybe the light was an angel. Did it smell? I hear angels smell like baking bread."

Miryam laughed. "No, it didn't smell. I don't know what an angel looks like, but this light that swirled around inside and around me was full of color—flaming orange and bright green and deep violet and sunrise pink. And full of sound, too. Babies laughing. Water lapping the shore. Doves cooing. It was full of life and so, so lovely. Then, gently, slowly, the light swept back to the cloud it had come from and disappeared."

"Were you sad when it left?" said Naomi.

"No, I was happy! My fears were gone. A peace settled upon my heart, a certainty that The Holy One cared for me and for all of our people, each one of us. And I knew that I was pleasing in His eyes. And I knew I should marry Yosef."

A bitter taste, as if I had sucked on the rim of a metal pot, puckered my mouth. The dust clouds had not swept me up. They had swirled off to the caves of Arbel without me.

"I was hoping that, coming to this same spot and hearing what happened to me, maybe you two could feel the peace that settled on me here. Of course we're all anxious, but I think that the light's message was that Adonai loves us, each one of us. I know He will be with each of us on every step of our journeys. The psalm says, '*I sought the Lord, and He answered me, and delivered me from all my fears.*' Pray with me, will you?"

Naomi laughed that ridiculous giggle of hers. "Delivered from all my fears sounds good. I'll give it a try."

To please Miryam, I prayed with them, though my prayer brought me no peace. I left the Nazareth ridge in anger and confusion. Miryam had sought answers, just as I had, and The Holy One had sent her a sign. She was pleasing to Him, even though she was a girl. He had a plan for her. She had been given the very blessing I had sought but been denied.

THE JOURNEY TO JERUSALEM

Another week passed as I prepared our household for our journey to Jerusalem. Father was of little help, consumed as he was by his fear of an imminent retaliatory invasion. He roamed the hilltops around Nazareth, scanning the horizon for signs of a Roman column on the march. He wandered from house to house in the village, monitoring each family's preparedness. When one family we planned to travel with encountered difficulties selling its livestock, and another had a sick baby, he decided we could wait no longer. Instead we would set out on our own and find other countrymen to travel with once we were out on the main road. With great care, he rolled protective calfskins around his scrolls and sealed them tightly into stone jars. The old donkey bore only this precious load. The younger one carried all our other provisions.

Naomi's parents and the few of our friends who had not yet departed walked with us to the edge of the village. Naomi and her mother wept and clung to each other, and Amos had to pry his wife and daughter apart so we could proceed. The familiar loneliness of having no mother seeped into my chest once again, but I clutched my father's hand and didn't look back. In my other hand I cupped some soil from our courtyard. I will return, I will return, someday I will return, I told myself with each step. Though my heart pulled backward, my feet moved forward, one regretful step at a time, throughout the whole long morning. Naomi sniffled for a long time until Father put her between the two of us and asked her to sing to cheer us all up.

We traveled east, which surprised me, because Lev had told me that a good road led straight south from Sepphoris to Jerusalem. But Father explained that the southern route passed through Samaria, considered a dangerous and unclean land. We would travel east to the Jordan River and follow it south almost to Jericho, then turn back west to Jerusalem.

All across Galilee, olive trees and trellised grapevines graced every hillside. Grain crops, mostly wheat and barley, flooded the valleys. Healthy pomegranate, almond, and fig orchards clustered around the villages. But the prosperity of the land did not match that of the people. In village after village, the children, listless with hunger, did not smile or raise their hands in greeting to us. Beggars squatted along the roadside. The first one we spoke to told us a bitter story, later repeated by others we met.

"I was a farmer. Rome demanded one-fifth of my crops as tribute; King Herod imposed other taxes; the Temple and its priests required its offerings and tithes." He stopped to gulp down the date cake we gave him, then held out his bony hand for another. "I had to borrow to meet all these obligations, and the debt crushed me. My creditors took over my land."

"Were your creditors Romans?" Father demanded.

"No. Jews. Wealthy Jews."

Father's eyes narrowed. "Was your land that of your ancestors, land given to your people by The Holy One?"

"Yes."

How strongly my father's scowl resembled Lev's.

We met men heading in the opposite direction, on their way out of Galilee. They, too, had been farmers, but, after losing their land, had left their families behind to migrate from estate to estate surviving on seasonal fieldwork. Others were heading to Caesarea Maritima to search for employment on the building projects there. Some were sharecroppers on the very land they used to own. They seemed to be the fortunate ones.

The afternoon sun shone harshly as we crossed our sad, beautiful land. The soles of our feet ached from the heat and the hard paving stones though only Naomi complained aloud about this. Passing carts raised a dust that lodged in our nostrils and wedged between our fingers. Dirt and perspiration clung to our clothes. We longed for shade and rest.

As we approached the town of Beit Yerah, an oak grove in the distance promised refreshment. Father said it contained a well and a space where we could spread a mat, eat some loaves and figs, and rest. However, as we drew closer to the grove, an odor of decomposition fouled the air. We slowed our steps. As we entered the grove, all was eerily silent. Women and children should have been drawing water, washing clothes, and gossiping there.

And then we saw them. Lashed to several of the smaller trees were the corpses of four crucified men. Their limbs were tied in grotesquely twisted positions, as if mocking their inability to flee their ghastly fate. One was postured against a tree trunk with his right knee raised and his left leg behind him like a runner's. The arms of another victim were tied to a tree's spreading branches and mimicked a bird's wings. Rats and dogs ravaged the naked corpses. Some of the beasts slinked off as we approached, but the vultures remained, hovering above the treetops, jealously guarding their food. The flies and maggots did not stir from their hideous work.

A board proclaimed in Latin and in Greek, "REBEL BANDITS. ENEMIES OF ROME." Lev. One of these putrefying corpses could be Lev! I closed my eyes and burrowed my head into Father's chest. Naomi shrieked and clutched him too. "It's not Lev," my father whispered over and over as he pushed us past this horror.

A short distance up the road, upwind of that grove of death, another beggar squatted and reached his hands imploringly towards us. Father extracted a loaf of bread from a pack on the donkey's back. "Why has no one from Beit Yerah buried those men?" he asked the crippled man whose eyes sank deep into their sockets

"The soldiers forbid it," said the beggar. "The rebels must stay on the trees until their bones are picked clean by the beasts, they say. The Romans swear they will return, and, if the crucified have been cut down, they will take innocent men from the town as replacements."

Father gave the man a loaf, and he tore into it ravenously. He looked like the starving beasts ripping into the corpses. Naomi and I fled, choking on our tears. Father hobbled along as best he could. Even the normally reluctant donkeys bolted ahead of us.

Eventually we caught up to a group of about fifteen refugees from Cana, a village not far from ours. Like us, they had stumbled onto the atrocity in the oak grove. Mothers and fathers held their children in their arms, even those far too old to be carried. We joined the stunned villagers from Cana and staggered on, mute with horror, until we reached the pebbly shore of the Sea of Galilee. The vast blue lake welcomed us, and we rushed into it, removing our head coverings, ladling cool water on our necks and faces, washing the images of death from our eyes, and calming ourselves until our exhaustion overcame our terror.

We dried off and set up a camp. From the donkey packs, I pulled out extra mantles for warmth and reed mats for ground cover. We didn't want to attract attention with a fire, so we ate stale barley loaves. I chipped a tooth on the hardened crust of mine. Darkness fell. I let Naomi put her mat next to mine, even though she kicked at night, and I held her until she stopped trembling. A line of clouds rolled across the moon; my eyes finally closed.

Sometime that night, before dreams had formed, I was awakened by fingers clutching my throat. A torch flared in the darkness. A faceless voice announced, "Give me your food, and I will not harm her."

Naomi whimpered beside me. Most of the group woke up in a daze. But Father stood up, fully alert, and fixed his gaze on the man who held me hostage. "Shalom, Judah ben Hezekiah," Father said calmly.

Judah ben Hezekiah, the leader of Lev's rebel band? Though one of my captor's hands was clasped around my neck, I could turn my head enough to see a red curl flashing out from under the man's head covering. It must be Judah ben Hezekiah. Lev might be close by!

Father opened his palms in appeasement. "We are poor people fleeing from Nazareth and Cana, driven from our homes by the threat of Roman vengeance. We're happy to share what food we have, though we don't have much."

Judah released me to draw his sword on the circle of people tightening in around him. He kept the torch in his other hand and ordered me to bring him the food. I fetched a sack of raisins, cakes of dried fruit, and a bag of barley flour. When I approached him with these, I could see his eyes in the light of his torch. A few nights ago from a distance, his eyes had seemed hard as stone. Tonight they looked like softened clay. That emboldened me, as did Father's presence right behind me. "Where is Lev ben Micah of Nazareth?" I asked.

Judah spat on the ground. "Lev deserted, the coward."

I remembered Judah's foot in Lev's stomach. "My brother is not a coward! You were cruel to him."

"How do you know?" Judah said. "Ah, so you were watching us that night?" He smiled in a way I didn't understand. He had all his teeth, and they were white and straight. "Lev told me he had a little sister with courage and dreams of being a revolutionary."

Then he softened his voice, speaking to me as if I were the only person there. "I disciplined your brother only that one time. He left my band after our attack on a Roman supply convoy. Some of my men were killed during the ambush. A few were captured and crucified by the Roman dogs." His eyes filled. The skin in the half moon below his lids was raw.

My hands shook as I held out the food to him. "We saw them at Beit Yerah."

But he turned from my offering and lowered his sword. "Since you are Galileans, you have suffered enough. Keep your food."

I knew then that all his men had deserted him. If he had troops to feed, he would have taken the food for them. Pity crowded against my anger. "What will you do now?" I said.

"Gather a new band and continue. I will not stop until the Lord's Kingdom has been restored to Israel. I have been chosen for this." Judah's voice was strong and heavy with conviction. So he, too, had been chosen. The Holy One had entrusted him with a special task. He was favored.

To me alone he whispered, "Maybe you should replace your brother." The soft rustle of his breath stirred through my hair. "In any camp, there is women's work that needs doing." His lips pulled out into a wide smile, revealing the long, sharply-pointed teeth farther back in his mouth.

Judah both attracted and repelled me. I couldn't determine whether he was a hero or a devil. An anointed one or a murderous brute. His suffering eyes said one thing; his hands around my neck another. A chill crept up my spine, but stopped at the spot on my throat where his fingerprints still burned. From there, a flame flashed through my entire body. Was this the call I sought? Was I being given another chance?

Father placed his hands firmly on my shoulders. "Come, Danya, our friend has to leave."

"Your brother has probably gone to the Essenes," Judah said, and withdrew into the darkness.

I heard him drag a boat from the shore and launch it into the Sea of Galilee. I imagined myself wading into the water and climbing into his boat. But I stayed on the shore as he rowed himself away, the light from his torch flickering faintly until it died.

The next morning, the group from Cana separated themselves from us. They believed it was too dangerous to travel with anyone associated with Judah ben Hezekiah. Alone again, Father, Naomi, and I turned south and followed the paths along the Jordan River for three days. Walking was easier for me than it was for Naomi and Father. I have big feet, and trailing after Lev had accustomed me to sustained physical exertion. Naomi complained that she was hot; then she was cold. She couldn't get to sleep; she couldn't wake up. She was frightened; she was bored. Father developed a limp and leaned heavily on his walking staff. He needed to rest often. Each time we stopped, he checked his treasured scrolls to make sure they were securely bound to the old donkey's back.

On our third day along the Jordan River path, we came across a forest ravaged by wildfire. The groundcover and shrubs had been reduced to ash; some of the trees still smoldered. Had we arrived there a day earlier, we could've been caught in those flames. Naomi and I held hands as we picked our way through the blackened landscape.

All along the Jordan River, Roman forts, menacing reminders of the crucifixions we'd witnessed, loomed above us. At night, jackals and leopards hunted in the nearby hills, and the screeches of their victims pierced our restless sleep. We knew that thieves preyed on pilgrim groups enroute to Jerusalem, and this threat gnawed away at us. Our only weapon was Father's staff.

Throughout our long trek along the river, I often thought about Lev, and wondered where he was and what he would be doing now. Father must know more about this than he was telling me. "Are the Essenes foreigners, Father?" I asked.

"No," he answered sharply, maneuvering around a huge rock that had fallen onto the path.

"Magicians? Bandits? Soldiers?"

"No. No. And no."

"Who *are* they then?"

"Jews, like us. I need to catch my breath. Sit on this log with me and be quiet."

"What kind of Jews—Pharisees? Sadducees? Zealots?"

"None of those."

"Why are they called Essenes?"

"I don't know. Please get me some water."

While I filled the water jug, Naomi stayed on the log with Father. "My father calls the Essenes 'Sons of Light," she said.

"Some do call them that."

"Where do they live?" I demanded.

"Qumran."

"Where is Qumran?"

"In the desert."

"Do they live anywhere else?"

"Probably. Let's just keep walking. I'm getting no rest anyway."

His habit of secrecy infuriated me. The parents of my friends told stories about growing up in Nazareth, marrying the spouse chosen for them by their families and gradually falling in love with that person. They talked about their aunts, uncles, cousins, and in-laws. I knew more about Naomi's and Miryam's families than I did about my own. I knew only that Father and his first wife had had one child, Chuza, and that they had lived in Jerusalem. After this wife died, Father and Chuza moved to Nazareth, where Father met and married Mother, who had fled from the country of Nabatea to our village. Mother was much younger than Father, closer in age to my half-brother Chuza than she was to Father. Her name was Nahara, which means "light." I couldn't remember what she looked like, but my fingertips still held the memory of the soft curve of her cheek and the dip of the dimple in her chin. I longed to know more about her. And about Father. I began to suspect that Lev was wrong: Father was silent not because he was thinking great thoughts, but because he was keeping great secrets. I would not give up.

"What do the Essenes, these 'Sons of Light' do?" I asked Father, as we waded across a flooded stretch of the pathway.

"They prepare to fight the Sons of Darkness."

"Who are the Sons of Darkness?"

"Their enemies, of course."

"I'm tired of hearing about these strange people," Naomi said. "And look, I dropped my sandals and now they're soaked."

"Who are their enemies?" I probed. "Romans? Other Gentiles? Jews?"

"They have many enemies."

"Do you think any Essenes live in Jerusalem?"

"Probably. We should sit and dry our feet now."

The tiny possibility of finding Lev with the Essenes in Jerusalem caused my feet to dance along the gnarled river path. For the first time since we had left Nazareth, I didn't worry about thieves, Romans, snakes, or thunderstorms. I carried the hope of seeing Lev again with me, in my hands. My hope was a real thing, warm and soft and pliable, like a wineskin.

After we had hiked in silence for some time, Father spoke without my having to prod him. "Danya, the Essenes are a male sect. Women can't be members. You weren't thinking you could join them, were you?"

"But surely, Father, there are some women. Lev and the other men don't know how to bake or spin or weave. How could these men survive without women?"

Father shook his staff at me. "They will survive without you, Danya. That is certain!" Losing his balance, he turned his ankle. "*Ouch*! Now look what's happened." He hobbled to the riverbank and soaked his leg in the cold water. Naomi clucked over him, binding his ankle tightly in thin strips of cloth. I dropped the subject of the Essenes. No one could win an argument with Father, Lev always said.

At daybreak on the fifth day, we split away from the Jordan River where the pilgrim path turned towards Jericho and climbed to the top of a cliff. From that height, we could see the Jericho oasis, improbably lush and green, springing up from the brittle desert besieging it on all sides. But columns of smoke smudged the sky over the city.

Naomi scurried forward. "My father told me that King Herod had three palaces in Jericho," she said. "And a swimming pool. And a sunken garden, whatever that is. There's even a bathhouse, like the Romans have in Sepphoris, that my father says is the work of the devil. Please, please can we see it?"

Father said, "Naomi, child, I'm afraid that you won't see a bathhouse or anything else in Jericho. That smoke is a bad sign." A foul odor, like the diseased figs we had to burn a few harvests ago, hung in the air.

The footpath that led down from the cliff fed into a road that sliced across the Jericho plain. Smaller roads, coming from other directions, joined this one. Merchants and their wagons, farmers with herds of animals, and pilgrims bound for Jerusalem all crowded onto this passage through the date palm groves of the Jericho valley. As we drew closer to the city, the smoke smudges in the sky darkened and thickened. Our eyes watered; we coughed; we put our headcoverings over our mouths.

The gates to Jericho were locked. Roman soldiers, stationed an arm's length apart, guarded its walls. We were in a crowd of people who, silently and submissively, streamed by them. No one questioned or challenged the soldiers whose short, sleeveless tunics emphasized the bulging muscles of their arms and legs. They clutched spears whose iron heads were as long as my arm and, and the handles on their thick-bladed swords were wider than my fist.

Staring at the swords, I suddenly felt foolish. If I had joined the raid on Sepphoris, I might've accidentally wounded myself simply trying to lift one of them. And how could I have run lugging a sack full of these heavy weapons?

Each soldier looked just like the next as we passed meekly through their ranks. Helmets, complete with cheek pieces and nose deflectors, obscured each man's individual features. It seemed as if the same face, fixed in the same contemptuous sneer, glared out at us and at all of Judea. Naomi clutched at my tunic, and I clutched at Father's. Had Lev been as afraid as I was now when he faced the Roman supply convoy in Galilee?

At the far edge of Jericho, we stopped to fill our water jars from the Ein es-Sultan spring. Father approached a beardless young soldier and spoke with him in Greek. "What has happened here?"

"Rebels have burned the palace and gardens," the soldier said.

"What rebels?" asked Father.

"Maybe the traitors who follow the shepherd Anthronges. Or maybe Simon of Perea's rabble. Or Judah ben Hezekiah's bandits. It doesn't matter who did it. We'll kill them all." The soldier pounded the ground with the butt of his spear and, with his other arm, signaled for us to move on.

"But it does matter," Father said, keeping his place. "You must not punish one for the crimes of another. Judah ben Hezekiah didn't do this."

"How do you know?" said the soldier. He stepped back and sized Father up.

His stare chilled me. I tugged on Father. "Come. We must go."

"You must have evidence of wrongdoing before you punish," Father said sternly.

"Don't tell me what I must or must not do, old man," said the soldier. The arrogant young man, a boy really, gripped his spear crosswise and pushed it against Father's chest.

Father lost his balance and fell down. The soldier towered over Father and sneered at him as Father lay on his back in the dirt. I cowered, too afraid to help Father to his feet. It was I who clung to Naomi this time, our mutual fear wet and heavy in our palms. Shame filled me. I was too weak to defend my own father. No wonder I hadn't been favored.

Slowly and in obvious pain, Father rolled over and struggled to bring himself to his knees, then to his feet. He brushed the dust from his hands and squinted into the soldier's blue eyes.

"You know better than to treat an old man like this," Father said gently, as if chiding a student of his.

The young soldier's face colored. He hoisted his spear and glared at Father. No one breathed. Then he lowered his gaze, laid his weapon on his shoulder, and walked away.

My tongue stuck in my mouth. My legs felt like water, so I couldn't walk. But Naomi ran to Father and, swatting at the dust on the back of his tunic said, "You are the bravest man in the world. I am so grateful that you're my protector!" She hugged him tightly then reached out and pulled me to him also.

Father held the two of us and let me cry. He thought my tears were those of relief. "It's all right. You've been strong and brave throughout this hard journey, my little light. Just another half day and we'll be in Jerusalem."

Though I had been brave in some ways, some of my tears were those of disappointment. I had neither the physical strength nor the courage I thought I had.

In my heart, I cradled that image of my father standing up to the Roman bully. I would have to find some way to do the same, to imitate my father's courage and dignity. However, I would not share his willingness to put aside the cruelty shown to him.

We hurried to reach Jerusalem before sundown. Father leaned heavily on his walking staff but trudged along without rest. I didn't even stop to pick stones out of my sandals. Naomi kept pace, for once not whining about the blisters on her toes or any other malady.

My apprehension about living in Chuza's house had dissipated as a result of this frightful journey. Soon we would be safe in Jerusalem. And Miryam was right: I would be fortunate to have time to read, write, and search for answers to my questions. The Holy One had brought me this far unharmed. Perhaps He might still have work for me, a way I could help to liberate our people. I would pray and watch for such a sign.

When at last Jerusalem emerged on the horizon, I latched my arm through Father's. "Tell us about Jerusalem," I coaxed.

"It's large."

"And the people?"

"They're like people everywhere. People come here from everywhere."

He withdrew his arm from mine to shade his eyes and look towards the southwest. "Soon you'll see it for yourselves."

Naomi took his arm. "Did you like Jerusalem?" she asked.

"Yes, especially the Temple." Father smiled and his eyes drifted off.

Naomi tugged at him. "Then why did you leave?"

"I could no longer live in Jerusalem as a good Jew."

"Why not?" I demanded.

"It's complicated, child. You'll understand better when you know Jerusalem. And when you're older. Be patient."

Father's life, so simple on its surface, seemed to have a trapdoor leading to a secret place. From time to time, he would crack that door open but then slam it shut before I could accustom my eyes to its darkness and peer in. It made me miss Lev all the more. He could help me prop open the door.

We entered Jerusalem from the north, pouring through the Benjamin Gate with a lively, jostling crowd. The late afternoon sun was nestling itself onto the houses and shops, bathing them in soft tans and yellows. Father plucked us from the throng, and we stopped for a moment at a shaded vantage point under a shopkeeper's awning. Naomi clapped her hands and squealed. "We're here. We're finally here! I've waited my whole life, twelve years, for this, and now, finally, little Naomi from Nazareth is in Jerusalem!"

I was both relieved that our journey had ended and anxious about what lay ahead. We elbowed our way down a street cutting lengthwise through the middle of the city. Father's limp lessened, and he no longer leaned on his staff. His eyes, usually tired and faded with studying, brightened. Their color seemed a richer brown. It had been years since he had been to this city and seen Chuza, his firstborn.

The main street of the Tyropoeon Valley was crammed with shops and market carts. Exotic-looking people swarmed around us. Many women wore veils; a few had face coverings trailing all the way down to the ground. Naomi, giggling, pointed to a woman whose thin tunic clung so tightly to her breasts we could see the outline of her nipples. I saw my first wig. We howled in laughter at the hair on a shopkeeper's head, piled so high it looked as if she might topple over.

Besides hoods, turbans, and mantles, men wore hats of every description: hats with wide, stiff brims or flaps; hats pointed at the top like cypress trees; hats embroidered with the shapes of animals and heavenly bodies; hats tall and rounded like the necks of wine decanters.

Eight slaves in matching red pantaloons suddenly commandeered the whole walkway, shouting, "Make way, make way." On their shoulders they balanced a man reclining on a chair and wearing a white toga bordered in purple. He was holding a rolled document, sealed with a gaudy blotch of red wax. Father scowled. "Probably a Roman procurator."

Another litter, behind that one, bore a woman. An enormous turquoise brooch fastened her mantle, and I gaped in wonder. Surely she must be the richest woman in Jerusalem! But her skin was whiter than any I had ever seen. She looked as if she had never been warmed by the sun, and I felt a little sorry for her.

Clamorous Jerusalem: tools pounding, digging, sawing, splitting; animals barking, bleating, bellowing; people chattering, chanting, shouting and singing in Greek, Latin, Aramaic, Hebrew, and a hundred alien tongues. Our donkeys added their brays to the din.

Open stalls reeked with the odor of spoiling fish and meat. The sewers swirled with the blood of slaughtered animals. Naomi, feeling sick, asked to rest. As we turned away from the crowded market area, I almost collided with a camel. It hissed at me, and I backed away from its enormous teeth. We climbed a staircase and sat there while Naomi's stomach settled. By this time, I, too, welcomed the chance to get away from the rowdy crowds. The donkeys pawed at the ground, hoping to uncover a sprig of green to eat, but nothing grew up through the stones.

"Are you sure you know the way to Chuza's?" a very pale Naomi asked my father.

"Of course. It was once my house, and my father's and grandfather's before that." From a pack on the younger donkey's back, Father extracted the Sabbath lamp, carefully wrapped in sheepskin, and cradled it against his breast.

We climbed a second staircase then followed along a street to a third staircase and another street. Father never hesitated. He made no wrong turns. Up here we could barely detect the commotion below. In this section of the city, the houses were all large and walled. Father led us down a few more streets, through a gate, and into the courtyard of a private home. He eased himself onto a stone bench just as the sun's reflected glow expired. I sat next to him. Tears spilled onto his cheeks as he placed the Sabbath lamp in my lap. "You are home, my little light," he said.

An open window overlooked the courtyard. From within the house, we heard something crash onto a stone floor, then sharp whispers. A stout man with a closely trimmed, oiled beard strode from the house. He wore a linen tunic and smelled of soap. "Father," Chuza said, "Shalom."

MY BROTHER'S MANSION IN THE UPPER CITY

Chuza bowed to Father but did not embrace him. "I received your letter, though we hadn't expected you so soon. I'm saddened that Nazareth is threatened, but my wife and I are pleased that you've chosen to take refuge with us."

A dainty woman about twenty years old stepped into the courtyard and smiled warmly at my father. "We are honored that you have come, Father. Since your son and I were wed, I've prayed for this day."

Chuza turned to me and said stiffly, "Shalom, sister. You are welcome here."

Joanna embraced me tightly. "Chuza told me you were a strong, beautiful little girl, and I see you're now a strong, beautiful woman. I'm so happy to finally meet you, my dear Danya."

Joanna was the beautiful one. She had flawless light skin, perfectly arranged, honey-colored hair, and graceful eyebrows. "Delicate" seemed the best word for her features. I towered over her and felt awkward. When she reached out to Naomi, it was almost a relief to see that Joanna had an imperfection: ragged fingernails. "We're delighted you've brought your pretty young friend with you. Shalom, Naomi," said Joanna.

Chuza nodded at Naomi, then asked Father, "Where's Lev?"

"With the Essenes," said Father.

"Has he joined the monastery at Qumran?"

"We expect to hear from him soon."

Apparently, Father didn't want Chuza to know about Lev's involvement with Judah and the raid. Naomi and I would have to guard our tongues.

Servants appeared to tend to the donkeys and our possessions. Father gave them strict instructions about handling the stone jars containing his scrolls. Then, because he had been exposed to corpses on our journey, he asked Chuza to accompany him to the house's miqveh to purify himself. Watching the men leave, I was surprised at Chuza's size. He was wider and shorter than Father. Lev and I had always thought of our older brother as tall and lean, like us, though probably taller because he was older.

Joanna led us into the house, and we met her little dog, Dodi. Naomi fussed over the animal, burying her fingers in her white, silky coat and accepting her watery kisses. I found Dodi unappealing. When I tried to pat her, she cringed pathetically and flapped her tail in an overanxious desire to please. She neither herded sheep, nor chased rodents from the grain bins, so what purpose did she serve? I thought of her as merely an ornament.

In the reception hall, a room three times the size of our house in Nazareth, I was afraid to sit on a chair or to lean on a delicately carved wooden table for fear of breaking them. The floor, though, entranced me with its black and bronze mosaic tiles arranged in a pattern of interlocking shapes. Naomi and I each picked out a single line and walked along it, our footsteps twisting and turning until we made ourselves dizzy. Joanna joined in our little dance on the tiles and laughed along with us.

Despite its high ceiling, the reception hall burst with fragrance. "I keep it full of jasmine," Joanna told us, and only when I brushed against them did I notice the delicate, yellow-flowered branches planted in tall earthenware vases. I traced my finger along the pattern etched in muted red and brown lines on the vase's surface. Joanna lightly touched my arm and said, "Careful, sister. That one is a favorite of your brother's."

The frescoes adorning the walls of the hall reminded me of the hillsides of Galilee. The grapevines in these paintings were almost as beautiful as the real vineyards they represented. I couldn't imagine my father ever having lived in such splendor, and I wondered why he left this beautiful house for a two-room, dirt-floored village hut. He told Naomi he "could no longer live in Jerusalem as a good Jew." But there must be many good Jews in Jerusalem.

Joanna gestured around her as she pivoted in a circle. "This hall is no longer large enough for our needs, so we intend to build a second one. We also need to add more ovens to the kitchen because we entertain a great deal. Did you know that Chuza has been appointed Chief Steward to the new ethnarch, Herod Archelaus?" She lowered her voice and chuckled. "Chuza acts more like a Roman every day. He would prefer a colonnaded courtyard in the center of the house, a real Roman peristyle, but we can't do that without taking the whole house down and starting over."

Such extravagance left us speechless. Joanna didn't seem to be boasting but only explaining the way they lived, which made it all the more astonishing.

"Come along and let me show you the bath." As we passed the stairway to the rooftop, Joanna hesitated and then said, "We'll add a second story when we need the space for children."

"How long have you been married?" Naomi asked.

"Five years," Joanna said quietly.

"Oh, sorry," said Naomi. For once she had enough sense to say nothing else.

The bathtub, which ranked its own room, was supplied with water from its own cistern. Joanna ordered a servant to warm some water and fill the tub for us. "Miryam's never going to believe this," Naomi whispered to me.

As we passed the hallway that led down to the purification pool, Joanna said sheepishly, "You should know that we are not very religious, not like your father, anyway. Chuza hardly ever uses the miqveh, though he wants people to think he does."

In Nazareth, there was one miqveh for all the men of the village and one for all the women. As we wandered through Chuza's house, I began to understand how distasteful he must have found our two-room, dirt-floored home in our village. Most of Chuza's childhood had been spent in this home in Jerusalem. It was only after his mother had died that Father and he had moved to Nazareth where they had to share a well, an olive press, a miqveh, and almost everything else of value with several hundred people. For the first time, I realized we were poor and I felt embarrassed about it. I also felt a surge of resentment towards Father for having chosen the life that he had when we could have had this. I began to view Chuza's sudden departure from Nazareth and his return to Jerusalem in a new light.

Joanna led us on to the bedroom Naomi and I would share. It was large enough for a family. Joanna said, "Enjoy your bath and then we'll dine."

Naomi protested. "But we haven't seen your rooms. Or your clothes."

"Tomorrow," promised Joanna. "You can try on anything you like. My clothes will look prettier on you girls than they do on me."

Prettier on Naomi maybe, but not on me. Naomi and Joanna were both tiny. Though Joanna had lighter, straighter hair, the two of them could have passed for sisters. Joanna's clothes would be too tight across my shoulders and hang immodestly far above my ankles. But it was generous of her to offer to share.

After Joanna left, Naomi poked around the room until she found a hand mirror, something we had heard about but never seen before. She held it up to her face and patted her bushy hair. "My mother tells me I have beautiful hair. Do you think so?" Naomi did have a perfect nose, slightly dipped at the end, and large sparkling brown eyes well accented by dark eyebrows that were neither too thick nor too thin. "You are pretty, Naomi. Your mother's right about that. Let me look now."

Naomi held the mirror up for me. I frowned at my eyebrows. They were so long and thick that now I would worry about them growing together. I put my finger on the little dent in my chin, an impression like my mother's.

Naomi turned the mirror back to herself. "My mother says that I'm pretty, but that you're striking, Danya,"

"Let's hope that your mother's right about us," I laughed.

Naomi and I flopped onto sleeping platforms heaped with soft cushions and blankets. How lovely it would be to sleep here, rather than wrapped in a dusty woolen cloak on the ground. Peristyle or no, it didn't matter to me: Chuza's home was the loveliest place I had ever been in. And Joanna, even though she was more like Naomi than me, could not be kinder. I had missed something by not having a sister.

That night Joanna and Chuza served us a lavish dinner, though Joanna apologized for its simplicity. "If only we had known you would arrive today," she kept saying.

"Hush, wife," Chuza said. "Our guests understand." He ignored the women after that and conversed only with Father. Once I heard him remark, unfavorably I felt, that I didn't resemble my mother.

Their dining room was furnished with couches, in the Roman fashion, but Father requested a stool and sat erect as the rest of us reclined. This unfamiliar position resulted in bits of our food slipping to the floor, but Dodi cleaned up after us. Joanna laughed with Naomi each time the dog darted after a dropped delicacy.

We ate foods we rarely indulged in, such as hen's eggs and apricot cakes. Joanna said that the salted fish, served whole on a copper platter, was a delicacy, but I found it as distasteful as the fish we had at home. She extravagantly praised the walnuts we contributed to the feast. We had carried them all the way from Galilee, knowing they were scarce in Judea. Chuza helped himself to a third helping of the fish and asked Father, "How long will you be staying in Jerusalem?"

"The women, until it's safe for them to return. I need to get back to Nazareth as soon as I can. To see that those who stayed behind get out safely. I'll be here only long enough to rest and to visit the Temple."

Chuza frowned. "Better only to rest. Don't go to the Temple."

"Don't go to the Temple! Why not?"

"There is great unrest in Jerusalem these days. Since it's Passover, huge crowds throng the Temple's courtyards. Crowds can be dangerous. Our Roman occupiers do not like crowds."

Father pulled a bone from his teeth and said calmly, "The Temple is the earthly dwelling place of the Divine Presence. We can't be harmed there."

Chuza fixed his small but intelligent eyes on Father. "Because of the unrest, Roman soldiers may be sent to help the Levites keep order on the the Mount."

Father looked up from his fish. "Roman soldiers on the Mount? Surely you're mistaken. Herod Archelaus is a Jew. He wouldn't permit the Temple Mount to be defiled in that way. Jerusalem is full of rumors."

"My information is reliable," Chuza said.

Father slammed his right hand on the table. "You may work for Rome, but you are first of all a Jew: how can you permit pagan soldiers on our most holy site?"

Chuza pawed at his beard, trimmed, Roman-style close to his full face. Joanna tried to change the subject. "Try this," she said, offering us a serving plate with yellow wedges on it. "A trader from the East sold me this fruit, called a lemon. Its juice is supposed to improve the flavor of salted fish."

Obediently, we squeezed the lemon over our fish.

In the silence that followed, Joanna, Naomi, and I looked from father to son, our hands clenched in our laps. My throat hurt, as if I had swallowed an underchewed lump of goat meat. I had forgotten how often I used to feel this way when Chuza lived with us. The tension between them, lurking in the background from the moment Chuza had greeted Father in the courtyard, now sprang from its weak confines.

"I have no voice in this matter," Chuza said, breathing quickly, in and out.

We finished our meal in silence, and then Father said, "We leave for the Temple Mount at dawn."

Chuza slammed both of his hands down on the table and pushed himself up from his couch. Scowling, at last bearing a resemblance to both Father and Lev, he stormed out of the room. Joanna shrugged her shoulders. Even in Jerusalem, I thought, salted fish is salted fish. Lemon juice cannot remove its bitterness.

We rose early the next morning, having barely slept anyway, and met Father for breakfast. Joanna, obeying her husband's orders, would not accompany us; nevertheless, she wanted to make sure we were well fed before setting out. Warm wheat loaves and freshly ground hummus dispatched the lingering foulness of last night's salted fish. A platter of perfectly ripened melon slices sweetened our anticipation of the glorious day awaiting us.

Suddenly, Chuza appeared in the doorway to the dining room. He pulled up a stool, sat next to Father, and waited until his breathing evened out before speaking. "I am only Herod Archelaus's steward. I manage his estates. I have no influence over any of his other affairs."

"But surely he confides in you," said Father.

"Yes. And that's why I'm begging you not to go to the Temple for the next few days. Wait until the Passover pilgrims leave the city. Then you can go and offer sacrifice and pray in the Temple all you wish. The protests will have died down. The Temple Mount will be peaceful once again."

Father stiffened. "What protests?"

Chuza whisked a fly from the fruit with the back of his hand. "Protests over some executions that took place a year ago."

"Who was executed?" asked Father.

Chuza poured water for Father and spoke reassuringly. "Two foolish teachers, believing King Herod, Archelaus's father, had died, incited their students to tear down a meaningless symbol over the Temple gate. Herod, though very sick at the time, was nevertheless well enough to order that the teachers and their students be burnt alive."

The melon in my mouth soured. Even in remote Galilee we had heard tales of the late king's brutality, but I hadn't imagined Herod capable of such an atrocity.

"The golden eagle is not 'meaningless,'" Father said quietly. "It's the official emblem of Roman imperial authority."

"We Jews are not forced to worship that image, just to tolerate it," argued Chuza. "In Jerusalem we have to accommodate to Rome. We don't have the luxury of living in a remote village that Rome cares nothing about."

Father's voice rose again. "The Roman eagle, mounted over the great gate of the Temple, mocks the power of The Holy One."

"The Holy One is all-powerful, of course," said Chuza. "He can't be mocked by a golden eagle. It's a reasonable accommodation to Rome to let their symbol stand. By permitting them their silly bird, we're able to run our Temple without their interference. Usually. Not today."

"The anniversary of this martyrdom is all the more reason to visit the Temple Mount today, then. We must honor the brave men who died trying to purify it," said Father.

Chuza threw up his hands in disgust. "I see there's no convincing you, as usual. Go to the Temple, then, but go yourself. I will not permit you to take the women!"

Father turned to Naomi and me. "You may come with me or stay here, as you wish." He proceeded through the doorway and out to the courtyard.

THE TEMPLE MOUNT

Despite Chuza's warnings, Naomi and I chose to go to the Temple. Passover was our greatest feast. To celebrate it in this most sacred place with Jews from all over the world was an event we had dreamt of all our lives. We trusted Father's judgment and believed he would keep us safe.

We could've taken a shortcut to the Temple Mount, using a bridge that connected its western gate to the Upper City, but Father insisted we enter from the south, the traditional access for pilgrims. From this direction in particular, the Mount, a hill between two valleys, dominated the landscape of Jerusalem. We shaded our eyes and gaped at its glistening walls. They were constructed of enormous blocks of white stone. About halfway up, carved columns protruded from the flat surface of the stones, extending all the way to the top of the wall. Each ashlar was so perfectly cut and placed that no mortar was needed between them. Not even a knife blade could slide between any two stones.

Though it was still early in the morning, people flooded the streets and market stalls. Merchants sold expensive grain, oil, wine, and animals to be used as sacrificial offerings on the Temple's altar. All goods were guaranteed ritually pure. Father bought a pair of doves and a covered basket to transport them.

Before ascending to the Temple Mount itself, we were required to follow the rite of ritual purification. Naomi and I approached one of the women's bathhouses scattered around the huge square below the Mount. Many women coming out of it wore rented white tunics, symbols of their pilgrim status.

"Did you get money from your father to rent clothing for us?" said Naomi.

"No, he only gave us coins for our purification bath." I wished we had the money. In pilgrim clothing, we wouldn't have looked as poor as we did in our yellowed flax tunics and gray wool cloaks.

In the bathhouse, we took off our clothes, asked an attendant to hold them for us, and completely immersed ourselves in the pool's chilly water. It was no place to linger, so we quickly climbed out. As we dried ourselves off with the worn flax towels the attendant provided, Naomi said, "You never told me your brother was so mean."

"I told you I don't know my brother. Besides, was he being mean? Or just careful? After all, we came to Jerusalem to be safe."

"I thought he'd be sweet, like Lev. Maybe he doesn't like me."

"There seems to be much he doesn't like."

Because everyone was required to remain barefoot on the Temple Mount, we carried our sandals as we emerged from the women's bathhouse. We waited for Father at the bottom of the wide staircase at the Mount's southern entrance.

Naomi squealed. "Here I am, finally, about to enter the Temple in Jerusalem. And during Passover. I never, ever, thought this would happen!"

Father joined us in time to hear Naomi's delight and smiled. He stepped between us, hooked his arms through ours, and led us onto the staircase. He recited one of King David's psalms as we walked up it.

Who shall ascend the hill of the Lord? And who shall stand in his holy place? Those who have clean hands and pure hearts . . .

Those who do not lift up their souls to what is false, and do not swear deceitfully. They will receive blessing from the Lord, and vindication from the God of their salvation.

The staircase ended at the Huldah Gates, enormous gilded doors that opened into a tunnel. *"Lift up your heads, O gates! And be lifted up, O ancient doors!"* Father chanted as we entered this spacious underpass to the courtyards above. Torches glowed along the passageway, but they weren't bright enough to fully illuminate the elaborate carvings on its columns and domed ceilings. I could distinguish the shapes of vines, leaves, and flowers, all intertwined and flowing into one another, on the columns, but I couldn't follow the complicated patterns of shapes and forms on the domed ceilings.

A ramp from the tunnel swept us up to the Temple Mount itself. As we emerged onto it, my eyes ached with the sudden brightness of the vast courtyard and its stunning structures. Covered colonnades rimmed three sides of this outer court. On the fourth, the western side, lay a series of three successively smaller courtyards. Many times when I was a child, Father had drawn the design of the Mount in the dirt for me. Today I followed his finger as he pointed out its features for us. I hadn't understood until now that each successive courtyard was higher than the one preceding it, symbolizing the increasing sanctity of each enclosure.

Overcome with awe and gratitude, Father dropped to his knees and kissed the holy ground. At that moment, a clot of sun-blinded pilgrims surged from the tunnel ramp; several of them accidentally trampled on Father's prostrate body. I screamed. Naomi and I struggled to steer the crowd away from Father. The Levite Temple guards quickly came to our aid. They lifted Father to his feet as we asked him, over and over, "Are you hurt?"

Dazed and shaken, he said, "It was foolish of me to attempt that in this crush of people. I'll be all right after I rest a little."

The Levites guided Father to a bench and eased him down onto it. Naomi and I retrieved his sandals and the basket of doves he had been carrying. We sat with Father while he gathered his strength again.

The huge plaza on which we sat was called the Court of the Gentiles because non-Jews were permitted here. On its west side, a stone balustrade sectioned off a smaller courtyard called the Court of Women. A silver-and-gold-plated gate allowed access to its raised confines, but only to Jewish men and women. Beyond that area, up a staircase, sat the Court of Israelites, which was restricted to Jewish men. A gate on its west side led to the Court of the Priests. Within that final courtyard gleamed the Temple itself, a structure almost blinding in its white and gold splendor. Rising more than thirty cubits above the court where we stood, the Temple sanctuary reigned as the highest point in Jerusalem. The white marble of its walls and the gold of its facade and rooftop powerfully and gloriously reflected the sun's light. The sight of it took my breath away. Of course The Holy One would choose this place as His own in all the world, I thought. And here I was, on the Temple Mount, close enough to the sacred sanctuary to bask in its brilliant glow, to smell the roasting meat of the sacrifices offered to Him, and to hear His praises sung in all the languages of the world.

This Court of the Gentiles throbbed with the movements and sounds of the multitude it contained. There were many, many more people here than I could count. Naomi said, "Once I was in the Sepphoris market during a festival and I thought most of the people in the world were there. But now I see they must've been here!"

Father laughed. He was feeling better. "Come," he said, "let's cross the courtyards to the place of sacrifice."

Our destination was the Court of Women, where Naomi and I would wait while Father proceeded through the bronze Nicanor Gate to the Court of Israelites. There he would pray with the assembly while priests offered our doves on the enormous altar in the Court of the Priests.

A long line sagged outside the Beautiful Gate, the opening to the Court of Women. Next to this gate hung a sign in Latin and Greek. "NO GENTILE ALLOWED BEYOND THIS SIGN UNDER PENALTY OF DEATH." We joined the line, and I studied the other visitors around us. Most people respected the admonition not to spit, which was posted on signs in several languages. I noticed a large number of Gentiles. Many men and even some women strolled about the huge courtyard with uncovered heads, eating and exchanging money as if they were in a marketplace. Their children misbehaved, the girls playing tag and the boys tussling with one another. Some of the women were even bare-shouldered!

I'd expected a respectful quiet on the Mount, an undertone, perhaps, of voices engaged in prayer and chanting. I had hoped to feel Adonai's presence here, but the clamor and irreverence shocked me. This holy place was as noisy as the streets of Jerusalem.

The smell of incense and the smoke from the roasting sacrificial meat intensified as the sun rose higher. After standing in line until the sun reached its highest point in the sky, both Naomi and I developed headaches. We asked Father for permission to sit down in the shade of the Eastern portico, but he didn't think it would be safe, even though Chuza had been wrong. There were no Roman soldiers here.

A headache didn't prevent Naomi from observing and commenting on the young men. "Look at that fat-legged one. He should wear a longer tunic." And, "Oh, see the sweet puppy eyes on that long-haired boy? Do you suppose he needs a wife?"

A man in a tunic shabbier than ours strode across the courtyard speaking loudly to some groups of people. He seemed to address young men who, judging from their clothing, looked like Jews from our own country of Galilee. Several of them broke away from their groups to listen to the ragged-looking man. As he worked his way closer to us, Naomi said, "Look at that fierce-looking one with the red curls falling onto his forehead. Wait. Is that Judah ben Hezekiah?"

I spotted the man with the undisciplined red hair. My fingers touched the place on my throat that Judah had clutched and bruised.

"He wouldn't look so bad if he'd smile once in a while," Naomi babbled. "Ugh. Never mind. He looks like a wolf when he smiles."

"Turn around," Father ordered. "Don't attract his attention. Don't speak to him."

I obeyed but wondered what I would do if Judah found me. I imagined the moment when his eyes, roaming over the crowd, found and locked on mine, and when his breath once again stirred through my hair. An unfamiliar but pleasant flush raced through me.

"One year ago today," Judah proclaimed, now close enough for us to hear his shout, "two brave scholars and their students were burnt alive here on the Temple Mount. Their only crime was to tear down the Roman emblem that profaned this holy place. Join me. Avenge this outrage against The Holy One and our people!"

Some young men left our line to answer Judah's call. He and his cluster surged across the courtyard. Like a tangle of brush rushing downstream, they ensnared the loose and the rootless in their powerful flow.

At the same time, approaching from the opposite direction, a man in a bright white turban wended his way through the throng. "Over there," Naomi said, pointing at the man who had just captured my attention. "That tall one is handsome. No. Too old."

The turbaned man wore a pure white linen tunic. A blue sash wound across his chest and hung almost to the ground. I supposed he was a priest. He was even taller than Lev, standing at least a head higher than everyone around him. He gestured constantly, sweeping his arms out and drawing people into a circle around him. When he had a group assembled, he pointed one long-fingered hand to the south. These groups began hurrying towards the Huldah Gates. He must have known many languages because he spoke with people of every description.

The white-robed priest approached our line and shouted in Greek to the people standing in it. "Leave the Mount now. Peacefully. Roman soldiers are on their way. Do not cause a disturbance. When they see we are peaceful, they will not harm us."

But even as he spoke, Roman foot soldiers poured from the portico on the east where Naomi and I had wanted to rest. Perspiration trickled down my back as I recalled the crucified men in the oak grove and my father splayed out in the dirt in Jericho. But these soldiers, armed only with undrawn swords, didn't wear helmets or carry shields. They formed a thin line along the eastern side of the courtyard and appeared to number no more than a hundred.

The clamor in the massive courtyard died down as the throng on the Mount, which numbered in the thousands, scrutinized the soldiers' movements. After a few very anxious moments, it became clear that the Romans did not intend to attack but merely to stand guard. Many people returned to their prayers and sacrifices. But some began grumbling, and the grumbling soon turned to shouting. "Go away, pagans!" "You don't belong here." "Get out of our Holy Temple!"

The white-robed priest gestured urgently and announced again in Greek, "Leave now, pilgrims. Leave peacefully."

But in Aramaic, Judah roared louder than the priest. "These Romans defile The Holy One's throne on earth. We must cleanse the Temple of them." He picked up a stone and raised his fist into the noonday sky. "No master but God!" he cried.

I felt a pull to join the young men who followed Judah. It was as if a rope had been tied around my waist, and Judah, hand over hand, steadily drew me nearer to him.

Now less than ten paces away from me, he would be close enough to hear my call. I felt his name in my throat, a pang throbbing for release. My mouth opened, and my lips shaped the beginning of his name. But I couldn't sound it, couldn't say, "Judah. Judah, here I am!"

How different my life might have been if, at that moment, I had spoken and he had heard. But Judah's name stayed bound within me and twisted itself into a question that haunted me for a long time. Was my silence a rejection of The Holy One's call, a "No" to His plan for me?

The priest tried unsuccessfully to stop several men from joining Judah and then he noticed us. His eyes widened as he looked at Father. "Rabbi, do you remember me? Have you returned to your position in the Temple?"

Father smiled. "Of course I remember you, Tobiah. I've returned, but only as a humble pilgrim." The hinges of the trapdoor creaked again.

Tobiah embraced Father. Then, taking notice of me and Naomi, he said, "Come, you have young women to protect. Let me lead you off the Mount." He took Father by the arm. Naomi, anxious to flee this tumult, grabbed Father's other hand.

Father, Tobiah, and Naomi began wending through the mass of people. I lagged behind, waiting there for Judah to find me, wondering what he would do when he did. What I would do. Tobiah let go of the others and hurried back to me. "You must be Micah's daughter." He smiled politely with closed lips. "Please, come quickly. Your father is anxious about you. He needs you."

Though a part of me begged to turn back towards Judah, I accepted Tobiah's argument: my father needed me. I fell in behind him. He strode through the chaos with a calm dignity. People gave way to him. With Tobiah leading, my retreat seemed sensible, even honorable.

Tobiah brought the three of us, unharmed, to the western gate. "Leave the Mount from here," he said. "It's closer and not so crowded. May Adonai protect you." He plunged back into the screaming throng though by now any effort to tamp its rage seemed impossible.

Before passing through the gate to the bridge, I turned around. No smoke ascended from the sacrificial altar. No songs of praise to Adonai emanated from the mouths of His people. All devotions had ceased, and the Temple Mount, whose stones my father had kissed just a few hours before, had been transformed from a holy ground to a battleground. A shrieking, cursing mob hurled a barrage of rocks at the Romans. As the deadly weights rained down upon them, the vastly outnumbered soldiers dropped like birds shot from the sky. I was surprised that I felt a pang of pity for those Roman soldiers.

We passed through the Temple's western gate and onto the bridge. There I opened the basket to free the pair of doves we had planned to offer in sacrifice. One of them bit my hand before taking off, reminding me that my compassion for those Roman pagans was misplaced.

ACTS OF VENGEANCE

With hearts pounding, Father, Naomi, and I pushed through the throngs in the streets and made our way to Chuza's house. My pale, heavily perspiring half-brother awaited us at his gate and hustled us into his courtyard. "I'm so relieved to see you unharmed! A messenger has just informed me that a mob is rioting on the Temple Mount."

Father coughed, trying to catch his breath. "The Roman guard provoked it."

"I told you not to go!" Chuza turned on his heel and hurried off to the Royal Palace.

Joanna brought us into the reception hall and sent a servant for water and fruit. Father rendered an account of the chaos on the Mount to Joanna while Naomi sat upright in her chair, gripping the seat as if to keep it from taking flight. I sat on a couch, but my legs shook uncontrollably.

What would the new king do? Would he understand that, by ordering the Roman guard onto the Mount, he had incited the mob? Would he restore order and round up the perpetrators and those who stoned the soldiers? Would he act justly by punishing the guilty and sparing the innocent?

We soon found out. The wind whipped through the Upper City, carrying in its lash the cries of war horses and the shrieks of their victims. The Roman cavalry was charging the Temple Mount. To block out the terrifying noises, I pushed my fingers into my ears. Judah's words echoed in them. "Avenge this outrage! "Cleanse the Temple!" After the stoning, Judah would've stayed there and tried to rally more rebels to his cause, making himself a prime target for the charging cavalry. I pushed my fingers deeper into my ears and heard Tobiah's words, "Come, your father needs you." Tobiah's gentle urging, though unwelcome at the time, may have saved my life. I wondered if the priest who saved us had taken his own advice and fled the Temple Mount himself.

Naomi and I ran to our bedroom, closed the door, latched the windows, and hid under a pile of blankets. When I closed my eyes, I saw the massacred: the heads of handsome young men smashed by horses' hooves; the bare-shouldered women, now completely exposed by swords tearing at their clothing; the puppy-eyed boy, his severed head staring at his torso; heaps of hacked-off arms that would never again bathe babies or light the Sabbath candles.

The wails and screams of the cavalry's victims punched through our barriers. Naomi's teeth chattered. "So cold," she said, over and over. I wrapped some blankets around her and brought her to Joanna, then huddled by myself, chanting prayers that I knew would not stop the massacre.

At nightfall, the cries ceased and Chuza returned. In a slow, controlled voice, as if he were dictating to a scribe, he described to us the merciless bloodbath on the Mount. With their swords and lances, the soldiers gored, beheaded, and disemboweled hundreds of people. With their horses, they trampled hundreds more. Panic-stricken Temple visitors stampeded to the gates, hoping to escape, but succeeded only in crushing the life from one another. No effort was made to distinguish the guilty from the innocent, or even the Jews from the Gentiles. Those who had no part in the madness were slaughtered along with those who had. The "crime" of being present on the Temple Mount this day had condemned two thousand souls to their deaths.

Sleep that night was impossible. The wailing of the innocent resounded in my ears: their pleas for mercy, their prayers to their God for deliverance, their sudden silences. Naomi called out to her mother in her restless dreams. I left the bedroom and roamed through the house touching its unfamiliar treasures. Oil lamps, left burning in the evening's confusion, guided my footsteps. In a room next to the kitchen, four bronze thimbles lay on a long table. Joanna had needles in many lengths and thicknesses. Each one could pierce flesh as easily as a sword. Why had I been spared? I pricked my finger and imagined my blood, with the blood of so many others, oozing into the cracks between the stones on the Mount; martyr's blood, now mortar for the stones that had not needed it.

I found a cabinet in which Chuza kept his pens and other writing materials. I dipped my pricked finger into the dried gummy powder in the inkwells and discovered that one was red. My blood mixed with the powder and made an ink. With it, I retouched the spots where Judah's fingers had clutched my neck and considered the ink spots insignia of my revolutionary resolve.

When I heard voices in the still night air, I followed them to their source. Chuza and Father sat together on the bench in the courtyard, their backs to me as I stood in the doorway. I almost chose not to listen, fearing they would argue, and then, in addition to sleeplessness, the painful lump in my throat would return.

Chuza massaged his temples. "I promised Herod Archelaus we could find the ones responsible for the stoning, so that he could punish only the guilty. But he ordered out all the cavalry quartered in and around Jerusalem."

"A stupid, brutal boy," said Father. "Only twenty years old. Yet Rome thinks he can rule all of Judea, Samaria, and Idumea!"

"He wouldn't listen to any of his advisors. He said he didn't need our opinions, that he had his father's example of how to control these lands." Chuza imitated a lisping Archelaus. "'I will teach the people that I, Herod Archelaus, am just as strong a leader as my father!'"

"Another ruler who thinks he can please Rome by murdering his own people," said Father.

Chuza ran his fingers through his hair. "I had such hopes. This Herod was raised and educated in Rome. He should be wiser and should know how to treat his people"

"Being raised and educated in Rome doesn't make a man civilized," said Father.

This would start the fight. Chuza, who wanted to design his house around a Roman peristyle, would challenge Father's criticism of Roman culture. I tensed and readied myself to leave.

But Chuza kept pulling on his hair. "I tried to prevent this, but I failed." His voice began to crack. "Look what has happened. Thousands have died! I failed. I failed." Then he wept.

I had never imagined so much as a tear welling in Chuza's eyes, but here he was, wracked with shuddering sobs, nose running, gasping for breath.

"Not your failure, my son." Father put his arm around Chuza's heaving shoulders, and his son leaned into him. "How I wish you didn't work for this tyrant. . . . But I know I drove you to it. What a jealous fool I was!"

Chuza dried his face with his sleeve then said quietly, "It's no longer important, Father. That was many years ago."

As I tiptoed off, they were still enfolded. That this most terrible day could produce harmony between my father and my brother seemed a miracle. The comfort of witnessing their embrace allowed me to finally fall asleep.

The Roman soldiers had heaped their victims onto carts and rolled their cargo through the Dung Gate into the Valley of Hinnon. There, in the area reserved for burning refuse, they had dumped the corpses. They had left the job of identifying and burying their slaughter to others.

Father insisted on going with Chuza to tend to the dead. As they were leaving I whispered to Father, "Will you look for Judah ben Hezekiah?" And, as an afterthought, "And the priest Tobiah?"

Chuza overheard me. "Judah ben Hezekiah? How would you know him? And why would you care what happens to him?" he said.

I weighed my words carefully. "He's from Galilee. We all know of him."

Chuza laughed. "Are you one of those foolish Galileans who thinks that cutthroat is your Savior?"

"No, not my Savior," I said, as evenly as I could. But I must have blushed.

"You fancy him then?" said Chuza. "I've heard that women find him attractive."

I didn't know if he was menacing or mocking me or just joking, so I stayed quiet and nudged myself closer to Father.

"Hush, Chuza," Father said, good-naturedly. "How old do brothers have to be before they stop teasing their sisters?"

Chuza didn't laugh. He frowned at me, and then they set off for the gruesome task that laid before them. My stomach stirred uneasily, as if some rodent were prowling about inside it.

Joanna sent servants all over the city to buy linen. While father and Chuza tended to the dead in their way, Naomi, Joanna, and I cut and stitched the linen into shrouds for those whose remains could be identified and claimed. These shrouds would cover the lucky ones, those for whom a proper Jewish burial could be arranged. Many victims of this slaughter would have to be buried in mass graves. Their bodies had been hacked or crushed beyond recognition, or they had no family left to identify and bury them.

At the end of a sad, tedious day of sewing, Joanna suggested that we meet Father and Chuza on their way home from their awful chore. Knowing they would be hot and very weary, she filled water jugs for us to carry to the Lower City plaza. There they would be able to rest and refresh themselves before the climb to the Upper City.

The plaza was almost empty. People were keeping to their houses, hiding or mourning. A fig tree, hanging over the last stairway leading down to the plaza, shaded us as we sat under it and waited there with our water jugs. Soldiers milled around, eyeing with suspicion each person who crossed the plaza. "I hate their sandals," said Naomi. "Why do they have to wind those straps all the way up to their knees? They look silly. The straps must tug at the hair on their legs!"

We smiled behind our hands until we noticed one of the soldiers staring at us. "That looks like the one from Jericho," Naomi whispered. "The one who shoved your father down."

"It can't be. They all look alike with their helmets on." But my palms began to sweat.

Father and Chuza trudged towards us, looking like corpses themselves. Their tunics were stained with dirt and blood. Their mantles, which protected them from the impurities of their work, were still tied across their noses and mouths.

We rose and lifted the water jugs as they drew closer to our stairway.

But at that moment, the soldier Naomi had pointed out strode over to Father and yanked on his arm. "Stop and remove your head covering," he ordered.

Father pulled his mantle down from his face. The soldier scrutinized him, then drew his short sword and pointed it at Father's throat. "This old man here," he said to the soldier with him, "told me that Judah ben Hezekiah didn't burn the palace at Jericho. The only way he could have known that is if he were a conspirator of Judah's."

Chuza tore off his own face covering. "I am the chief steward of Herod Archelaus. Put your sword down and release this innocent man. You don't know what you're talking about."

The soldier then pointed to us. He said to his companion, "He travels with those two young women over there. Probably spies. I saw them all at Jericho, hanging around after the rebels had destroyed it."

"I command you to release this man," shouted Chuza. "He is my father. He has no affiliation with Judah ben Hezekiah!"

The soldier kept his sword on Father's throat. "Herod Archelaus has ordered us to root out all the rebels. He didn't exclude the fathers of minor palace officials."

Chuza lowered his voice and filled each word with menace. "Herod Archelaus is the Roman appointed governor of all of Judea, including the ground you are standing on. Release my father or Herod will hear about this directly from me."

The second soldier grabbed Chuza from behind and, pushing his thick forearm against his throat, choked off his speech. Father turned his head to say something to us. As he did, the young soldier drew the tip of his sword across Father's neck and raised a thin line of blood on it.

To the soldiers, Father said, "These women have nothing to do with our business here. They're just women. They're not capable of revolution." To us he called sternly, "Go. Now. Get our supper prepared, women."

"Your father is trying to protect us," said Joanna. "And himself and Chuza. The soldiers know they are in the wrong, but they need to save face. They'll release Micah and Chuza if we leave."

I stiffened and stood my ground. Joanna and Naomi put down the water jugs and dragged me up the first flight of stairs. At the top, I pulled away from them and turned around to watch. The second soldier still held Chuza but had loosened his grip. I heard my brother entreat and threaten the soldiers. "He's a harmless old man. I have power and money. Release him and you will be richly rewarded. Harm him and you will pay with your lives!"

"We'll see who has power and who'll pay with his life," jeered the soldier holding him, squeezing his arm against Chuza's throat and silencing him again.

Father shouted a second time. "Women, go!"

Joanna and Naomi started up the next flight of stairs, but I didn't. This time I would not fail to help my father. I took three steps down the stairway and then heard the soldier holding my father declare, "You are guilty of inciting revolt against Rome. I should have done this in Jericho, but now I do know better, old man."

With that he slit my father's throat.

The other soldier released Chuza who threw himself on Father's lifeless body and wept. The murderer called to me, "Here's woman's work for you: make him a shroud." Then the two butchers walked away laughing.

I stumbled down the stairway and ran to my father and brother, but Chuza pushed me away fiercely. "So you *do* associate with Judah ben Hezekiah," he hissed. "Go. Go make a shroud."

In the funeral procession, Naomi, Joanna, and I walked behind the flute players and in front of the litter bearing the body of my father. I put one foot in front of the other, as I had the day we left Nazareth. Fleeing my home was an easy journey compared to this one. Naomi's wails overpowered the plaintive tones of the reeds. She rubbed dust in her hair and rent her clothing, something I, too, should have done, but those symbols of mourning couldn't begin to express my grief. I wanted to throw myself down and beat my head against the paving stones.

Many, many other funeral processions passed and crisscrossed ours, heading to the cemeteries outside the city walls. Jerusalem was burying its beloved dead, and the lamentations from its streets and plazas rose on the hot dusty air all the way to the heavens. Our long walk brought us to the kokhim of Father's family, a tomb cut into the rocky slope of the Kidron

Valley. Father's body would join the bones of his father, his father's father, and those of many of his ancestors. In this holy necropolis in the Kidron Valley, we believed that the just ones awaited the Messiah, who would one day descend from the Mount of Olives to enter the Temple. On His way, the Savior would raise the dead He passed there. Father and I believed this, anyway. I doubted that Chuza did, since he wasn't religious.

The stone seal of the tomb had been rolled back and secured with a wooden wedge. Lowering my head, I descended a few stairs and entered the cave. The men bearing Father's body followed. When I moved aside to make room for them, my foot bumped against an ossuary on the floor. I shuddered. Flesh decomposed in a year, and, in another twelve moons, we would return to this place and seal Father's bones into one of these stone containers.

The sweet scents of nard oil and myrrh, with which Joanna had anointed Father's body last night, permeated the small room. The men slid him off the litter and into a kokh carved into the wall, hitting his head against the rock. I winced, even though I knew he felt no pain. I longed to crawl into that niche and share the aromatic darkness with him, to smooth his hair, to close his wounds, and to feel the embrace of his strong arm around me.

Chuza wept and tore at the sleeves of his tunic. As he did this, he scowled at me. To appease him, I tore a hole in my mantle. I dared not anger Chuza.

A thin strain of chanted prayer ended our formalities in the chamber.

May His great name be blessed forever and to all eternity. Blessed and praised, glorified and exalted, extolled and honored, adored and lauded be the name of The Holy One, blessed be He, beyond all the blessings and hymns, praises and consolations that are ever spoken in the world; and say Amen.

We climbed out of the crypt, and Chuza removed the wedge. The stone rolled along in its groove and settled with a thud across the entrance, sealing Father into the cool vault with his ancestors. I had never felt so alone in all of my thirteen years of life.

As we processed back to Chuza's house, I recalled some verses Father had once made me commit to memory. One rainy afternoon, I had been inside the house spinning wool while Father copied these writings onto a new scroll. He called me over to read them aloud to him.

The souls of the righteous are in the hand of God, and no torment will ever touch them. In the eyes of the foolish, they seemed to have died, and their departure was thought to be a disaster; their going from us to be their destruction; but they are at peace. For though in the sight of others they were punished, their hope is full of immortality.

"Always remember this, Danya," Father had said. "Do not see death with '*the eyes of the foolish.*'" I knew I shouldn't see his death through such eyes, but my foolish eyes kept weeping, and nothing could stop them.

At Chuza's house, visitors who were impatient to offer their condolences and return to their other business awaited us. Quickly, we washed and ate the bread of mourning. Naomi went straight to our bedroom then, knowing that Chuza didn't want her with the family. Chuza probably didn't want me, either, but my absence would've been an impropriety, so I was tolerated. But I knew none of these people. They couldn't be any consolation to me.

I sat in a corner and tugged on the silk tunic Joanna had loaned me. The sleeves didn't cover my arms completely, which embarrassed me in front of these beautiful, elegantly dressed guests. At Chuza's order, Joanna had also provided me with a veil, something I thought I would hate wearing. But the dark veil proved a blessing. Behind it, I felt removed from this event, as if I were watching from a distance. I could pretend I was not sitting shiva but was at home in Nazareth, lazily surfacing from sleep. A pitcher of fresh goat's milk sat on the table, and Father and Lev were saying that the blackberries would soon ripen. . . .

Joanna interrupted my dreaming to introduce me to an older man on her arm. "Danya, this is Efron, my father." The eyebrows on Efron's small copper face flew up onto his forehead and laugh lines jumped out from the corners of his mouth. His nose curved like the handle of a water jug. But even at this solemn moment, he couldn't compose his face into a truly sad expression.

"My dear Danya," he said, plopping onto the bench next to me. "I am so very, very sorry for you. I am sorry for me, too, because I didn't have the honor of meeting your most righteous father. Just today I've returned from a long business trip and heard the terrible news. Joanna's mother, Yona, sends her deepest sympathy as well. She couldn't accompany me here today because of her illness."

"Thank you," I said. His sweet, kind speech did offer me a bit of solace. People who didn't know my father had missed something. Joanna hadn't mentioned that her mother was ill, but we'd only been in Jerusalem for five days, though it seemed like years.

Efron and I sat in silence for some time. I was comfortable with him and pleased to have someone with me among all those strangers. Then, attempting to distract me, Efron asked, "Who do you think are the best-dressed men here?"

I surveyed the twenty or so people in the reception hall and pointed out two men whose silk pantaloons were the color of olive leaves. Silver pins bunched and clasped their sleeveless tunics at the shoulders.

"You have a good eye," said Efron. "Those men are my customers. Very wealthy Phoenicians. They come to my shop twice a year to purchase my silk."

Watching his daughter with her visitors, Efron's eyes danced. "Joanna is my prize. I chose her name, Greek not Hebrew, because it sounds more fashionable. I've worked my whole life to help her rise in Jerusalem society, and look at her today: she certainly looks like an aristocrat! She has wonderful posture. Straight as a Roman column, even when she was a little girl. Ha, ha!" He bounced a little on the bench.

When later his eye snagged on Chuza, he frowned. "Chuza and I have little in common except for Joanna. Oh, and I'm not very religious either. When your brother talks to me, he looks around for someone more important. Except when he needs money! Ha, ha, then he pays attention to me!" He bounced again. "Oh, here he comes now."

"Efron, so good of you to come," said Chuza. "If Yona needs you to attend her, I hope you won't feel obliged to remain longer."

"That means I'm dismissed," Efron whispered to me as Chuza left us.

"I wish you could stay," I said.

He patted my hands. "Come by my shop when you feel up to it, and I'll have some tunics and mantles made for you." He winked. "And I'll only charge Chuza double what I should!"

I was alone again in my corner. The afternoon wore on and on, lonelier and lonelier for me. Just days ago, I'd lived in a village where I knew everyone and was protected by my loving father and brother. Now I resided in a city, among strangers, where death struck senselessly and changed lives in an instant. Chuza and I didn't know each other. I didn't love him, and he didn't love me. Yet, since I no longer had a father, I was the legal property of my elder half-brother. Chuza now had the power to determine the rest of my life. He had the right to decide where and how I would live, when and whom I would marry. The rodent, some demon form, crept about inside my stomach.

From time to time, Joanna briefly joined me in my corner. But Chuza would always summon her back to their guests. I noted that Joanna had to be very careful with everything she said and did in Chuza's presence. My brother's sudden angers frightened me, as did his coldness towards Naomi. The rodent's claws pinched as it prowled. Dodi jumped into my lap, and I leaned over her and placed her little panting body under my veil. With my face buried in her fur, I wept. She whined along with my soft sobs. I thought that no one could hear our strange animal dirge.

"I apologize for disturbing you, but are you ill? Can I help you?" I looked up—and up—at the man I recognized from the Temple Mount. The priest Tobiah, who had saved us. A dark bruise stained one side of his lean face, and his nose was swollen. Tobiah must have been caught up in the mob's frenzy on the Mount. But he had survived. Maybe Judah had too.

"You're not disturbing me," I said, wiping my nose with the edge of my sleeve, hidden beneath my veil. The light through the windows was fading, and the lamps had not yet been lit. The reception room held only the two us and, at the far end, Chuza and a man wearing a toga.

Tobiah clasped his clean hands. They bore no calluses from the plow or the hammer. Scholar's hands, like my father's. "Permit me to . . . um, I know you are Micah's daughter. . . . I am Tobiah."

He looked over my head as he spoke. My face was shrouded by a veil, and, though I thought of lifting it, I dared not. Tobiah continued, "Your father's death is a great sadness to me. Please accept my deepest sympathy.

Micah was the best teacher I ever had." Tobiah bowed. I thought I saw gray hair encircling a bald spot on top of his head. He began to walk away.

"Wait. I want to thank you for helping us escape the Temple Mount. And would you please tell me about my father? Tell me what you know about his life in Jerusalem."

Tobiah stroked his unfashionably long beard. "Your father taught at the beth ha-midrash on the Temple Mount. He knew the Torah in such depth that many who studied with him became doctors of the Law. Chuza studied there as well, though not with your father, and, as you know, he has chosen not to serve in the high priesthood."

Finally, someone who could prop the door open. I had so many questions to ask him. "Why did my father leave Jerusalem and go to Nazareth?"

Tobiah shook his head and turned his palms up. "That was the question we all asked. I know that corruption within the Temple leadership disturbed him greatly. His efforts to root it out failed. But it was more than that. Micah used to teach that we as a people would free ourselves from oppression not by warfare or accommodation, but by becoming more pious and righteous. He came to believe that communal village living was the way to attain such holiness. Other rabbis also taught this, but Micah was the only teacher I knew who actually tried this. After his wife died, he just took off to Nazareth."

"Why Nazareth?"

"'Because it is nowhere,' your father told me." Tobiah's smile was kind, more than a polite formality.

The strident voices of Chuza and the Roman abruptly stopped our conversation.

"That soldier was 'only doing his duty?'" shouted Chuza. "He murders my father, and his punishment is to be transferred to another province?"

"I did all I could, my friend," said the Roman. He avoided Chuza's eyes and concentrated on the creased folds in the front of his toga. "The new ethnarch wants all his subjects to know that no one is above the law, not even the family members of high officials."

"Lucius, my father adhered more strictly to the law, every law, than any man who ever lived."

"So you've told me, and I believe you. But some powerful people do not. Archelaus's spies have linked your father to Judah ben Hezekiah."

Chuza pushed out his words one at a time. "Father strongly disapproved of Judah. He opposed all violence!"

"Nevertheless, eyewitnesses say they saw your father and your sister with him," countered Lucius. "I'm sorry, my friend. There's nothing more I can do."

"After everything I've done for you," growled Chuza.

Lucius looked sternly at Chuza. "The truth is that it was all I could do to keep Archelaus from removing you from your position. Maybe someday you'll see that you do owe me your gratitude. I would advise you to hold onto your friends and make more of them if you want to maintain your position." The Roman's leather boots flapped on the tiles as he stomped out of the house.

Chuza folded himself into a chair, then changed his mind and headed over to my corner. I thought he was coming to commiserate with me because we would have no justice for the murder of our father. Even a man as important as Chuza was subject to a higher power's fickle will. I wanted to console him.

But Chuza was breathing heavily, and the vein in his forehead bulged. With its sharp nails, the rodent demon scratched at the pit of my stomach. Chuza pointed his finger at my veiled face. "You whore!" he said. "You and your ridiculous revolutionary notions. Father has paid for them with his life. And now you've dragged me into it as well. Curse you!" He raised his arm.

I flinched from the blow to come, but Tobiah intervened and stayed Chuza's hand. "Your grief is so great that it clouds your judgment, Chuza. A cruel, ambitious soldier killed your righteous father. No one else is responsible."

Chuza wrenched his arm from Tobiah's grasp and pointed again. His finger touched my veil this time. "You, Danya. You had something to do with this."

The demon slashed and ripped inside me.

LETTERS, BETRAYALS, ENSLAVEMENT

After Father's funeral, Chuza locked me in a storeroom off the kitchen. He claimed the reason for my confinement was to hide me from Roman soldiers who, believing I was also a member of Judah ben Hezekiah's band, might kill me as they had Father. But I believed Chuza was punishing me.

Wine amphoras with seals from Rhodes, Chios, Cos, Lesbos, and other places I had never heard of filled most of the space. The servants pushed them aside to make room for a sleeping mat, a small table, and a bench for me. Each day Chuza brought me food and allowed me out to empty my chamber pot, but the only thing he would say to me was that I would be released "as soon as it was safe."

Naomi stationed herself outside the storeroom door the first day of my imprisonment. She slid her fingers under the door, and I held onto them. Together we quietly mourned for all we had lost. I longed for her to chatter as she always had, but all Naomi could muster was sighing, muffled weeping, and a whispered dream. "When you get out of this room, Danya, we will find a way to sneak back to Nazareth."

But my grief so exhausted me that I couldn't imagine formulating such a plan. "We're stuck here for a long time, Naomi. We must learn how to survive in Jerusalem."

The afternoon of the second day, Joanna pounded on the door. "Danya, are you all right in there? Answer me! Danya, wake up!"

"I'm awake. Now."

"You mustn't sleep so much. Here is something to keep you occupied." Joanna slid a tablet and stylus under the door.

"Wait. Stay and talk to me. Why am I here? What's going on?"

"I don't know. This is all a mystery to me, too. Chuza has forbidden me to visit with you. I am sorry, dear one. I must leave now."

"Then send Naomi."

"I can't even do that for you. Chuza has moved her to the servant's quarters. She'll be very busy and probably unable to visit you."

As Joanna predicted, Naomi didn't come. Not that day or the next. Near the end of the third day I turned to the writing materials Joanna had smuggled into my cage. At least the storeroom had a window, so I had some light. I touched my forefinger to the wedged point of the stylus and smoothed the palm of my hand across the wax. I used to love practicing my letters and words. Last year my writing had become so proficient that I had done some of Lev's schoolwork for him. I wondered now if Father had known.

I punctured the soft wax in firm, deliberate strokes and soon a letter took shape.

Danya to my dearest Father, greetings

I know you will never read this, but it will comfort me to talk to you on these tablets. When you allowed me to learn to write, did you ever think I would use my skill in this way? I miss you so much, Papa. And Lev and Nazareth and the happy life we shared there. Papa, one good thing about being locked up by myself is that I have figured something out. Your death was not my fault. At first I thought Chuza might be right, that my interest in Judah ben Hezekiah and his movement somehow caused the soldier to kill you. I hated myself. And I hated Judah, worse than I hate scorpions. But I no longer blame myself or Judah. I blame the soldier. And The Holy One. You always told me He has a plan for us, so this must have been His will for you. He sent the soldier to you. How else could he have been on that plaza just at the time you were crossing it? This makes me very angry. I don't understand The Holy One. Now when I think about His plans, dust swirls around inside my mind. I can't see anything because the dust obscures all. It fills

my lungs as well, so it becomes hard for me to breathe. Breathing is making me tired now. I have to stop and lie down.
Farewell.

I awoke to find Chuza standing under the oil lamp in its niche in the storeroom wall. He frowned as he read my letter to Father. The embers of my anger flared into rage.

"Give me those," I screamed as I snatched the tablets.

He folded one on top of the other and held them behind his back. "Who taught you to write?" he asked.

"Father. And Lev," I answered, standing and putting my hands on my hips. I was not going to let him criticize me for my literacy. Chuza might be one of those people who insisted that the Torah did not permit women to read and write, but Father told me those people were wrong. And Father, I now knew from Tobiah, was a true doctor of the law. He handed the tablets back to me. "Don't tell anyone that we have a brother named Lev."

"Why not?"

"Just don't tell anyone in Jerusalem that you have another brother."

"I'll decide what I say to people in Jerusalem!" I was tired of Chuza's orders. Tired of being pushed around by someone who was, after all, just my half-brother, not the ruler of all Judea. I pulled at the door latch. "And I won't be penned up like a goat anymore."

"I came to release you. I'm hungry. Get me some food, and I'll talk to you."

It was late, and the servants had retired. Joanna joined us, and we sat in the kitchen by the cook stove. I heated loaves of bread over still-warm embers. Joanna poured wine for Chuza and cut up chunks of cheese to melt on the bread.

"So why are you releasing me, O merciful one?" I said, not caring about the consequences of my fresh remark.

Joanna dropped the cheese knife and covered her mouth, but Chuza ignored my insult and swilled his wine. He belched and settled himself more comfortably on the bench. He seemed very pleased with himself. "This week I demanded a hearing before the Great Sanhedrin to address the accusation that Father was a revolutionary," he said.

"Everyone knows your father being a rebel is nonsense," said Joanna, soothingly.

"That doesn't keep people from saying so, wife," he snapped. "And in Jerusalem, it can be convenient to accept rumors as truth. This had to be dealt with. Swiftly."

Joanna folded her hands in her lap. "Then you were wise to do so, husband."

"Do you want your father-in-law to be remembered as a revolutionary conspirator? My enemies would leap at the opportunity to brand me along with him! Is that what you want?"

Joanna's color deepened. "No, husband."

Dodi backed into a corner, out of the range of Chuza's foot.

"What is this Great Sanhedrin?" I asked, trying to divert Chuza's attention away from Joanna. Managing his temper, and mine when I was with him, was a skill that I, too, would have to practice.

"Our highest court, which is seventy members when all are assembled. But this matter required only twenty-three. Pour me more wine, wife."

Chuza recounted his frantic efforts to obtain a hearing before the Sanhedrin on short notice. "I had to promise, pressure, bribe, call in favors. You can't imagine the work it took." Then he explained how he had evaluated the possible accusations against Father, gathered witnesses, and formulated shrewd arguments.

As he washed down several rounds of bread and cheese with more wine, he rendered an account of the enquiry itself. Only one credible piece of evidence had surfaced. Some pilgrims from Cana testified that they had witnessed Father speaking to Judah ben Hezekiah near the Sea of Galilee. But, when pressed for details at the hearing, they admitted Father did so only to prevent Judah from harming them and me.

An enemy of Chuza's had brought to light the fact that Father and Judah's father had been students together at the Temple's beth hamidrash. But Chuza's enemy was ridiculed by the court when three witnesses, high priests themselves, swore that Hezekiah and Father had always been enemies, each holding sharply contrasting views on how to re-establish The Holy One's kingdom in Israel. Father was a Pharisee; Hezekiah a revolutionary. Chuza laughed until he coughed while rendering his account of this part of the hearing.

"In the end, the court found Father blameless, completely innocent," he concluded. "When Herod Archelaus received the ruling from the Sanhedrin, he ordered that the soldier responsible for Father's death should suffer further punishment and declared Father's honor fully restored.

"So that's the report," said Chuza, draining his fifth cup of wine. "It's safe for you to stay in this city, thanks to me. Our family has no ties to any rebels. But to associate with one could mean death to all of us. You understand that now, Danya?"

I nodded. Chuza's chin dropped to his chest, and he fell asleep. Dodi darted for the crumbs that dropped from his lap.

"Please understand that your brother does care for you," said Joanna. "Your father's responsibilities have suddenly fallen to him, and he's inexperienced in caring for other people." She paused and pried the empty cup from Chuza's hand. "He's doing what he thinks is best, though we may not agree with all of his decisions."

Having slept so much over the course of the last three days, I couldn't fall asleep that night. So much had happened over the course of the last month. So many complicated, confusing, terrible things had happened. So much I couldn't understand. Once again, I wandered sleeplessly through the house until I stood before Chuza's writing cabinet. Perhaps someday if I had a record of the events of the last month, I would be able to sort it out and make sense of it. I took a pen, ink, and some sheets of papyrus from the cabinet, brought them to my room, dipped the pen into the inkwell, and began my account with the night of the raid.

My first sensation upon awakening that night was an unusual silence, the absence of my brother Lev's restless sleep-breathing. His empty mat signaled that the moment had finally arrived: the raid on Sepphoris, the Roman capital city of Galilee, would take place tonight. But Lev had snuck off to join the rebels without me! I tightened the combs in my braided hair and donned the clothing I'd hidden under my mat. Disguised in the head covering and tunic of a young man, I crept by my father, sleeping in the other room, and slipped out the door. I was a swift runner; I would catch up to Lev and participate in this holy adventure with him.

I wrote all night, words tumbling out faster than I could form their shapes. Once the sheets had dried, I hid them under my sleeping platform. Feeling like I had broken a fever, I slept soundly.

I awoke late the next morning, roused finally by my anxiety about Lev. He should know that Father had died. And, if he was in Jerusalem, he needed to leave because he was putting all of us in danger. Herod Archalaus had spies everywhere, Chuza said.

Judah ben Hezekiah had said that Lev had gone to the Essenes. Perhaps Joanna knew something about them or even knew some of them. Maybe she would help me search for Lev.

I found her in the dining room, counting the soup bowls in a storage cabinet. I told her only that Lev, as far as we knew, had recently joined an Essene sect somewhere. And that I longed to see him.

"I know it would be a great consolation for you to see him, Danya. And Lev should know his father has died, but Chuza has decided not to seek him out right now."

"Why not?"

"He thinks it would bring Lev to Jerusalem, and that Chuza's enemies would try to link Lev to Judah ben Hezekiah, as they did with your father. Chuza would have to fight all over again, this time to prove his brother's innocence. What if he failed?"

He probably would fail, I thought. "But if Lev is with the Essenes in Jerusalem, he would flee the city once he knew this. Then all of us would be safer," I reasoned. "Let me look for him, please! Tell me how to find the Essenes."

"I see what you mean. And a son should know that his father has died. There is an Essene quarter not far from here." Joanna put the bowls back and closed the cabinet door. She explained that I couldn't roam the streets and alleys of Jerusalem unaccompanied. That might be dangerous, and, anyway, Chuza wouldn't permit it. But I felt that she was wavering and that I might yet persuade her when we heard heavy footsteps in the hallway outside the dining room.

"Here he is now," said Joanna, and she began straightening the sleeves of my tunic as Chuza entered the room. "Your sister needs some clothing that fits her better and is appropriate to her station in life here," she said. "You don't want her looking like the poor relative from Galilee in front of our friends, do you?"

I was the poor relative from Galilee, and, though Joanna was joking, it stung a little to hear this said aloud. Chuza frowned, but Joanna persisted. "My things are too small for her, and hers are wearing out."

"All right," Chuza sighed. "Off to your father's shop, but I don't have time to accompany you. Take one of the male servants with you."

"The servants are already overburdened with preparations for tonight's dinner. Better not to tie one up waiting around for us. Father's shop is close, and we'll be safe with him."

While Chuza considered this, Joanna shifted from one foot to the other. "Just see that the old crook doesn't overcharge me like he usually does," said Chuza finally.

She gave him a quick kiss. "Of course, husband. Thank you."

After he left, I said, "Should you be doing this for me? What if Chuza finds out?

"Even if he does, which is unlikely, he'll eventually see the propriety of it. A son should know when his father has died. Chuza believes this, but he's not himself right now. He's anxious because so much has changed in Jerusalem of late. Staying in favor becomes harder every day."

Before we set out, Joanna gave detailed instructions to her servants about the dinner preparations. I admired her air of confidence as she did this. When she wasn't with Chuza, she seemed so competent. Though she was small-boned and delicate in her mannerisms, she carried herself with authority.

Joanna knew her way around Jerusalem. Because Efron had no sons, he had schooled Joanna in his business. Before she was married, she often accompanied him on his business affairs around the city. The Essene quarter was close to her father's shop though Joanna had rarely gone there because Essenes do not wear silk. But she assured me that they were pious, righteous people, so we would be safe among them.

A stairway at the southern edge of the Upper City brought us down to some twisting alleys and into the Essene quarter. The houses here, with their tiled roofs and plastered stone walls, were smaller but still elegant by my standards. We knocked on doors, intending to ask if anyone knew of a Lev ben Micah from Nazareth. But, in house after house, no one answered our knocking. The aroma of baking bread and grilled vegetables drew us to a long building, which turned out to be a dining hall where most of the quarter's residents were enjoying a meal together. Men, women, and children, all dressed in white linen, stood and sang a hymn of thanks. *"Thou hast redeemed my soul from the Pit, and Thou hast raised me up to everlasting height. I walk on limitless level ground . . ."*

When the singing ended, the servers brought food to their tables, and all eyes turned to us. Joanna stated our business to one of their leaders. He went from table to table asking if anyone had heard of a new member named Lev, from Nazareth. But, even in this large group, no one had heard of him. They suggested we try the monastery in Qumran, whose ranks grew daily with young men from all over the country. But Qumran was more than a half day's walk from Jerusalem, and it would be impossible for us to go there. Another of their leaders suggested we write a letter to Lev and entrust it to him in case he ever came across my brother. But I dared not accept his kindness. He, too, would be tainted if such a letter were to go astray. We thanked them for their time, and, discouraged, hurried back to the Upper City. We still had to go to Efron's shop and order some clothes for me, so Chuza wouldn't become suspicious of our whereabouts.

In Efron's shop, sheets of silk lined the walls, hanging from pegs fastened near the ceiling. Long lengths of saffron, pink, red, and blue-hued silks spilled down to the floor and rustled with each breath of wind flowing through the door. Entering his shop was like walking into a fluttering rainbow.

"Joanna, my love." said Efron as he popped out from a curtained back room. "And Danya. Is today the day you join the ranks of the most beautiful women of Jerusalem?"

I managed a polite smile. "Today is the day I stop borrowing Joanna's clothing, at least."

Efron told me to pick any color, and I chose the saffron. He wafted the length of silk over my palm; it was so soft I felt my touch might melt it. The women tailors clucked and measured and fussed over me. Joanna advised about trimming the cut. But I had no heart for this business.

My heart had been fixed on finding Lev. When Efron asked me to pick a color for my second tunic, I listlessly pointed to the white. "How about something more striking? This crimson perhaps? Look how gorgeous it is against your skin."

Crimson reminded me of Naomi. A light crimson tinted her cheeks when she laughed. "No thank you. The white will be more useful," I said. "But could we also order something for my friend Naomi? Her clothes are as worn as mine, and she would be so happy to have one of your beautiful tunics, Efron."

"Surely, my dear," said Efron.

Joanna took my hand. "Danya, Naomi won't need . . . I'm so sorry to have to tell you this, but Naomi is no longer staying with us. Chuza has found her. . . a position."

"What do you mean 'a position'? What has he done now?"

Joanna cleared her throat. "Chuza has sold Naomi to Plotinus Metellus, a Roman friend of his. His wife just had triplets, all boys who survived their birth. Most extraordinary and unplanned for. Plotinus needed an extra caretaker for his daughters so that their nurse could care for these infants. He was willing to pay a very high price for Naomi given the circumstances. Chuza thinks Naomi's father will be grateful for the money. Amos had given your father permission to sell her, as I understand."

I threw the crimson silk on the floor. "But not to a Roman! Surely Chuza could've found something better for her if he had only waited a little longer! Father would never have done such a thing!"

Joanna tried to hug me, but I turned my back on her. "He didn't even allow me to say farewell to her."

"He didn't tell me either. She was sent away before I knew about it. I know she's like a sister to you, Danya. I'm so, so sorry for both of you."

Efron's ever-present smile had sagged into a frown. "How could my son-in-law have done such a thing? He never told me about this poor girl. I could've found her a position with Jews."

Joanna moved to the wall and stroked the crimson silk. Quietly, bitterly, she said, "And how would that have benefited Chuza? No, Chuza used Naomi's unfortunate situation to curry favor with a Roman."

I was shocked to hear Joanna criticize her husband so harshly. I had only seen her accommodate or conciliate in matters relating to Chuza.

"I worry that he'll mistreat you, too, my pet," said Efron. His eyebrows wilted. "Did I make a mistake in choosing him for you? I thought there could be no greater blessing than to have you marry into an aristocratic, priestly family."

Joanna pulled at the corners of her eyes to stop the tears that had begun spilling from them. She straightened her back. "It is a blessing, father, and I am determined that you will one day have grandsons, and they will serve as leaders of the land of Judah. Chuza can be very difficult, but I'm not mistreated."

Efron's frown deepened. "I wish I could ransom this girl myself, but I don't have the money. Even if I did, it's not my place. It's her family's."

"Then I'll write a letter to Naomi's father," I said. "Amos will return the money in order to buy her back."

Joanna considered this. "He's a poor man, badly in need of money. He might not."

"He will," I insisted. "He loves his daughter. He would never consent to her bondage in a Roman household."

Efron produced a pen and paper and sat me at a table. "Write to her father. I'll engage a messenger to carry it to Nazareth and bring back his reply."

Danya to Amos of Nazareth, greetings
Do you know that Chuza did not sell Naomi to a Jew but to a Roman? Please, take the money you received for her term of servitude and buy her back. I will help with anything you ask. Send your answer back with this messenger.
Farewell

Then I had another idea. Efron came in contact with many, many people from all over the world. He was a good man, someone I knew I could trust with my secret about Lev, so I asked Efron for a second sheet of papyrus.

Danya to my dear brother Lev, greetings
I hope this will find its way into your hands soon. My message is urgent. When you read what follows, you will want to come to Jerusalem, but, if you do, you will endanger your life and mine.

With the deepest sadness I tell you that Father is dead. He was killed by a Roman soldier and buried here in Jerusalem. Do not try to visit Father's tomb. No one here knows that Chuza has a brother who was a member of Judah's band, most importantly not even Chuza. Spies are everywhere. You must stay in hiding, though my heart breaks to have to tell you this. Let Efron know by letter or messenger that you are safe. I worry about you all the time.
Farewell

Efron pledged to make discrete inquiries about Lev and see to my letter's safe delivery when it was appropriate. I sealed my letter with wax which I softened with the flame of an oil lamp. Like the wax, I could feel the shape of my life changing. It was being molded into something new, though I feared the hand that held the softening flame and the seal to be imprinted upon me.

Against Joanna's counsel, I waited for Chuza to return home that evening and confronted him in the courtyard, making no attempt to check my anger. I grabbed at the sleeve of his tunic. "Father would be ashamed of you. Naomi is twelve years old! How could you sell her to a Roman?"

"And how old are you? Thirteen? Fourteen? You understand so little of the world, village girl. I see I'll have to explain its ways to you: Naomi became my responsibility when Father died. I decide what's best for her. This is a good situation for your little friend. Soldiers won't break into the home of a high Roman official and drag his slaves off as suspected revolutionaries. She'll be safe in the household of Plotinus Metellus. And after she has completed her seven years of service there, she can lead her life as a free Jewish woman."

"Seven years in a Roman household! They keep graven images in their homes. They eat pigs. What Jewish man would marry her after she had lived with Romans?"

"That's not my concern. You, however, are. Remember that I make all decisions for you. You have no rights other than the ones I choose to grant you. Now let go of me."

He brushed at the dusty print my hand had left on the sleeve of his otherwise spotless tunic and stepped around me to enter his house.

"I will take this matter to the Sanhedrin. They will hear me."

"Ha, ha, ha. Since when does a woman, much less a girl, who owns no property be allowed to testify in a court of law?"

"Father would be ashamed of you," I repeated.

He continued to laugh even after he slammed the door on me.

When we returned many days later to pick up the clothing tailored for me, Efron produced a letter from Nazareth, still tied and sealed. "The messenger brought this just today."

Amos to Danya, greetings
This letter comes written by the hand of a scribe in Sepphoris. I did not know Chuza had sold my daughter. I received no word or money from him. What has happened to your father? Micah would not sell my daughter to a Gentile. I will come to Jerusalem after the harvest to see to this matter. I cannot leave Nazareth until then. If I fail to bring in the harvest, we will lose everything. We live in constant fear that the next day will bring the Roman legions down upon us.
Farewell

"What deception is this?" exclaimed Efron. His hands shook as he clasped and unclasped them. "Chuza didn't tell Amos he had sold Naomi? Didn't send him the money?"

Joanna's voice was faint. "There must be some misunderstanding. Chuza wouldn't be so dishonest. He wouldn't sell a man's daughter and keep the money for himself. It can't be!"

As I rolled up Amos' letter, my feelings towards Chuza darkened and tightened with each rotation of the parchment.

During the next two months of that hot, dry season, Chuza and Joanna entertained almost every night. Planning and supervising the preparations for these lavish feasts occupied Joanna's days, so we spent very little time together. I worried incessantly about Naomi, but when I tried to talk to Joanna about her, she suddenly had some pressing matter to attend to. It was as if the word "Naomi" summoned a wind that blew my words away before they reached Joanna's ears.

Father's ears would listen. He would care about what was happening to Naomi and to his family. I wrote to him again.

> **Danya to my dearest Papa, greetings**
> *Chuza tells me that Plotinus Metellus has not yet paid him for Naomi. When he does, Chuza says he will send the money on to Amos. But I wonder if Chuza has received the money and pays for all these feasts with it. Amos promised to come here after the harvest, but he has not arrived. When he does, Chuza will be very angry with me. But how else could I help Naomi? I wish I could find more ways. There is more you should know. Chuza is often hard-hearted towards Joanna. She says this is because she has not borne him a child. She seeks the help of physicians, and they make her drink foul-tasting potions. But Joanna is always kind to me. She shows me how to dress and fix my hair and how to talk to people. I am grateful for her. She is my only friend and I am less lonely when I am with her.*
> **Farewell**

Chuza never invited Efron and Joanna's mother to his parties, so Joanna had to see her father at his shop. Sometimes I accompanied her on these visits. One time as we were crossing the Upper City's market square, we thought we saw Naomi. A slight girl with bushy hair was clutching a child in one arm and dragging a second one, crying, with her other hand. I felt a stab of joy and called out, "Naomi, Naomi," and pushed my way through the crush of market-goers. Naomi had truly loved Father, had lost what I had lost. At least we could comfort each other even though I couldn't free her.

I thought the girl turned at my call, but I lost sight of her as the crowd folded around her. Joanna, a few steps behind me said, "That couldn't be Naomi. That girl is too thin." But she paled and her voice cracked as she said this. We both knew we had seen Naomi.

Danya to my dearest Papa, greetings

I saw Naomi today. She is starving or sick or mistreated in some way. Chuza continues to entertain. He says he needs to make more friends and to keep the ones he has because these are very danger-ous times throughout the land of Judah, and only those who know the right people will survive. Chuza compares our land to a kettle beginning to boil, with clusters of bubbles rising in different sec-tions of the pot. Another stick of wood will make the fire so hot that the whole pot will churn up and spill over. Joanna and I are afraid. Chuza carries a knife.

Farewell

One letter, more than any of the others, occupied me throughout those sad, lonely months. On my wax tablets, I would add some words, take others out, then wipe them all away and start over, time and time again. Finally, when the letter said exactly what I wanted, I copied it onto a sheet of papyrus.

Danya of Nazareth to The Holy One, greetings

Look at all the bad that has happened since I sought to do Your Will! Lev is lost, Father is dead, and Naomi withers away in slav-ery. The people of Nazareth have had to abandon their homes and now wander the earth seeking refuge. Thousands of innocent people were killed in the Temple courtyard within sight of the Holy of Holies. You say You love Your people, and yet You permit these terrible things to happen. When are You going to save us? You spared me, but was it only so I might suffer more? Why do You keep Your plans a mystery? I can only try to save myself now. And Naomi. I must save Naomi.

Farewell

I waited for a clear, star-filled night. While the household slept, I car-ried my letter and a lamp up to the roof. With steady hands, I joined the page to the wick's flame and inhaled the fumes of my acrid words as they rose up to the heavens.

BETROTHAL AND FREEDOM

Five guests lounged on the dining couches: Lucius, Plotinus Metellus and his wife, and two managers of Archelaus's farming estates. Languorously, they wended their way through the heavy meal with Chuza, Joanna, and me. I resented Chuza's demand that I sometimes attend his Roman-style dinners, feasts that I considered unseemly by Jewish standards. Unrelated men and women shared the same table, consuming excessive quantities of wine and rich foods. The Jewish guests often ignored our dietary laws to keep up with the Romans.

Though a breeze occasionally wafted through the open windows, it failed to cool us. Its arrival only irritated the oil lamps and propelled dark clouds of smoke into our flushed faces. Midway through the dinner, I developed a pounding headache.

As Chuza carved a joint of roast calf, he and his guests gossiped about political leaders. "At first I thought Archelaus was a genius," said Chuza. "When he took office, he displayed brilliant leadership by abolishing some of our taxes and tolls and freeing most of the political prisoners."

"Yes," said Lucius, "but those moves exhausted his fund of brilliance. The massacre on the Mount, then deposing two High Priests showed him to be the fool he really is." With his fingernail, Lucius flipped the body of a crawfish from its shell. "Even we Romans meddle more successfully in Temple affairs than that boy has. Are you sure he's one of yours?"

Chuza snorted. "Unfortunately he is a Jew. His father had a habit of murdering his sons but died before getting to this one."

"Speaking of Herod's sons," said one of the estate managers, "I hear good reports about the one ruling Galilee and Perea."

The other manager reached for a stuffed hen's egg and popped it whole into his mouth. "My money's on that one, he said, spewing bits of yolk as he spoke. "Herod Antipas knows how to collect taxes, just like his father did. He'll last in Galilee. He might even expand his territory. He'd be a good one to work for."

Grease had congealed on the platter of sheep's tails; my stomach turned. The sight of Plotinus, busy gorging himself on Chuza's bounty while Naomi starved under his roof, sickened me further. When Plotinus heaved himself across the table to stab at a platter of bull's kidneys, I excused myself to step out of the dining room for some fresh air.

Out in the courtyard, a breeze freshened the air. Stars gleamed in a clear sky. How I missed the open spaces of the country. In Jerusalem, I spent most of my time indoors. Even when I was allowed out, I had to be veiled, accompanied, and restricted to areas within the Upper City. What I would've given for a long walk by myself over the hills with the sun or the rain kissing my skin. It seemed as if I had lived in Chuza's house for years instead of only months.

"Beautiful night, isn't it? The party should move out here."

Lucius startled me. I hadn't heard him enter the courtyard, and, since we were alone, it was inappropriate of him to speak to me. Or was it? Jerusalem's customs frequently differed from those of my village's. I nodded at Lucius and started back into the house.

"Why hurry off?" he said. "It's so hot inside. Stay a minute. I don't bite."

Perspiration and wine stained his toga. My instincts said to flee, but it might be rude for me to leave. It might be considered an offense against my brother's friend. If only some of the others would join us.

"I saw you looking into the sky," said Lucius. "Do you know that heavenly bodies interpret the present and foretell the future?"

"I know only that the heavens are the creation of The Holy One," I said quietly.

He laughed. "The heavens are much more interesting than that. I'll demonstrate. Find Mars."

I'd never heard of Mars. Lev hadn't taught me the Roman names for the stars. Embarrassed by my ignorance, I shrugged my shoulders,

Lucius grabbed my wrist and pointed my hand at a reddish body in the sky. "That one. That's the planet Mars."

My arm froze, then recoiled. Lucius clenched my wrist tighter, lowered my hand into his, and pried open my fist. Lightly, he ran his fingers across my palm. "A virgin's hand," he said. "It needs a man to teach it women's work."

He was breathing hard; my breath stopped. Beads of sweat dripped from his hand into mine. I yanked my hand away and started towards the door. He blocked me. I tried to scream but couldn't summon the breath.

"Danya, are you bothering my friend Lucius?" said Chuza, entering from the doorway into the courtyard. "You should be with the women in the reception hall. Go, Danya. My apologies, Lucius. My sister still practices some of the improprieties of village living. I hope she didn't offend you."

"It's forgotten," said Lucius.

I almost cried with relief, but, feeling shamed for no good reason, I slunk inside. I wasn't sure whether Chuza had saved me or betrayed me. I went directly to my bedroom, bolted the door, and slept fitfully until a nightmare ripped me from my rest. Judah's teeth tore at the ropes binding my hands, but his sharp incisors also cut my wrists. My blood flooded down the side of a hill, polluting a vineyard and the vast field of grain below it.

My bed cushions were damp as Lucius' toga, and I couldn't get back to sleep. In this city, people slept on rooftops on nights as hot as this, so I carried a light blanket and a pillow up the staircase to the roof. As I neared the top, I heard Chuza and Joanna talking above me.

"This tile is so hard," said Chuza. "Spread out another blanket for me, wife."

"You know," said Joanna, "there will be more and more of this with Danya."

"I should lock her in her room when we entertain," Chuza grumbled.

"It's not Danya's fault that she's a beautiful young woman. Men are going to desire her. Your job is to protect her. Here, try this pillow under your head, husband."

"Ah, that feels much better. Come and lie down next to me. And you should know that I have to protect myself as well. I can't offend my friends by bashing in their skulls when they try to seduce my sister, even though I may want to. That damn Lucius thinks every unattached woman is his plaything."

"Then maybe it's time for Danya to marry. A husband would protect her, as you do me."

Oh, no. Time for me to marry? After everything else that had happened! I was still in mourning for Father! I should announce my presence and end this discussion immediately. But knowing what they were thinking might give me some control over the matter. I curled up on a step and made myself quiet as a fox.

"That has crossed my mind. Being responsible for her is a burden, and she's costing me a fortune. The jewelry and the clothes. I can't afford her!"

"Nonsense. I loan her my jewelry. You agreed to the clothes. She costs you next to nothing. My father, you remember, made no profit on her wardrobe."

"I know, I know. 'Only a shekel or two to cover the cost of the fabric.' Hmmmm. If I found the right match for Danya, the bridewealth she might command could be considerable."

"Bridewealth is money you must hold for her, should her husband divorce her. It doesn't become your money. You can't spend it."

"I know, wife. Don't lecture me on the law."

"The match must be to someone with whom Danya can find happiness. A good man. A good Jew. She is not going to the highest bidder!"

"I know that, too. I'm not a barbarian."

"Naomi."

"Stop reminding me of that girl! Naomi is not my sister. Once Plotinus finally pays me, Amos will appreciate the money I get him for her. If only that fat Roman would stop making excuses. You must show more respect for my judgment, wife. Move over. It's too hot to have you so close to me."

"Promise me, Chuza. No marriage unless it's a good match."

"Stay out of my business."

Once Chuza was snoring, I crept back to my sweltering room and climbed onto my bed. I tossed and turned. I certainly did not want to marry at this time. Other girls thought marriage was The Holy One's plan for them, though I had always believed I was meant for something grander. However, perhaps marriage was now my punishment for not following Judah when I had the chance, for saying "No" to The Holy

One. And with whom would my brother match me? Someone old, fat, cruel, stupid, or ugly, but rich? Chuza did have the power to marry me to anyone he chose, even to Lucius. I was trapped. But I vowed to find a way to slip my foot from this snare.

Several weeks later, before the Sabbath sundown, Joanna's ivory comb tugged and snagged at the tangled knots in my hair. "Ouch! Be careful," I complained.

"Sorry. Sit down. This is going to take some time," Joanna said.

I pushed aside a linen sleeping tunic and sat on the dressing table's bench. Joanna's closet was crowded with chests and cupboards of clothes, but she reserved a corner of the room for grooming. "Work in small sections, so it won't hurt so much," I said, enduring a slash of the comb's prong along my scalp.

"Don't pull away," said Joanna. "I'm about to tell you something that may hurt you, but you must hear it." She took a deep breath. "Danya, Chuza has received a proposal of marriage for you. He didn't seek this man out. This man came to Chuza."

"A marriage proposal! I'm much too young to marry. And I'm in mourning for Father."

"You're fourteen, Danya. Not too young to marry. And this man will wait until the mourning period has passed. You must at least consider his proposal."

I sighed. "Who is it? It can't be anyone I know because I hardly know anyone. Oh, not a Roman, is it?"

"No. It's Tobiah."

"Tobiah? The priest with the bald spot and the long beard?" I squeaked.

"Yes, that one, though there are better ways to describe him."

"The tall one. With the long, clean hands? That I met on the Temple Mount? That came to shiva after Father's funeral?"

"Yes, that one. Tobiah is a good man. And a good Jew."

"But he must be at least twenty years older than I am! He's older than Chuza!"

"When you're fourteen, most people are older than you."

My stomach dropped. Tobiah probably had scraggly gray hair on his chest. And yellow teeth. Judah's chest would be smooth and hard, and his teeth white and straight as cut limestone.

"Uh oh. Hold your breath: here comes a huge knot," said Joanna. "Why do you let your hair get to be such a mess?"

"There's too much of it and it's too much trouble. I'll chop it all off and then no one will want to marry me." I wanted this marriage talk to end. Now.

"Oh, hush," Joanna giggled. "You should be grateful for your beautiful hair. And grateful for such a good proposal."

"I'm not interested in any proposal, good or bad. Tobiah as a match for me is a ridiculous idea." I'd distract Joanna and let the subject drop. "Will you oil my hair? Now that the knots are out, I see that it could use something to make it shine."

Joanna removed the stopper from one of her glass vials.

"Not that flowery-scented one." I pointed to another flask. "The cinnamon, over there."

"Older men can be sexy, you know," said Joanna.

"What older men? Chuza? Ugh."

"You told me your friend Miryam was happy with her older husband."

"Miryam is favored. The Holy One gave her someone that He chose especially for her."

"Oh, nonsense. Her parents chose her husband, and, wisely, she accepted their good judgment. Anyway, this match does favor you."

"Can I look at your makeup, Joanna?" Joanna's cosmetic pots and boxes with their spoons and spatulas and tiny sponges were tidily laid out on the dressing table before me. She showed me kohl to darken the eyelashes and eyebrows. Sikra to redden the lips and cheeks. A reddish-yellow dye to tint the nails. "Never mind. It's all too complicated for me. I'm too young for makeup. And for marriage. Would you do my nails instead?"

Joanna indulged me and dug in a basket for a pumice stone. "Tobiah is a scholar, like your father. From a priestly family, same status as you. You are not inferior to him."

"I am inferior. I'm a poor girl from a little village in Galilee." I held out my hand for her to work on my fingernails. "And I don't love him. I can't imagine ever loving him." It wasn't right, was it, to marry one man if I loved another? *If* I loved another?

"Tobiah said very flattering things about you. He said that his world has been turned upside down since the moment he saw you on the Temple Mount, and that you have permeated his thoughts since then. 'Permeated.'" Joanna sighed. "That sounds so romantic. Remember that this match is all Tobiah's idea. He says he won't be at peace until he marries you." She sighed again. "'Permeated.'"

"That's all very nice, but why would such a distinguished older man want me? I don't have a dowry. Father left no property that could match me to a man of Tobiah's stature."

"Tobiah says he doesn't require a dowry. And why wouldn't he want you? You're beautiful and wellborn and literate. You're the daughter of a priest, which means Tobiah's sons would be eligible for priestly status."

When Joanna finished with my hands she said, "I want to see if pumice can smooth out some other rough places on you. Why, I could grate cheese on these ragged elbows of yours!"

"I'm not wellborn. Not really. Though Father was of a priestly family, what about my mother? She was a foreigner, from Nabatea."

"True, but Chuza told me she was a member of the elite there."

"Really? What else do you know about my mother? Father told us so little. Why did she leave Nabatea and come to a poor village in Galilee?"

"It had to do with politics in her country. Nahara told Chuza that a powerful pagan clan, seeking a Jewish alliance, attempted to coerce her family into giving her in marriage to one of their sons. She went into hiding to avoid this, and little, remote Nazareth turned out to be a perfect place to hide. It's quite a coincidence, now that I think about it. Your mother was living in Nazareth during political unrest when your father met her. Hmmmm. And here you are, living in Jerusalem during a time of turmoil when Tobiah meets you: clearly, this match is destined to be!"

"The only coincidence is that, like my mother, there is an attempt to coerce me into an unwanted marriage," I said sourly.

Joanna dropped the pumice into a bowl of water. "There, all finished. You should pay more attention to your grooming. You're so pretty when you do."

I stared down at my hands and fingernails, turning them over, back and forth. They did look nice, but they looked nicer to me when they were pruning grapevines and shaping dough and drawing water from the well in Nazareth. A wave of homesickness drenched me, as it often did since I'd come to Jerusalem.

"Look at yourself." Joanna held her mirror of finely polished metal up to my face and stood behind me. "This is how I'll fix your hair on your wedding day, flowing over your shoulders in sparkling black waves."

I rubbed at a blemish on my chin.

Joanna continued, as if recounting a dream of hers. "The bridegroom and his friends will carry you on a litter to his house. People in the streets will sing, '*Who is this coming up from the wilderness, like a column of smoke, perfumed with myrrh and frankincense and all the fragrant powders of the merchant?*' And then of Tobiah, they will sing, '*See how he comes leaping on the mountains, bounding over the hills.*'

"Your bridesmaid, me, will be dressed all in white. You will look like a queen sitting under the huppah. Tobiah will sing: '*Arise, my love, my fair one, and come away; How beautiful you are, my love, how very beautiful! Your eyes are doves behind your veil. . . . Your lips are like a crimson thread, and your cheeks are like halves of a pomegranate.*' Ahhh, we'll sing and dance and feast for seven days."

We both laughed and, for just a moment, I believed such joy was possible. Then I swatted the mirror away from my face. "Oh, stop it, Joanna. I'm not going to marry just so I can be a bride."

Joanna laid the mirror down and lowered her voice. "There are worse things than being a bride, you know. Like not being a bride."

This had gone far enough. Why did Joanna keep pushing this match with Tobiah? He wasn't the only man in the world, after all. "I just can't be a bride now. I'm not ready to marry."

Joanna shrugged her shoulders and bit her lip. I must have offended her. "Joanna, I appreciate that you're so good to me and that you want me to be happy. But can we stop talking about this? Would you let me try one of your perfumes? Please?"

She nodded.

Joanna's favorite, I already knew, was the jasmine. I sniffed an alabaster flask of lily essence and wrinkled my nose, then reached for a little container in the back. When I removed its lid, the aroma of balm filled the closet room. "Ugh," said Joanna, "It reminds me of medicine. I don't even know what it is."

"This is balm, an evergreen that grows wild in Galilee. It smells like home. I love it."

"Then take it, please." She took my hands in hers and looked into my eyes. "Danya, my dear sister. No more playing. You must grow up. Tobiah is a righteous, gentle man. His family has property, and he will provide well for you. Don't be afraid; your marriage will be happier than mine, and soon you'll know the joy of children."

I shook my head. "Thank you for consulting with me, Joanna, but my answer is no."

She dropped my hands and covered her jars, vials, and boxes. With her back to me she said, "Danya, I thought you should be allowed to decide about your marriage. Chuza did not." She took a deep breath. "The fact is that Chuza and Tobiah have already drawn up a contract. Chuza has received a mohar of five hundred denarii. You are betrothed to Tobiah."

A rough-rinded melon on the kitchen table fell victim to one of my fits of temper over this betrothal, this betrayal. With one sharp stroke of a long-bladed knife, I stabbed into the fruit's core: betrothed without my knowledge, without my consent! I sawed into the melon, and my knife mired in its flesh: marriage to a stranger, an old stranger. Juice and seeds oozed from the table onto the floor, much to Dodi's delight.

Though my heart was filled with anger, my thoughts were split like the melon. I righted the half of the fruit that had flipped over in my attack. Reasons favoring a marriage to Tobiah: union with a good Jewish man of status and property; freedom from Chuza's unpredictable, harsh control; protection from the attentions of hyenas like Lucius. And there could be a worse match.

The other half, reasons opposing this marriage, lay face up: I didn't love Tobiah and I might even love Judah; Tobiah might not love me once he realized how uncultured and childish I was; the possibility of joining Judah ben Hezekiah's movement would have to be put aside once and for all. And there could be a better match.

But really what could I do? I had no father; Lev, my other protector, was lost; I had no way of escaping to a remote village in a foreign country; my oldest brother had legal control of me. The law offered me no recourse in this matter.

My jealousy of Miryam flared again. She had asked for help in her unhappiness over an offer of marriage, and The Holy One had answered her plea. During her betrothal to an older man she didn't know or love, Adonai had sent Miryam a light that brought her comfort and assurance. But prayer wouldn't help me. The Holy One wouldn't listen to me now, if He ever had. The burnt offering of my bitter letter surely had turned Him away from me.

On the other hand, even King David had had dark days, believing that Adonai had abandoned him. Yet he still prayed. *"How long, O Lord? How long will You hide Your face from me?"* I had missed talking to The Holy One. A prayer couldn't hurt, anyway. I put the knife down, closed my eyes, and whispered, *"Do not let the flood sweep over me, or the deep swallow me up, or the pit close its mouth over me. Answer me, O Lord, for Your steadfast love is good; according to Your abundant mercy, turn to me. Do not hide Your face from your servant, for I am in distress—make haste to answer me."*

When I opened my eyes, the answer lay on the table before me, so obvious and so simple that I had to laugh. Both sides of the melon were equal. Marriage or no marriage, each possibility contained a portion of sweetness. And each had a disagreeable component, an inedible rind that would have to be disposed of. The answer was to accept what had been served me, enjoy its goodness, and cut away its distastefulness.

I found my wax tablets and wrote the same thing, over and over, as if it were a school exercise. With each repetition, my stylus dug deeper and deeper until it scraped into the wood beneath the wax:

Danya of Nazareth to Judah ben Hezekiah,
Farewell

In the weeks that followed, I sometimes dreamt of dust clouds receding into the horizon, but the nightmares of my bleeding wrists ceased. Though I didn't feel the conviction of The Holy One's favor, as Miryam had, new dreams began to form when I was awake. I would be the wife of a righteous, powerful man. Perhaps I could have some influence over the lives of our people after all. Both Judith and Esther had been married, and that had not prevented them from acting heroically in a great cause.

My marriage to Tobiah was to take place after the feast of Sukkot and before the rains began. Except it almost didn't.

By the end of that dry season, Jerusalem teemed with rebels Herod Archelaus had failed to root out. The slaughter on the Temple Mount had served to only strengthen the rebels' resolve to drive the Romans from our land. Shortly after my betrothal, Rome lost patience with its seditious province of Judea. Quintilius Varus, the Roman legate of Syria, swept down from Antioch with an army of twelve thousand men to punish the enemies of the Empire.

Chuza told us Quintilius Varus looked as if he were carved from stone: cold, unmoving eyes, a severe mouth, and a uniform that never wrinkled. Chuza also said that Varus's shoulders were twice the breadth of Archelaus's, and that the young ethnarch trembled in the legate's presence. As soon as Varus arrived in Jerusalem, Archelaus vacated his own palace to make room for Varus and his tribunes.

The soldiers sealed off the city and launched a house-to-house search for rebels and their accomplices. No sections of Jerusalem were spared. Chuza locked Joanna, me, and the servants into the house and hurried off, carrying the bronze key to the courtyard gate with him. Joanna paced all morning, peering out windows and scratching at the red bumps that had arisen on her neck and arms. I recalled one of Chuza's justifications for selling Naomi to Plotinus Metellus: "Soldiers won't break into the home of a high Roman official and drag his slaves off as suspected revolutionaries." This one and only day I was grateful for Chuza's betrayal of my friend.

In the afternoon, Chuza returned with Efron by his side and Yona, Joanna's mother, in his arms. "Your parents will be safer with us," he said to Joanna as he settled Yona onto a couch. "I thought you would want them here."

Joanna threw her arms around him. "My dear husband."

Chuza smiled broadly. Then he deposited Joanna's parents into our care and left, locking us in again.

When we were introduced, Yona smiled a sweet, crooked smile. Her right side was paralyzed, and she had lost her ability to speak. But she had lively, expressive eyes and she pointed excitedly at me with her one good hand.

"She thinks you're beautiful, Danya," said Efron. "I told you proper clothing was all you needed. And now you're betrothed to a Temple priest! We wish you much happiness with Tobiah. It's an excellent match."

"Thank you, Efron, but at this time I really can't think about my own happiness."

"This will pass. Jerusalem has survived worse. Take heart, my dear."

Privately I asked Efron, as I always did, "Lev?" And, as always, he gently shook his head and patted my shoulder. "But I keep your letter safe and ready to send on a moment's notice," he reminded me.

Joanna sat us all in the reception hall and chewed on the stumps of her fingernails. "I'm so relieved that Chuza has brought you here. I was losing my mind with worry over you, Mother and Father. What's happening in the streets? We've been locked in here all day and know nothing."

"Terrible things," said Efron. "Soldiers storm into houses, shouting in Greek, or Gaulish, or Latin—who knows what they're saying—and drag men off to prison in the Antonia fortress. Or they torture someone until the victim produces the name of some suspected rebel. Even women and children are forced to name names."

At the thought of being tortured, fear clamped my tongue to the roof of my mouth. I vowed to myself to die rather than give up Lev's name. But I had been such a coward at other times.

"I think we're safe here," Efron said, unconvincingly. "At least we're together."

The rest of that day and the next, Chuza tore from the palace to the army camp, to the Temple porticoes, to the houses of his friends and enemies. Late each night he reported to Efron on his activities before sleeping a few hours and going back out.

Efron tried to soothe our anxieties with reports of Chuza's maneuverings to keep the soldiers from our door. "Chuza is valuable to Rome, and he's making sure Varus and all the Roman armies know this. He wants no mistakes as there were with your poor father."

Efron's respect for Chuza surprised me. I had never heard him speak highly of my brother. "Chuza's job is to oversee the revenues from all of the ethnarch's estates. He makes sure that the taxes levied upon them are collected and that Rome gets its share. And your brother can pressure, bribe, cajole, and even blackmail with the best of them. We're in good hands."

The arrests continued. Even in our section of the city, we heard the wails of women as soldiers dragged their husbands and sons from their houses. Efron reported that these arrests also were based on the flimsiest of evidence, often the perjured testimony of tortured witnesses. I admit I felt grateful to Chuza and was content to stay behind our locked gate.

The morning of the third day of Varus's rampage, Efron was restless. "My business has been left unattended too long. Mother will stay here, but I must go out for a while. I have urgent matters to attend to."

Joanna and I pleaded with Efron to stay, but he kissed each of us, promised to return before sundown, and left with Chuza. We worried all day about him. Joanna and I didn't speak of my father who, in the midst of Jerusalem's last crisis, had ventured into the city and never returned. The red bumps on Joanna's skin darkened.

In the afternoon, while I was cutting fruit and cheese into tiny pieces and Joanna was feeding them to Yona, a servant brought us some news. "I heard it from a delivery boy who heard it from the butcher who heard it from a camel driver who had entered the city through the Gate of Ephraim on the north: the crucifixions have begun. Outside the western and northern walls of the city, they have lashed hundreds of suspected rebels to crosses." Joanna's fingernails bled.

To our enormous relief, Efron returned unharmed, though greatly agitated, at nightfall. His business had taken him outside a northern gate where he had witnessed some crucifixions taking place. He told us that most of those executed were followers of the shepherd Anthronges, whom they believed to be a messiah. Anthronges and his four brothers had led raids on palaces and military outposts all over the land of Judah but had managed to avoid capture themselves. So the Roman army ended his revolt by executing anyone suspected of being a follower of Anthronges.

These unfortunate souls suffered the torturously slow death of asphyxiation. Their bodies hung on the crosses until the birds and beasts of prey picked their bones clean. The sight of the ravaged corpses at the entrance to the city was intended to teach a lesson: do not challenge the power of your Roman overlords. Efron said the only thing we could do now was "learn how to live with the Roman heel on our neck." Certainly the slingstones and captured spears of our peasant revolutionaries could never defeat such an adversary. Only the direct intervention of The Holy One could work such a wonder.

Quintilius Varus and his army spent several weeks ridding Jerusalem of its rebellious elements, and we women never once left the house during that terrible period. The day the last of the soldiers pulled out, Chuza summoned me to the reception hall.

I was surprised to find Tobiah there. Though we were engaged to be married, we hadn't seen each other since the day of Father's burial. In village life, with its trips to the well, the fields, and the market, encounters between betrothed men and women were natural and inevitable, but, in Jerusalem, couples often didn't meet before their wedding day. Tobiah and I had not had the opportunity to exchange the glances and shy smiles that spark the longings to touch and talk that are often love's tinder. In any event, the Roman terror had preoccupied us both. As I entered the reception hall, Chuza, at eye level with Tobiah's chest, was stabbing his finger into it. "The ketubbah is valid. We will take this matter to the Sanhedrin, not to a woman, and they will rule it lawful."

Tobiah looked even older than I had remembered him. His beard was longer and more unkempt. Deep circles rimmed his eyes. A shameful thought surfaced: I could be a widow before I was twenty years old.

Tobiah removed Chuza's finger. When he saw me, his face opened into the warm smile he had showed me on the day of Father's funeral. He extended a rolled sheaf of parchment to me. "The matter of my marriage proposal rests in your hands, Danya. Please read this."

I felt young and ignorant as I unrolled the formal document on one of the stone-topped tables. I began to read the page aloud, fervently hoping

I wouldn't stumble over its unfamiliar words. At least it was written in Aramaic and not Greek. "Female children which you shall have by me shall dwell in my house and receive maintenance from my property until they marry husbands. You shall dwell in my house and receive maintenance from my property so long as you remain a widow in my house. Male children which you shall have by me shall inherit—"

Chuza interrupted me. "This is a standard betrothal and marriage contract. You don't need to read the whole thing. The problem is this: Tobiah thinks this agreement is no longer binding."

"Yes," said Tobiah. "Since this document was drawn up and signed, my circumstances have changed. I want to know what Danya thinks."

"What Danya thinks!" Chuza spat out the words as if a fish bone clung to the tip of his tongue. "She's not permitted to think. 'Change in circumstances' doesn't change the agreement." Chuza turned to me. "The only difference is that after your marriage you and Tobiah will live in Sepphoris, not Jerusalem." He grabbed the ketubbah from me and tossed it on a wooden chair. It rolled off. Dodi scurried over to sniff it.

Live in Sepphoris, the gleaming limestone city on the hill. Yes, it was a Roman provincial capital, but it was the capital of Galilee, and most of its inhabitants were Jews. It was less than four Roman miles from Nazareth. I'd be surrounded by real grapevines, not the ones on frescoed walls. I'd be close to my own people, and far from Jerusalem's violence, restrictions, and confusing customs. I could hardly believe my good fortune. The only better thing would be to return to Nazareth itself. I smiled at Tobiah. "Living in Sepphoris would be fine."

Tobiah didn't return my smile. He rubbed at the back of his neck. "Danya, it's not the Sepphoris you knew. Chuza hasn't told you? There's been a disaster there."

"A disaster?"

Chuza suddenly became preoccupied with the pattern of shapes on the mosaic tile beneath him. He wouldn't look at me.

Tobiah clasped his hands together and pushed them against his chin. "This is such awful news, Danya. Perhaps your brother thought he could spare you the sadness of hearing it. But you must know what has happened." His voice quavered. "On their way to Jerusalem, Varus and his legions marched through Galilee. In retaliation for Judah ben Hezekiah's raid on Sepphoris, they burned much of that city and enslaved its Jewish leaders."

"No!" I exclaimed. "Why would the Romans destroy their own capital?"

Tobiah lowered his hands and clenched them. "Rome requires the local aristocracy to keep order. To keep the peasants under control. The Jewish leaders of Sepphoris failed to do this and so they were punished. I went there and saw the devastation for myself."

I shivered. If the Romans had done this to their own capital, what had they done to its surrounding villages and its "uncontrolled" peasants? I could hardly get the question out. "Nazareth?"

Tobiah's face tightened. "Your father was wise to bring you here." He covered his eyes and turned away.

Chuza spoke softly, but his words fell hard as a hammer on me. "Nazareth was leveled. No survivors. They even found those hidden in the caves."

Blackness flashed in front of my eyes. So this is what fainting is, I thought as my legs crumpled beneath me.

Lying on the floor, I heard Chuza scolding a servant for being too slow in bringing water. I couldn't move my limbs, but curiously, my mind remained active. My imagination filled with visions of the hacked and bleeding bodies of those I loved, the vineyards reduced to ash, the olive press smashed into pieces, our courtyard littered with the rubble that was my house and Naomi's and Miryam's. Dodi licked my face. I heard Chuza's voice again, surprisingly gentle. "Let me help you to a chair."

I waved him away and stood up by myself. But my knees trembled, so I sat down, picked Dodi up, and clutched her to me. "Father, in his wisdom, made sure you weren't there, Danya." Chuza patted my shoulder as if it were a hot pan that he might burn his fingers on. Dodi barked at him.

"There's more you must know," said Tobiah. "My brother Ezri lived in Sepphoris and managed our family's estates nearby. He, his wife, and his children have been enslaved." Tobiah stopped and took a deep breath. "Hoping to ransom them, I went to the slave market in Tyre where the Romans had sold their captives. But I was too late. Ezri and his family had been purchased by an Egyptian slave trader and put aboard a ship.

That trader could have sold them at any of the dozens of slave markets polluting the Mediterranean coastline." Tobiah steadied his trembling lip with his teeth. "Until Ezri is located and ransomed, I must live in Sepphoris and take over his work there."

I looked at Tobiah and the blackness began to curtain my vision again. Guilt snatched my breath. Lev had raided Sepphoris, and Tobiah's brother had been punished for this. My brother had, in a way, enslaved his brother.

"Deep breaths," Tobiah said. "Like this." I heard him demonstrating. "Breathe. Breathe."

I followed his directions, breathed when he did, and managed to stay awake. Poor Tobiah. His life had changed in an instant, just as mine had. At least the two of us shared something, though it was troubled hearts, the sudden loss of loved ones, and the burden of displacement.

"Keep breathing, Danya. One breath at a time. One breath at a time."

The dark circles under Tobiah's eyes were moist. "I can't offer you the life I'd planned. If you marry me, you won't be the wife of a Temple priest and scholar."

Before I could say, "I never dreamt of being the wife of a Temple scholar, anyway," Chuza broke in, the firmness restored to his voice. "We had an agreement. A contract is a contract. There's nothing in the ketubbah that promised Danya a life of wealth and leisure in Jerusalem."

Now Tobiah stabbed his finger into Chuza's chest. "If you're worried that you'll lose the bridewealth, keep it. It will provide for Danya's maintenance in your household." To me he said, "I'll understand either way. It's your choice, Danya."

My choice? It was my choice? I could not recall ever being told something was my choice and not my father's or my brother's or The Holy One's. My choice. . . . Perhaps someday I could love a man who would allow me a choice. A man who could stab Chuza in the chest and insist that I had a choice. . . . My head felt as it did when Lev and I raced to the top of the ridge on fresh, cool mornings: full, yet light and clear. Lev called this feeling "free."

However, I might be just as responsible as Lev for the enslavement of Tobiah's brother. Justice would demand that I tell him of my effort to participate in the raid. But if I told him, would he terminate our engagement?

I also feared for Naomi. Since her parents had elected to stay in Nazareth, they must be dead. If I left Jerusalem, she'd have no one here. "I need time to think about it," I said.

Chuza stomped up and down the length of the reception hall. "Time to think! Here's what you need to think about, Danya: you are a burden I will no longer bear. I never asked you, or Father, or your friend Naomi to come here, and I am finished with you. My life was fine until you arrived. Nothing I have done since has been right. My colleagues no longer trust me, my wife questions my decisions, and even the dog defies my authority."

Tobiah stifled a laugh. "Enough, Chuza. Besides this terrible news about Galilee, your sister needs time to think about me as a husband. Does she want to marry someone who has been set in his ways for so long and now must adapt himself to a whole new way of life? I will give your sister all the time she needs."

"And I will grant her one month. She either marries you or leaves my household with some other husband. And I no longer care who that is!" Chuza tromped out of the reception hall, bumping into one of the tall earthenware vases. His clumsy exit disturbed the jasmine it contained, and a burst of its sweet fragrance floated around us.

Tobiah bowed. His bald spot wasn't so large after all, and I was mistaken about the gray hair. He only had a few. "There's another thing you should know, Danya. When I was in Sepphoris, I learned that your brother Lev was involved in the raid. But I don't consider him my enemy. I hope someday he and I will be brothers." Tobiah pulled the ketubbah out from under Dodi who had settled herself upon it. He rolled it up and placed it back in my hands.

Tobiah's generosity of spirit ignited mine. I couldn't keep my secret from him. I forced myself to show him my face, even though I felt it sting with embarrassment. "I tried to join that raid, but Lev didn't allow me to. I thought it would free us, reduce the suffering of our people, not add to it. But now many innocent people, including your brother, have suffered because of it. I am deeply sorry about your brother and his family."

"Shhh. Shhh." He placed a warm finger on my lips. "I'm not surprised you would've wanted to do that. Being your father's daughter, I know you must care deeply for our people. That's one of the reasons why I want you for my wife."

His eyes were a light, soft brown, the color of Jerusalem the first time I saw it in the setting sun. The feeling of a long journey ending settled over me again. I did not lick away the salt spot his finger left on my lips.

My only remaining reservation to my marriage was leaving Naomi behind in Jerusalem. With her father and mother dead and having no other kin, Naomi would have to endure the full seven-year term of her servitude in Plotinus' household. She couldn't survive that long. Even though I couldn't help her now, a way might present itself if I stayed in Jerusalem. I felt I must not abandon her. On the other hand, how could I turn my back on Tobiah? Joanna was right; he was a good man. Didn't I have some obligation to make amends for the devastation the Sepphoris raid had caused his family? Settling in Sepphoris and helping Tobiah rebuild its Jewish community and re-establish his family there would be an appropriate act of reparation.

This dilemma tortured me, and the month Chuza had allowed me to make my choice was nearing its end when Efron sent a servant requesting I come to his shop. When I got there, Efron was occupied in the back and called out for me to wait. No one else was there. His inventory had been greatly depleted since my visit several months ago. The pegs were empty; only a few bolts of white silk rested on a small table in the long display room. Perhaps the caravans from India and other places hadn't been allowed entry into Jerusalem, or had bypassed it during Varus's purge of the city, and that would explain the lack of inventory.

Efron wrestled a large wooden box through the curtained doorway of his backroom. "Danya, my dear, a wedding present for you. You'll need some silks for your life in Sepphoris, and shopping opportunities there will be rather limited for some time." Efron's face was drawn and serious as he dropped the box on the floor in front of me.

I dared not lift its lid. An elaborate gift could only compound my marriage dilemma. I was still a poor girl and not above being swayed by beautiful things. "You're most generous, Efron. But I can't accept this. I haven't yet decided if I'll marry and go to Sepphoris."

"So Joanna tells me. But, dear one, you must be sensible."

"I am being sensible. Leaving Naomi in Jerusalem would not be sensible."

"Oh, nonsense. You never see her anyway and you shouldn't pass up the opportunity of this match with Tobiah. The Romans are fond of quoting their writer Horace: 'Carpe Diem!' Seize the day, Danya." He waved his hands around his head as if swatting away a flying insect.

"Oh, Efron, since when do we take the advice of some Roman? What has gotten into you?"

Efron's mouth drooped, and his shoulders sagged. "Since when, indeed. I am a foolish old man. Don't listen to my babble. I'm not only a fool; I'm a sinner."

"What do you mean? You're a kind and generous man. Look at this extravagant present you're trying to give me."

"Which you won't accept. So therefore The Holy One will continue to punish me. My attempts at restitution do not please Him." Efron pleaded. "Please accept my gift, please, Danya. This is a sin offering."

"How could a wedding gift be a sin offering?"

"It's complicated, but when I explain, you'll agree I am a sinner." He motioned for me to sit down on the box and joined me on it. He hung his head and told his story. "When Quintilius Varus and his legions occupied the city, once Chuza had assured our safety, he and I bought up every yard of luxury fabric, not just silk, but fine linen also, from every merchant in Jerusalem. Then, using Chuza's contacts, I sold these goods to Roman army officers for three times their customary price. It was all my idea. Chuza and I split the profits down the middle. It's true that the officers still paid a lower price than they would've in Rome, but it was evil of me to profit from the torture and murder of our people."

It was. Chuza's profiteering didn't shock me, but Efron's did. So this was what he meant by learning "how to live under the Roman heel." And no wonder Chuza had been so unexpectedly generous in looking out for Efron's welfare.

"I've slept poorly, when I can sleep, ever since," Efron continued. "My sin follows me everywhere I go. It hovers over me like the vultures I saw over those crucified people. I even tried making a sin offering at the Temple, something I'd never done before. I bought a fine ram, washed my hands, laid them upon the animal, and confessed to a high priest the reason for my sacrifice."

Efron put his elbows on his knees and rooted his head in his hands. "But after all that, I still couldn't sleep. I heard, I still hear, the wings of the vultures flapping over me. I returned to the Temple and consulted with Tobiah. He told me I should find the officers and reimburse them. I told him it would not be possible to find them, and besides, what keeps me awake at night is my sin against our people and The Holy One, not cheating some Romans. Tobiah then told me that the Law would require me to take my unjust profit, add one-fifth interest, and use the money for an act of justice. So I thought of giving you these silks for a wedding present. Let me do this, please. It might stop the flapping wings."

Efron looked as if he were about to cry, but I didn't pity him. His actions shocked and disgusted me. I rose from the box containing his "sin offering" and called for the servant to accompany me back to Chuza's home. Efron reached for my hand and captured it. "Please."

"Efron, your gift is a kindness, but it's not an act of justice. An act of justice. You need to perform an act of justice." . . . An idea suddenly struck me. This was the opportunity I'd been seeking! "An act of justice would be to get Naomi back from Plotinus. Go to the courts and correct the injustice that was done to her. As a woman, I can't do this, but you can advocate for her. Plotinus Metellus may have never paid Chuza for her. Even if he did, Naomi's father was the one entitled to Plotinus's money. Everything about her sale was unjust!"

"Danya, we have no evidence of their transaction to present to the court. And, frankly, I won't bring my son-in-law into court over this matter. Politically very unwise."

"I see what you mean. And I suppose we'll never know if Plotinus paid Chuza for Naomi. Whether or not he did, the only way to ransom her is to pay Plotinus. And that will take a great deal of money."

Efron jumped up from the box. He paced the length of his shop several times. "Naomi has no kin to ransom her, so I am legally permitted to. It would correct an injustice, the sale of a Jewish woman to an abusive Gentile master. Chuza would suffer no public embarrassment by having to appear in court, and he could keep his ill-gotten gain, if he ever received it, and therefore would not object."

Efron started to brighten. "Naomi can live with us. She'd be good company for Yona. We'll fatten her up, and, when the time is right, return her to Nazareth. It'll take me some time to get that much money together. You may have left for Sepphoris, but, yes, I can do this!" Efron's leaping smile returned. He hugged me tightly. "Now I can sleep again! Thank you, my dear one. You have the gift of wisdom. The Holy One has sent you to me."

I had no sense of that. But I had told Him I needed to save Naomi, and now she would be freed. My heart danced with joy for the first time in many months.

Back in my bedroom in Chuza's house, I took my father's knotted walking stick from the corner. As I clutched the spot darkened by his grip, I felt the presence of his strong hand. On our journey to Jerusalem, Father had leaned on this stick while resting in the forest ravaged by wildfire. A plane tree in that forest had been scorched badly but it had survived. The blaze had licked at its leaves and branches but left its core untouched. Father told me that if a tree is strong enough, flames might jump over it and consume less resistant prey.

The image of the plane tree suffused me with hope. I determined to be that tree. I would not yield to the fire. One day, new leaves would bud on me, and wildflowers would burst from the charred ground on which I stood.

PART II:
1 CE TO 8 CE

WIFE OF A PRIESTLY ARISTOCRAT

I lay on the bed cuddling our baby, Mattityahu, and trying to rouse myself from a night of interrupted sleep. Our firstborn was still young enough to require several feedings each night. My enchantment with the fragrance of his sweet baby breath and my reluctance to stir and awaken him also bound me to the bed.

I watched my husband, Tobiah, begin his morning prayers by holding his tallit in both hands and reciting the prescribed blessing: *"Blessed be Thou, Lord our God, King of the universe, who sanctified us with His commandments, and commanded us to wrap ourselves in the fringed garments."* He wrapped the prayer shawl around his head, and the long knotted threads of its fringed corners swayed with his movements. This white silk tallit with the blue stripes had been Father's. Chuza had presented it to my husband on the occasion of our son's brit milah. Though Joanna had remarked, "Chuza will never miss it since he never prays anyway," I considered the gift a precious one.

My husband had chosen Father's tallit especially for this occasion. Every twenty-fourth week, for a week at a time, Tobiah took his turn serving at the altar of the Temple in Jerusalem with his group, or "course," of one hundred priests. He had been excused from these duties while we settled in Sepphoris and our first child was born, but he would now rejoin his course for his Temple service rotation. This would be the first separation of our marriage. Tobiah's choice of Father's prayer shawl was intended to please me, and it did. But I also felt some shame because he was a more thoughtful spouse than I was. He always waited to eat until I was ready. Every decision he made concerning the reconstruction of the Kamith family home took into account my needs and preferences. And he asked so little of me. Last night at bedtime as I was donning the worn, colorless shift of my childhood, Tobiah said, "I want to buy you something beautiful in Jerusalem. How about a few bolts of colorful linen for some sleeping tunics?"

He wasn't asking much of me, only that I not dress like a beggar in our private moments, but I preferred to sleep in my childhood garment and replied, "No, thank you. I'm content with the clothing I have."

In bed, Tobiah politely asked for permission to touch me and would handle me gently. Since the birth of our son, he had become reluctant to "bother me," as he put it. I suspected this might be my fault, but I didn't know what to do about it.

This morning I watched Tobiah wind the thin leather straps of the tefillin around his left arm, binding a tiny parchment of Torah to himself. I also was tied to this man, bound by the restraining straps of marriage. As Tobiah would ponder the interpretation of Torah text, I puzzled over the meaning of marriage. Having no mother and no close female relative nearby, I often fretted over what my obligations were. What was permitted and what was forbidden? How do I uphold the covenant I have formed with this man?

As he prayed, Tobiah faced south, towards Jerusalem. Nazareth was also situated south of Sepphoris, though it was only a few Roman miles away. This morning, like every morning, I gazed through the window in numbed sadness towards the village where I'd grown up. Some mornings a misty rain shrouded my view and my memories; but on sharp, clear days, I could spot the rocks on the crown of its bordering ridge, and recollections of Nazareth cut me with their clarity. The other towns in the Beit Notofa and Tiran valleys had recovered soon after Quintilius Varus's army had finished with them. However, they had not suffered the devastation that Nazareth had. In those places, the Roman marauders contented themselves with burning the crops and stealing some livestock, raping a few women, and killing only the men who were defiant enough to fight back. But whether because it was so close to Sepphoris, or because Varus knew of our village's complicity in the raid, Nazareth bore the brunt of the Roman legion's vengeance on Galilee. Tobiah and I had ridden through my village in a carriage on our move from Jerusalem to Sepphoris. Piles of stones and blackened timbers, which had once been homes, lay scattered about like the garbage in Jerusalem's Gehenna. A few scorched trees listed in the charred courtyard of my childhood. Heaps of ash were the only reminders of the vineyards that had once flourished on the hillside. The soldiers had slaughtered, burned, or crushed every living and non-living thing in Nazareth.

I had wept so profoundly at the sight of these horrors that Tobiah lashed the horses and drove them straight to Sepphoris without stopping. I hadn't gone back there since. No one had returned to resettle the village, though Tobiah had hired teams of workmen to tend to the grisly tasks of decontaminating the well and burying the bones of those who had attempted to hide in the Jebel Qafzeh caves.

Tobiah continued with his prayers this morning. He adjusted the tallit down around his shoulders, positioned the second tefillin over his forehead, and began to recite the 'Amidah. *"Grant us, O Father, the knowledge which comes from You, and the understanding and discernment which come from Your Torah. Blessed are you, O Lord, who grants knowledge."*

I needed knowledge. Though Tobiah never said so, I believed he must think me ignorant. After our brief coupling last night, I'd tried to make intelligent conversation.

"Will you meet with the High Priest Eleazar while you are in Jerusalem?" I asked.

"I hope to."

"You must advise him to forbid Roman troops from ever again entering the Temple courtyards."

He rearranged the pillow under his head. "He doesn't have that power, Danya. The High Priest is no longer the leader of the land of Judah. He's appointed by our king, who is himself appointed by Rome. Since we are an occupied country, Rome can put its troops wherever it chooses."

"But we must resist Roman rule. Our leaders must not allow Rome to trample on us."

Tobiah's voice lowered as his irritation mounted. "We need our leaders to help us survive Roman rule, not rebel against it. We cannot win a war against them. Would you please try to understand this?"

I did understand Tobiah's point of view, but I didn't agree with it. I still believed, as did many of our people, that the day would come when The Mighty One would lead us in triumph over our enemies, as He had in the past. The twelve tribes would be restored, the Gentiles subjugated, and the Temple purified. But to succeed in this great mission, peasants and aristocrats would all have to join together under Adonai's laws.

"Yes, husband. I will try," I said.

He rolled over onto his side and faced the wall.

Deep down, I knew Tobiah resented foreign rule as much as the rest of us. To a Roman's face, Tobiah might praise their architecture and engineering; in private, he prayed, *"May the arrogant kingdom be swiftly uprooted, in our day."* However, our differing beliefs about how to uproot this arrogant kingdom had become a source of contention between us.

Tobiah concluded his prescribed rituals this morning with a prayer of his own. *"I give You thanks, O Lord God, for my virtuous wife, my healthy son, and the rich harvest of the fields, orchards, and vineyards which You in Your Goodness have bestowed upon me. I seek the blessing of safe travel to Jerusalem where I will praise Your Blessed Name in the timeless place that is Your throne on earth."*

Tobiah's irritation with me last night had apparently dissipated. Mattityahu opened his sparkling brown eyes and smiled at me before rooting for my breast. Grateful for Tobiah's patience with me, I said, "Will you stay your departure until I feed the baby? Then I can walk with you to the city gate."

"I'd like that," he said, as he folded Father's tallit carefully and placed it in the storage chest he had commissioned especially for it. He tickled his son's dimpled legs, and the baby kicked in pleasure.

After breakfast, our servant Zohar brought Tobiah's carriage around to the outer courtyard gate. Two new horses, the color of almond shells, shook their heads and pawed at the ground. "They're all yours, Master," said Zohar, passing the reins to Tobiah. Zohar was small, and even though he was strong, he could barely maintain control of these spirited stallions.

Only a handful of Romans and three other Jews in this city owned horses. Tobiah was the only Jew with a carriage. He had bought it and the team to reduce the time it would take him to travel between Sepphoris and Jerusalem and therefore shorten the time of his absence from us.

"I'll worry about you all alone on your journey, husband."

He stroked the huge chests of the handsome pair. "No reason to worry. I can outrun any bandit, beast, or Samaritan with this fine pair." He stepped up into the sturdy, metal-wheeled cart. "Come, I want to show you off. Ride through town with me."

"Oh, but it's not appropriate. Everyone will stare at us. I'll walk behind your carriage."

"I want them to stare. They'd only glance at an old gray man, even one in a carriage, but an old gray man with a pretty young wife will give them something to talk about. Come, ride with me. Zohar will follow behind us to accompany you back."

I stepped into the carriage and sat next to him. It was embarrassing to make a spectacle of myself like this, but it made me proud too. Tobiah had a distinguished bearing, and he handled the horses skillfully. "You're not old and you're not gray, much. You're just fishing for a compliment when you call yourself that," I teased.

He laughed and put his arm around me until the horses required both his hands on the reins. We proceeded towards the city square, which here they called by its Greek name, "agora." Herod Antipas had chosen Sepphoris to be the capital of his kingdom, and he had engaged legions of workers to rebuild it after Quintilius Varus and his legions had pillaged it. Its two main streets, the cardo and the decumanus, were paved with limestones. Aqueducts carried water into the city, and sewers removed its waste.

From everywhere, eyes turned to us. I melted into my mantle. All these people staring at me were strangers.

"Will you stay with Chuza and Joanna in the Upper City?" I asked.

"No, I need to stay in the Temple precincts. But I'll visit them, of course."

"Will you check on Naomi?"

"Who?" He couldn't hear me over the clanging of hammers on chisels, as stonemasons roughed out the supporting columns of the cardo's covered sidewalks.

I cupped my hands and shouted. "Naomi."

"Yes, if she's still with Efron and Yona."

We abandoned our attempts to converse over all the construction noise. As we approached Antipas' palace and the basilica that would soon house the courts and administrative offices, hundreds of workmen swarmed in and on these structures, shouting, hammering, and sawing. It saddened me that the men who were reconstructing this city would never inhabit the structures they built. These crews moved from one place to another, wherever there was work for them. In Nazareth I had lived among people who worked with their hands and enjoyed the fruits of their own labors. They had names I knew, like Leor, Yoel, Abir, Shamir, and Niv. They prayed in our assemblies and haggled with me over prices in the market. I played with their children. But the workmen of Sepphoris were all strangers to me, as I was to them. They cast their eyes down in deference to me as the wife of an aristocrat. I was not Danya to them; I was a rich man's wife. Sepphoris, like Jerusalem, was a lonely place for me.

As we continued down the cardo towards the southern wall, the construction and its clamor tapered off, so we could hear each other speak. Before we parted, I wanted to show my husband that I was trying to accustom myself to life in this city. I pointed to the southwest. "There's a rumor that Herod Antipas will build a theater over there that will seat a thousand people. Can you imagine something so grand?"

"His plans have grown even grander! He told me he'd prefer it on the north side of the city, and it'll hold four thousand," said Tobiah.

What did I know? I associated with servants and shopkeepers and the beggars and peddlers who came to my gate. Tobiah was the chief magistrate of this city, a powerful landowner, an aristocrat from a high priestly family. I stopped my foolish chatter and turned away from him to wipe the tears that had suddenly welled up in my eyes.

Tobiah reined the horses to a halt and studied me. "But, wherever the theater is built, it will be my honor to escort my beautiful wife to the performances there."

"Thank you, husband." I could never match his thoughtfulness. How many times had I hurt his feelings and not realized it? How many amends had I failed to make? Since our baby's birth, I often neglected to properly care for my husband. An example stood out right in front of me: I should've thought to trim his beard before he left. I wanted to kiss him goodbye and remind him to go to a barber in Jerusalem, but, on the streets of Sepphoris, couples didn't touch or kiss. I stepped down from the carriage. "May heaven be with you, husband."

"And may Heaven bless you, wife."

The next morning I was nursing Mattityahu when our servant Razi interrupted. "Excuse me, Mistress, but there's a peddler at the gate who insists on speaking with you. He refuses to leave a message with me." Razi dug her hands into her wide hips and sniffed. "He thinks he'll get a bigger tip from you, I suppose."

Though Mattityahu protested the interruption, I propped him on my hip and ran to the gate, praying this was the moment I had been waiting for. Every peddler and other itinerant in Galilee knew that I wanted to be informed of the first sign of life returning to Nazareth.

The peddler, stooped with the weight of the pots hanging from the pole across his shoulders, shouted over the baby's cries. "They've come back to Nazareth, lady. A big family with a father Yosef, a mother Miryam, and four fine boys."

Four boys! One more than Miryam left with. She was still being favored. "Oh, you've brought the best news I've heard in years! Put those pots down. I'll buy every last one of them!"

I dashed back into the house. "Razi, tell Zohar to load the donkey. I'm going to Nazareth! And pay the peddler twice what he asks for those pots."

I finished feeding my baby while Zohar tied supplies onto the donkey. The new pots joined the sacks of grain and seed, dried fruit, cheeses, and jars of olive oil I had been storing up for the first villager's return. I tucked my now-contented Mattityahu into a sling and hurried to the gate.

Zohar was waiting for me there with the tallest, strongest donkey we owned. Its overburdened back swayed. "Perhaps you should wait until the master can go with you," cautioned Zohar, a proper, solemn man. He and his wife Razi had served Tobiah for many years in Jerusalem. They were still ill at ease in Galilee, a region they considered alien and backward.

"Tobiah will be gone for more than a week. I can't wait that long to see Miryam and to help her family get settled," I explained.

"I should accompany you," said Zohar.

"No, thank you." I could make this journey blindfolded, having traveled between Sepphoris and Nazareth so many times when I was a girl. I didn't want this older, cautious man slowing me down. "It's less than half a morning's walk, Zohar. Don't worry about me."

I clutched the donkey's lead and headed along the same street Tobiah and I had traversed in his carriage the day before. Heads turned today at the unusual sight of a woman traveling by herself. I fixed my eyes straight ahead and imagined I was passing along a dusty street in Nazareth where a woman and a donkey would be unremarkable.

As we picked our way down the hill on which Sepphoris lay, clouds began to cluster in the blue sky over the valley. Though white and seemingly harmless, they were a reminder that anything could happen with the weather on a day this late after the harvest. The steepness of the hill and the weight of the load caused the donkey to lose his footing several times. I stumbled once myself; I'd never done this with a baby cradled under my breast. But Mattityahu slept peacefully, unaware of the added burden his weight placed on me.

We reached the bottom of the Sepphoris mount and started across the Netopha Valley. The footing became surer, and our speed increased. Still, my body confounded me. Not even three years ago, I could've run the entire distance between Sepphoris and Nazareth and not become fatigued. Today I was breathing heavily and needed to rest when we reached the Nahal Zippori wadi.

I took off my sandals and lowered my swollen legs into the stream's cool water. They hadn't returned to their normal size since my pregnancy. During this month of Kislev, early in the rainy season, the wadi was still shallow enough to wade across. So, with one hand on the donkey's lead and the other tucked under my baby's bottom, I planted each foot firmly, taking care not to lose my balance in the slippery stream bed. The wind whipped across the shallow water and stirred up a chill. I pulled my mantle around us.

The clouds darkened to the color of sheared sheep's wool before the washing as we trudged to the top of the ridge overlooking Nazareth. There, between its two largest rocks, I again stopped to rest. The donkey grazed on a few sprigs of green poking out of the gritty ground. I remembered what I had witnessed from this spot: the raiders leaving Sepphoris, Lev's departing kiss, Miryam's account of her apparition. The feelings of intense disappointment, anger, and jealousy that had gripped me at those times sprang up again, but I pushed them aside.

I kissed the dark curls on Mattityahu's beautifully shaped head and repositioned him so he wouldn't feel the wild beating of my heart. My legs bent like willow whips as I started down the hill into Nazareth, and I fell to my knees. Mattityahu wiggled and kicked in his sling. Then, from the wasteland where our old courtyard used to be, a plume of smoke rose from a fire, enlivening this bleak, sorrow-filled place. I picked up a handful of soil and clutched it in my palm as I had done when I had left my home more than four years ago, stood up, and led the donkey down the rock-strewn path towards the life signaled by that flame.

"Danya!"

"Miryam!"

We ran to hug each other. I didn't release her until her children wriggled their way between us. Miryam shrieked. "I'm so happy to see you. And with a baby!" She pressed a roughened palm to her red-rimmed eyes. "Who is your husband?"

"I married Tobiah ben Mattityahu of the Kamith family."

"You've never looked more beautiful, Danya. I can see you're happy."

A child who was too old to be sucking his thumb removed it and asked, "Who is the rich lady, Mama?"

I wore a yellow linen tunic, a finespun wool mantle, and sturdy new traveling sandals. Maybe I no longer looked like a peasant girl, but I was certainly not a "rich lady." A rich lady was the woman carried on the litter in Jerusalem, the one with the turquoise brooch and the face unkissed by the sun. Surely I was nothing like her.

Miryam presented each one of her children to me. The tallest boy, who had the presence of mind to grab the donkey's lead when I'd dropped it to run to Miryam, stepped forward. "Yaakov, this is my dear friend Danya. Her house was in our courtyard, over there, before we moved to Egypt. Remember?"

Yaakov, the oldest and now six years old, said, "I think I remember you. Maybe I do."

Miryam continued, touching the thumb sucker on the head. "This is Joses. He's almost five now."

Joses removed his thumb from his mouth. "Will you live in our court-yard again?"

"No, I live in Sepphoris, but it's not far away. Just a little over the ridge." I pointed.

"And this is Yeshua," continued Miryam. "He was only a baby when we left. And the one who is just about to trip and hit his head"—she grabbed the toddler's arm just in time—"is Shimon."

Miryam's face had thinned, and her hair had lost its luxurious waves. Motherhood had taken its toll on her. Other trials must have burdened her as well.

I leaned over to show them the face of my handsome baby. "This is Mattityahu. He's almost six months old, and you'll hear from him soon. Almost time for him to eat."

"Big boy," said Shimon.

"He has the head of an aristocrat," said Miryam.

I cringed, hoping Miryam would not think that, since I had married an aristocrat, I was now "too good" for Nazareth and the likes of her. But, of course, that wouldn't be Miryam.

She instructed the children to continue collecting the rocks they would need to build a house. The boys jumped to the task, impressed with the importance of their mission. "No shortage of materials," Miryam said to me, her voice breaking.

"You hadn't heard, then, that Nazareth wasn't resettled?"

"No. I expected that we would return to a livable village. But it wouldn't have mattered anyway. We would've come back when we did. Yosef had another one of his dreams, this one directing us to return to Nazareth." Miryam quieted until her lip stopped trembling. "But we were right to obey his dream commanding us to go to Egypt, so we'll be fine in following this dream's bidding to return to Nazareth. So here we are." She shrugged her shoulders. "We arrived just yesterday, and already my dear friend has come to visit. Welcome to my kitchen." Miryam smiled weakly and pointed to a boulder. "Please, rest while I boil some water for us." She placed a pot on a grate laid across a small wood fire pit and began to ask about people.

"Naomi's mother and father?" she asked. "I remember they stayed behind."

I shook my head slowly. We both began to cry, but Mattityahu distracted us by awakening and screaming. I let my baby cry hard. He didn't have to hold anything back. Then I changed his cloth and fed him.

Miryam's children called to her. While she was checking on them and I was nursing my baby, I watched the charcoal edging of the clouds leak into their centers. I looked around for shelter should the rains come. Miryam's "home" was a few pieces of hide fastened between two burnt tree trunks. One goat, tethered to a stake and looking starved itself, appeared to be the only source of food. I wouldn't tell Miryam that Tobiah had sent a team of builders to repair his brother's, now our, home in Sepphoris before I journeyed there from Jerusalem. I wouldn't tell her that I arrived, with my trunks and chests, to a house well-stocked with food and drink and that I had had servants to help me with my settling-in chores.

When Miryam returned, she poured water into clay mugs for us. "We'll pretend it's wine and celebrate our reunion," she said. Then, wistfully, "I remember the wonderful wine your father used to make. How is he?"

I conveyed my sad news just as I'd practiced. Speaking quickly, I said, "He died almost four years ago. Killed by a Roman soldier, shortly after we got to Jerusalem."

Miryam dropped her mug, and it broke into pieces. "Oh, Danya. I'm so sorry. I loved Micah. There was no better man in this whole village." She bent to pick up the shards of the shattered mug.

"Here, leave that broken one. I've brought plenty of mugs and dishes. Can you take the baby for me?"

Miryam dried her tears on the sleeve of her tunic. She grinned and babbled at Mattityahu, who wiggled his whole body in pleasure, while I struggled with the ropes on the donkey packs. Their knots had tightened on the way from Sepphoris. Undoing them was like trying to open a walnut. Annoyed with the task, I asked Miryam, "Can your husband help me with this?"

"Yosef has gone out to the vineyards and the orchards to see if anything can be saved. But, speaking of absent husbands, where's yours?"

"This week he's in Jerusalem because it's his turn to serve in the Temple." Jerusalem reminded me. "Naomi is also in Jerusalem. She's living with Efron and Yona, the parents of my brother Chuza's wife." I paused and looked at the dirt caked on my sandals. "She's not well enough to return yet."

"Not well enough?"

Before I could explain, Miryam's children reappeared bearing a treasure they'd found in the weeds: an intact wooden door. Her four handsome boys wrestled this gift over to their mother and presented it to her as if she were the queen of all Israel and the rustic door a gold-threaded tapestry.

"Thank you, noble princes," she said solemnly. "This will hang in the place of honor at the entrance to our palace."

The boys giggled. A twinge of jealousy pricked me. Miryam's sons loved her so much. Would I ever be loved so deeply and by so many?

"Danya has brought gifts," Miryam told them, "and we need help unpacking them." She handed Mattityahu back to me, and she and her boys worked on the ropes. Chaos followed as the knots loosened and the boys grabbed at the bags. "Carefully. Carefully!" she shouted at them. To me she whispered, "Thank you. We've been living on goat's milk and some very hard cheese these last few days."

I pruned off the bud of my envy. Miryam battled the boys away from the food and dug into the sacks herself. She issued each of them two dried figs and a handful of raisins. "Eat these, and then put everything except one sack of wheat flour under the tent. I'll bake some loaves with that flour, and soon your tummies will be full again."

Miryam added a little water and salt to the flour to make dough, then kneaded it on a stone and shaped it into small loaves. While she worked, she told me about the troubles that had befallen her family in Egypt. Yosef had been arrested shortly after they arrived there. An informant had accused him of plotting against the Pharaoh. Maybe because he was such an outspoken critic of Rome—they never knew why. But the charges were false. After a few very anxious weeks, he was released from prison, though he had been severely beaten. Then Miryam's elderly parents, who had accompanied them to Egypt, had died. She had to leave their bodies buried in that foreign land.

"How terrible," I said. "Anna and Joachim were always kind to me."

She placed a shallow bowl upside down over the fire pit and laid the flat loaves on it to bake. I wanted to help her, but Mattityahu began to fret. Usually he was happy to sit in my lap, scrutinizing and reaching for the things I dangled before him. But sometimes he complained from one feeding to the next. I hoped this wouldn't become one of those times. I wanted to show Miryam what a good mother I was.

To calm Mattityahu, I jiggled him on my knee. He spit up. I cradled him on his stomach across my forearm. He stiffened and screeched. I held him on my shoulder and crooned a lullaby. He drowned it out with his shrieks. Miryam's children, gathered around the oven to pounce on the baking loaves, backed away. Embarrassed by my own incompetence, I stepped away from Miryam and them.

Yeshua brought me the sling that I'd removed when I fed Mattityahu. "He wants this," said Yeshua, grinning confidently.

I'd tried everything else, so I took the sling, tossed one end over my shoulder and tied it under my arm. I placed my distressed baby in it. He fell asleep instantly, just as the edges of the wheat loaves browned.

"Look, Mama. Other people are coming!" shouted Yaakov.

Three men of various ages, all so short their heads barely topped their donkeys' backs, plodded towards the village. Even from a distance, I knew who they were. Their stout legs and out-turned toes distinguished them as did the position of their women. They always walked behind their men, balancing heavy loads on their heads. This was Samuel's family.

Samuel and his father Ze'ev had accused Father of instigating the raid, and we had left the village on bad terms with them. Seeing them returning to Nazareth while my father lay in his tomb put a sour taste in my mouth. However, Miryam greeted Samuel's family hospitably and offered them food from the supplies I'd intended for her family alone. They dove into it like dogs and snatched the hot loaves from the fire even before Miryam's hungry boys had a chance to indulge themselves. Samuel groped about in the sacks of raisins and dates and extracted fistfuls of them while Miryam's children, their two dried figs and raisins long gone, waited empty-handed.

Raisins snagged in the beard of Ze'ev, the twisted, toothless grandfather.

I was considering yanking them off and giving them to Miryam's children when he spoke to me. "And where is your father, Danya?"

"He was murdered by a Roman soldier in Jerusalem." The fact that these louts had survived seemed so unfair that I couldn't stop my tongue. "Though he was innocent, he was not spared from Roman vengeance, as you were." Even the ravenous Samuel stopped eating and stared at me. Finally Ze'ev said, "We had our differences, but I respected Micah."

I turned away from him, but my foot caught in the handle of a broken grindstone. I lost my balance and fell down. Startled by my fall, Mattityahu began crying again. I scrambled to stand up on my own before Samuel or Ze'ev could help me and threw the grindstone handle as far as I could. Miryam and I had spent so many hours of our girlhood milling grain. Hot, dirty, work which produced only a coarse, barely edible barley meal. I didn't eat barley loaves anymore; I didn't have to. In Tobiah's house we ate wheat bread, ground and baked by someone else while I read, or supervised the servants, or played with my fat, healthy baby.

I suddenly wanted to go home, to my home in Sepphoris, with its ten solid stone rooms, plastered walls, tiled floors, servants who acquired and prepared my food, and hired workers who farmed our estates. Though I missed the many joys of my childhood, I would no longer pine for Nazareth, with its hungers, brutish labor, and narrow-minded, back-biting villagers.

"I have to leave. I can beat the rain if I do," I said. A dark-tinged cloud covered the sun and bolstered the timing of my excuse. "But, Miryam, I'd like your family to stay with us in Sepphoris until Nazareth can be made more habitable for you."

"That's a most gracious offer, but this is where we've been directed. We'll be well-settled here soon. So please stay longer today. We've only just begun to visit. And you're better off being with us if the rain comes. There's protection here." She pointed towards the pathetic strips of matted goat hair drooping in a little stand of dead tree trunks. She dropped her hand. "No, run, Danya, while you still can. You've always been lucky. You can make it."

Miryam clutched me tightly as we said goodbye. I had always thought Miryam was the lucky one. She had a mother; a light had appeared to her; she had sons. The fact that my blessings were now many compared to Miryam's did not please me, though once that might have.

I whispered because I didn't want Samuel to overhear. "I'll send goats and sheep tomorrow and wheat flour and fruit every week. Send word of anything else you need, and I'll get it to you." With my baby tucked in his pouch, I climbed onto the donkey. As we trotted up the overgrown trail to the Nazareth ridge, I kept turning back to look. Miryam threw dirt on her cooking fire and herded her boys and supplies under the goat hide tent. Samuel's family proceeded on to the miserable plot of hardened grit that had been their family's land for generations. The men sat on its rubble while their women unloaded the donkeys.

I stopped at the top of the ridge where the shower of light had assured Miryam that The Holy One had marked her as special, a gift that I had craved and been denied. I would no longer seek such favor. It carried too dear a price. I didn't want a life as hard as Miryam's. Suddenly, having not been chosen seemed a blessing. I would number it among my others: a beautiful son, a good husband, and a life free from want.

I kicked the donkey to hurry him down the hill. The wind lashed the hem of my cloak against the beast. He bucked his head and sidestepped, almost losing his balance. Near the bottom of the hill, I thought better of crossing the valley in the storm that was now about to strike. A few olive trees had escaped the Roman torch and could provide us some protection. I tied the donkey and covered Mattityahu's head with a cloth to keep him dry. We crouched down in a patch of deep weeds further protected by the overhanging branches of a triangle of olive trees and waited.

From behind me, a hand pressed lightly against my throat. "We meet again," said a low, intimate voice.

My breath stopped. I turned around and faced Judah ben Hezekiah.

He threw back his head and laughed out loud. "So, Lev's little sister is a mama now."

I was speechless. I had said farewell to Judah when I agreed to marry Tobiah. But the truth was that sometimes on market days or passing through the noisy agora, my eyes roamed over the crowds for this red-haired, roughly dressed leader of men. And on soft nights when moonlight illumined the inner courtyard and the wind rustled through my loosened hair, my scalp tingled as I recalled Judah's breath on it.

"You're still alive!" I finally said, then felt foolish.

"Are you disappointed?" he teased.

"I only meant . . . so many others have perished. And I heard that Rome had crushed out all resistance."

"Don't be fooled by Roman lies. The resistance grows every day. We're everywhere, hidden and cared for by the people we will one day liberate." For a man on his own in the countryside, Judah did look well maintained. His tunic, though worn, was clean and patched; his beard and hair were trimmed. He still possessed a forceful, muscular build, so he could not be going hungry.

Judah clenched his jaw and crossed his arms across his chest. Quietly, solemnly, he repeated his call to arms on the Temple Mount: "No master but God! This is what I live for and I still believe that day will come."

I hadn't stopped dreaming of being a part of the liberation of our people. Judah's call stirred the embers of that dream in me.

The Holy One had a special mission for Judah, and he seemed to shoulder this burden lightly. Or maybe not so lightly, after all. I noticed that he was missing a few of his white teeth, and a thick red scar wandered crookedly down his cheek, as if it had lost its way. I puzzled over what would maim like that. A pottery shard? A dull knife? I shivered.

Judah reached around and pulled back the covering on Mattityahu's head. "What's his name?" he asked.

"Mattityahu."

"Mattityahu. 'Gift from God.' A fine, strong name. Perhaps God has given him to you for now, and you will give him to my army when he is grown."

I shivered again and covered my baby back up. "Not my son. He has another destiny. My husband is a priest. He owns estates in this valley that our son will inherit."

Judah scowled. His russet eyebrows almost touched each other. "So you are the wife of an aristocrat?" he jeered. "Then more likely your son and I will one day meet in conflict."

He had put his finger directly on my unhealed wound. Around peasant people, my people, I felt guilty about my comfortable life. Though I had never sought to live the life of an aristocrat, I now did. But the fact that Judah was a peasant and I was now an elite should not make us adversaries. We were both Galilean Jews, both oppressed by the same enemy. "My family desires freedom and prosperity for our people just as you do. We, too, long for the coming of the Kingdom of God."

"Provided you aristocrats still rule that kingdom."

"No, Judah. The Mighty One rules this land, and we obey His laws for it just as you do. My husband pays his workers just wages and provides for their widows and orphans. In Sabbath years his fields and orchards rest untilled and he cancels all debts. Our slaves are treated as family."

"Then he'll be poor himself. Those strict religious practices and Roman taxation will soon put him out of business."

"No. God will reward those who follow His commands."

Judah chewed on the side of one fingernail as he stepped back and looked closely at me. I met his gaze. "Ah, he's probably lying to you about all his righteous acts," said Judah. "Most rich men lie to their wives."

Like so many peasants, including me at one time, Judah couldn't accept the possibility of an honorable Sadducee. I resented his insulting my husband and resolved to say nothing more about him. Judah would only revile Tobiah further. In the silence that followed, I thought of the other rich man I knew well, my brother Chuza. I suspected that Chuza did lie to his wife. But Tobiah was different. Comparing him to Chuza was like comparing a fine horse to a goat.

Lightning flashed, and I counted to two before thunder cracked. The rain that had threatened for so long finally began to fall, though softly at first. I watched it for a time as Judah silently poked a stick into the dampening ground. Finally he tossed the stick away and said, "I apologize for saying that about your husband. Perhaps he is an exception."

"He is."

More thunder boomed behind us, sounding as if it came from the other side of the hill. "Nazareth," Judah said, his voice heavy with sadness. "Your village didn't deserve such cruel treatment from Rome. I, too, am from a small village, Gamla, in Galilee. How I miss that life, digging and planting and pruning. And the harvest: there is nothing so sweet and satisfying as the harvest."

I was determined not to talk to him. He would only attack me or my husband or anyone else who did not agree with him. The rain hardened into a downpour. Judah chewed more on his fingernails. "Have you heard from Lev?" he asked, his voice softening sympathetically.

I shook my head.

"I look for him as I travel about."

It had been four years since the night of the raid and my last glimpse of my dear brother. "Why hasn't he sent us some word of his where-abouts?" I asked. "He should have written a letter or told someone pass-ing through to let us know he is all right."

"Too dangerous. Letters fall into the wrong hands. No one can be trusted with messages because spies are everywhere. Lev is doing the right thing, for you as well as for him, by staying hidden."

"I pray every day that is the reason."

"It is. I know in my heart that Lev is still alive. I promise to bring you word of him." Enormous wind-sharpened raindrops flung themselves upon us like the points of spears. Mattityahu howled, but I dared not unwrap him and expose him to this assault. Judah and I each huddled under the hoods of our mantles, listening to the storm and Mattityahu's distress. "I've always wanted children," Judah said.

I pulled my cloak tighter, leaned my head farther over my baby, and tried to soothe him with murmurs.

Judah reached over and patted Mattityahu on the head. "You're safe here, Matti."

Matti. What a sweet name for my little man, I thought. His cries inten-sified, and I tried to soothe him by humming the familiar tune of "The Lily of the Covenant." Judah joined in and sang words to my melody.

> *My heart overflows with a goodly theme;*
> *I address my verses to the king;*
> *My tongue is like the pen of a ready scribe.*
> *You are the most handsome of men;*
> *Grace is poured upon your lips;*
> *Therefore God has blessed you forever.*

Mattityahu's cry withered to a whimper as he turned his ear to Judah's strong, clear voice. Judah repeated the last three lines until the baby quieted completely. For a few minutes, the only sound was the rain. Then Mattityahu began to kick and cry again.

Judah laughed. "Your little king is hungry. Tunes won't fill his aching belly, any more than Rome's empty promises will fill a peasant's."

My face and neck warmed, and my breasts leaked, but I was not going to nurse my baby in front of Judah. The rain lowered into a steady downpour; the baby's screams heightened.

With a bored sigh, Judah removed his mantle and held his cloak around us, exposing himself to the storm. "Here. This'll keep the rain off the blessed one's face while he suckles." When I hesitated, he said impatiently, "I've seen plenty of women's breasts, you know. You aren't the first woman to feed an infant."

I felt foolishly modest and unsophisticated. I settled myself with several deep breaths, untied my swaddled baby, and put him to my breast.

Under Judah's protection, my baby sucked hard and rhythmically. Judah stood over us and watched. Once he murmured, "Beautiful," and again, "beautiful."

His skin and clothing smelled of balm, Galilee's native evergreen. Judah must sleep under the stars on a bed made of this wild shrub's boughs. How freeing it would be, I thought, to sleep in the open air, far away from any lonely city or stifling village.

As Judah watched me nurse, my embarrassment faded. In its place I felt pride. I was proud of being a woman and proud of the gift I had to calm and nourish this infant who, moments before, had been suffering. My child needed and appreciated me, and I loved the fact that no one else could provide for him as well as I.

Matti hated even the slightest interruption in his nursing, so, when it was almost time to transfer him to my other breast, I uncovered myself. Before I could move the baby to my other breast, Judah reached down and lightly brushed his fingers across my exposed nipple. His touch was as soft as the silks in my wedding trunk.

Blue-tinged drops of milk oozed from my stimulated breast. Judah trapped them on his fingertips and raised them to his lips. He closed his eyes and sucked intently. The vein in his forehead pulsed. Then he opened his eyes and locked them on mine. "I want you," he said, his voice breaking in shallow heaves. "Will you have me?"

My body responded with a longing unfamiliar to me, but I knew it was a hunger I should have only for my husband. I looked into Judah's hungry eyes. He leaned over to kiss me and waited. Raindrops from his hair fell onto Matti's forehead. The baby raised his eyelids. He looked from Judah to me.

I lowered my head over my child to block his view of Judah and of the shame that was spreading across my face. Judah stood over us, waiting for my response. He didn't touch me with his hand, but I felt the cord stretching between my heart and his tighten until there was no slack.

I kept my eyes down and they found Judah's bare, bruised feet. His toes were knotted and twisted; some had obviously been broken more than once. These were violent feet, feet that kicked and stomped, that battled the sandal-strapped feet of Roman infantrymen.

Matti's chubby hand found my lower lip and pulled on it. He giggled, put both of his hands on my cheeks, and patted them.

I looked up at Judah and shook my head no.

"The faithful wife of a priestly aristocrat, eh?" He snatched back his cloak and, without bothering to cover himself with it, set off bareheaded into the rain.

I didn't offer my other breast to my baby. I was afraid the soured milk would sicken him.

I huddled in the olive grove, not knowing what to do or where to go. I wouldn't go back to Nazareth since I didn't belong in my village anymore. But the prospect of going home to Sepphoris paralyzed me. I didn't belong there, either. I considered running after Judah, thinking of the freedom I would have in a life with him. Wandering from place to place in the countryside, not tied to Sepphoris and its restrictive conventions. Shedding the unworthiness I felt around Tobiah. Sleeping without a baby's constant demands. No, no! Of course I'd bring my baby. But a baby living in a band of rebels, hiding by day, stealing around at night, living off the land?

The rain continued, sometimes swelling into a downpour, then shrinking to a drizzle, then pouring hard again. Now thoroughly drenched, the soil released its long buried odors of death and decay. We were soaked to the skin, but at least Mattityahu, accustomed to soggy cloths, didn't seem to mind being wet. He sat propped between my crossed legs, and I stretched my mantle around the two of us. From this nest, he reached out, laughing, to capture the raindrops and taste them. He also dragged my finger to his mouth and bit down on it. A tiny sliver of tooth had broken through his gums. It imprinted itself into my flesh, like a seal in wax.

Should I tell Tobiah about Judah? I'd promised myself there would be no secrets between us. But pardoning my brother for insurrection was one thing; forgiving me for desiring another man was something else. However, if I didn't tell him, he might find out anyway. Something in my eyes or manner or lovemaking might expose my guilt.

I was still shaking all over when I heard my name being called from far away. "Dan-ya. Dan-ya." The voice, muffled by the storm, seemed to call from another world. For an instant, I thought it might be an angel, who might guide or punish me, but then I recognized the voice as Miryam's. I stood up and spotted my friend walking atop the ridge above me. I waved my arms, shouting, "Down here, in the olive grove."

Miryam ran all the way and arrived out of breath. "We worried about you," she gasped. "Oh, no. You're shaking. Something awful has happened!"

I nodded.

"Here. Sit," Miryam said, struggling to get her breath under control. She pulled a dry blanket from under her cloak and wound it around me and Mattityahu, sitting with us and holding the blanket tightly in place with her strong arms. The baby snuggled into the cocoon she formed for us. I continued to shiver. "Tell me," she said.

My story spilled out. How I had first met Judah and later had longed to join him on the Temple Mount. How I had failed to extinguish my desire for him since my marriage. How I had almost allowed myself to be seduced. "I'm a terrible wife," I concluded. "Unworthy. Unthoughtful. Ungrateful. And now lustful. I should be stoned." I hunched my shoulders, preparing myself for Miryam's attack of me and my sinfulness.

But she took an edge of the blanket and wiped my eyes and cheeks with it. "Why should you be stoned?" she asked. "No law has been broken."

"But I wanted him."

"So? You refused him."

"But I desired Judah when I'm married to Tobiah. That means I'm a sinner."

"That means you're a grown woman, Danya." Miryam kissed the top of my head.

"But everything will be changed. My breast will forever hold the memory of Judah's touch."

"I doubt it. Hush now. You haven't sinned."

She readjusted the blanket, covering my head as well as my shoulders and back with it. We sat in silence while she rocked me, and I began to warm up. "How did you know to look for me?"

"When you didn't come back after the rain started, Yosef said I should go after you. He packed some food and thought of the blanket."

"It was exactly what we needed." At the mention of food, my stomach pinched. I hadn't eaten since breakfast. "Did you say you had food?"

From a hide pouch strapped over her shoulder, Miryam removed a perfectly baked wheat loaf. I devoured it like Samuel had his.

"Will I always desire him?" I asked, licking my finger and capturing the crumbs that had dropped into my lap.

"Probably not." She reached into her pouch again. "There's one more loaf."

"Thank you." I nibbled on this bread. "Naomi always said you were in love with Lev," I said. "Are you in love with Yosef now?"

"Yes, but it took time. You'll love Tobiah someday."

I finished the bread and brushed the crumbs to the ground. "How can you be so certain I'm like you? Chuza once called me a whore."

Miryam just smiled. "Danya, go home and take care of your family. You're an adult now. Stop thinking like a child."

The sky was brightening. Miryam fetched the donkey. I stretched out my cramped legs and folded Mattityahu back into his sling. Miryam hugged me once more, boosted me onto the donkey's back, and handed me the reins. She slapped the animal on its haunches. "Shalom, Danya of Sepphoris." I rode back to my home there, determined to make myself a better wife.

Night after night, while I waited for my husband to return from Jerusalem, I lit the oil lamp in his library and sat at his desk. I needed to find a way, once and for all, to put Judah out of my mind. With pen and papyrus, I carefully reconstructed, in words, the paths I had walked since the day I had turned away from Judah on the Temple Mount. My account would demonstrate to me that, in not following Judah, I had acted wisely and should have nothing more to do with him. Ever. I wrote about my unexpected betrothal to Tobiah, about marriage, motherhood, and settling in Sepphoris.

But, as if the papyrus had been incompletely washed before its reuse, Judah's words leaked up from the layer below the one I wrote on. His question, "Will you have me" left a stain on every page that my blotter could not absorb.

I rolled my manuscript tightly and shoved it into a storage niche. Miryam told me to stop thinking like a child. She was right: I was seventeen years old now. Any woman of sound mind and virtue would think she was fortunate to have a husband like Tobiah. I should respect and obey him in all matters and devote myself to his happiness and comfort. But I didn't know how to do this. Since my mother had died when I was so young, I had no memories of how she'd behaved as a wife. I would not emulate Naomi's mother. She and Amos fought so loudly they'd often awakened the whole courtyard at night. Miryam's parents were old and quiet, nothing like us. Chuza and Joanna? Certainly not. There wasn't a single marriage I had closely witnessed that I could use as a model for ours.

I searched through Tobiah's collection of wisdom literature. Perhaps the writings of the sages would tell me how to make myself a better wife. I found a parchment of Ben Sira's wise sayings. He had much to say about wives and marriage. *"A woman's beauty lights up a man's face/And there is nothing he desires more."* I could pay more attention to my grooming. In a corner of the bedroom sat my dressing table, coated with dust. Without Joanna around to instruct and nudge me, all I had been doing was combing my hair twice a day and bathing before each Sabbath. I could do more. It wasn't vanity to enhance the looks I had been granted. If my appearance could light up Tobiah's face, then I should try to improve it. My heroine Judith was beautiful and used her beauty for the good of our people. I could use mine for the good of my marriage. I yanked open a dressing table drawer that had been stuck closed for years to search for the lotion that made Joanna's skin soft and for the perfume she'd given me. Never mind the perfume. Its fragrance was balm, Judah's scent.

I returned to the library to continue my study of Ben Sira's counsels. Over and over, he criticized wives who talked too much. *"A loud-voiced and garrulous wife is like a terrible trumpet."* Talking too much was a great fault of mine. I must learn to hold my tongue. From now on, I would not vex my husband by wrangling with him, particularly about affairs of the world. He knew far more than I did on that subject. He should advise the High Priest any way he chose.

"A silent wife is a gift from the Lord/And nothing is so precious as her self-discipline." I could show self-discipline by no longer robbing Tobiah of his quiet moments. So often when he was studying or resting, I would draw him into debates about subjects such as the afterlife or the Roman occupation or the way to holiness. Usually these disputes made Tobiah throw up his hands and say, "Just like your father," which made me feel both happy and sad. Convincing Tobiah of the error of his views was impossible anyway, so I resolved not to risk destroying my marriage with my intemperate tongue.

An instruction of Ben Sira to husbands chilled me: *"Do not leave a leaky cistern to drip/or allow a bad wife to say what she likes. If she does not accept your control/divorce her and send her away."* All Tobiah had to do was serve me with a get, and our marriage would be dissolved immediately. Even Tobiah's patience must have its limitations, I feared.

I put Mattityahu down for the night in the cradle next to our bed. I'd been trying to accustom him to sleeping alone all week. He rolled over onto his back and held his arms up, whining for me to lift him out. Swallowing my croon of sympathy and reminding myself that this was best for my marriage, I turned him back on his stomach. He found his thumb. I rubbed his back until he fell asleep and dozed off myself. I awoke to find Tobiah standing over us. Creases of fatigue lined his forehead and eyes.

"I'm home at last and happy to be here," he said. "But why have you moved our son from our bed?"

"It was time. Matti rolls over now and kicks like a goat. Soon he'll be crawling all over us, and we'll never get any sleep." Oh, no, I thought. Maybe his expression is a frown rather than fatigue. Maybe he doesn't want to be in bed alone with me. My voice became as small as a bashful child's. "I thought you would be pleased."

"I am. I've missed him, that's all." Tobiah patted our son's head, and the baby cried out in his sleep. I tucked the blanket tightly around him, and he settled himself.

"But I've missed you more, Danya." He hugged me, but then slumped onto a bench explaining that, on the last afternoon of his two-day journey, one of his horses had come up lame, and he had to walk them and the carriage all the way across the Jezreel Valley to get home.

"Let me bathe your feet for you, lord." I rarely addressed my husband with this formal term, though many wives regularly did. Joanna could sometimes placate Chuza's temper by salting her speech generously with "Lord" and "Master." Razi had placed a jug of water and a basin on the bedroom table for me. I carried them over to the bench where Tobiah rested and, kneeling in front of him, poured the cool water over his blistered feet.

"When did our son's name become Matti?" Tobiah asked.

My hand froze on the handle of the jug though heat flashed through the rest of my body. Judah had been the first to call my son "Matti."

"Just a mother's term of endearment," I explained.

"The name sounds sweet when you say it, though, as his father, I should address my son by his given name."

My hands loosened, and I set the jug down. I rubbed water on a dark spot that I thought was dirt on Tobiah's ankle.

"Ouch, careful. I burned myself there. Cinders from the sacrificial fire," he said. While washing his feet, I found other burn marks, five in all. Tobiah's feet had been singed from his service at the holy altar in the Temple. Judah's had been disfigured from combat.

In the medicine niche in the bedroom wall, I found a jar of healing salts and added them to the water. "Ahhh, better, much better," Tobiah said.

While he continued to soak his feet, I unpacked for him. I lifted a sack of his clothing, loosened its rope tie, and reached in. I assumed this sack contained his priestly clothes, the dazzling white linen tunic and blue sash he had been wearing the first time I saw him on the Temple Mount.

Instead I pulled out a short tunic and breeches that were stained and smelled of soot and blood. Reaching in again, I extracted a sash, which may once have been blue, and a brownish heap of unwound turban. His priestly garments must be in another pack.

"I am sorry," Tobiah said. "I should've had my clothes washed in the Temple laundry, but I was in a hurry to get home."

"You wore these clothes in the Temple?"

"Yes. All week I've been butchering lambs and calves, washing the blood of the sacrificed animals down the drains, and removing ashes from the altar. It's a great honor to serve The Holy One in sacrifice, but it's also messy work!"

That Tobiah could work with his hands as well as with his mind pleased me. I put a towel down on the floor. He lifted his feet out of the basin and lowered them onto it.

"What's the news from Jerusalem?" I asked, carefully patting his feet dry. "Did you see Naomi?"

"No. Efron has taken her to Rome. He thinks the physicians there can heal her. She's still very ill: withdrawn, unable to concentrate on any kind of work, terrible dreams at night."

I wanted to object that Rome would be the last place Naomi could be cured since it was a Roman who made her ill in the first place. However, bringing her there wasn't Tobiah's decision. But I managed to hold my tongue for a change. "Chuza and Joanna? How are they?"

"Chuza and Joanna send their love, though there's little love between the two of them. They've been married eight years and, if she has borne no children after ten, the law permits divorce. But I doubt he would that. He'd have to return her dowry, if for no other reason."

"Joanna should appreciate her husband more."

"What?" Tobiah's voice lifted in surprise. "You're taking your brother's side in the matter?"

"No, but, never mind. Any other news of them?"

"Chuza doesn't like working for Archelaus. The ethnarch is unpopular with the people. And Rome thinks he's weak."

I returned to the medicine niche and picked out a vial of the purest olive oil, the first pressing. I knelt down again to massage Tobiah's feet with it. "And Joanna, did you speak with her alone?"

"She still hopes to bear a child. But she's given up on physicians. Some healer had her eat the fruit of the mandrake plant to cure her infertility but to no avail. Now she consults with magicians. Jerusalem teems with such people, promising cures and miracles through the power of their charms and potions."

"Joanna should occupy herself with charming her husband, not with searching for magical cures."

"Hmmmmm. Your skill with massage is charming me, anyway," said Tobiah. He bent forward and kissed the top of my head. "This is the first time in a week my feet haven't been in pain."

His approval sparked a glow of relief within me. I shifted my position on the uneven stones of the bedroom floor to ease the aching in my knees and doubled my efforts to soothe my husband's wounded feet.

"So you're familiar with the sayings of Ben Sira?" he asked.

"I've been studying them, trying to make myself a better wife."

"But I was happy with the wife I had!"

"You were?" I didn't look up at him but focused on massaging his feet.

"Yes, I was. And the wife I had would show compassion for her sister-in-law. Some rabbis teach that a woman's barrenness is the result of the husband's disrespectful treatment of his wife, you know."

"Of course I sympathize with Joanna, but I'm starting to understand that some of her troubles are of her own making. She often criticizes Chuza, though rarely to his face. I now see their marriage in a new light."

He lifted my face up with his fingertips and frowned. "Danya, something is wrong. What happened to you while I was gone?" he asked gently.

I didn't want him to see into my eyes. They might reveal a sign of my moment with Judah. I lowered his hand from my chin and examined the back of it. "Your hand has been singed, lord. Let me find something for that." I stood and picked through the medicines again, searching for my answer to his question. There must be no secrets between us. Or at least no lies. I opened a jar of purple aloe and dabbed some on the burns on the backs of his hands. But I felt Tobiah waiting for my answer. With the towel, I dried the ointment from my fingers. "I thought a great deal about you while you were away and realized that I haven't been a good enough wife. I lack wisdom and experience. But I'm determined to improve." While waiting for him to say something, I wove an edge of the towel under and over my fingers, avoiding his gaze.

Tobiah cleared his throat. "Well, if it's wisdom you seek, Danya, there are better places to look than Ben Sira. The collection of writings your father worked on for so long might be a better place."

No lies between us. Secrets maybe, but at least no lies, so I said, "The truth is that I never understood most of Father's writings." Though it was painful for me to admit this, I would no longer feign an intelligence I did not possess.

Tobiah paused, and then laughed loudly. "Honestly, I never did either. His writings are difficult for me, too! But I'd appreciate your help in my study of them. You must have some insights into them."

I blushed. My brilliant husband seeking to learn from me, a woman whose education was pieced together by looking over the shoulder of her brother. "Sometimes as he wrote, he'd talk about the passages to me. Maybe I could remember some of his explanations if I went over the text with you."

"Good." Tobiah rose and pushed open the wooden shutter on the south window. "It's getting stuffy in here," he said.

Now that the subject of our conversation seemed to have shifted from what had happened to me, I felt giddy with relief. I stood by Tobiah at the window. Clouds obscured the half-moon's light; the hills of Nazareth were invisible tonight. Tobiah wrapped his arms around me and teased, "In your quest to become a better wife, you're not going to turn into one of those capable wives from Proverbs, are you? They're so busy being capable, they never have time for their husbands."

This was so confusing. I thought men wanted capable wives. Or did they want only beautiful, silent ones? I stepped out of his embrace and teased him back. "Though I'm not happy with myself as a wife, I'm not happy with you as a husband, either."

He clutched his heart. "Have I transgressed?"

"Yes. You've let your beard get so bushy, you look like one of the ancient prophets!"

"But their beards made them strong!"

"No, their young wives did."

Tobiah laughed and stroked his unkempt beard. "If I let you trim my beard, will you make me strong as a prophet?"

I had my opportunity. Tobiah's long full beard made him look years older than he really was, and I had always wished he would keep it shorter. "I believe I can," I said in a voice I hoped was seductive. Then before he could change his mind, I sat him back down on the bench and dampened his face with a cloth. I fetched my comb and scissors from my dressing table. "Ready?" I said, poised to snip.

"Not quite. My neck hurts."

Was he teasing or had he changed his mind? "Shall I first massage your neck?" I asked.

"That'd be good."

I stood behind him and warmed the back of his neck by holding my hands on it. The heat from the pressure I applied released a minty scent from his skin. "You smell like a Passover morning in Nazareth," I said, inhaling deeply and brushing my nose along his shoulder.

"Before I left Jerusalem, I bathed with a sponge soaked with rosemary water and then rubbed myself down with the herb. I was hoping you'd like it."

"I do." I hadn't smelled rosemary on skin before. Its essence contained a hint of new beginnings. After Tobiah's neck had warmed, I kneaded it and his shoulders. His body moved at the will of my fingertips. His taut skin and the muscles beneath it softened. Even his face relaxed; the lines on his forehead smoothed out. Except for that beard, he looked almost like a boy.

"Ummmm," he groaned. His pleasure emboldened me. I expanded my massaging down his arms. His muscles had hardened from his physical labor. My fingers lingered on their firm roundness. Tobiah's head slumped back into the pillow of my soft belly, and he sighed. At the spot where his head rested against me, a pool of warm water formed within me. It overflowed its banks and meandered downstream, spreading through me in warm rivulets. I forgot everything else in my joy at feeling such pleasure.

"Well, are you going to trim it, or not?" he teased.

I waited a moment for my hands to steady. "Close your eyes," I cautioned. Best he not see what was being lopped off. I worked silently, my mind and body still thrilling with the desire I felt for my husband.

"When are you going to ask me about the High Priest?" asked Tobiah.

"You can tell me if you want," I replied absently, as I toed large chunks of hair under the bench and out of his sight.

"As it turns out, Archelaus had deposed Eleazar ben Boethus and appointed Yeshua ben See as the new High Priest.

That news brought me back to the present moment. "No! Yeshua ben See doesn't have a religious bone in his body. He's not even from the Zakodite line of priests," I complained. But then I remembered Ben Sira's admonitions about being a terrible trumpet and I stopped talking. If they wanted to appoint a rooster to the position of High Priest, I would hold my tongue.

Tobiah laughed. "I thought that wouldn't please you. But Yeshua ben See knows all the influential Romans. He moves easily in their circles and understands how to work with them."

"Then, if you approve of him, so do I." I settled into the finer trim work on what was now a youthful beard on the face of this man who, after all, was only in his thirties.

"That's all? You're not going to argue further about this?" Tobiah wondered.

"Yes, I mean no. No arguments." I combed through his tidy beard. "*A sandy ascent for the feet of the aged—such is a garrulous wife to a quiet husband.*"

"I may be older than you, but I'm hardly 'aged.'" Tobiah sat up straighter. "Ben Sira also says, '*Happy is the husband of an intelligent wife.*' I thought I had married an intelligent wife."

The only sound in the room was the snip, snip of my scissors as I puzzled over how to respond to this. On the one hand, wives were not supposed to argue. But on the other, wives are supposed to obey their husbands, and if he wants me to argue, then maybe I should.

Tobiah stayed my hand and took the scissors. He looked at me kindly but said firmly, "Danya, I could have married a woman who agreed with everything I said. One reason I chose you is that you have your own mind and your own opinions, even though, I confess, those opinions sometimes annoy me."

"I'm only trying to please you, lord. To be a proper wife to you."

"Then please me by being my dear Danya, not some puppet of a wife. And stop calling me 'lord.'"

I felt an enormous weight lift from me, as if I were a peddler setting down a load of pots and coming to rest. "Gladly, Tobiah."

Then I handed him the mirror and winced. Silently, he stroked the air under his chin where his beard had hung only minutes before. I covered his face with kisses and told him that, having such a handsome husband, I would be the envy of every wife in Sepphoris.

"I may get used to it. I promise to try. And now you must keep your promise to make me strong." He put the mirror down and rose from the bench. He crossed the room, lay down on the bed, and patted the empty space next to him. "Come, wife."

"Ahhh." It was a pleasure to lie next to him and a pleasure to be off my feet.

"Are your legs still bothering you?" Tobiah asked.

"When I'm standing. Not much otherwise."

Tobiah rose from the bed and retrieved the olive oil. He poured a small amount of it into his palm, then rubbed his hands together. Gently, he began to massage my legs. Starting at the tips of my toes, then slowly ascending to my ankles, then calves, then thighs, he caressed me with long, slow strokes. He quoted Ben Sira one last time. *"Like a golden pillar on a silver base, is a shapely leg with a firm foot."*

Tobiah slid his hand higher up my thigh and stroked there in short, vigorous circles. He kissed me deeply. Without his bushy beard, I could feel every muscle in his lips and tongue pushing their way into me. I pulled my childish sleep tunic off and tossed it on the floor. His hands, still warm and moist with oil, found my breasts, which, it turned out, did not hold the memory of Judah's touch after all. We sank deep into the cushions and blankets of our bed.

That was the night I fell in love with my husband.

TIMES TO LAUGH;
TIMES TO WEEP

The next morning, Razi's bustling about in our bedroom awakened me. I reached to the other side of the bed for my husband, but a tray occupied his space there. I sat up and asked Razi where he was.

She winked at me. Matti lay in the crook of her fleshy left arm as she opened the shutters and poured water into the basin with her right. "I'll keep the little one," she said as she withdrew with my baby. "You enjoy your breakfast in peace." I'd never had breakfast in bed before; I hadn't even imagined such a thing. But I set the tray across my knees and inhaled its aromas: warm bread, hummus spiced with roasted eggplant, fresh goat's milk, and the first ripe figs of the early harvest. While the bread and hummus melted on my tongue, I savored the little mystery of Tobiah's absence. Was he reciting his morning prayers in the synagogue? Today, when my husband thanked God for the graces he had been granted, would I be considered one of those graces? Perhaps he had already said his prayers and gone out to the farms. In any event, I hoped he was as happy as I was now.

As I bit into the juicy flesh of a fig, Tobiah entered our bedroom carrying two roses. He dipped his finger into my hummus and snatched a taste of it. I swatted his hand, and he laughed. "Where did you find roses blooming at this time of year?" I asked.

"My secret. And Razi's." He kissed me and set the flowers on my tray. "Two roses, dear Danya, for our two children."

"Two children?"

"Razi thinks your legs are swollen because you're pregnant again. She insists that she's always right about such matters."

In my ignorance, I had assumed I couldn't become pregnant while I was still breastfeeding, but this surprise pregnancy delighted both of us. Tobiah hovered over me for the next six months, encouraging me to rest and eat. Though he'd treated me this way during my first pregnancy, I'd attributed his efforts then to his desire for a healthy heir. But now I understood it was because I was loved. I was loved. I was loved!

Matti offered gifts to his unborn sibling. I would awaken from a nap to find pretty stones or an almond blossom or slivers of his little fingernails on the altar of my enlarging womb. Tobiah hired Alona, the best Jewish midwife in Sepphoris, to care for me throughout this pregnancy. Her name meant "oak tree." To keep me from miscarrying, Alona directed me to avoid strong odors, so I kept away from newly fertilized fields and, often, the kitchen. Alona taught me that I was exempt from religious fasts, except those on the Day of Atonement and the ninth of Ab. She insisted that I adhere to other pious practices that would ward off the possibility of my dying in childbirth, so I faithfully lit and tended the Sabbath lamp. I stayed strong and healthy throughout my pregnancy, and Alona smiled broadly each time she put her ear to my belly.

Tobiah prayed the Seventeenth Benediction each night, and I felt as if this prayer perfectly expressed the song resounding in both of our hearts.

> *We praise you, O Lord our God, and the God of our fathers, on account of all the goodness, grace, and mercies which you have granted us and to our fathers before us. . . . Blessed are You, O Lord, the All-good; You are to be praised.*

After prayers, my husband and I would make love and then fall asleep together. Throughout those star-filled nights, I breathed his air, and he mine, leaving no space between us. So this is what the word happiness means, I thought, though a single word seemed insufficient to express the fullness of my spirit.

The only shadow on our lives was our mutual sadness over our lost brothers. Tobiah now missed Ezri more than ever. Perhaps the thought of Mattityahu having a brother or a sister intensified my husband's yearning for his own brother. Ezri was Tobiah's only sibling who had survived into adulthood. It had been four years since Ezri and his family had been enslaved during Quintilius Varus's retaliatory raid on Sepphoris. Everyone who had experience with the system of Roman political enslavement had advised Tobiah to give up his search. "You will never find them, though you will make yourself poor trying," they said. "Learn to accept your loss."

But Tobiah had not given up and, during my second pregnancy, he intensified his efforts to find them. He sent letters to every port on the Mediterranean, inquiring about Ezri and his wife and children, and promising to pay a ransom for any or all of them. He addressed these letters to the leader of each of these cities and paid professional messengers to deliver them. Tobiah wrote in Greek, on sheaves of expensive parchment, his texts all similar to this one he wrote to Phraates.

To The Mighty Phraates, Ruler of the Great City of Sidon, greetings

I seek my brother, Ezri ben Mattityahu, of the Kamith family of Sepphoris in Galilee. He and his wife and two sons were sold into slavery more than four years ago. My brother is tall, gray-haired, and well educated. He is knowledgeable in philosophy and mathematics and speaks and writes Greek, Latin, Hebrew, and Aramaic. His wife is fair-haired, of average size, and skilled with the needle. His boys are eight and ten years old. I will negotiate a ransom for the return of any or all of them.

Farewell from Tobiah ben Mattityahu of the Kamith family, of Sepphoris, in Galilee

Tobiah sealed these letters with the Kamith family seal, a vine lying atop a scroll. He noted its destination on a list that grew longer with each new moon. The list began with the cities around the Mediterranean where Ezri's learning might be valued: Rhodes, Cyprus, Crete, Tripolis, Ptolemais, Olympia, and Athens. It expanded to places I had never heard of, such as Byblos, Phrygia, Ascalone, Pergamum, and Risidia, as well as to cities with familiar names like Antioch, Damascus, Alexandria, and, of course, Rome.

I stubbornly nurtured the dream of my own brother's return. From Nazareth to Jerusalem to Sepphoris, I carried the warm wineskin of my hope for a reunion with Lev, and I would not set that vessel down. Ezri's enslavement was a graver situation than Lev's self-imposed exile, so I didn't write letters seeking information about Lev, nor did I ask Tobiah to include my brother in his letters of inquiry. But I believed that Lev was still alive and must be living outside of the purview of the ruler of any city or country. Efron kept my letter to Lev; he kept watching for any hint of Lev's where-abouts for me. And I trusted that Judah ben Hezekiah did as well.

After Matti's first birthday, during the wheat harvest in the month of Sivan, my labor pains began as dull throbbings. Since it was a Sabbath day, this caused me great anxiety because our laws forbade working on the Sabbath. I feared Alona, my midwife, my sturdy oak, would not be able to help me deliver this baby, and that I might have to allow a Gentile midwife to attend me. But Alona came as soon as she was asked. Helping a woman in childbirth, she said, was the equivalent of saving a life: both overrode the law forbidding work on the Sabbath.

As it turned out, I was blessed with a swift and almost painless childbirth, "the reward of a righteous woman," Alona told me. After a morning of mild pains, I sat on the delivery seat and pushed three times. Our daughter dropped into the midwife's steady hands. After Alona had washed her, Tobiah laid our baby on his knee and claimed her as his own, naming her "Mariamme," after his mother. Then, with brimming eyes, he embraced his daughter. I had to pry my baby from her father to nurse her for the first time.

When she was only four days old, Mariamme smiled at me. Razi declared her toothless grin a grimace caused by indigestion, but I knew otherwise. Her smile reminded me of Miryam's. Its lively, generous curve entwined itself around my heart. Mariamme also had my own mother's dimpled chin. All in all, she was the most beautiful baby in the entire world.

For almost two moons, Mariamme smiled for me and me alone, and I felt a wild joy each time she did. But my baby's merriment also pained me in an unexpected way. Her smiles made me grieve for my mother. Fever had taken Nahara slowly. She must have known she was dying. How sad it must have made her, knowing she would have to relinquish the joy of basking in her daughter's smiles and guiding me through my childhood.

For years, I had been haunted by the questions "Why did the fever take my mother and not take me?" and "For what purpose was I spared?" I finally had at least a partial answer: The Holy One in His goodness had spared me so that I could know a daughter's love.

Around the time Mariamme began sleeping through the night, a messenger arrived from Jerusalem reporting that Chuza would visit with us the following evening. My brother was accompanying Herod Archelaus from Jerusalem to the coastal palace in Caesarea Maritima where Archaelaus would escape Jerusalem's dusty dry heat. But he and his retinue would stop along the way in Sepphoris so that Archelaus could visit with his brother Herod Antipas.

The next afternoon, as Razi was preparing a festive dinner for Chuza's visit and I was spinning in a workroom connected to the kitchen, a servant of Chuza's interrupted our work. "My master Chuza says that you must take her," he announced in a loud, agitated voice.

"Take who?" said Razi irritably, as she hoisted a lamb hind onto the spit.

"My master says you must take charge of this woman immediately. He will join you this evening." Within a few eye blinks, the gate slammed and there, in my kitchen, stood Naomi.

"Naomi!" I said, dropping my wool and wrapping her in my arms. Naomi stood stiffly with her arms at her sides as if steadying herself during an assault. "How wonderful to see you!" I said, releasing her from my embrace.

She greeted me with a nod in my general direction, as if I were a neighbor she loathed but had to endure. "Danya."

Her black curly hair, unkempt and uncovered, hung all the way down to her waist. This was the girl who used to decorate her hair with wild-flowers. No respectable woman would show herself on the streets of a city this way. But at least she was no longer wasted by starvation. Her body had matured beautifully under Yona and Efron's care. The loose draping of her tunic couldn't conceal the fullness of her breasts. A belt accentu-ated her rounded hips.

Razi gaped at us through the kitchen doorway, shaking her head at Naomi's disheveled appearance. "Our guest has traveled all the way from Jerusalem, Razi," I said, excusing Naomi's dirty face and clothing. "Please bring her some water so she can wash."

Naomi's eyes roamed over the contents of my workroom with its loom, spindles, and piles of unspun wool, but they seemed dead as stones. Their utter lifelessness unsettled me. Suddenly, I felt younger than Naomi, even though I was eighteen, her elder by two years, the mother of two children, and the wife of a respected aristocrat.

Razi carried the water and a cloth into the workroom and plunked them down on the table. Naomi ignored both her and the water. With downturned mouth, Razi returned to the kitchen.

I reminded myself that travel was arduous and could put a person out of sorts. Here was my dear friend whom I had not seen in four years. This should be a moment of great joy. "Naomi, you are most welcome in our home. To see you looking so well and here in Galilee is an answer to my prayers."

"Show me the servants' quarters," she said flatly.

"As our guest, you'll have your own room in the family quarters. It's an honor to have you here."

"An honor." She mimicked my tone, and then snorted, mocking me. "An honor indeed."

She was angry. That was understandable. While I had been living comfortably in Chuza's house, she had been a slave in Plotinus's. On the other hand, that had not been my doing, and I had agonized over her misfortune. Rather than leave her alone and enslaved in Jerusalem, I would have ransomed my own future and not married Tobiah. "I did all I could to free you, Naomi. I battled with Chuza over you. I wrote to your father. I convinced Efron to buy you out of slavery."

"Yes. I was told." She returned to her survey of my workroom: its beaten earth floor, single window, and the table littered with weaving and sewing materials.

So that was all she had to say. Not even a small expression of gratitude. I felt a pulsing in my ears as my temper rose. No, I told myself, do not be angry with her. She has been sold into slavery, starved, abused, and orphaned. Be patient with her. "Come, my friend, I'll show you to a comfortable room and draw you a bath."

"I'll stay right here," Naomi announced. She dropped the small pack she carried onto the floor. "You'll soon change your mind about having me as a guest." She snorted again.

When we were young, her girlish giggle used to flutter up and out of her, irrepressible and light as a hummingbird's wings. But this new laugh emerged from a dark place within her, flapping its way out like a startled vulture.

"Whatever you want, my friend." I kissed her cheek, but she withdrew, repulsed by the touch of my lips. A chill seeped into my bones, and I withdrew to my sun-filled courtyard to warm myself.

Raw stripes of red-orange light slashed across the western sky that evening as Chuza, Tobiah, and I sat down at the dining table in the inner courtyard. Razi removed the place at the table set for Naomi when our guest ordered her meal be served to her in the workroom. I hadn't expected Naomi to consent to dine with Chuza, so I didn't press her to.

My brother perched uncomfortably in the tall dining chair with his toes barely touching the ground. He preferred to recline Roman-style at the table, but we didn't have dining couches in our home. Though Tobiah had business and legal dealings with the Roman military and administrative officials who dwelled here, we certainly didn't entertain such people, as Chuza so often did in his home in Jerusalem. My half-brother fingered the rim of his wine cup while Tobiah said the blessing over the food.

I wondered if Chuza would remember and comment on the soup, a leek and lentil specialty that Father used to make for us years ago. Chuza slurped it down quickly without comment, then held his empty wine cup towards me and waited to have it filled. He took several swallows before answering my inquiry about Efron and Yona.

"They're both very ill. One morning last week, Efron was in his shop by himself. He collapsed and tumbled into a table of fabric bolts and lay there until his workers found him. They told Joanna he looked like a broken-winged bird in a colorful nest."

I dropped my soup spoon. "Poor Efron. Did he break any bones?"

"No broken bones, but he hasn't moved his limbs or spoken since then. With great difficulty, he can swallow a little water and broth. We don't think he can live much longer. Or Yona, either. She's become very frail." Chuza held his cup out, waiting for me to pour again.

"Oh, no. Both of them." I wiped my eyes and nose with a linen cloth. Efron had comforted me at Father's funeral, showered me with wedding gifts, and ransomed Naomi from slavery. He and Joanna had been my only friends in Jerusalem. And despite her handicaps, Yona reached out with her generous heart to me and Naomi and all who entered her circle. But their son-in-law Chuza was concerning himself only with his own business. "You should've stayed in Jerusalem to help them," I said, making no effort to hide the reproach in my voice.

"I thought I could help them most by placing Naomi in your care. She's a burden they can no longer bear. Though Joanna would keep the girl, I won't allow it. She's completely occupied with the care of her parents. I will not continue on to Caesarea with Archelaus but will return to Jerusalem tomorrow." He pointed to his empty wine cup. "Now, is that being dutiful enough to get me another cup of wine, sister?"

Tobiah took up the wine decanter and poured for Chuza since I wouldn't. Why should he receive such gracious treatment? He hadn't treated Naomi graciously. Nor had he been good to Joanna, for many years now. He should've done her the kindness of divorcing her, so that she could've found a more suitable mate.

The sun set, though its rash still stained the horizon, reflecting my gashed, inflamed heart. I needed to control my anger at Chuza and concern myself with Naomi's welfare, so I busied myself with the task of lighting the oil lamps until I could speak civilly again. "Why does Naomi need to be cared for?" I asked. "What's wrong with her?"

Chuza swatted my question away as if it were a fly on fruit. "She has some difficulty concentrating. And she needs to learn a skill to occupy herself. Otherwise, she's fine."

"If she's fine, why isn't she helping with Efron and Yona?"

"She's not that fine. Though she looks pretty fine, doesn't she, Tobiah?" He smirked.

Tobiah cleared his throat. "I think these cucumbers are the best I've tasted in years. What's this seasoning you have on them, Danya?"

"Olive oil, garlic, and wine vinegar, as usual."

Razi served the lamb she had roasted all afternoon on a spit over the wood fire. The meat's crust, spiced with mint and salt, perfectly preserved the moistness of the tender flesh sealed within it. Our talk switched to appreciation and praise for this exceptional meal until Chuza brought up politics. "Herod Antipas has gained my respect. He's a master schemer. His nickname, The Fox, suits him well. Though he praises his brother Archelaus and appears to be helping him, all the while he's subverting him." Chuza licked meat juice from his fingers and slid another hunk of lamb onto a round of bread.

"What do you mean?" asked Tobiah.

"I think Antipas plots to become King of the Jews, as his father was. It's always needled him that, when his father's kingdom was divided among the three sons, he didn't get Judea and its jewel, Jerusalem. To accomplish that, he has to get Archelaus removed. Then he can convince Rome to assign those territories to him."

I had drunk a cup of wine and felt bold enough to interrupt them. "About Naomi. Why do her eyes look so empty? When did she develop that horrible laugh? Chuza, what has happened to her?"

Chuza raised his eyebrows. "Is there a salad course?"

I placed some lettuce and endive on plates, then spooned a honey of crushed dates over the greens. "And where is the money Plotinus paid for her? Tell me the truth: did Plotinus ever pay you for her?"

"Naomi, Naomi, Naomi," said Chuza. "Is that all you can talk about, Danya? Let me remind you of something: against my wishes, at Father's death, I became her guardian. By the time Plotinus actually produced the coin for her purchase, her parents were dead. I had the right to keep that money. If Efron wanted to pay Plotinus for her release, who was I to stop him? I don't make the rules, so I'm not ashamed to admit that, in this case, I profited from them."

"You feel no shame." I said. "Then why is your face purple?"

He slammed his cup down so hard that most of his wine sloshed onto the table. "Danya, Naomi is now your problem. Once you see more of her, you won't want her either!"

How dare Chuza accuse me of being as selfish as he was! I turned in my chair, placing my back to him.

Chuza ignored my slight and spoke to my husband. "You're missed at the Temple, Tobiah. The corruption there is enough to scandalize even me. Priests are taking Gentile wives; money is missing from the treasury." He stopped and whispered something in Tobiah's ear.

"Things only heathens would do," Tobiah said darkly.

"Yes," Chuza said. "In Father's time, there were similar problems, which was one reason he left Temple service. But the solution is for the dedicated priests to stay and clean things up, don't you agree?"

I peered over my shoulder to see Tobiah's reaction.

Tobiah didn't answer him, so Chuza leaned over the olive pits and gnawed bones on his plate and brought his face closer to Tobiah's. "Many influential people are hoping I can persuade you to return to Jerusalem. What do you say to that?" Chuza poked Tobiah in the chest with his forefinger.

Tobiah didn't pull back from Chuza's coarse touch. He held his wine cup to his lips and drank thoughtfully. "Jerusalem. I do miss life in Jerusalem." Then he blinked rapidly and shook his head as if to clear it. "But I have responsibilities here, and we are content in Sepphoris, aren't we, wife? Aren't we?"

During her first night with us, I heard Naomi rustling about. Thinking she might need some help, I hurried to the workroom. I found her pacing back and forth, back and forth, as if in a trance.

"Naomi! Are you all right?" I called.

Pace, pace, pace, pace; stop, turn; pace, pace, pace, pace.

"Do you need anything?"

Pace, pace, pace, pace; stop, turn; pace, pace, pace, pace.

So I left her until the morning when Tobiah and I together checked on her. At some point, she had finally fallen asleep on the mat I had placed in the workroom for her. Tobiah, deep in thought, pulled on his lower lip.

"What's wrong with her?" I wondered aloud.

Tobiah said, "Once a woman with eyes as hard as stone and an evil-sounding laugh appeared before me in my courtroom. Her accusers believed she was possessed by devils. They wanted her stoned to death."

"Stoned to death! You didn't permit it, did you?"

"No, but, I exiled her. She frightened them. They would have killed her if I hadn't sent her away."

"Naomi couldn't be possessed. She's not a sinner. Neither were her parents. I can point to many sinners, beginning with my brother Chuza, whose souls could harbor a devil. But not Naomi's."

Tobiah twisted his lip until it was white. Then he said, "You and Razi must watch her carefully."

Naomi frightened me, but I wouldn't admit that to Tobiah. I'd begin her weaving instruction this very day. Chuza was right that an occupation would be good for her.

In the afternoon I found Naomi in the children's room hovering over Mattityahu who was napping on his cot. She did not take her eyes off of him, even when I entered and stood beside her. "Please," I whispered. "Leave him. He needs his rest now, or else he'll be very crabby at dinnertime."

I tugged at her sleeve and led her away, but she walked backwards out of the room, staring at my boy. She never even glanced at my baby girl.

Naomi told me she already knew how to weave. She took up a spindle of gray wool and announced she would weave a shirt for Matti. I shivered. I told her that he didn't need a shirt, but that Razi needed a tunic. Naomi refused to weave anything for Razi, complaining that the servant held a grudge towards her. So, after his nap, I sat Matti on my lap while Naomi measured him for his shirt. She stretched long threads of wool across his chest and around his little arms, then carelessly cast her precise measures into a pile of scraps, losing them among the other odd strands. Her hands running across my son's skin cast a shadow on him. When she had to repeat her measurements, I captured each length and set it safely aside, so she wouldn't have to touch him again.

For two days, on my many trips in and out of the kitchen, I stopped in the workroom and tried to converse with Naomi. She never responded to my comments or questions. I kept Matti away from her, making the excuse that he was ill.

Her weaving didn't progress. Occasionally she sat on the stool in front of the loom to string a few threads of warp. But most of the time, she occupied herself with other pursuits, such as pulling her hair across her face and then picking through it, strand by strand. Or licking her finger-tips and catching dust motes floating in shafts of sunlight. She also slept a great deal of the day because she slept so poorly at night.

Naomi wouldn't bathe or change her clothes. This offended Razi, who, though her work was often messy, maintained herself meticulously and believed everyone else should also. Naomi wouldn't speak to Razi, not even to thank her for serving her all her meals and removing her dirty dishes. Razi, who was usually talkative and cheerful, carried out her duties sullenly.

To separate my friend from my servant for a time, I asked Naomi to accompany me to the market. She had always loved shopping. Though some of the stores in the market area were still being constructed, the streets had been paved and the covered sidewalks along them were fin-ished. Merchants brought their wares into the agora and the market streets by cart twice each week, and today a caravan from Batanea was passing through as well. We'd find the perfumer, for, in her hasty departure from Jerusalem, Naomi had failed to bring her scent. Then we'd examine the fabrics of the silk merchants, which surely must be inferior to Efron's goods, but were still worth seeing. Finally we'd stop at the sandal makers where I'd buy Naomi a pair to replace the ones she'd damaged on her journey from Jerusalem. With these lures, Naomi consented to go. She allowed me to tie up and cover her hair, but not to braid it. She accepted my loan of a clean tunic when I told her we could try on brooches and necklaces at the stall of a jeweler I knew. As children, we would search for the ruddy sandstones we called "rubies" and tie them to our necks with strands of grape vines. When I reminded her of this game, she even smiled once, a vague shadow of a genuine Naomi smile.

We walked from our house, near the eastern wall, along the decumanus, the main east-west street of the city. The small limestones in the Sepphoris walkways had been chiseled flat and laid close together, so toes couldn't snag in the spaces between them. A column of heavy carts, each drawn by four oxen and hauling white ashlars from the quarry outside the walls, stopped at various sites along the street to drop off their loads. Oak beam cranes lifted the huge stones from the carts to form the walls of stores, houses, and apartments. The construction noise was deafening, and the sun blazed hot. We looked forward to the shade and the relative quiet of the colonnade rimming the agora.

However, when we did reach the shelter of the colonnade, Naomi's breathing suddenly became short and shallow. She said she needed to rest and stopped to lean against one of the limestone columns. My eyes wandered up to the decorative curls at the top of the column. They looked like ram's horns. Naomi's eyes must have followed mine. "Ionic columns," she said. "Another thing the Romans stole from other peoples." Then her eyes darted from column to column. Her face flushed. She breathed faster and faster. "Hate Roman columns, Roman buildings, Roman houses, Roman rooms . . ."

Sweat drenched her face. "Must leave. Feel sick." She uncovered and unbound her shock of bushy hair and began to run.

I hastened after her, as unobtrusively as possible, but she quickly outdistanced me. People everywhere turned at the sight of a woman running along the decumanus with her hair unbound, bumping into people and failing to apologize.

I caught up with Naomi in the workroom at home. She was curled into a ball near the loom and appeared to be sleeping. "Naomi," I whispered, shaking her gently. "Are you ill? What happened to you?"

One eye opened. It was blue. No, impossible. A sunbeam pierced the window at a peculiar angle and must have made her eye appear lighter than it was.

"Naomi is not here," she said in a raspy voice. The blue eye shut, and she tightened the coil of her body.

I hugged myself to stop my violent shaking and then sent Zohar to find Tobiah, even though it meant going into the courts to do so. Tobiah arrived within the hour and joined me in our bedroom. He held me and stroked my back, trying to calm my tremors. "Now, tell me what happened," he said.

As I spoke, my chest tightened as if my heart was shrinking inside it. When I finished my explanation of Naomi's strange behavior, he drew his lips tight. "Perhaps Naomi is possessed. There may be an evil spirit dwelling within her."

"No," I insisted. "She's not lame, or dumb, or fitful, like other possessed people. Just a few years ago, she was a funny, carefree girl. Why would a demon bother with her? The Merciful One wouldn't permit it, would He?"

Tobiah didn't answer my question. He narrowed his eyes. "The problem is her strange, unreliable behavior," he said. "Think of our children and their safety. You've told me how she acts around Mattityahu. And we've seen that she cannot occupy herself, and that she paces all night and lies about all day."

I nodded my head in agreement. "I especially fear the way she looks at Matti."

"Yes, it's unnatural," he said. "And many people saw her today in the agora. They'll think she's possessed. Or a prostitute, parading down the streets of the city with her hair streaming behind her."

He stood up and paced the room, ticking off Naomi's deficiencies on his fingers. "She will never be accepted by people in Sepphoris. She has been the slave of a Roman master. People will make assumptions, which will probably be correct, about her purity. They will judge her unclean and sinful. And judge us likewise since she is living in our house. One of my scribes told me today it's already whispered in the courthouse that she is my mistress."

So it was not just the safety of our children that concerned my husband. It was his reputation. He did not want people associating his name with this woman with the unloosed hair. My sympathy for Naomi weakly rebounded. "But it's our duty to help her. No matter what other people may think."

"But what will help her? Efron took her to the best physicians in the world. He even took her all the way to Rome. Chuza told me that every possible cure has been attempted: Temple sacrifices, medicine, spiritual healing, exorcism, even magic. What else is there?" He turned his palms up and rendered his judgment, like the magistrate he was. "We cannot keep Naomi with us. She is dangerous."

Since the moment Naomi had arrived, my fear of her had gnawed away at my judgment, and I no longer knew what to think. Maybe she was possessed. Maybe I should trust Tobiah's evaluation of her condition. He was experienced in such matters. The truth was, I now admitted to myself, that I didn't want to help Naomi anymore. I hadn't trusted her from the moment she arrived in Sepphoris. The Holy One had granted me a good husband, healthy children, and a comfortable life. Naomi put my blessings in jeopardy. I, too, wanted her gone. I was grateful that Tobiah was insisting on it so that I didn't have to.

I began to cry with relief, but Tobiah misunderstood my tears. He squeezed his hands together, as if pleading with me. "Please understand, Danya. You have a good heart, but you cannot help her. We must send her away now. It's what is best for her as well as for us. You'll see this in time. Trust me."

I did not have a good heart. My heart had hardened, so much so that I understood and sympathized with Chuza's cold heart. Both of us had been forced to care for Naomi against our own wishes. She arrived unbidden into our homes; she upset the peace and harmony of them; she brought no resources and consumed ours ungratefully; she had needs we could never fill.

The blood in my veins turned cold as well water. Thoughts clicked smoothly and logically through my mind. Naomi is dangerous. She is a threat to my whole family. I have done what I can for her. I am being wise not to risk my happiness for this girl again. I must send her away.

But where to send her? Back to Jerusalem? No one there can care for her. To a foreign country? Even Chuza hadn't been so cruel. She would starve, suffer mistreatment, and quickly die away from her own people.

So I had Zohar bring Naomi to Nazareth that same day. I stood at the gate and watched them start down the street, Zohar leading and Naomi sitting upon the donkey, while I thought of the times she had been led away before: by my father, by Chuza, and now by me. Pity for her should've filled my heart, but it didn't. When I told her to prepare herself to leave my house, she snorted and said, "*An honor* to have me, wasn't it?" She reminded me of the dove on the Temple Mount that had bitten my hand as I freed it.

REVELATIONS

Early one warm morning in Ab, I brought the children with me to our garden plot outside the city walls. Though our servants maintained the garden, I still loved working with my hands in dirt from time to time. A village girl at heart, I suppose. Ever since Matti could walk, his chubby hand had transformed any long object, such as a tree twig, a cooking spoon, or a clutch of dried wheat stalks, into a blade. Last month, as a sixth birthday present for him, Zohar had carved two blunt swords from olive wood, one for Matti and a second one for Mariamme. Matti had appointed his little sister his permanent opponent, a Roman centurion. My son carried his sword everywhere, cinched in a rope around his waist. Since Mariamme so often misplaced her weapon, he graciously toted hers for her, in case an opportunity for swordplay should present itself, as it did today.

He circled his wooden blade over his head until it whooshed, then glided it down close to, but not touching, Mariamme's slender neck, neatly dispatching her to Hades. Though she was a year younger than Matti, Mariamme was taller than her big brother, which must have made his conquests all the more satisfying for him.

As a child, I, too, had been my brother's favorite adversary and victim. Lev had schooled me in the art of dying dramatically: bulge the eyes, gasp for breath, convulse, drop to the ground and stare, face up, at the sky. A longing for Lev and for my childhood swept over me, as it frequently did these days. Matti and Mariamme played so much like Lev and I used to.

After dying a few more times, Mariamme consigned her weapon to me and wandered off in search of more dignified pursuits. I took up her sword and dealt King Matti a near-fatal blow when I cut off his arm. But, while I was distracted with another enemy, he recovered, and I was slain by my one-armed foe. Matti's victory pleased him, so he agreed to sheath his sword and see what occupied his sister.

Mariamme stood in a blister of sunlight holding a stick. In sure, steady strokes, she pushed the tip of her stick through a little plot of smoothed soil near a clump of wild mint.

Mattityahu Mariamme

Tobiah Danya　　　*Ezri Adira*

Mattityahu Mariamme Gad　　*Yochanan*

"What's this scribble?" asked Matti, waving his sword over the markings in the dirt.

Mariamme calmly pointed to each name as she read it. "This is Papa's father and this is his mother. We're named after them. And here are Mama and Papa, and Papa's brother and his wife. What was the name of their other boy, the other cousin we never met?"

I was so astonished, I stuttered the child's name. "N-N-N-Naor."

Mariamme dropped the stick and with her four-year-old finger formed the letters of her cousin's name as competently as a Temple scribe. She stood and showed me the smudge of dirt on her forefinger. I hugged her so tightly she squirmed in my arms. I was still stuttering when I asked, "M-M-Mariamme, how did you learn to do this?"

"I watch you and Papa sometimes."

"Yes, but it took us years to learn to write."

She shrugged. "I think it's easy."

I hugged her again, careful not to squeeze her too tightly. "I'm so proud of you."

I knew that this gift was not her doing, or mine, or Tobiah's. This could only be the work of The Highest. "Praise Him who gave you this gift, Mariamme," I whispered against her warm little neck as I kissed it.

Matti scowled and kicked out the letters in the dirt. "Play with me now," he said to Mariamme. "You can kill me this time."

She shrugged and grasped the sword he offered her.

"Wait." I stopped them. "Who's Gad?"

"The one in your belly," Mariamme explained. "I call him 'Gad,' the happy one."

The child in my womb kicked at that moment. Had Mariamme, my quiet, self-possessed little girl, also been given the gift of prescience? I spread my hands across my tight stomach. "How do you know it's a boy?"

"I don't know. I just hope it is, so he can swordfight instead of me."

The baby quieted. I captured the swords and herded my children from the garden into Tobiah's library. Tobiah was hunched over his desk, squinting at the farm accounts in the dim lamplight. I opened the shutters. A light breeze freshened the stale indoor air. I grabbed a wax tablet and stylus from his desk. "Look, look what your daughter can do, Tobiah."

I handed Mariamme the writing materials and told her, "Write the names like you did with the stick in the garden."

Mariamme sat on the stone floor and rested the tablet across her knees. In calm, confident strokes, she repeated her genealogy record, identifying each name as she etched it into the wax. "Mattityahu was the husband of Mariamme and the father of Tobiah and Ezri. Tobiah is the husband of Danya and the father of Mattityahu and Mariamme and maybe Gad. Ezri is the husband of Adira and the father of Yochanen and Naor."

Tobiah jumped up from his bench and examined the marks on her tablets. From the storage shelves against the wall, he selected a scroll and rolled it open over the farm ledgers. He sat Mariamme on his lap and pushed his finger across the page. "Do you know what these words say?" he asked.

Without any hesitations, Mariamme read them aloud in her high, little girl voice. "*Happy is the man whose heart is fixed to call upon the name of the Lord; At what he sees in his bad dreams, his soul shall not be troubled; When he passes through rivers and the tossing of the seas, he shall not be dismayed.*" She frowned. "What does dismayed mean, Papa?"

Tobiah scooped Mariamme up in his arms. "Dismayed means worried, but we will not be dismayed, will we?" Then he spun his daughter in circles until the two of them, giddy and dizzy, fell to the floor.

"What's happening?" Matti asked, turning his head from me to his sister to his father.

"Mariamme can read and write," I explained.

Matti's full, round cheeks reddened. He set the wax tablet across his knees. With the flat end of the stylus, he obliterated his sister's letters, drew a sword into the wax, and showed it to his father. Tobiah leaned over to look and smiled at him. But he didn't spin his son in circles.

Matti took up the stylus again, and, biting on his tongue, dug the outline of a javelin deep into the wax, then a lance. He lowered his head in concentration, and his dark curls fell across his eyes. He brushed them back and drew a shield, a bow, and a sling.

"That's very good, Mattityahu," said Tobiah. "I see you're ready to begin your schooling. We'll start after the next Sabbath."

Again, Matti looked at Tobiah and then at me. He threw the stylus down and wept.

Tobiah stood over him. "Mattityahu," he said sternly, "Your sister's gift is cause for rejoicing, not crying. You have your own blessings." Tobiah reminded Matti how, sitting with him on the horse, the two of them would take inventory of the estates. Matti counted the sheep and goats and rows of vines and hectares of wheat. And how Tobiah didn't need to record them until he got home because our son always remembered the numbers.

Matti's ears turned purple, and he wailed even louder. I understood the heat of jealousy, so I carried him from the library out to the inner courtyard where I maintained a small vegetable plot. "Count for me, Matti," I said. "I'll pick the beans that have ripened and put them in this basket. I need you to make an accounting of how many there are."

Matti's heaving sobs simmered down into sniffles, but the redness in his face remained, as if steeped into his features. He softly hiccupped and counted each bean pod. But from that day on, in Matti's eyes, his gift never again sparkled as brightly.

After I had comforted my little boy, Zohar took him and Mariamme to the stables, located outside the city walls. Tobiah still kept horses for his trips to Jerusalem, and the children loved to brush and nuzzle the handsome pair.

I returned to the library, excited to discuss Mariamme's gift with my husband. The scroll Mariamme had read from had been reshelved. Tobiah was again hovering over the farm ledgers, his elbows up on the table and his forehead propped in his hands. On the day after the Sabbath last week, our farm manager, Otzar, had suddenly departed for the northern Galilee town of Gischala to tend his dying father, and so, for the past three days, Tobiah had immersed himself in supervising the estates and their accounts. I stood in the doorway, reluctant to disturb him.

He lifted his head and saw me. "Come in, Danya. You brought me such wonderful news this morning, but I have only bad news for you." He looked back down at his papers. "Tare was mixed in with the corn. Anyone who eats it will get sick. The entire corn crop must be burned."

This could happen if a farmer wasn't vigilant. Seed selection was one of Otzar's responsibilities. Fortunately, corn wasn't a major crop on our estates. "Even good farmers make mistakes," I pointed out. "But it's unfortunate to lose any crop just before the Sabbath year."

The Sabbath year was to commence in Tishri, the month after next. The Holy One's Law required that every seventh year the people and the land of Israel rest. Jews, their servants and slaves, and even their animals were commanded by The Holy One not to work. The land itself must not be tilled: no grain planted, no vines or fruits harvested. In Sabbath years, we were to live off the abundance of the prior year. In the Torah it is promised that *"I will order my blessing for you in the sixth year, so that it will yield a crop for three years."* Some landowners had abandoned the pious practice of keeping the Sabbath year, but Tobiah's family had honored it, and, for generations, they had thrived.

"Having adequate supplies to carry us through the Sabbath year is beginning to worry me," said Tobiah. "Yesterday, after I'd been to the cornfield, I rode through the vineyards. Some of the grapes are turning sour. The workers told me that Otzar should've begun the harvest last week." Tobiah rubbed at the crease between his eyes. "This is my fault for not paying closer attention to the farms."

Actually, the farms had done well without Tobiah's attention. Since Tobiah had been raised to be a scholar and teacher of the Law, he knew almost nothing about farming when he arrived in Sepphoris, so he had wisely relied on the skills of the stewards he hired. These managers had come and gone over the years, but Tobiah thought he had finally found an expert in Otzar. This clever, industrious young man had been an assistant steward on one of Archelaus's estates in Judea. When Otzar expressed a desire to live closer to his family in Galilee, Chuza had directed him to us with his most enthusiastic recommendation. This past year, Tobiah had left our estates almost entirely in Otzar's talented hands while he turned his attentions to the civic and religious undertakings for which he was suited and which he vastly preferred.

"Don't blame yourself, Tobiah." I stood behind him and kneaded his neck. "You've been occupied with good, holy work. Don't worry so. There are always difficulties in farming. We'll recover."

"There's more to recover from than the grapes and the corn," said Tobiah, shaking his head in disgust. He spread more of the farm accounts out on the table before me. "Sit down and look at these. In going over these records, I've learned that Otzar was not the farmer or the business-man I thought he was."

I pulled up a bench and sat next to him at the wood-topped table. Tobiah shuffled through the sheaves of papyrus until he found one in particular. His long, thin finger pointed at two columns of numbers. "See here: Otzar didn't set aside enough grain from last year's harvest for this year's seed. It takes a bushel of seed to produce four bushels of grain. So he had to buy a large amount of seed this year. And then he paid too much for it. I should've checked all of this sooner."

"But overall it was a good harvest, wasn't it?" I wished I had left the shutters closed. Heat now poured into the library.

"Yes, but the profits will be small. So much of the harvest is already appropriated. The first twenty percent to Rome for taxes, the next forty percent to the tenants, then from our forty percent, I must deduct Temple taxes and offerings. Celebrating the Sabbath year is going to strain our resources."

"Temple taxes and offerings are not that onerous," I pointed out.

Tobiah shrunk down a little on his bench. "There is also debt repayment."

"Debt?" I asked, trying to keep my voice steady.

"Yes, I've had to do some borrowing." Tobiah must have detected the criticism I tried to conceal. He sat up straighter and defended his deci-sion to borrow. "Two years ago, you must remember, locusts ate most of the barley and half the grapes. And every year, despite too little rain, or too much heat, or pests, or vandalism, or lazy workers, and everything else that plagues the farms of Galilee, I must still pay taxes to Rome and to the Temple while also supporting this large household. To meet these obligations, yes, I have had to borrow some money."

"From whom?" I asked.

Tobiah's voice lost some of its force. "From Salvius Marcellus."

"You borrowed money from a Roman?" Such a thing was just not done.

"Yes, from a Roman. What faithful Jew would loan money in the sixth year when he knew I couldn't pay it back quickly? In order to follow the Law, he would have to cancel the debt during the Sabbath year and would therefore lose his investment."

The loan had been made. There was nothing to do but repay it as soon as possible. Keeping the Sabbath year was the more important issue. "The soil needs its rest, Tobiah. When we celebrate the Sabbath year, the land rewards us with great abundance the following year."

"Yes, the following year. I'm worried about this year." He slapped his hand down on the table, almost overturning an oil lamp. "Caesar Augustus may no longer grant the exemption his predecessor did in Sabbath years. It's likely he'll tax us despite the Sabbath year. How will we pay the taxes if we don't till the land?"

I shrugged and shook my head, though I felt like crying. I wasn't accustomed to fits of temper in Tobiah.

He straightened the lamp and took a deep breath. "I apologize. None of this is your fault. You manage the household very well." Tobiah closed his eyes and rubbed his temples. "Give me some of your wise advice. What would your father have said about this Sabbath year?"

My lip was still trembling. "'Follow the Law,' I suppose. That's what he always said." I was reminded, then, of the sacrifices Father had made in his observance of the Law. He'd given up a privileged life in Jerusalem to live on two hectares in Nazareth. Insecurely, as it turned out. Father's strict adherence had alienated his sons from him, and he'd died a senseless, violent death.

"I could sell one of my estates," said Tobiah. "That would give us the money we needed at this time. But I think it would be wrong to give up any of my patrimony. That land was entrusted to my ancestors by The Holy One."

"Do not sell one cubit." I held to the peasant understanding that the only truly valuable possession was land. Peasants knew that selling land was "eating the seeds that should be sown next year," and would soon result in a family's starvation.

"We can limit our expenses," I pointed out. "There are household costs I can cut. And you could set the slaves free, so we wouldn't have to support them. It's the custom in the Sabbath year to do so, anyway." We had about ten men who, to pay off their debts, had sold themselves to Tobiah for seven years in his service. They were treated as members of our own extended household, in accordance with the Law, and had to be fed, clothed, and housed by us. "The grain allotment for each of them is almost forty-five seah a year."

The corners of his mouth pulled down. "Set them free? To do what? Starve in the streets of Sepphoris? Become bandits and prey on the countryside? I'd hoped to give each of them a small plot of land upon completion of his service, but I can't do that now."

He rose from his bench and paced. We were both quiet while we tried to think.

Increasing income by leasing out more land was not a possibility in the Sabbath year. No one would lease land in a year they did not intend to till it. Gentiles would, but that was unacceptable. This was our sacred land, held by us in covenant with The Holy One. We would not lease, much less sell, our lands to pagans.

I tried to squelch the alarm rising in me. "I know how much grain, oil, and produce we'll need for the Sabbath year and for the following year until we can harvest again. But how much do we have in storage? Even if there isn't much grain to sell, don't we at least have enough stored for our own use?"

Tobiah thumbed through all the sheets on the table. He licked his fingers and rippled through them again. "Those numbers aren't here. Strange, they should be. I'll go to the storage chambers and check the grain supply right now."

Tobiah and several other large landowners in Sepphoris, including Herod Antipas, stored their barley and wheat in large silos beneath the Acropolis. These underground chambers had been hewn out of bedrock and plastered, so the grain would stay dry during the rainy season.

Guards, stationed every fifty paces atop the walls of the Acropolis, protected these storerooms from bandits. From one harvest to the next, our grain harvest was portioned out from these silos. The household consumed relatively small amounts of it. Most was sold for cash as need and the market dictated.

While I waited for Tobiah to return from the silos, I looked over all the accounts again. Perhaps Tobiah had made some arithmetic error. Maybe some expense was deducted twice or some income item overlooked. But I found no evidence of this.

Within the hour, Tobiah returned. He looked as if he had just hit his head against a beam. He sat down and buried his face in his hands. "Empty," he groaned. "Not a kernel."

"Empty? Nothing? In any of the silos?" The words scraped at my throat.

"Nothing." He kept his face in his hands.

Though such depravity seemed inconceivable, this must have been Otzar's doing. Tobiah had given his steward a house to live in, taken him into his confidence, and entrusted him with the care of his precious lands. We expected deceit and violation from our Roman occupiers and strangers from other countries. But not from one of our own.

Later, we would piece together the full account of Otzar's underhanded dealings. He paid too much for seed just to test the extent of Tobiah's supervision of the accounts. Once he knew Tobiah trusted him and was not paying close attention, Otzar hired several foreign field workers who agreed to do his bidding and keep silent. By day during the months of Iyyar and Sivan, Otzar and these men worked side by side with our loyal slaves and honest hired workers to harvest, thresh, winnow, sift, and temporarily store the grain in sacks. He also collected Tobiah's share of each tenant's harvest. By night, instead of hauling the grain to our storage chambers, these thieves hid it in caves until they found itinerant merchants willing to purchase the smuggled grain. Otzar, and the embezzlers who had colluded with him, then scattered across the countryside and seas like our grain. Not surprisingly, no one in Gischala had ever heard of a man named Otzar, much less his dying father. Neither the thieves nor the grain could be traced or recovered. I suspected that Chuza had a hand in this because he had recommended Otzar to us. But Tobiah said it was foolish of me to entertain such an idea.

But on this day in the month of Ab, we desperately needed a plan for surviving the coming year. We had no wheat, barley, corn, or seed. We would have a poor grape harvest. And debt. And taxes.

Through the library windows, I gazed out at the terraced hillsides and plains of Galilee, now scorching in the midday sun. It was rich soil, but always perilous for those who depended on it. No doubt there were also villagers in Nazareth wondering how they would get by in the Sabbath year. But they would. For centuries, no matter how difficult the circumstances, pious peasants had always found ways to abide by the Law and celebrate the Sabbath year. At least our household was fortunate enough to have animals for meat. And Razi had already stuffed the kitchen storeroom with large rounds of cheeses. The olive harvest next month would be plentiful, so we would have excess olive oil to sell. We had possessions we could part with, and their sale could provide us with much-needed coin.

"Look at me, Tobiah," I said, gently removing his hands from his face and holding them in mine. The lines in his high forehead were etched in as deeply as Matti's impressions in the wax tablet. How I loved those earnest, thought-filled lines. I kissed them. "I've been much poorer than this before and still celebrated the Sabbath year. We can get by, I know it. Do not be 'dismayed.'"

He slipped his hands from my grasp. "I have not been poor. The Merciful One has blessed me with wealth. My duty is to manage His blessings wisely, providing for the people I am responsible for." Then he straightened himself up on the bench and laid his palms flat on the table, as if bracing himself for a blow. "*For the Lord is good to them that endure chastening.*" Do you believe that, Danya?" he asked.

I hesitated. "Yes, I believe the Lord is good."

"Because I may have to endure His chastening." Perspiration rose on Tobiah's ashen face. "I will not sell my land, nor can I afford to let my farms rest untilled, nor my animals or slaves or orchards be unproductive. I am not going to observe this Sabbath year. May Adonai forgive me." He walked out of the library, tall and stiff-necked.

I was stunned by Tobiah's decision. But it was made with such firmness, I knew it was useless to try to change his mind. I stayed behind in the library, and my eyes came to rest on the scroll Mariamme had read from. That joy-filled moment of discovering our daughter's gift seemed like a long time ago, though the sun had moved only half a day in its path since then. The dry parchment crackled in my fingers as I laid it out on the desk again.

This scroll had been Father's. He had wrapped it in calfskin and sealed it in a stone jug when we brought it from Nazareth to Jerusalem with us, and I had done the same to carry it to Sepphoris with us. Father called these writings "The Psalms of Solomon" to honor our great king of antiquity. Onto this parchment, Father copied the verses he had collected from various sources over many years. He had also added verses of his own. I thought of him sitting over these writings, pen in hand, still and expectant, as if waiting to hear a knock at the door. He waited for enlightenment, for Adonai to tell him what to write.

I found the passage his granddaughter had read. *"At what he sees in his bad dreams, his soul shall not be troubled; When he passes through rivers and the tossing of the seas, he shall not be dismayed."*

Father had recited this to me when I was little and interpreted it for me. "It doesn't mean that we won't have difficulties. It means"—here he tapped his staff on the floor to emphasize what was to follow—"that the Holy One will help us to stand fast when we do."

Tap. Tap. Tap. Father's staff. After his death, I kept that knotted stick with me throughout those lonely months in Jerusalem. His hand had stained its grip. Though this staff had long since been misplaced, Father's hand had also gripped this scroll. His fingers had labored over these very words. I placed my fingers lightly on the characters, careful not to smudge the ink. Yes, here he was, reminding me: "The Holy One will help us to stand fast."

BIRTH, SIN, PIETY

On a cold, rainy afternoon in Tetbeth after the winter grain sowing, my midwife, Alona, arrived to help me deliver my third child. I labored all night, but this baby would not give up the safety of my womb. Worry clouded Alona's face as she wiped my face with a cool cloth. She suggested calling in a second midwife, a Roman named Marcella, whom Alona thought was the best midwife in all of Galilee.

I closed my eyes and watched colored stars explode behind them while I counted out the length of my next contraction. Fifty. Still fifty counts long. After all these hours, my pains should be longer. And stronger. Exhausted and now unnerved by Alona's fear, I consented to the Gentile midwife. Tobiah sent the carriage for Marcella.

Combs bound Marcella's straight yellow hair tightly to her head. I could almost feel the stick of their tines in my own scalp. Her eyes were turquoise. Marcella frightened me, but her small, nimble hands turned the baby inside me, and my pains grew more frequent and more intense. I thought I would begin pushing soon.

However, as the sun rose that morning, my labor pains lost their power. Marcella's brows knit together, and her lips disappeared as she examined me. She dug into her calfskin sack and removed a two-pronged instrument that I had never seen before. She instructed me to push, and, with her jaw firmly set, inserted the cold metal tongs into me and dragged my baby from my womb.

Alona caught him. I held my breath and prayed to hear a cry. Alona turned the gray-skinned infant upside down and smacked his bottom.

He gasped for air, sputtered up mucus, and pushed out a weak whimper. My child lived.

I wanted only to rest, to close my eyes and sleep for days, but Marcella gave my face a sharp slap. "Not now. You must deliver the afterbirth."

I had no strength left. I couldn't even lift my head to look at my baby. Marcella's hands pressed down hard on my womb, and sharp pains ripped through it. The Gentile commanded, "Push, push, push," and I finally expelled the bloody sack. Then I floated into a half-waking, half-sleeping state. Blurry images washed through my waking moments.

Alona rubbed the white, sticky coating from the baby's skin, then wiped her own eyes with the back of her hand. My eyelids drooped heavily.

Marcella whispered, "Now! Before your wife takes to it." I tried to raise my head, but blackness pushed it down.

My whole body shook with cold. Someone wrapped me in a warm sheepskin.

Tobiah hissed at Marcella, "Leave us. Your work here is finished." Marcella packed her instruments into her bag. Footsteps sounded on the stone floor.

My husband paced with his arms crossed tightly against his chest. My eyes finally stayed open. I longed to hold my baby and to be held by my husband. Razi and Alona propped me up in the bed by placing cushions behind my head and back and under each arm. Matti and Mariamme burst into the room and crawled up onto the bed by me. They positioned themselves one on either side of me, and we cuddled around the cushions. But the recollected sounds of crying and hissing frayed the edges of my joy. Matti made a space for Tobiah who continued pacing. The children called to him, "Are you going to name the baby now, Papa? Name him Gad. Mama wants that name, too."

Tobiah took the infant from Alona and laid him on his knee, as he had done with our other two newborns. "You shall be called Gad, the happy one," he said solemnly. He did not hold the tightly swaddled child to his heart, but carried him to my bedside and placed him in my arms. He touched his lips to my forehead. "I was so worried about you, my dear one. But they tell me you'll be all right. I must go out now and tend to some business."

"Where's Papa going?" asked Matti. "Doesn't he want to play with the new baby?"

Uttering his children's names for the first time had made Tobiah so happy before. He had hovered and fussed over Matti and Mariamme at their namings such that I had to beg for a turn to hold them myself. But I told Matti, "Your father's very tired. He stayed awake all night waiting for Gad to come."

"Then he should be glad because the baby is here now!" objected Matti.

Yes, he should be. This long and difficult birth was not Gad's fault. Or mine. We were the ones who had suffered the most, but Tobiah had left us both unembraced. "There'll be plenty of time in the days ahead for your father to play with Gad," I assured Matti.

Mariamme squeezed her hands under her little dimpled chin. "Can we look closer?"

I laid Gad down on my legs and unwrapped some of his swaddling. He arched his back and flung out his arms and legs, yelped, and coughed up more mucus. Good, I thought, Matti and Mariamme had also done that as newborns when they were suddenly exposed to chill air.

Gad's skin color improved, a reddish-purple tinge replacing the mottled gray of his complexion in his first minutes. I studied his face. It was unusually flat, and his eyes slanted upwards. His ears were tiny, but his tongue was large. This baby did look a little peculiar. The frowns, the whispers, the tears, the midwife's hasty dismissal: perhaps all of that had something to do with his odd little head and face. But when I put Gad up on my shoulder and embraced him, his body shaped itself nicely into mine, just as it was supposed to do.

Matti said, "Oh, I think he's going to be very strong. He looks like a fighter." Gad's nose, flattened and skewed to one side, his puffy, swollen eyelids, and the bruises on his cheeks and temples from the forceps Marcella had used did make him look as if he had been in combat.

"He had to fight hard to come out and meet his brother," I said, kissing the beautifully rounded curve of the back of my sweet Matti's head.

"I have a present for him, Mama." Matti brandished a small olive branch whose bark he had peeled off. "See, my brother's first sword." I lowered Gad into the crook of my arm, turning him towards his brother.

Matti held the yellow branch up to Gad's face. The baby brightened. When Matti slowly swished the sword from side to side, Gad turned his head as if following it.

"See that, Mama! He wants it! He's a fighter. I like him."

Mariamme carefully uncovered more of Gad's swaddling. She pointed to the dark, fine hair on his shoulders. "Oh, he looks like a little marmot," she cooed. We turned him over and found dark hair on his back also. "Did I look like a little furry animal when I was born?"

Yes, she had. The soft down that had covered her sloughed off after a few months. I was relieved that Gad looked like his attractive sister had, in this way at least.

Mariamme placed her hand next to Gad's tiny one. Three creases crossed Mariamme's palm, but Gad's had only one long crease. His fingers were short and stubby, different from the long tapered fingers of my other babies. But when Mariamme stroked the palm of Gad's hand, he grasped her finger like a newborn should. "Matti's right, Mama. Gad is strong. And he's the cutest little baby I ever saw."

Matti, our lover of numbers, counted Gad's heartbeats. Then he put his other hand on his sister's heart and counted. "He's twice as fast as you, Mariamme!"

My arms tightened, and Gad squirmed in discomfort in them. But then I remembered that a newborn's heartbeat should be rapid. I relaxed, and Gad again nestled comfortably against me.

With his thick fingers, Matti undid the rest of Gad's wrappings. He pointed to the baby's enlarged scrotum, and both children giggled and covered their mouths. "That's how a baby boy is supposed to look," I told them, pleased with yet another sign of Gad's normalcy.

My baby was alive. He was beautiful to me and to his brother and sister, if not to his midwives and father. He did look peculiar, but he was a newborn, and I believed he would soon outgrow the drubbing he had suffered during his difficult birth.

The morning my milk came in, a messenger brought a letter for Tobiah from a man named Dardanius Cimber from Pompeii. The messenger said he did not need a reply, so I left the unopened letter on a table in the bedroom. All day, its garish red seal disturbed me because I remembered that Tobiah had sent an inquiry to the leaders of Pompeii seeking information about his brother Ezri.

When my husband returned from his work at the courts, he frowned at the letter and then at Gad. Gad was not eating. I was sitting in a chair in our bedroom, trying to get him to nurse by stroking around his mouth. He took my nipple, but after a feeble tug or two would drop it.

Tobiah picked up the letter and broke the wax seal. It was written in Latin, but Tobiah translated as he read it aloud.

> **To Tobiah ben Mattityahu of Sepphoris, in Galilee, greetings**
> *A man named Ezri ben Mattityahu served as tutor to my sons. He was tall and learned, though white-haired, not gray as you described. I bought him at a slave auction about nine years ago. Ezri's wife and two sons died on the sea voyage to our country.*

"Oh, no! Finally, news of my brother and it's of the worst kind. Adira, Yochanen and Naor. All gone." Tobiah slumped down onto the floor next to my chair. I wrapped my free arm around his shoulder and pressed him against my leg. He held the letter up again and continued to translate slowly and cautiously.

> *After six years as my slave, I freed Ezri, but he did not want to return to his country. He said he no longer worshipped the Hebrew God who had abandoned him and permitted his wife and children to die. Ezri applied for Roman citizenship and chose to remain here in Pompeii as a teacher.*

Tobiah and I gasped. Although Ezri's afflictions must have caused him overwhelming pain, even Chuza would not repudiate his God and seek Roman citizenship. Gad began to whimper. Tobiah's tears splashed onto the parchment. He blotted the letter with his sleeve. "His suffering is so great, he despairs." He continued, slumping deeper with each line he read.

Unfortunately an illness of the heart claimed his life shortly there-after. His body was cremated, according to our custom, and his ashes were buried in our city cemetery. This was his last wish.
Farewell from Dardanius Cimber, Pompeii

"Buried in a Gentile cemetery." Tobiah turned the letter over and wept bitterly.

For years, my husband had borne the sadness of his brother's enslavement. That burden had been heavy enough for him to bear. But now he would have this heavier cart of sorrow to draw, the knowledge that Ezri died renouncing his people and The Holy One of Israel.

Gad, hungry but unable to fill himself, wailed. Over our baby's frantic screams, I said, "I'm so sorry, husband. Better that you had never found out what happened to him." For an instant, I let myself consider the possibility that my brother Lev could have done something equally sinful, but I cast off the thought.

Tobiah stood and reread the letter to himself. His face hardened. I tried, again unsuccessfully, to tease Gad into nursing.

"Can't you get that child to stop screaming?" Tobiah snapped. He read the letter a third time with his back to us. Finally, he tore it to pieces. "My brother died a sinner, and his punishment has been passed on to our family. Now I understand that it was his iniquity that caused the troubles with the farms. Then I transgressed further by violating the law of the Sabbath year. And so . . . this baby."

"What do you mean, 'this baby'?" I pulled Gad tightly against me, muffling the intensity of his screams.

Tobiah pointed a long finger at him. "This baby, he is my family's chastisement."

"Chastisement? You call our baby a punishment?" I stiffened.

"This child is not right, Danya. After three days, surely you must see that. The midwife Marcella did as soon as he was born. She told me that Romans expose children who look like him because they suffer from ills that can't be cured, and they don't live long, anyway. I refused to expose him. Jews do not engage in such barbarities. But now I know Adonai is angry with me. He sent this child to me and to the Kamith family as a chastening."

Gad suddenly stopped crying and snuggled his loose-jointed body against me. "You're overwrought with grief for Ezri. You know our child is not a punishment. He's a blessing, as are all our children." My heart tugged away from Tobiah's, but I reached my hand out to him.

All he had to do was take it in his. That would draw me back to him. "You don't mean what you just said, Tobiah. It's your grief speaking."

But Tobiah again pointed his trembling finger at Gad and backed away from us. I dropped my outstretched arm and wrapped it around my child.

Alone with my baby, I stroked his cheek over and over. Finally, his lips locked onto my nipple, and he began to suck, strongly and rhythmically, for the first time in his short life. With each tug of Gad's mouth, I felt a sharp pain in my breast, the sweetest pain I'd ever had. Milk spilled from the corners of his mouth, dribbled down his chin, and dropped with my tears onto his bravely beating heart. Chastisement, indeed!

Tobiah noted each sign of abnormality and slowness in Gad and used them as further proofs of Adonai's punishment of him. He frequently brooded over Ezri's apostasy and believed it was meant to be a lesson for him: if he continued in his lax observance of the Law, he would end up like his brother, a sinner who had broken his covenant with The Holy One.

Tobiah began to tighten up his and the whole household's religious observance, starting with the kitchen. One night I went there for some fruit after feeding Gad and found Razi grumbling and puttering about.

"Razi, what are you doing here so late?"

She tossed her hand in the direction of the storage shelves. "Ask your husband. Twenty years I've worked for him, and now all of a sudden, the storage vessels are impure? Clay is no longer good enough, 'Too porous,' he says. 'The impurities in the liquids will soak into the clay and pollute the next batch they contain.' He says all the wine and oil have to be stored in stone or metal containers." She pointed to an assortment of jars and decanters piled in a corner. "He bought those new containers today. Can you imagine what they cost? And what am I going to do with all of this old pottery? He says I should break it up and throw it away. I can't break up perfectly good jars. I'd sooner sell them to Gentiles!"

Some members of Pharisaic sects concerned themselves with such strict observances of the purity laws, but Tobiah was a Sadducee and never had. And neither had I. In Nazareth, people couldn't afford stone and metal storage vessels any more than we could afford a miqveh in each house. It didn't make us less pure or less holy than those who could.

"Razi, this can't be done in one night. Go to bed. I will help you with this in the morning."

"What has gotten into my good master?"

In the past, I had admired Tobiah's piety. He prayed twice a day, honored the Sabbath, followed proper dietary practices, circumcised his sons, and paid his Temple taxes and offerings. Twice a year he served in the Temple. Tobiah loved The Holy One and acted justly in his dealings with people. He, like me, believed Adonai had given us the Law to bring us closer to Him. The rites and practices we engaged in served that purpose. They were sensible, if sometimes inconvenient, but they marked us as a people set apart and reminded us of the special covenant we had with Him. There had always been those living around us, in Nazareth as well as Sepphoris, who carried things too far and became enslaved by rites and practices not required in Torah. And there were people like Chuza who ignored virtually every commandment and pious practice. But Tobiah had always placed himself between these extremes and tried to follow the heart of the Law, if not every external detail of it. Until now.

The children and I were eating breakfast one morning when we heard the chink, chink, chink of a stonecutter's hammer below us. Matti and Mariamme came down to the miqveh with me to investigate the source of that sound. When Tobiah's great grandfather built this house, he had this ritual purification pool hewn into the bedrock beneath it. Tobiah was now standing in this miqveh, which had been emptied, supervising a stonemason at work.

"What are you doing, Papa?" asked Mariamme.

"Our family is becoming more observant," Tobiah replied with great enthusiasm. "We are building a second stairway into this miqveh. One set of steps will be used to enter the immersion pool and a second set, the ones we are cutting in now, will be used to leave it after the ritual cleansing."

For generations, the Kamith family had descended into the pool using one side of the stairway and ascended using the other side of the same steps. Apparently, a single stairway was no longer pious enough for us.

Mariamme's little face pinched in consternation. "But what if people mix up which stairway is which? Can we go up the down?"

Tobiah laughed. "You won't have that problem, my daughter. You remember everything."

"I can help you build it, Papa," said Matti, contending with his sister for Tobiah's approval. "See, I'm going to be more o'servant." With a sweep of his thick, short arms, he dug a sharp chisel into the original staircase, chipping a chunk of stone from the top step.

"Stop," Tobiah shouted and snatched the tool from Matti. "This is very important grown men's work, Mattityahu. Not for you."

Matti's cheeks flamed, but he did not cry. He stayed by my side during the entire period of the miqveh's reconstruction. He said he thought the house was going to fall down.

I shared my son's reservations about this "improvement." When I had used the miqveh after childbirth and my monthly periods, I had never felt unpurified when walking up and down its single staircase. I had always felt ritually cleansed, as well as grateful that we had our own pool and I did not have to share a single miqveh with all the other women in the village, as I had done in Nazareth. Stone and metal storage vessels. A second staircase in the mikveh. All of this seemed unnecessary to me. But I didn't object. If more elaborate purification rituals would help Tobiah reconcile himself to The Holy One, I would go along with them.

An advantage to delivering a male child was a shorter confinement than that prescribed for a female's birth. So, forty days after Gad's birth, the period of my childbirth impurity ended. After I had ritually bathed, complimenting Tobiah on the new staircase in the miqveh, I expected my husband to desire me. I had looked forward to renewing our lovemaking. The conflicts between us over Gad and Tobiah's grief over Ezri would be set aside, at least for a time. In the past, intimacy had brought peace between us.

But that night, Tobiah clung to his side of the bed, gripping it as if he were about to tumble off it. The next morning, he announced his plan for yet another act of piety involving the family. He wanted us to go to the Temple and offer the sacrifice after childbirth. When Mattityahu and Mariamme were born, we hadn't done this. We had stayed home and offered prayers of thanksgiving and praise, as many parents do when their children are born in places far from Jerusalem. Travel was always dangerous and especially difficult for a mother and a newborn.

"All purity regulations should be closely followed," the now rigorously pious Tobiah declared. "At the Temple, I will make a guilt offering to atone for my sin of violating the Sabbath year, and you can offer the woman's sacrifice after childbirth."

I had rolled a stone across the memories of my journey from Galilee to Jerusalem so many years ago. Tobiah's request released those long entombed frights: the sight and smell of the twisted, crucified corpses in the oak grove, the burn of Judah ben Hezekiah's fingers on my throat, the cries of the wild animals at night, the taste of my cowardice in Jericho, and of course, witnessing the murder of my father shortly after our arrival in Jerusalem.

But even my pious, observant father had not demanded that his wife and babies journey to Jerusalem for this rite. I also wondered about our safety in Jerusalem because, once again, the political climate had heated up there. Caesar Augustus had removed Herod Archelaus and exiled him to Gaul. The Roman legate Quirinius had come down from Syria to seize Archelaus's territories and keep order in Jerusalem. A procurator, a Roman, would be appointed by the Emperor to govern Judea, Samaria, and Idumea.

No one had approved of Herod Archelaus. But at least he was a Jew and had that link to our people. Replacing Archelaus with a Roman could be dangerous. His father's death had incited the rebellions led by Simon of Perea and Anthronges the Shepherd. And the raids of Judah ben Hezekiah.

However, it was now clear to me that there would be no peace within himself or between the two of us until Tobiah resolved his relationship with Adonai. "If it will reconcile you with The Holy One, I'll go."

I also had sins to atone for: my cruelty to Naomi and taxing an already-overburdened Miryam with her care for the last four years. Yosef and Miryam had built a small house for Naomi around their courtyard and cared for her. I hadn't seen Naomi in all this time.

To prepare for his sacrifice, Tobiah spent two days inspecting each yearling in his flocks for a perfect, unblemished animal. My husband thought it more pious to offer a lamb or calf of his own. In the end, he found that he didn't own an unblemished yearling, so he'd have to purchase one in Jerusalem. He would bring his perfect lamb or calf to the Court of the Priests where it would be inspected for its suitability for sacrifice. Then he would confess his sin and assist the priest in slitting the animal's throat. The priest would sprinkle the victim's blood around the altar, then clean, salt, and dismember the animal, and lay it on the altar to be burnt. The flames would consecrate it while burning the offering in its entirety. Adonai's displeasure would be placated, and Tobiah's sin forgiven at last. I fervently hoped and prayed.

A cold mist dampened me as I hurried to the stables to say a hasty good-bye to Tobiah as he prepared to leave for Jerusalem by himself. Matti and Mariamme had come down with fevers the day before our scheduled departure, and I had been up all night with them. We dared not subject our little ones to a long journey in their condition, but I had begged Tobiah to go himself since he so desperately needed to offer sacrifice to The Holy One at the Temple's altar.

After embracing me coolly, Tobiah mounted his horse. At that moment an almost-breathless messenger stopped him with the demand from Herod Antipas that Tobiah go immediately to the basilica for an emergency meeting of the leaders of the city. He set his traveling bag down and hastened away.

When Tobiah returned from that meeting late in the morning, I had fallen asleep because my children had. Tobiah's changing out of his traveling clothes awakened me; he told me why Antipas had called the urgent meeting.

"Quirinius has called for a census to be taken of Judea, Samaria, and

Idumea, the territory he is now temporarily governing. Some people in Jerusalem have begun to oppose the census for religious reasons. Others oppose it just because they know that a census will lead to more taxes. Antipas's concern is that this unrest in Jerusalem will spark rebellion in Galilee."

"Rebellion over a census? No one is stupid enough to risk his life over such a thing," I yawned. I got out of bed and washed my face as Tobiah unpacked his travel sack. But I began to wonder who would lead a movement to resist this census of Quirinius's. Surely neither Judah ben Hezekiah nor Lev would concern himself with defying a census.

So many years had passed since I had seen either of them. Nevertheless, I didn't accept the possibility that one or both of them had died. I often daydreamed about Lev living in the monastery at Qumran, observing the regulated life of that desert community. He would be an Essene scholar who copied Scripture, prayed frequently throughout the day, and prepared himself for the great and final battle to come. I imagined Judah living as a farmer in a village over the Galilean border where his past remained hidden. He would dig and plant and harvest the earth's rich soil with dirt, not blood, wedged under his fingernails. Occasionally he might steal off on a secret revolutionary mission. Rumors circulated that corrupt Jewish leaders, Roman collaborators, had been executed here and there by unknown assassins. I suspected Judah ben Hezekiah might be one of these assassins. But neither Judah nor Lev would be involved with a census revolt. Nevertheless, I had to know. "Who is leading the resistance to the census?" I asked as casually as I could.

"A Pharisee named Saddok, considered to be a holy man by all who know him. He calls for nonviolent resistance to the census. His teaching is that tithes and taxes are to be offered only to Adonai. Therefore, Temple priests and Jewish rulers can collect tithes and taxes, but Jews must not give money or offerings directly to the pagan Romans."

In Galilee we paid our taxes to the Jewish tetrarch, Herod Antipas. True, he had been appointed by Rome, and most of this money made its way to Rome as tribute; but, since our coins clinked into the coffers of a Jewish ruler first, we believed we were following the Law and our hands were clean. But with the removal of Herod Archelaus, the coins in the territories he ruled, including Jerusalem, would fall directly into a Roman's hands.

I dried my face. "I think I understand now: Saddok thinks Jews should resist the census that will determine the taxes because these taxes will go directly to the Roman infidel, not to Adonai first. So again: this doesn't sound like much of a revolution. And, anyway, it doesn't concern Galilee."

Tobiah tightened and re-tightened the drawstring on his empty travel sack as he paced.

"We don't know that. Rebels and self-proclaimed messiahs still roam the countryside in hiding, and they will take advantage of any shift in power. We will not allow revolutionaries to gain a foothold in Sepphoris. I cannot leave Galilee now."

"But what about making your sacrifice in the Temple? Isn't reconciliation with Adonai far more important to you?"

Tobiah scowled. "I won't make the same mistake my brother did. He ignored the signs of unrest among the peasants. It's our duty to deal with these matters. Uprisings must be stamped out before they begin."

"Surely a few more days won't matter," I said timidly.

"Do you want your children enslaved?" Tobiah barked. "Because that's how they, and you and I, will be dealt with if this revolt spreads into Galilee."

STORMS

It rained for weeks. Wadis overflowed and rampaged across the Netopha Plain. The wheat seedlings, which Tobiah had planted during the Sabbath year in defiance of the Law of Moses, washed away in the flooding. The rains and failed grain crop provided Galileans with more immediate concerns than fighting the injustice of Judea's census mandate.

The fevers would not leave the restless, fitful bodies of my children. They complained that their bones ached, and they didn't want to eat. Razi made Matti and Mariamme drink fish brine to ease the swelling in their joints, but it made them vomit. One day while I was tending to their sickly stomachs and the mess they'd made in their bedroom, Tobiah looked in on us. He felt the children's foreheads with the back of one hand. In his other, he clutched a small scroll, sealed with blue wax.

"What's that?" I asked.

Quietly, so that the children wouldn't hear him, he said, "A deed. I have to go." He started for the doorway.

I put a basin under Matti's chin and another one under Mariamme's and hurried after him, closing the bedroom door behind me. "A deed to what?" I said, feeling as if my stomach might sicken like the children's.

"I'm selling twenty hectares to Salvius Marcellus."

"Twenty hectares—to a Roman?" I covered my mouth to smother a scream.

"Yes, to a Roman. His terms are generous. He'll forgive my loan and supply us with coin for our taxes and maintenance until we have another profitable harvest."

"But, Tobiah, surely selling land is not necessary at this point."

He shook his head. "The decision has been made."

I couldn't keep my voice down. "But Kamith ancestral lands have never been sold!"

"Hush, Danya. The children," whispered Tobiah. "You must understand. There's nothing else I can do."

"Surely that is not so," I objected.

"This is Kamith family business, not yours," he growled. "Stop interfering. You should be nursing the children. Why haven't their fevers left them by now?"

A fever began to rise in me, but at that moment Mariamme cried out to me as she began vomiting again. I hurried away to help her.

I couldn't stop the sale of land that wasn't mine. And my children were in great need of me, so I did what I could. I spooned date palm honey into their mouths to heal their raw throats and settle their stomachs. Then I dampened linen cloths with cool water, wrapped the sheets around their overheated bodies, and laid them on their cots.

My mind drifted to the possibility of Judea's census rebellion spreading to Galilee. I couldn't participate in it anyway, confined as I was by my husband's position and with the care of my sick children. Why, I could venture no farther than the walls surrounding my house. Nevertheless, my dream of being a part of a freedom movement for our people stayed entangled in the web of my thoughts. Like caterpillar netting clinging to a tree, it lodged high up in the leaves and branches of my mind. Neither the driving rain nor the high winds could displace it.

Herod Antipas and the local Jewish elite, including my husband, moved swiftly to prevent Judea's rebellious sparks from igniting Galilee's tinder. The construction of Sepphoris's new synagogue, which had proceeded sluggishly due to limited funding, picked up at a furious pace after Antipas made a large financial contribution to the effort. He made sure that huge stones, quarried and cut right outside the city walls, were transported up the cardo for all to see. And hear. The bellows of heavy-laden oxen and the shouts of enthusiastic, newly employed workers accompanied the transport and placement of every ashlar. The walls of the synagogue rose higher each day, a vivid display of our leader's "affection" for us.

Herod Antipas tripled his spy system throughout Galilee. Informers nested among us, and agents investigated anyone reported as even slightly suspicious. Disguised as a turbaned Parthian trader, Antipas infiltrated the crowds in the Sepphoris marketplace. He engaged strangers in idle chatter, eliciting their opinions about the tetrarch of Galilee. Many men, who were innocent of any wrongdoing other than disapproval of Herod Antipas, were arrested and exiled. No one in power, including Tobiah, objected.

During the remainder of the rainy season and beyond, Tobiah pushed himself farther away from the children and me. On the third and fifth days of each week when the courts were in session, he left the house before we awakened and returned very late. After the children were settled in for the night, I'd leave a few lamps lit for him and try to sleep myself, turning and reaching over to the empty side of the bed for hours. I dreamt of the shore of the Sea of Galilee, the shore Judah ben Hezekiah had rowed away from. The children and I stood on a dock watching Tobiah drift away from us on a boat that had slipped its mooring. We threw a line out to him. Though it landed at his feet, he didn't pick it up. He was distracted by something on the horizon and didn't seem to see it.

On the mornings he didn't go to court, Tobiah tutored Mattityahu whose fever now waited until the afternoon to rise. Matti had a gift for numbers and a remarkable memory for the spoken word, so teacher and student flew through mathematics and Torah recitation. But during the time devoted to reading, Tobiah closed the library door and shuttered the windows because Matti was so easily distracted: an insect buzzing or a bird perching in a nearby tree too easily drew his attention from the jumble of letters he was supposed to decipher.

One morning, as I was passing by the closed door of the library, I heard Tobiah shout at Matti, "Tomorrow you will read this passage without error or suffer three strokes of the rod."

My heart pounded as if the rod were striking my own legs. I dreaded the possibility of replicating the conflict between father and son that had occurred between Father and Chuza in my childhood.

Matti stumbled from the library. When he saw me, he grabbed me around my waist. Beads of sweat dotted his arms.

"I can't do it, Mama. I know each letter by itself, but when he puts them together, I don't know what they say!"

I brushed his damp curls back from his forehead. "Keep trying, Matti. It will get easier in time."

"Papa gets so angry with me." His chest heaved. "He says I'm lazy." Matti pulled away from me. "I hate reading! I won't do it anymore!"

My mind churned with uncertainty, but I couldn't stand by and risk a hatred developing between these two people whom I loved so much. I knocked softly on the library door and let myself in.

Tobiah had opened the shutters and was checking the height of the sun. "Yes, wife?"

"Husband, you're burdened with so many duties," I said, then stopped because my voice sounded like Joanna's addressing a foul-tempered Chuza. I cleared my throat and started over. "Maybe I could lighten your burden by instructing Mattityahu in the basics of reading. Until he surpasses my simple abilities, of course, and then you would have to take over."

A crevice, deep as a stab wound, formed between Tobiah's eyes. "It's a man's sacred duty to instruct his son."

"Of course," I said, swallowing the urge to address him as lord. "This arrangement would only be temporary. Until Mattityahu could benefit from your superior knowledge."

Tobiah rolled up the scroll that Matti had been struggling with. "I will teach my son to read. And to accept chastening. He will be taught as a man, not as a girl. Stop intruding in my business, wife. First you tell me I can't sell my own land and now you want to teach my son. Enough!" He turned around and occupied himself with the arrangement of the scrolls on the storage shelves.

Of course I preferred that he teach our son. Just not to punish him while he did so. And, yes, I did think ancestral lands should never be sold to Gentiles. My husband used to value my opinions, but it seemed he no longer did. Tobiah was now treating me like so many men treated their wives. I had no influence over matters of importance even inside my own home, much less outside of it.

In the end, I had to leave Mattityahu's education in Tobiah's hands. I submitted to Tobiah's will and didn't challenge his decisions, hoping my forbearance would relieve a portion of my husband's misery. He had lost ancestral land, money, and his brother. Of course he would grieve, and I should be understanding and sympathetic. Waking three times each night to feed Gad and tend sick children tired me, but Tobiah's unhappiness exhausted me.

In the month of Nisan that same year, Tobiah journeyed to Jerusalem to celebrate the feast of Passover and, after that, to serve his week in the Temple. He wanted to try again to offer an unblemished lamb in sacrifice for his sin of violating the Sabbath year law.

During his month-long absence, the air on our hilltop city lightened. The persistent mist, which had hung on long after the rains had ceased, finally lifted. Released from the lessons he failed and the punishments he suffered, Matti had no nightmares. He followed Zohar around and helped with the outdoor chores, something he had loved doing before his schooling began.

Mariamme continued to squint over her tablets. Tobiah had written down the Greek alphabet for her, and she was determined to master this before he returned. I couldn't lure her outside for a walk, even on the finest of mornings. Silently, she endured helping me prepare the vegetable beds for planting. Her stubborn refusal to enjoy physical activity worried me. One day, I confiscated her reading and writing materials and insisted she spend the day outdoors. She snatched up her baby brother and the mat he lay on and stomped out into the sunny inner courtyard with him. Soon they were both laughing, and Mariamme began to spend a part of each day playing with Gad.

She made up all kinds of games for him. In one, she placed Gad on his stomach and propped his head up on his chin. Then, quickly before his head flopped sideways, she held a toy butterfly at his eye level. Gad loved to look at its wooden wings, painted bright yellow and edged with black. Mariamme held the butterfly higher, and Gad lifted his head from the mat to follow it. At first he held his head up only for an instant, but gradually his muscles strengthened, his head steadied, and his gaze lengthened to the count of fifty. Neither Mariamme nor Gad seemed to tire of this game, and it brought delight to the whole household.

I hadn't understood until then how difficult it could be for a baby to hold his head up. Mariamme had shown me that we could figure out how to teach Gad the skills that the other children had learned on their own. Why, by the next moon he could be rolling himself over; by the one after that, he could be sitting up!

My heart lightened like the freshened hilltop air. Gad began to sleep through the night, allowing me to. Deep, satisfying sleep restored my energy. Though during the day my responsibilities consumed most of my time, I could stay awake long enough at night to reflect and write a little. I wrote about the difficulties that had beset us during the last year—learning of Ezri's death and apostasy, Gad's difficult birth and slow growth, Tobiah's religious crisis, the precarious finances of our estates. Seeing these crises as small letters on paper made them less formidable. I felt that Tobiah and I could overcome them and be the stronger for it. I still loved my husband deeply and believed that he still loved me.

I harbored the hope that Tobiah would return from Jerusalem with his guilt offering accepted and his troubled soul healed. He would marvel over Gad's newly acquired skills. I pictured our family in the warm months to come walking together in the cool of the evening, Matti, fully armed, leading our little army, Mariamme wearing a kiss of sunburn on her nose from her day outside, Tobiah proudly carrying Gad on his shoulders. All along the decumanus and the cardo, heads would turn at the sight of our beautiful family. And after our walk, Tobiah and I would talk and laugh quietly in our bed while we waited for the children to fall asleep. Outside our bedroom window, the moths would stretch out their silken wings, and the little animals of the field would emerge from their hiding places. Darkness would protect us all from the teeth of our predators. Tobiah and I would make love as the night breezes licked the lengths of our bodies.

My husband returned home from his Temple service after nightfall, as he had that first time after our marriage. He glanced at Gad, who was sleeping soundly in his cradle, then plopped himself down on the bench in our bedroom. I had many questions to ask and a hundred things to tell him, but I held my tongue. Quickly, I got up from the bed and filled a basin of water to bathe his feet in.

A prickly silence accompanied my ministrations. He smelled not of soap and fresh rosemary, as he had other times upon returning from Jerusalem, but of soot and blood and sweat. After I had washed and dried his feet, Tobiah finally spoke, but only to ask me to tend the burns on his ankles that he had sustained while working near the altar's sacrificial fires.

As I knelt there, dabbing the purple aloe on his injuries, I couldn't wait any longer. "Did you make your offering, husband?"

"Yes, I offered it, but I don't think my sin has been remitted. I feel unforgiven. I may have to endure more chastening."

I looked up into his eyes. They seemed muddied with confusion, and his eyelids drooped. I desperately wanted to soothe him, but I didn't know what to say or do. I had failed at this so many times of late. "You're a good man, Tobiah," I offered. "You're righteous and '*when the righteous cry for help, the Lord hears.*'"

"Am I righteous?" he said sharply.

"Of course you are. You treat people fairly. You try to do Adonai's will."

"What is His Will?" he said. "I used to think I knew, but now I'm not so certain."

This unsettled me. I was the one who still searched for The Holy One's will. I had long relied on Tobiah's certitude about religious matters, as I had relied on Father's when I lived under his roof. Tobiah studied the nature of The Holy One. He contemplated what Adonai expected of a good Jew. I didn't always agree with my husband's ideas, but his strong, sure convictions reassured me that answers could be found. "What do you mean? You know His will."

He closed his eyes. "Ah, it's nothing. I'm very tired and don't know what I'm saying." He pushed his hands against his knees and stood to undress.

I unpacked his traveling sack. I was disappointed that he hadn't hurried home with his priestly garments unwashed this time. The white linen tunics, the blue sash, the headcloths, and all the clothing he wore for his Temple service had been laundered, so I had only to lay them in his storage chest.

"How are the children?" he asked at last, as he shook out his dusty traveling tunic.

"All well. Mariamme has been playing more and not overstraining her eyes with study. Mattityahu has been sleeping soundly. Their fevers are completely gone." I paused before making my grand announcement. "And Gad can hold his head up!"

Tobiah tossed his tunic into a corner. "He should've been doing that months ago."

Tobiah might as well have heaved a boulder into my chest. I went to the window for air.

Perhaps he noted my distress because he joined me at the window, fingering the edges of the folded sleep tunic he held in his hand. "But it's good news that Gad can do that now. It sounds as if the children have flourished in my absence. Perhaps they hardly need me."

"That is not so, Tobiah," I managed.

We said nothing more about the children. As Tobiah pulled his tunic over his head, he relayed some astonishing news. "Herod Antipas has appointed your brother his new Chief Steward. Chuza and Joanna will be moving to Sepphoris."

Having Joanna, my kinswoman, close by would be a joy! I'd been so lonely for so long. But Tobiah didn't seem pleased with his news. "Are you upset that Chuza will be living in our city?" I asked.

"It's not Chuza, but Joanna who upsets me. Your brother's wife acts more strangely each time I see her."

"I thought you liked Joanna. You said her eccentricities were Chuza's fault. You've always defended her in the past."

"I've lost patience with her. Her latest folly is to follow the healer Hanina ben Dosa around as if she were his lapdog. Hanina is a madman. He is so observant that he won't permit his donkey to eat untithed food! Joanna runs all over Jerusalem to purchase food for his beast. Chuza puts up with it, but he shouldn't."

Hanina ben Dosa was a mystic of great renown. He performed miraculous healings and was respected throughout the land of Judah. I had dreamt of meeting him myself one day. But I still hoped that Tobiah's homecoming could occasion a reconciliation between us, so I kept my views on Hanina ben Dosa to myself. "It'll be good for the children to have their aunt and uncle living nearby," I said by way of compromise.

Tobiah shrugged and sat on the bed. He didn't signal me to join him. I longed to be embraced. We hadn't made love since Gad's birth and the news of Ezri's sinful death. I needed to keep my husband from turning to the wall and going to sleep.

"Before you lie down, would a massage please you?"

He nodded and returned to the bench. I poured some massage oil into my hands. When I stood behind him and rubbed my hands together, he dropped his head back into the pillow of my belly. I laid my warm oiled hands on the back of his neck and I felt a spot inside me stir and heat.

Tobiah suddenly straightened his head and sat erect. "There's something you should know." He took my hand and led me around to stand in front of him. Now would he say how much he loved me, despite our recent difficulties? That we would once again know deep happiness?

He spoke slowly and watched my face closely. "The census rebellion in Jerusalem has been crushed. Its leaders are imprisoned in the fortress at Machaerus. A number of other bandits and rebels from all around the country have been captured and imprisoned there as well. Including Judah ben Hezekiah."

Undoubtedly his eyes were probing for my reaction to Judah ben Hezekiah's imprisonment. I turned my head to scratch an insect bite behind my knee and tried to keep my voice from quavering. "The Romans haven't killed them?"

"They dared not incite a mob by executing Saddok the Pharisee. He's holy and much loved. Fortunately for the other captured rebels, they share his fate."

I dug my fingernail into the itchy bump on the back of my leg but felt no release from my discomfort. As calmly as I could, I said, "So, no executions now. But later?"

"The new procurator will decide their fate when he arrives."

"And what will that be?" I shut my eyes.

"The Sanhedrin recommended death," Tobiah replied quietly.

The Great Sanhedrin Council. Seventy-one Jewish aristocrats who represented the interests of the powerful. And acceded to Roman wishes.

I couldn't conceal my disgust. I straightened myself up and faced my husband. "And what about you, Tobiah? Would you have advised that Saddok the Pharisee be executed? You said that he's holy and nonviolent."

"We can't have a rebellion over a census. Too many lives would be lost."

"What lives would be lost? Their revolt is a peaceful one, you said so yourself. They're only pious people who refuse, on legitimate religious grounds, to be counted!"

Tobiah clenched his fists and set them on his knees. "Rome considers the refusal to be counted a crime against the republic. Treason. These pious people will be slaughtered. We have to consider the consequences."

"Yes, the consequences. Constantly submitting to Rome will never result in freedom! How can The Holy One save us from our bondage if we do nothing?"

"We are not doing 'nothing!'" Tobiah straightened himself higher on the bench. "We're doing everything possible."

Except acting. At least Judah ben Hezekiah acted on his beliefs. Though Tobiah prayed for the salvation of our people every day in the Seventh Benediction, praying and accommodating were all he ever did to free us. And, since I had married him, all that I had done. Like every other married woman in this land, I could act only through my husband. I had to get Tobiah to act!

I put my hands on his shoulders and squeezed them. "Tobiah, perhaps now is the moment of our redemption. Remember the prophesies of Isaiah? Jerusalem has *'received from the Lord's hand double for all her sins.'* Our people have certainly suffered greatly. Jerusalem has *'served her term, her penalty is paid.'* We've held true to our covenant with Him and our penalty must surely be paid by now. Furthermore, our peasants are starving, Tobiah! They don't have land to sell to survive these times, as you do."

He removed my hands from his shoulders. "There are no such signs. You're mistaken."

"This is a peaceful revolution, led by a man *'without horse and rider and bow* and *without gold and silver for war.'"*

Tobiah threw his head back and laughed derisively. "Ah, another of your father's daydreams: a savior with no resources, a king with neither soldiers nor money. I loved your father dearly and respected his wisdom, but he was wrong about the kind of man who'll lead us to freedom."

"It's actually not a man, but Adonai who will free us," I said firmly. "When He chooses to lend us His power, the Roman legions will flee in terror."

Tobiah stood up and towered over me. "And what man will He work His wonders through? You don't really believe it will be Saddok, do you? You still think it'll be Judah ben Hezekiah! Let me tell you something: Roman legions have not cowered before Judah ben Hezekiah. He is not the man Adonai will work His wonders through. Judah is impious and heedless of the safety of those he promises to free. Look at what his holy war in Galilee did to our own family. Ezri, his wife, and his children were enslaved and are now dead; your brother Lev is lost; your father was slain. That man is not from God."

I made myself stand as tall as I could before my husband. "You condemn Judah, but at least he shows courage. He stands up to our oppressors, rather than cowering to them!"

For long moments we stared each other down. Like the hard-backed, luminescent insects of the dry season, Tobiah's eyes flashed bright with the light of anger, then darkened with the shadow of hatred and pain. Once he lifted his arm, as if to strike me. I didn't flinch, and he dropped it back down to his side.

The heat left Tobiah's eyes and frost settled in them. "You think courage is leading people to their deaths. It is not. Courage is the harsh, distasteful business of keeping our people alive. Someday the Romans will be finished with Israel, as were the Egyptians and the Assyrians and the Babylonians and the Persians and the Greeks. My duty is to make sure our people are not annihilated before that day comes. This is courage, but you think it cowardice!"

He gathered a cushion and a blanket from the bed. "I won't allow you to teach our children that their father is a coward. If you want to join the rebels who bring death to our people, I'll divorce you and you'll be free to do so. If you stay, you must renounce your peasant dream of an imminent revolution. It's your choice."

The cushion dropped on the floor. He stooped to pick it up and pounded it back under his arm with his fist. "If you go, take Gad with you. You can't have the other two."

He left with his bedding and slept in another room.

FEVER'S ONSET
AND DELIRIUM

I wrestled with the possibility and ached for the freedom to act on my own beliefs. I gathered strength by reminding myself that my mother had resisted an unjust demand and fled to a foreign land. She had started a new life for herself. Since her blood coursed through my body, I should have the courage to do the same.

But abandon my children and settle among aliens? Nahara wouldn't have left Lev and me in another country. Our separation from her was caused by her death, not by a choice she'd made. I knew the pain of losing a mother. I could not imagine afflicting that heartache on Matti and Mariamme.

As the writings counseled, *"If she does not accept your control/divorce her and send her away."* Tobiah could write a get, that is, a bill of divorcement, and our marriage would be dissolved. Since I had brought no goods to my union with Tobiah, none would be restored to me upon its dissolution. I would have no home, no land, and no money of my own. Gad and I might end up completely dependent upon my brother Chuza for our survival. What choice did I have?

So I kept what Tobiah termed my "peasant revolutionary dreams" to myself, rather than risk losing my children and becoming a beggar. I never again spoke of freeing our people from Roman oppression or uttered the name of Judah ben Hezekiah.

But my soul was still my own, and there I continued to harbor the hope that one day I could help to liberate my people. My heroine Judith accomplished this, but only after her husband had died. Tobiah would likely die before me; I might still be called, as was Judith, once I was widowed.

Tobiah's giving me a "choice" to remain his wife did not spark love as my choice to marry him had. This choice smothered love. Our marriage became a bizarre reflection of the politics of our sorrowful land, with Tobiah, the haughty Roman conqueror imposing his will and ways upon me, the subjugated, resentful peasant.

The illness that had shadowed Matti and Mariamme now descended on me. One moment I would be drenched in a fiery sweat; the next I would be encased in a listless chill. My fever fueled the resentment I felt towards my husband.

In front of the children and other people, Tobiah and I treated each other with respect. But occasionally I indulged in one of the limited forms of protest available to my peasant self. I would serve a supper of only root vegetables, knowing full well that Tobiah had difficulty digesting these. I feigned inexplicable memory lapses relating to pious religious practices. "Where has my mind gone?" I would wonder aloud, after serving milk with meat or mending a torn seam on the Sabbath. The sour expression on Tobiah's face that such actions produced would perversely sweeten my dreary day. Climbing up from the miqveh on the staircase he had built for descending into it afforded me another childish, private satisfaction.

Joanna wrote to me that she and Chuza planned to move from Jerusalem to Sepphoris in a month's time. Her note that she would precede Chuza in order to prepare the house for "her lord" greatly annoyed me. Why was Joanna still trying to please him? She would never know happiness or peace with Chuza. She should take advantage of Roman law, which permitted a woman to divorce her husband. Joanna's dowry of two thousand denarii would provide her with enough money to live comfortably for the rest of her life even without a husband.

I began to dread Joanna's arrival. She would disapprove of my appearance and pry into the source of my maladies. I would have to disclose my troubles with Tobiah. She would counsel me to accept her solutions to marital unhappiness: accommodation and submission.

On the afternoon Joanna arrived, I was dozing on the couch in the reception room. A cool hand on my arm roused me. "Danya, wake up!"

I lifted an eyelid. There stood little Joanna, her fair hair swept up from her shapely neck and held with a tortoise-shell comb. Not a single strand of it fell from its appointed place. She carried jasmine blossoms that matched the color of her silk mantle. Her eyes glowed like roasted almonds. I closed my eyes tightly and curled up tighter.

She nudged herself onto the couch and pulled me up to sit. "Oh, my poor sister. What's happened to you? You're ill!" The jasmine stems dropped from her lap onto the floor.

I had practiced the answer I would give to her. Tobiah and I are having a difficult time. It will pass. You need not concern yourself. But when she held me in her arms, and her voice broke in compassion for me, I couldn't remember my speech. I rested my head on her bosom and lamented that my once happy union with Tobiah had become a resentful, duty-driven chore, and I didn't know whose fault it was or how to fix it. She stroked my back. When I finished my plaint, she simply dug into her bag and pulled out a hairbrush. "Let me fix your hair," she said. "It's full of knots."

Joanna's way of straightening out life's entanglements, I thought, but I allowed her to comb out the back of my head so she wouldn't study the imperfections of my face.

"It's useless to sort out who's to blame," Joanna advised. "In the eyes of a husband, the wife is always the one at fault, so you're the one who must fix things."

"But he—"

"Tsk, tsk, no buts. What choice do you have?"

I bit my lip and nodded. Joanna's brush slid easily through my thinning hair.

"Since Tobiah is angry with you," she continued, "you must change yourself to make him happy with you. All wives have to do this." Her tone of voice sounded like mine when I was patiently explaining to Mariamme why she must spend more time outdoors. "Much of Tobiah's displeasure can be traced back to Gad's birth. When you have another baby, he'll see that he can still father healthy children. That will lift his opinion of himself. And of you."

"He's moved to his own bedroom," I said softly, swallowing a sob. Tobiah's sexual rejection of me caused me great shame.

Her hand stopped. "Well, then, it's up to you to get him back into your bed. And to accomplish that, you'll have to do something about your appearance, dear."

She began to braid my hair for me. I sat there like a compliant child, though I was twenty-four years old, a grown woman, and the mother of three children. She wove tightly, taking no notice of the hurt her tugging caused me. "One could hardly blame Tobiah for not wanting to make love to you with the way you keep yourself."

"It's not what I look like," I protested. "It's who I am and what I believe in. He demands that I believe what he does. We can't live in peace with the differences between us."

"Stop fretting about beliefs. You can't do anything about the Roman occupation and neither can he. Tobiah can't help being who he is, and you'll never change him. Nor he you. You *can* change what you look like, however, beginning with this hair of yours." She dug into the brush and extracted a wad of limp, faded fuzz. "See this? I used to need a whip to tame your hair, but now it breaks off at my touch. I'm going to help you, sister. I won't take 'no' for an answer."

That very day, Joanna abandoned her current obsession, the study of astrology, and devoted herself to improving me. She and her cook baked a handcart load of date cakes and sweet loaves for me. Joanna delivered them herself, still wearing the beautiful linen clothing she had soiled with flour and oil. "You're too thin, Danya. At your height, you should be eating twice what you do. Don't try to hide yourself under that oversized tunic," she scolded, as she heaved her bounty onto my kitchen table. "A husband doesn't want a wife who's nothing but bones."

For months now, anxiety had filled my stomach. Since I wasn't hungry and food had no taste, I couldn't eat her offerings. But I knew Matti would enjoy them.

Joanna shifted to my other defects. "Your eyes are sunken. Men find that undesirable. The best cure is more sleep, so I'm going to mix you a sleeping potion."

Restorative sleep had become impossible for me. Since I could no longer supply Gad with all the milk he needed during the day, he had begun to feed at night again. My fever made me fitful, and when I did doze off, Gad would rouse me for a feeding. I'd taken to resting on the bench in my bedroom between feedings because I couldn't bring myself to lie down on our bed alone. However, I knew that my sunken eyes weren't what Tobiah found undesirable, so I poured Joanna's potion into the courtyard soil. Joanna hauled in baskets of other foods, praising their restorative qualities. "Cheeses and butter for your nails. Greens to thicken your hair and brighten your skin. I remember that Tobiah used to admire your beautiful complexion. Take heart, you'll win him back. Just make yourself pretty again and do what he says."

Joanna would never understand. I didn't either, except that I knew that looking pretty and obeying my husband would never close the great divide between us. But Mariamme would benefit from these healthy foods, so I accepted them gratefully.

Joanna fished a few small items from the bottom of one basket and carefully unwrapped the calfskin protecting them. "I've also brought powder and a cream for the circles under your eyes."

What would stop her fruitless, exasperating meddling? "Just leave me alone!" I shouted at her. "I don't care what I look like!"

Joanna withheld her ministrations for a few days, and I returned to the comfort of my isolation. But then she reappeared with a wet nurse in tow, insisting that I should stop breast feeding my baby in order to regain my strength. However, nourishing Gad was the only thing I did that filled the emptiness inside me. I was certainly not going to give that up.

A swish of air across my face awakened me from a nap the next day. Joanna was swinging a huge, star-shaped copper charm, suspended from a pole, back and forth across my body. "What are you doing?" I gasped, as I covered my face to protect it from the sharp metal points swinging dangerously close to my nose.

"Drawing the fever from your body with this charm. Yesterday, I saw a wandering magus cure a woman with this. Now, what were those words?" She stamped her foot. "Oh, I can't remember the incantation. It was something in Greek." She lowered the amulet and sighed. "It's no use without the incantation."

"Or with it," I pointed out, and rolled on my side to continue my nap. She shook me. "No sleeping, Danya. Hear me out. I have one more idea that I promise will be my last." She set the copper star down on the floor. "To rid yourself of this fever, you must purge the foul vapors from your body. All this construction dust in Sepphoris is terrible for your skin.

And the noise in this city causes a strain that puts lines on the face." She sat me up and smoothed my unwashed hair. "You and the baby will both benefit from long walks outside the city. I'll mind your children and your household while you do this."

I did miss the countryside and outdoor exercise. And Joanna could certainly manage my household in my absence. She had managed her father's silk business after his death while caring for her ailing mother and pacifying her husband's temper, each a formidable accomplishment on its own. She was far more suited than I to supervise my household. "All right, Joanna. I give in."

So, with Joanna in charge, I followed a routine of strapping Gad into his sling each morning and escaping Sepphoris while my two older children delighted in Joanna's company. As soon as Tobiah finished the tortured tutoring sessions with Matti, Joanna swept my son out of the shuttered library and brought him to the shops in the agora. She boosted the boy's spirits by entrusting her coins to him and by having him calculate the daily expenses of the household. Joanna endeared herself to Mariamme by whispering grownup tales to her about the physicians, teachers, healers, magicians, and mystics she had consulted with over the years. She marveled at Mariamme's ability to write and had my daughter teach her the Greek alphabet. Joanna confided to Mariamme that, if she ever did get pregnant, she would want a daughter just like her. With Gad cradled close to my heart, I hiked through the pomegranate, walnut, and fig orchards of the countryside around Sepphoris. Though I still felt like a foreigner among the Greek-style buildings of our city, I was at home out here. We emptied our ears of the city's discordant clamor and filled them with the songs of the birds. We exhaled the dead odors of dust and sewage and inhaled the lively scents of soil and grasses. Since it was a Sabbath year, many of the fruit trees and vines had not been pruned or harvested. They seemed to relish this rest, for they had grown as wildly as the weeds in the fallow grain fields. Only birds, animals, and poor people would harvest these fruits, but they would have a feast. I held Gad up to show him how sunlight sharpened the silvery green on the leaves of the olive trees, and how it revealed the red buried in the purple of the grapes. Each morning, once the dew burned off, I loosened my mantle so that the sun could warm my neck as well as my face. Slowly, the blessed heat melted the captured sobs which had swollen my throat.

Sometimes, though, my fever still robbed me of much of my energy. On one of those days, when I was too tired to walk any distance, I asked Zohar to saddle a donkey for me. With our mount doing the work, Gad and I ranged farther than we usually did. As the morning wore on, we edged closer to Nazareth. Old nagging questions scraped at the surface of my pleasant thoughts. What had become of me, the girl from Nazareth, who was so determined to seek and carry out Adonai's will? Was The Holy One displeased with me? Would I ever be the woman I had dreamt of becoming? The questions saddened and depleted me. To quiet my anxieties, I sang to Gad the first thing that came into my mind. *"You are the most handsome of men/Grace is poured upon your lips/Therefore God has blessed you forever."* Judah had sung this as a lullaby to Matti. I hushed myself and rode on, burdened with questions and bittersweet recollections of my childhood. One memory of my village arose which I savored: I was not a stranger there. I knew those people, and they knew me. I had been loved in Nazareth.

I nudged the donkey farther along the path across the valley until he suddenly took off at a run. So did my heart. Yes, we should go to Nazareth today. On to Nazareth! It was as if I were rolling down a hill, arms folded around me and my head tucked in. Unstoppable, I was giddy with glee. On to Nazareth! I would visit with my friend Miryam and talk with her about unforgiven sins and punishment, about the death of love and the possibility of its rebirth. Miryam wouldn't care how ugly I was, inside or out.

Suddenly I yanked on the reins with all my strength. No, I couldn't go to Nazareth. Naomi lived in Nazareth, in the same courtyard as Miryam's family, in the house they had built for her. I couldn't avoid seeing her. And she hated me. I had driven her out of my house because she was an inconvenience. Because her presence threatened my blessed family life. Because my husband suggested that she was possessed by evil spirits, and I found it advantageous to believe him. I had cast her out.

Finally, I understood my own monstrous cruelty. Now that Tobiah had turned his back on me, I felt Naomi's suffering. The desert I lived in, created by love's removal, had been unimaginable to me when I had banished her. But now I shared the same wasteland as she.

But I longed to see Miryam and my village. Facing Naomi was not impossible. I would have to do it sometime. Perhaps that time was now. I'd go first to Naomi and beg for forgiveness. "I have sinned against you," I would say. "Forgive me. I have treated you with great injustice. Please, forgive me."

I held Gad tightly against me with one arm and urged the donkey into a trot. "Forgive me, forgive me, forgive me," I practiced, as we bounced though the olive groves. The words weren't so hard to say. I shouldn't have kept them buried all these years. Even if Naomi didn't grant me forgiveness, it would lift my heavy heart to ask for it. The beast slowed to a careful walk as the hill to Nazareth steepened, and he strained on the climb up through the vineyards. I gazed at the grapes ripening in the afternoon sunlight. When I was a child, we shared these hillside vineyards with many families. During Ab, which was coming up soon, we harvested the grapes. The whole village engaged in the happy business of picking and pressing and storing the wine that would sustain and cheer us for the coming year. The girls and the younger children made the raisins. We spread the picked grapes out to dry on roofs and in sunlit courtyards. Lev was learning the intricacies of the winepress and had promised to show me how it worked, until the raid changed everything. . . .

The donkey lowered his head and exhaled in loud snorts. He needed rest. Gad would soon clamor to be fed. And my fever was making me dizzy. Rather than arrive in Nazareth with a screaming baby and a lathered donkey, I decided to stop and refresh ourselves before descending into the village.

Goats and sheep bleated in the distance, but it was blessedly quiet at the top of the Nazareth hill. The breeze barely bent the tops of the grasses. I dismounted, tied the donkey to a stubby oak, then searched for a place to sit. I chose a smooth, flat boulder and loosened the tie around my waist so I could nurse Gad. At seven months, he had finally mastered the skill of sucking and was making up for lost time. Joanna said he seemed to gain weight and length each day. My friends in Nazareth would love my sweet-natured baby boy. As I nursed him, I took a few swigs of water from my jug. My fever had risen higher, as it usually did late in the morning. My vision blurred, so I cupped water in my hand and rinsed my eyes. When they cleared, I looked at the big rocks rimming the hilltop and remembered watching from there as Judah and Lev's raiding party left the valley in a swirling tower of dust. So many memories clustered here. Miryam, Naomi, and I had wedged ourselves between those rocks shortly before we had to flee from Nazareth. There Miryam had her encounter with "the angel," as Naomi called it. "Light," was Miryam's description. Miryam knew from that moment on that she was pleasing to The Holy One. If only I knew that. If only Tobiah did. There was still so much that I didn't understand.

I felt very drowsy. I shook my head to clear it and splashed more water on my face. Today those rocks looked like sentinels, standing back to back, only a few paces between them, as if they were guarding some valuable treasure. Something appeared to be stuck between them, but I was feeding Gad, so I stayed where I was and puzzled over what it might be. Perhaps another smaller rock fallen in that space. Maybe it was a stray sheep.

It stirred. It might be a person. I put both of my arms around Gad and stood. It sat up. It was a person! Be calm, I told myself. My heart pounded. Be calm. It's probably just a weary traveler or a drunken peasant.

"Stay. I won't harm you," said a man's familiar voice. I shaded my eyes, but I couldn't see his face with the sun shining so brightly above him. He leaned heavily on both arms to support his torso, while his legs stayed crumpled beneath him. He must be crippled. His tunic was torn and splotched with reddish-brown stains. I squinted to get a better look at him. My head throbbed with the heat of my fever. Blood. His clothing was tainted with blood!

I must help him. Bring him water, call to shepherds for help, put him on my donkey and carry him down to Nazareth. I told my feet to walk, to run, to do something, anything, but they remained stuck on the ground. I was the cripple.

But my mouth wasn't paralyzed. I could form words. "What do you need?"

"I need you to know something, Danya."

Judah ben Hezekiah! Even though the sunlight obscured my vision, I knew his voice and that intimate tone he used when he wanted something from me. Sympathy, forgiveness, sexual union. This was certainly Judah. I trembled. "What are you doing here, Judah?"

"Bringing you a message: Know that God walks with you. Walk humbly and you will see Him. Do not carry a sword, as I did. *'This and only this The Lord asks of you: act justly, love kindly, and walk humbly with your God.'*" He then coughed uncontrollably. His head and chest quaked with spasms.

Poor Judah. So wounded, he must be close to death. The least I could do was to hold his head and provide him with comfort as he struggled to take his final breaths. Sensation returned to my legs. I laid Gad on a cloth and scurried the short distance to the boulders.

But Judah wasn't there. Perhaps he had slipped over the edge of the cliff and was pitching helplessly down the hillside. But in the vineyard below, each vine, neatly draped across its own forked stick, swayed gently in the light breeze. Row after row of vines, entirely undisturbed. I searched the length and breadth of the hilltop, checking behind every rock and shrub, scrutinizing the soil for markings. How had Judah gotten himself up here in the first place? He must have pulled himself along with his arms. There should be drag marks in the dirt, or a scrap of his clothing caught on a thorn, or a dusty handprint somewhere.

I found nothing. I returned to Gad and the boulder I'd been sitting on and reviewed the whole encounter in my mind. "Walk humbly, and you will see Him," he had said. . . . But Judah couldn't have said that because he hadn't been here. I must've fallen asleep and dreamt it. Or I was hallucinating. My fever must be getting dangerously high.

Or maybe he was here, as a spirit. Perhaps I had finally been favored by The Holy One. But I hadn't seen a dazzling light or an angel or the spirit of a deceased great one. I had seen Judah ben Hezekiah, who, I knew, was imprisoned in the fortress at Machaerus. No, this couldn't have been a vision. Adonai wouldn't speak through the image of this flawed man.

I must've imagined the whole event. Of course I imagined it. This very spot marked the turning point of my young life, and it would always resurrect strong feelings in me. My exhaustion, my fever, the deep disturbance of my soul over my marriage, my anxiety as I approached Nazareth: these must have caused me to conjure up an apparition.

My fever must be getting out of control. I had to care for Gad! I must hurry down to Nazareth, beg Naomi's forgiveness, and ask Miryam to help me and my baby. I placed Gad back in the sling. He patted my face.

If Gad had seen the crumpled, bloodied man, surely he would have cried out in alarm. I untied the donkey and looked back one more time at the point between the rocks. A blotch on the ground I hadn't noticed before attracted my attention. I led the donkey over to the stain so that I could examine it. When we got close, the animal tossed his head to loosen my pull on the lead rope, then planted his forelegs and refused to advance. I stretched out my hand and pinched some of the moist dirt between my fingers, brought it to my nose, and sniffed. Balm. Galilee's wild, scrubby evergreen shrub. Judah's scent.

· · ·

. . . Where am I? Mud-packed stone walls and a thatched roof. Is this the tiny room I slept in as a girl? The voices in the next room must be Mother's and Father's. . . . But there is Judah ben Hezekiah. He walks towards a distant light whose flame glows red and throbs like a beating heart.

· · ·

A dampened towel cools my face and chest. Such blessed relief from this breath-robbing heat. I must be awake, though I cannot lift my eyelids. Weights seem to press them shut. I hear people talking. Whose voices? Tobiah's, yes—Miryam's—Joanna's—and maybe Naomi's. They murmur, so I cannot understand what they say. But I hear their worry. It thickens the air like strands of wool during sheep shearing.

They are praying loudly now, imploring The Holy One. "*Blessed are You, O Lord, who hear our prayer. Blessed are You, O Lord, trust of the righteous. Blessed are You, O Lord, who heal the sick of Your people Israel. Blessed are You, O Lord, who make the dead alive.*"

· · ·

"Please, please drink this tea, Danya," Joanna begs. "It has qinghao in it. The traders from the East swear this herb will cure even the worst of fevers."

My mouth cannot open. Is it sewn shut? Joanna leaves my bedside. Come back! I am all alone. Am I going to die?

· · ·

Joanna rubs an ointment all over my body. "Since Danya cannot swallow," she tells someone, "I crushed the qinghao leaves and put them into this salve." Her ointment smells like evening, when the day's heat has lifted and the earth begins to breathe again.

· · ·

My breasts leak milk. I must feed my baby. Where is Gad? Let me get to my baby. My arms feel as if they are pinned under a pile of dirt. Please, please, Holy One. Send an angel to dig my arms out and lift me from this pallet. Gad will starve without me or he will die of exposure, like the Gentile midwife wanted. He will shrivel up and blow away in the raw east wind.

I shake all over with cold. I need my mantle to smother the chill of this wind, the qadim, a whirlwind. Whirlwinds can sweep me away, out of this life. No, no!

"Here are the blankets you asked for, Naomi," someone says. Strong arms tuck thick sheepskins around and under me. Naomi's arms are bony and hard. I did not act justly or love her kindly.

· · ·

It is hot and hard to breathe in this tomb. Father is gone. His flesh has decomposed, and Chuza has sealed his bones into an ossuary. Do not roll the stone across the entrance, Chuza! Can't you see that I am in here?

I must get out or I will suffocate. Hurry, hurry. But my legs will not move. They cannot get to the dying Judah. I walk too slowly, too proudly. I am the girl who can do things boys can do. I am married to an aristocrat. I am the mother of beautiful children. If I die, they will be motherless and alone, like I am. The only way out of the tomb is to walk humbly. The stone begins to roll in its track. Help me, Mother. Do not leave me again. Help me!

· · ·

My spine is rubbed raw from lying on this cot. The bones in my body prick at my skin. My fingers will break off if I wiggle them. Tobiah tells someone that Judah ben Hezekiah is imprisoned in the fortress at Machaerus.

"Danya admires him," says Tobiah.

"She admires his cause," says Miryam.

"I think she loves him," says Tobiah.

I must object, but my tongue is chained. "She loves only you," says Miryam.

Her footsteps cross the tiny room and fade away. Tobiah stands over me. His breath blows hot, like the Khamsin wind. "Haven't You punished me enough?" he asks. His anger singes my eyelashes.

"I am not Job. If You test me further, I will fail. Like my brother Ezri, I will renounce You." Tobiah's hands slap against the dirt floor as he prostrates himself. "Do not punish me this way," he warns. "Take me instead."

Tobiah addresses The Holy One, but he does not praise Him, nor does he seek forgiveness. His scorching demands will displease Adonai. I will not be spared. My bones smolder. I am going to die.

· · ·

I must purify myself before I die. Wait! I am ascending, but the purification pool is below me. I leap to the other stairway and descend to the miqveh. The surface bubbles and steams. I bend to put my hand in. The water scalds me. If I submerge, I will boil. I climb up the stairs, accepting my punishment: I will die unclean.

· · ·

"She is near death," Miryam says.

A hand takes mine. It is a boy's hand: grit stuck in the lines of the palm, a crusty scab on the pad of one finger. He prays in a whisper, addressing The Holy One as "Abba." I hear the quick intake of Miryam's breath, as if she is swallowing something sharp.

The weights drop from my eyelids, and I can lift them! An oil lamp casts a dim light. Miryam sits on a bench by my bed, chanting an unintelligible prayer. Her son Yeshua presses his palm against mine; his hand is the size of mine. Beads of perspiration glisten on his forehead. My eyes close again.

I dream that I am wading into the Sea of Galilee, as I did the day I left Nazareth. I submerge in the lake until the ghastly images of the crucified corpses are washed from my eyes. The terror subsides. My shaking stops. I am calm.

AWAKENING

I awaken to morning sunlight creeping around the edges of the shutters. My hand begins to tingle. The tingle builds into a flood of energy rushing through my whole body, as if the debris clogging a river has suddenly been cleared and the water now plummets wildly downstream. I try to stand.

"Praise Adonai!" Miryam exclaims. She leans out to steady me.

Tobiah and Joanna fling back the curtain to the bedroom. "What are you doing?" they ask. "Why have you taken her out of bed?"

Miryam embraces me. "Danya's fever has broken," she says. "She will live!"

Miryam rearranged the cushions against the wall behind me. Tobiah, Joanna, Naomi, and Miryam's family crowded around me, marveling at my sudden recovery. I credited the extraordinary care I'd received from my friends. Joanna argued the qinghao must have helped. "Our prayers were finally heard," Tobiah said. "The Merciful One's will has been done," Miryam concluded.

"How was I found?" I wondered. "The last place I remember being was on the hill above the village."

Everyone began nudging Yaakov, Joses, and Yeshua, three of Yosef and Miryam's sons. "You're the eldest, Yaakov," said Yosef. "You tell."

"That morning," Yaakov said in a high voice. He stopped, cleared his throat, and began again. "That morning, me and my brothers went to the lower slope of the hill to check on the early olive crop. Some were ripe enough to harvest, so we worked at that for several hours."

Joses cut in. "When we stopped to eat, we heard a baby hollering so loudly, he sounded like a flock of startled sheep. Of course we heard him! Gad was the one who saved you."

For once, Tobiah smiled at the mention of Gad's name. "Who would've thought that this little baby had such power?" he said.

"My brothers made a litter by cutting two saplings and tying Danya's mantle to them, and they brought her down," said Yeshua. "They're very strong. I carried the baby."

I looked closely at the boys. "No one else was up there?"

"No one," answered Yaakov, "The place was deserted. The donkey was a little spooked, though."

"It smelled nice up there. Like balm," said Yeshua.

A stain in the dirt. Damp soil on the tip of my finger. The distinctive, unmistakable aroma of balm.

Lightly, Yaakov slapped the side of Yeshua's head. "What're you talking about? There isn't any balm up there. It's the wrong soil for evergreens." Yaakov rolled his eyes. "I don't think you'll ever be a farmer, Yeshua. Maybe someone can make a tekton or a stone-cutter out of you yet, but even that'll be difficult."

"Poor me. I'll have to be a scholar, then," Yeshua joked.

Yeshua's laugh was like his mother's. It lightened and sweetened. Everyone laughed with him, except Naomi who stared intently at the boy. "Maybe you should be a scholar, Yeshua," she said.

"Well, first there are olives to be picked," Miryam said. "Come, children, Danya needs to rest and we have chores to do this morning."

Though I felt almost well enough to make the trip home, everyone insisted I remain a few more days in Naomi's house. Gad would continue to need the village wet nurse until I had enough milk to feed him myself again. Joanna promised to care for Matti and Mariamme. Tobiah consented to my staying. Once these arrangements were settled, I fell into a deep, dreamless sleep.

When I awoke late in the afternoon, I was ravenous. I hugged my complaining stomach. It was so lovely to feel hunger again. My appetite teased me into getting out of bed, but my legs wobbled, so I slid one hand along the wall for balance and slowly maneuvered myself into the other room of Naomi's house. A barley loaf, water, and cheese lay out on the table. My mouth watered at the sight of these simple foods. I tore the bread into pieces, saying the Ha-Motzi, then sat down and reminded myself to eat slowly and sparingly. I indulged in one small bite at a time while permitting my eyes to feast on my surroundings.

Beautiful tapestries brightened the mud-packed stone walls and the dirt floor of Naomi's little house. The complex patterns and the clever color combinations in these weavings dazzled me. Stripes, braids, triangles, spirals, waves. Rows of threads angling like the skeletons of fish, and others circling like snail shells. And each tapestry bore the same weaver's mark: a small gold egg in the center of a dark square.

Naomi came in, carrying a basket of freshly picked mulberries.

"This weaving is extraordinary!" I said. "I've never seen anything like these tapestries. They're brilliant! Whose mark is this?"

She placed her basket down on the table and, with her eyes on the berries, said, "Mine." She tossed off my compliment as if it were an unripe mulberry she would set aside for chicken feed.

Of course she would feel resentment towards me. She had taken me into her house when I was deathly ill and nursed me back to health whereas I had turned her out of mine. Just days ago, as I had ridden towards Nazareth, I had chanted, "Forgive me, forgive me, forgive me." At that time, the words had risen in exhilaration from me like trapped birds suddenly set free. But today the words caught in my throat and roosted restlessly there, like doves rustling their cramped wings in a covered basket.

I hobbled over to the tapestry that I found the most fascinating. "How did you learn to do this?" I asked, running my finger over its double-hearted design. Two hearts lay tip to tip. Spirals curled into their centers to form their tops.

She stopped her sorting and sighed impatiently. "My mother taught me to weave. I think she taught you as well."

It was true that, after my mother's death, Naomi's mother taught me to weave, sew, and bake. At the time, I chafed at the drudgery and at being kept from the more interesting things the boys were learning. The kindness Naomi's mother had shown to me had gone unappreciated, and Naomi must also resent this ingratitude of mine.

"Yes, your mother taught me many things, and now, too late, I appreciate her efforts. She was always very good to me. I wish I could tell her this."

Naomi's lower lip began to tremble. "I used to love helping my mother with the weaving. The times I wove with her were the happiest moments of my life." Naomi put the berries down, walked to the door, and stared out into the courtyard, the same common area our families had shared years ago. What did Naomi remember as she gazed out there now? She and her mother weaving together on a sunny morning? The two of them spinning wool, laughing, and whispering about the neighbors? Her mother kissing her head of wild curls as she braided them into captivity? When she was a girl, I knew everything that was on Naomi's mind because she was always talking, but now I had no idea what this silent, solemn woman thought.

I returned to the table and ate in silence for a few moments, hoping she would talk again. When she did, her eyes were filled with tears. "While I was his slave, Plotinus Metellus raped me. Many times over many months and always in the weaving room. I couldn't work at the loom after that. It overwhelmed me with shame."

A lump of bread swelled in my throat, and I felt it cut all the way down as I tried to swallow it. "The shame is not yours, Naomi! It belongs to the man who raped you and to my brother who sold you to him!"

"I knew that. And yet, I still couldn't."

"And I tried to force you to weave when you stayed at my house. I am so sorry."

"You didn't know."

"But I'm another one who's done something shameful. I had a choice to keep you in my house, but I turned you out of it. Can you ever forgive me for my cruelty?"

There, it was out. I waited for her to castigate me, to say, "Yes, Danya, you were cruel and unjust. You deserve the unhappiness you now suffer." She would be justified in throwing me out of her house now. I stood up and withdrew to the wall where the double-hearted tapestry hung and waited for her reaction.

Finally, Naomi spoke. "You saw to it that I was released from that monster. If you hadn't persuaded Efron to ransom me, I'd still be the slave of Plotinus. Or more likely, I'd be dead." Tears dropped from her cheeks onto the mulberries in her basket, darkening their tiny orbs. "For a long time, I wished I were dead."

I twisted the bottom edge of the rug hanging beside me, winding it into a knot between my fingers. "I'm deeply sorry, Naomi. I should have kept you in Sepphoris and cared for you there."

She wiped her face with her sleeve and straightened herself. "I forgive you," she said quietly. "As it turned out, sending me to Miryam was the best thing you could have done."

How could my doing the wrong thing have turned into the right thing? I glanced at the weaving I gripped. Upside-down hearts, touching at their tips. "What do you mean?"

She smiled down at the basket of fruit. How I wished she would smile at me. "For a long time, after I came to Nazareth, I couldn't sleep at night. For many months I wandered through the village until people complained to Miryam and Yosef that I was disturbing them. Their sons had to take turns guarding my door and keeping me inside. One particular night, though I was locked in by myself, I heard a whispering voice in the room with me. It repeated the same word, over and over: 'Forgiven, forgiven, forgiven.' The word touched something deep inside me. It released a joyful force I hadn't known was still in me. I went to my loom and began to work out a pattern. It's the one you're holding in your hand right now. I was drawn to it. No, drawn into it. I wove and wove, not thinking of my shame or missing my mother or anything else, until I completed that rug. And I've not stopped weaving since."

I ran my hand over all the paired hearts in the design. Standing out against the background with their triple layers of thread, the hearts seemed to pulsate. Naomi couldn't have learned the artistry displayed in these rugs from her mother. Like all the women in the village, Naomi's mother wove shirts and tunics and blankets to serve her family's needs, but not tapestries suitable for the finest homes in Galilee. I gave the handsome rug in my fingers a little shake. "What do you mean when you say the design drew you into itself? Surely you must've studied one like it somewhere. Maybe you saw something like this in a shop in Jerusalem or in the Temple itself?"

She squeezed a berry between her fingers, discoloring them. "I'm not certain. My mind was often in other places back then. I don't remember ever seeing anything like it. Miryam guesses that the idea might have come to me in a dream."

"Did it?"

Naomi filled her mouth with berries and merely shrugged.

I stood on a rug whose spirals of purple danced atop waves of yellow. "How about this one?" I asked. "Did this pattern appear in your dreams?"

She shook her head.

I pointed to a palm leaf design with an unusual diagonal twist in its paired pink and green threads. "Or this one?"

"No."

"And this?" Tendrils of vine leaves wound their way through a ribbed band.

"No, once I was finally freed from my shame, my mind flooded with ideas, my own ideas."

"Naomi, you're very gifted!"

She shrugged. "Maybe yes, maybe no. But it makes me feel better. I'm happy when I weave."

I spent my days in Nazareth resting and caring for Gad while Naomi and Miryam washed, wove, and sewed clothing, ground and baked grain, carried water, gardened, and performed many more of their daily tasks. But each evening, we women gathered outside in the courtyard to spin thread. While we worked, we watched the night sky deepen and the stars brighten. Miryam and Joseph had recently adopted two orphaned girls from their village. Assia and Lydia held the distaffs for us while we twisted strands of wool onto our whirling spindle sticks. These simple, repetitive motions required little attention, so my mind wandered freely between my private thoughts and the conversation at hand.

The struggles I would face when I returned to Sepphoris the next day hung like the distaff over my head, and I fingered the unruly, tangled fibers of my cares: my husband's displeasure with me and his sons, our conflicting views on the Roman occupation of our land, the unremitting sense of otherness I felt in Sepphoris, our financial difficulties, Tobiah's religious guilt.

Assia and Lydia began to yawn, and their heads bobbed. Miryam took up their distaffs, and the little girls laid their sleepy heads in her lap. "Naomi, would you make me a new tunic?" asked six-year-old Assia. "Any color except gray?"

"I can do that for you," said Naomi.

"For me, too?" asked Lydia.

"For you, too."

The threads we were spinning tonight would be woven into fabrics that would keep these loved ones warm in the cold, dry in the rain, and shaded from the sun's glare. I, too, wanted to weave a fabric that would shelter my family from the adverse weather to come, but I didn't know how to do this. Though I ached to embrace Matti and Mariamme again, my dread of returning to Sepphoris the next day thickened like the thread accumulating on my spindle.

Miryam's husband Yosef and their boys joined us and lit an oil lamp so they could see. Yosef and Yaakov whittled wooden nails, while Simon and Joses played dice. Yeshua attempted to carve a flute. He held up his hand to show us the nicks it bore, much to the amusement of those more skilled at working with the knife.

Yeshua had also smelled balm on the hilltop. Balm. Judah ben Hezekiah. Why was I so reluctant to believe that The Holy One had granted me a vision? Because the image wasn't a light or a holy being, but a blemished man? Because I was unworthy of His favor?

But think of the extraordinary events in the few days since I had steered towards Nazareth! I had hung over the precipice of death and been pulled back. Naomi had become an artistic genius and had forgiven me. Tobiah had even praised Gad. Such splendid blessings were not showered on the unworthy.

Simon shouted, "A pair! I win!"

Dice skidded across the hard ground. "No you don't. I have a seven!" said Joses, picking up the dice and holding them to the light.

"Double or nothing?" Simon challenged.

"Why not?" Joses answered. "What do I have to lose?"

Yes, why not, I thought. What do I have to lose?

Yosef spoke about the village. Many families had returned, and Nazareth's reconstruction was progressing well. Samuel's family, who had blamed Father for instigating the raid on Sepphoris, had risen to prominence. Samuel and his three sons were industrious and clever with money, though their women were still sullen and kept to themselves. Samuel had been chosen gabbaim, treasurer of the knesset, and therefore manager of the village assembly's leases. I disliked the idea of this greedy man having such power.

"If only Lev were here," I wished aloud. "He would be entering the prime of his life and would be a respected leader of this village."

Yosef nodded and said, "Yes, Lev's death is a loss to all of us."

I corrected him, pointing out that Lev was lost, not dead, and that it was easy to become one of the missing, especially if one wanted to. I told Yosef that Lev may have joined the Essenes or fled to Egypt or Syria. He could have stolen into Phoenicia and boarded a ship that could have taken him anywhere in the world.

Yosef was silent as I tried to convince him. And myself. But his silence struck home. Yosef's assumption made sense. We all knew that Lev could write. If he weren't dead, he would've gotten a letter to one of us sometime during these last twelve years. Even if he didn't know that I had married and was living in Sepphoris, Lev could've sent some word to Chuza or to Nazareth. Long-suffering peasant people like Yosef recognized hard truths: people who were "lost" were, in fact, dead. Lev could've been captured and crucified by the same convoy of Roman soldiers who executed those men in the oak grove at Beit Yerah. Or, traveling by himself, he may have been murdered by bandits who left his body to the wild beasts. He could've been on a ship that sank to the bottom of the wild Mediterranean Sea. He could've been among the hundreds slaughtered on the Temple Mount whose unidentified bodies were buried in a mass grave. Yes, if he lived, of course we would've heard from Lev by now. I needed to accept the fact that Lev had died.

No mother, no father, and no beloved brother. A husband who did not love me. I was alone again. It seemed as if the warp of my life's loom was strung with the fibers of loneliness. Weft threads of happiness, sadness, joy, and sorrow entangled themselves around the warp, but the constant cords of loneliness defined its pattern.

Yosef put his whittling down and sighed deeply. "Lev and so many fine, brave men have died. And now Judah ben Hezekiah."

I felt faint; my mouth went dry; I could utter only the words, "Judah, dead?"

"A villager who returned from Jerusalem just today told us that Hezekiah was killed last week while trying to escape from prison." Yosef clenched his fists. "I believe they murdered him. No one has ever escaped from the fortress at Machaerus. Judah wouldn't have been so stupid as to attempt this. But sooner or later, one way or another, the Romans butcher all who challenge them."

In my heart, I'd already known this, hadn't I? Last week, I'd seen the sun blazing around the wounded, crippled form of Judah. The light had throbbed like a beating heart, drawing him urgently on. And yet, Judah had paused to speak to me. The spirit of this flawed man had delivered a message to me on its flight to the next life. . . . Why not? Why not believe I had been granted a sacred vision? What did I have to lose?

I looked up at the night sky so that the tears pooling in my eyes would flow back into their well. The stars above us had not been extinguished. They were created by The Eternal One on the fourth day to illumine our way in the darkness. They still traveled their course under His watchful eye. So, too, did His people, even we insignificant Nazarenes. Our village had been rebuilt, and here we all were, gathered together again in the courtyard of our childhood under the star-laden mantle of His protection. Miryam had returned unharmed from Egypt. Her sons played at her feet and her daughters slept in her lap. Naomi had overcome her terrors and developed gifts none had known she possessed. Neither illness nor sorrow had destroyed me. Adonai granted me continued life and new insight into how to live it.

I kept my face lifted up to the lights He set in the dome of the sky. Even though I didn't understand Judah's apparition, I would trust it. Like Miryam, I would be led by the light. "Know that The Holy One walks with you," Judah had said. "Walk humbly and you will see Him." I stretched my feet out from under me. They had fallen asleep. I rubbed them until sensation returned and placed them out upon this path.

PART III:
13 TO 16 CE

PART III

THE FEAST OF BOOTHS
AND SPIDER WEBS

O ur family had first attended the Sukkot, or Feast of Booths, cel-
ebrations in Jerusalem five years ago, soon after I'd recovered from
the fever that had almost claimed my life. In gratitude to Adonai for sparing me and to our Nazareth friends for caring for me, we had all attended
the festival at Tobiah's expense ever since, and it had become our family's
favorite event of the year.

Since it was the month of Tishri, our bones still held the memory
of the recent heat, but the newly arrived crispness in the air quickened
our footsteps along the way to Jerusalem. Singing and conversation
with our friends also shortened the distance. Miryam and Yosef's two
older sons now had families of their own, so our group numbered
twenty. The size of our group and the presence of strong young men
in it discouraged bandits, so I felt safe. We traveled on well-populated
pilgrim routes, including some Roman roads. Even I conceded that
these well-built, patrolled stone roadways greatly reduced the hazards
and hardships of travel. Wines accompanied our evening meals and
honey sweetened our loaves. At night, pleasantly fatigued from the
day's hike, we wrapped ourselves in lightweight blankets and slept
soundly.

On the last evening of our journey, while Mariamme and I cleaned the
supper bowls and stored them in hide bags, Gad stacked, unstacked, and
restacked the pile of palm and willow sprigs the children had collected
along the way. We would use them in our Temple worship.

"He's telling us that he wants to make his lulav now," Mariamme said. "Can we?"

I gathered the family inside our tent to assemble the lulavim. Gad couldn't hold the leafy sheaves in one hand and tie them together with his other, so Matti held the bundle while Gad wound, then dropped, wound, then dropped again, then finally knotted the twine around its base. Matti often had no patience with himself, but he heaped an abundance of it on Gad.

Once his lulav was finally assembled, Gad slowly waved the sheaf up and down in front of him. "Sound like wain," he said in his thick-tongued, shortened way of speaking.

Tobiah was pleased at Gad's observation. "Yes! It's supposed to sound like rain. In the Temple, we'll use these when we bless the coming of the rainy season."

Gad smiled. His crooked little teeth gleamed. If he couldn't understand his father's words, he certainly sensed the approval in them. Hungry for more praise, Gad repeated, "Sound like wain, sound like wain, sound like wain," until Tobiah's smile turned weary, then disappeared.

Mariamme halted his repetitions by hugging him. "'Sounds like rain.' How smart you are. I didn't know that the lulav represented rain until I was seven!"

Gad waved his lulav over and over, giggling with pleasure at its sound. His delight infected us. Mariamme, Matti, and I joined him in producing the sweet, trembling, expectant tones made by air rippling through leaves. With each sweep of the bundled twigs, we heard the music of the rain as if for the first time. Once again, Gad reminded us of the beauty in the simplest of things.

Tobiah looked around at the four of us, playing our lulavim. "I'm going to make sure the animals are securely tied for the night." He departed and rolled the tent flap down, separating himself from the beautiful noise within.

Tobiah was not unkind to Gad. He no longer called our son his chastisement, but I didn't think he loved him. I told myself this was because Tobiah couldn't understand Gad. Intelligence was of such importance to my husband, he couldn't comprehend anyone who had so little of it. Despite his coolness towards Gad, I tried to love Tobiah kindly. Gad certainly did.

After my convalescence in Nazareth, Tobiah and I had established a truce. The family was well served by this pact because there was peace in our house. Over time, our truce had become friendlier. He returned to our bed, though we couldn't rekindle the deep desire we'd once felt for each other. We weren't granted another child.

I attempted to live by the directives Judah's spirit had given me: *"Act justly, love kindly, and walk humbly with your God,"* the message similar to the one the prophet Micah had delivered to the people of Israel hundreds of years ago. Father's scroll containing Micah's words read: *"He has told you, O man, what is good and what the Lord requires of you: Only to do justice, and to love goodness, and to walk modestly with your God."* When I first meditated on these words, I was euphoric with relief. I finally knew with certainty what The Holy One required of me—and it was so simple! I didn't need to puzzle out His plan for my existence, or join a revolution, or carry out a grand mission. No, to please Him, I needed only to follow these three simple guidelines.

But over time, confusing situations presented themselves as I attempted to live out this message. With the children, was it *loving kindly* to demand more of them or was it *loving kindly* to accept less? Should I grant them certain pleasures that might or might not weaken them, or should I withhold these pleasures in hopes of strengthening them? Also, these directives were often difficult to carry out. How could I *love* Tobiah *kindly* when something he did or said tore loose the scab on my unhealed heart? And how could I *act justly* when I knew I was being treated unfairly? What did justice demand of me and my people when Roman taxation snatched bread from the mouths of hungry children?

And *walking humbly with God* was the hardest directive of all because I didn't understand it. What did *humbly* really mean? Walk with The Mighty One, as if He were a companion? But shouldn't I walk behind Him, not with Him, because He is all-powerful and I am His lowly creation? But the directive was to *walk*, not crawl or grovel or cower. I am to walk with Him. *Humbly.*

At the Benjamin Gate in Jerusalem's northern wall, we separated from our Nazareth friends. The children would have preferred sleeping in tents on the Mount of Olives with them and the thousands of other out-of-town pilgrims, but we were staying with Joanna and Chuza. Though they now lived in Sepphoris, they still maintained their house in the Upper City and had preceded us to Jerusalem, speeding across Samaria with Herod Antipas' retinue in carriages drawn by teams of horses. Chuza attended all three of the annual festivals: Passover, Weeks, and Booths. It was politic for Jewish leaders doing Rome's bidding to be viewed as pious Jews, and attending these pilgrim feasts fostered that perception. The drinking and merry-making on these feast days also gave Chuza a good opportunity to mingle with city and Temple leaders.

My brother greeted us cheerfully, but hurriedly. "Quickly now, wash your feet and come with me," he said. "Joanna's gone to the market to find some citrons for the lulavim, but she said to start building the booth without her. 'All that are native in Israel shall dwell in booths,'" he reminded us, quoting an ancient directive for this festival. He led us to the rooftop and threw himself into the hut's construction with the enthusiasm he usually reserved for feasting.

"Tobiah, you stand right here and stretch your arms out sideways as far as you can. Good! Children, I'll have some very important work for you shortly. Danya, stand behind Tobiah. You may have to help him if his arms tire." My brother's boyish energy for this project puzzled me. In prior years, he had excused himself, pleading urgent business, while the rest of us constructed the family's booth.

Chuza lifted two thick olive branches, and his face flushed with the effort. He placed one in each of Tobiah's hands. "These will serve as the sukkah's corner posts. Hold them steady, Tobiah." Chuza began binding cross pieces to the posts Tobiah supported. My brother was so short that he didn't have to bend much to accomplish this, but nonetheless, reaching over his substantial stomach to lash the ties took a substantial effort. He mopped his jowly face with a towel. With a grunt, he eased himself into a chair and continued to manage the project from there.

"Mattityahu and Mariamme, it's your job to finish making the walls of our little palace here." Pleased with Chuza's uncustomary good humor, they plunged into their work, and I enjoyed watching them. Mariamme's fingers, long like her father's, delicately wove small strips of myrtle, palm, and oleaster into the larger branches that Matti wrestled onto the skeleton of the wall. Our son's childhood clumsiness had vanished. He was a solidly built, muscular youth, though a little shorter than his sister.

Gad sat on the floor in his usual pose: cross-legged, his tongue thrust out from one side of his mouth, and his head tilted to one side until Chuza involved him. "Down to the courtyard, Gad, and bring some branches up here to us." Chuza's servants had gathered the materials for the booth and, following Chuza's orders, had heaped them in the courtyard so that Gad would have work today.

As I observed a beautiful, leafy web begin to emerge on the booth's frame, I was reminded of the first time I had watched a spider construct its web. I was alone in the courtyard of my childhood home and I looked on in fascination as an orange spider fashioned a graceful, intricate design between two flower stems. Then the web entrapped a grasshopper. The spider scuttled over to the struggling insect and turned it round and round with its many legs, binding it in a shroud of silken threads, then sucked the life from its victim. I hadn't understood the web's purpose until that moment. The horror of that discovery had never faded from my memory.

An unreasonable fear gathered inside me today. A fear that my children were constructing a web for Chuza that they themselves would be trapped in. But I handed Mariamme another trail of myrtle and swept my dark thoughts aside. In Sepphoris, my brother enjoyed the reputation of being a gregarious, open-handed friend. Perhaps he had decided to treat his family as well as he treated his acquaintances.

Gad enthusiastically bore yet another armload of myrtle, palm, and oleaster up to the rooftop. "That's it, Gad, what a strong one you are!" Chuza said to the beaming boy.

Chuza's kindness towards Gad shamed me. A spider. No. It was unjust of me to have such a thought about my brother.

Joanna arrived and welcomed each of us with the formal greeting reserved for those who have come a great distance. "Shalom alekhem, Tobiah," she said. "Shalom alekhem, Danya, Mattityahu, Mariamme, and Gad."

"Peace to you also," we replied politely, wondering that she didn't also greet us with embraces.

As Joanna inspected our sukkah wall, Chuza said, "Some jasmine stems would brighten up the walls of our dwelling, wouldn't they, dear?"

Her pretty face darkened; her voice sliced the air like a knife. "A sukkah commemorates our people's experience in the desert after their release from slavery. Jasmine would be inappropriate." She grimaced at Chuza. "A booth is not a brothel."

Fingers stopped tying. Eyes widened. Gad said, "Uh oh." The little brown dog who had become Dodi's replacement scampered under a palm branch. None of us had ever heard Joanna belittle her husband to his face.

He colored deeply, as if straining to lift the weight of a waterlogged branch. But he stayed in his chair, wiping his face with his towel while Joanna nonchalantly picked through the citrons in her basket. Like a solitary drum, Gad's repeated "Uh, ohs" supplied an underlying rhythm to the long silence.

"No jasmine, then, wife," said Chuza quietly. He pushed a smile of strained civility onto his face. "Did you find enough citrons?"

Smiling, as if she were suggesting a pleasant outing, Joanna said, "You'll have to do without. There aren't enough for all of us."

The tendons in Chuza's neck splayed out, thick as the ties we were using to lash the sukkah together. "Of course. Our guests must be served first."

"Indeed. I'll go tie these fruits to the lulavim, then. Gad and Mariamme, will you come downstairs and help me with this?"

The children crept carefully around Chuza's chair, leaving a wide space between it and them. When they reached the stairway, they fled. Joanna descended with dignity.

Chuza was being gracious to us, and Joanna was reserved. Joanna gave orders, and Chuza obeyed, or rather groveled. It was as if the two of them had suddenly changed places, as if their souls had migrated from one body to the other.

Matti remained on the roof with us, and Chuza reached his arm out to him. "Mattityahu, give a hand to your fat old uncle who doesn't know a booth from a brothel." With a pull from Matti, Chuza rose from his chair and set back to work, soon chatting amiably again. As he supplied Tobiah with two more corner posts to steady, he said, "Brother, you're still greatly respected in Jerusalem. You should think about returning to Temple service. You know, you could rise to a position of enormous influence within the Temple priesthood. Some whisper about you as a candidate for High Priest."

Tobiah laughed. "Oh, Chuza, Chuza, Chuza. A brother-in-law in a position of power within the Temple priesthood wouldn't harm you, either, would it?"

"Ha, ha. Of course not, but my real interest is the good of our people and our family. There are two thousand priests living in Jerusalem, and you're a more righteous man than any of them. You should be using your talents of judgment and scholarship for the betterment of all. I also believe your family would flourish in Jerusalem. They'll languish in that bucolic outpost in Galilee."

"You certainly haven't languished there. And we're content in Sepphoris, aren't we, wife?" said Tobiah.

I pretended I didn't hear the question. "Content" wasn't true, but the children were rooted in Sepphoris, even if I wasn't. Matti tucked a piece of errant myrtle back into the section he was quietly working on and turned to catch his elders' every word.

"The Temple would support you, and you could live here in my house." With one hand, Chuza gestured to the elegant house beneath us. "*Ve-hayita akh same'ah,*" as we say during this festival. Ha, ha."

You shall have nothing but joy. The greeting when visiting someone's sukkah.

My husband responded politely. "A gracious offer, but I have to live near my estates."

Chuza persisted. "I could manage your estates for you while you were in Jerusalem. Herod Antipas himself will tell you what an outstanding steward I am." He grinned. "I could make some real money for you, a handsome patrimony for your son." He winked at Matti.

Tobiah maintained his grip on the pole, but his knuckles whitened. It was true that Tobiah struggled to make a profit on his lands. After Otzar, who'd robbed us and disappeared, Tobiah had employed several other honest but not particularly successful estate managers. The disastrous Sabbatical year, scanty rainfall, and another locust infestation had substantially reduced yields. And Tobiah scrupulously paid every tax imposed by civil authorities and every tithe and tax required by the Temple though some landowners didn't in such bad times.

"I'll get it right yet," said Tobiah. He didn't raise his voice, but I could feel the edge in it. "We'll stay in Sepphoris and handle our own estates, as my family has done for generations."

Chuza slapped Tobiah on the back. "Of course you will. I didn't think I'd convince you otherwise. No harm in my asking, though. You can count on me, brother, should you ever need it. And you, nephew, I pledge my assistance to you, should I be among the living, when you're steward of your family's sacred soil."

Before Matti could say anything, Tobiah replied curtly, "We're grateful for your care, brother."

That evening, Chuza and Joanna dined at the home of one of the many friends they still had in Jerusalem, so I had no opportunity to question Joanna about her shocking exchange with Chuza. After sundown, Tobiah and I sat on the bench in their courtyard, the same courtyard where I had witnessed the reconciliation between my father and Chuza so many years before. Tobiah and I gazed at the lovely city spread out before us. Oil lamps flickered in the courtyard and glowed from within the houses below, and the moon bathed all of Jerusalem in a soft ivory light. "I do miss living here," Tobiah said quietly. "Though I thought I could adapt to life in Sepphoris, I really haven't."

Tentatively, I took Tobiah's long, thin hand in mine. "I haven't either."

His hand grew warm. "I was so in love with you, Danya. I thought we could live happily anywhere. But I was wrong. We never should have moved to Sepphoris."

"You had no choice. But you gave me the choice to go or not."

"You were too young to understand the choice you were making. I was older and should've known myself better. My responsibilities in Sepphoris have turned me into a frightened man. I act out of fear most of the time now. Fear of losing my sacred ancestral lands. Fear of losing The Holy One's favor. Fear of violence between Rome and Galilee. Fear of losing you and the children to such conflict. And, in the blindness caused by my fear, I came to see you as a threat to me and all I possessed."

He took his hand from mine and bent to pick up a pistachio that had blown into the courtyard from a neighbor's tree. With his fingernail, he split open the pistachio's husk, extracted the tan shell from within it, and rolled the shell back and forth in his palm. "I'm sorry for so much,

Danya. I knew who you were when I married you, but as time went on, I wanted you to change: to think like me, believe what I believed, and fear what I feared. That was wrong. I've treated you unjustly." He looked at me with his soft brown eyes, eyes the color of Jerusalem in the setting sun, and pressed the nut, still in its shell, into my hand. I curled my fingers around it, and he squeezed my fist with both of his hands.

I felt that he was pleading with me to do something. Or to believe something. To crack open the shell he had pressed into my palm and to free its small green nut from its prison. "I'm sorry, too, Tobiah. I wanted *you* to change, to believe what *I* believed. But I have always loved you, even though it has been hard for me to do so for a long, long time now."

He kept my fist cradled in his hands, and his eyes fixed on mine for a long time. "Please be patient with me, Danya. In time, I will love you again as you deserve to be loved." Then, with a sigh, he rose and limped inside to go to bed, and I followed.

His knees had bothered him for a year. The long trek from Sepphoris must have been particularly hard on him, though he hadn't complained. The physical demands of life in Sepphoris had aged my scholarly husband. The hair on his chest and beard had turned white, as had the wreath of hair crowning the top of his bald head. The skin under his chin was gouged with lengthy rifts, like the barren hills on the eastern side of the Jordan River.

We lay down on the bed. I placed a small pillow upon his bony shoulder and set my head on it. "Maybe we should consider Chuza's idea," I suggested. "We could start over here in Jerusalem. You could live the life you are suited to here, the life you were raised to live."

Tobiah readjusted the pillow and my head on his shoulder. "No. I must carry out my responsibilities in Sepphoris, confront my fears there, and change my ways there. And Sepphoris is better for the children, especially for Gad. The boy is safer in a smaller city. Gad works hard and he's persistent, qualities that are especially useful for those who work the land. Perhaps we can prepare him for some occupation in the country-side around Sepphoris."

This was the first time Tobiah had ever spoken about a future for Gad. I lay next to my husband, squeezing back my tears.

"We must also stay in Sepphoris so that Mattityahu can learn to manage the estates," Tobiah continued. "He'll have more success than I've had. Though Ezri's sin fouls our ancestral lands now, that pollution won't pass into the next generation. Under our son's stewardship, I believe the Kamith family estates will flourish again."

"And Mariamme? What would be best for her?" I asked.

He sighed. "Best for me would be to keep her with us. Always."

As hard as Tobiah was on his sons, he was the opposite with his daughter. Men often teased him about his tender-heartedness for his female child, warning that it could cost him dearly when it came time to dower her. However, I thought that Tobiah's affection for Mariamme was one of his loveliest qualities.

"But that wouldn't be best for her," he continued. "We'll have to find her a husband while I can still provide her with a dowry sufficient to protect her."

I squeezed the pillow. "Mariamme is only twelve years old. She shouldn't marry yet."

"I agree. But we should begin to seek an appropriate match for her. Someone whose dreams and values she shares, so that she can know the deep joys of married love, as we once did."

I held my breath, hoping he would embrace me. He did, and we made love more tenderly than we had in years because we both knew that the delicious nutmeat of our love was still there. Because we had tasted it before, we knew it would be worth the sacrifices it would take to release it from its shell.

The next morning, the first day of Sukkot, the children and I wedged into a crowd forming near the Pool of Siloam. Soon a group of priests, including Tobiah, would draw water from this ancient pool and carry it to the Temple sanctuary for the Water Libation, the opening ceremony of this eight-day feast. As the priests began to fill their vessels, Joanna joined us. She was so poorly dressed and groomed that I almost didn't recognize her. "Joanna, what's happened to you?"

Joanna squeezed around behind the children and spoke to me in a whisper. "This is so humiliating, I can hardly bear to utter the words: Chuza says he's going to take a second wife."

"A second wife! He wouldn't dare!" Mariamme and Matti heard my exclamation. Their mouths dropped.

"He says he needs a wife who will produce an heir for him."

"But wouldn't a second wife make Chuza look bad in front of his Roman friends? They don't practice polygamy."

"Romans don't care who Jews marry. Chuza got this idea into his head just last week. I thought it would pass, but now he's been suggesting names to me. He says he wants the two of us to be 'friends' so that his home will be peaceful."

"Oh, Joanna. What an indignity!"

Gad turned to me and, giggling, put his fingers on my lips. "Shhhhh, Mama."

"Why doesn't he just divorce you? It's what I've wanted for you for a long time."

"Money, of course."

Gad, now making a game of it, tried to shush Joanna. I led him away from her. "The procession's starting soon. Look for a shiny silver bowl and tell me when you see it." He shaded his eyes and watched the procession emerge from the pool's portico enclosure.

"Money," Joanna repeated. "He doesn't want to return my dowry, as required by Jewish law. Also, my father was clever enough to prepare his will according to Roman law. Though Chuza has the right to use my inheritance as long as we're married, it reverts to me in the event of our divorce. So I've resorted to this outrageous behavior to force him to divorce me."

At that moment, the procession of priests and their sacred vessels passed in front of us. We fell in line behind the priests and walked up through the Lower City towards the Temple Mount, singing the Songs of Ascent. Though these psalms were meant for us as a nation, some seemed written for each of us personally. I thought of Tobiah's hopes for his patrimony during the song entreating *Restore our fortunes, O Lord, like the watercourses in the Negeb. May those who sow in tears reap with shouts of joy.* I thought of Joanna's yearnings when we sang *We have escaped like a bird from the snare of the fowlers; the snare is broken, and we have escaped.*

The procession ended on the plaza below the southern wall of the

Temple Mount. We joined the line for the ritual purification required for entrance to it. Matti led Gad to the men's bathhouses while Joanna, Mariamme, and I waited our turn at the women's. When Mariamme drifted far enough in front of us so that she couldn't overhear, Joanna pointed to her coarse wool tunic and slovenly hairdo. "I'm purposely disgracing myself in public, knowing it will get back to Chuza and embarrass him. I speak to him as if he were a slave. I'm trying everything I can think of to get him to divorce me."

It must have taken great self-control for Joanna to keep her hand from smoothing back the strands of hair that sprouted like wheat shafts out from under her head covering. "Perhaps now Chuza will. What people think of him, and therefore of his wife, is extremely important to him."

Joanna wiped her nose daintily, forgetting to do so crudely. "Humiliating myself like this may be useless, though. Even if he could bring himself to part with my dowry, he wouldn't be able to because he's probably already spent it. I may never be freed to have children of my own."

"Children of your own? But I thought you were barren," I said, too loudly.

That caught Mariamme's attention and she turned back to join us. I waved her away, but Joanna said, "No. Let her hear this. She's almost grown now and needs to know the truths of married life." Joanna continued in a whisper. "The woman is always blamed. When I think of what I allowed myself to be put through, all these years, to cure my presumed infertility—don't ever let yourself be fooled like I was, child, only to learn from one of Chuza's mistresses that she hasn't borne him a child, either. She says none of them have."

"None of them!" I almost bellowed, but held myself to a whisper. "How many mistresses has he had?"

"It doesn't matter. What matters is that Chuza is the barren one. I may still be capable of bearing a child. But I must be free to remarry."

"We'll help you, won't we, Mother?"

"I'll do anything I can for Joanna, of course, but this isn't your concern, Mariamme. Come, it's our turn for the baths." I wasn't going to involve my daughter in any matter relating to Chuza, no matter how bad we felt for Joanna.

As always, the water in the ritual baths was freezing cold. We were in and out, with a hasty prayer, in the blink of an eye. But before Joanna slipped back into her tunic, I looked closely at her beautiful, meticulously maintained body. She was close to thirty-five years old, but she had ample breasts and adequate hips. Maybe she could still bear and nourish a child. Such things happened, though not often.

Outside the baths, we pushed through a mass of foreign revelers to meet Matti and Gad at the bottom step of the southern stairway. We ascended to the Mount together. The Levite musicians struck up their lutes and harps, and the singing of the Hallel began. Because so many heads blocked our view of the distant altar, we couldn't see the rites, but this was nonetheless a joyous moment. We joined our voices to the many thousands in this holy, timeless place and waved our lulavim as we sang. *"From the rising of the sun to its setting, the name of the Lord is to be praised."* There was no mourning in the Hallel psalms. They were all songs of praise and thanksgiving.

"I walk before the Lord in the land of the living." Once again I was reminded of Adonai's mercy, for I was walking in the land of the living, though once I had stumbled at the edge of the dead.

"Who is like the Lord our God who is seated on high? He gives the barren woman a home, making her the joyous mother of children. Praise the Lord!" The Lord our God could make a barren woman fertile. He could make Joanna the joyous mother of children if it was His Will. I would have to help her. I squeezed Joanna's hand. "I promise I will look for a way to help you."

"Thank you, dear sister."

The Hallel singing continued. Matti's eyes scanned the crowd. I wondered what he was searching for. When I was around his age, I had waited on this Mount for Judah ben Hezekiah's eyes to find mine. Now that Mattityahu was almost an adult, was some young woman waiting for his eyes to find hers? Years ago, my call to Judah had gone unsounded here. Was Matti longing to call out to someone today?

It saddened me to realize that I had no idea. Since Gad's birth, I'd paid so much attention to my broken son that I had neglected my whole one. When Tobiah had demanded I withdraw from Matti's education, I didn't search hard enough for other ways to spend time with him. I'd lost track of Matti's heart, the heart that had once depended solely upon me for its beating. Now I didn't know him as I should have.

Chuza wandered through the massive pillars of the Royal Stoa and found us. With the exception of Matti, we were all surprised to see him here. My brother never attended festival events with us. Chuza sang the last psalm of the Hallel with us; hummed it rather, since he didn't know the words. Then the cymbals clashed. The singing of the Hallel was completed.

"Mattityahu and I have some appointments in the city today," Chuza announced. "Are you ready to go, my boy?"

"Yes, uncle."

I took Matti's hand in mine. "The sacrifices haven't begun yet," I objected.

"There'll be other sacrificial offerings the boy can attend in the next seven days. Our affairs can't wait. The important people we're meeting today won't be available tomorrow."

"But his father expects Mattityahu to meet him for Scripture study," I objected.

"I want to go with Uncle Chuza," said Matti. "I'll join Father for Scripture study tomorrow."

Chuza reached out for my son. The spider wrapped his arms around the grasshopper and encased it in a silken shroud.

"Sister, stop frowning. I won't harm your baby. I'm just an uncle who wants to spend a day with his nephew."

Matti extracted his hand from my grasp. "I'll see you tonight, Mother."

Chuza led my son away from me. I watched the two of them start down the stairway. I was startled by how much Matti's thick, compact build resembled Chuza's. My son's name throbbed in my throat. . . . This time on the Temple Mount, I would listen to my heart. My call would not go unsounded. "Mattityahu!" I shouted. "Come back here. *Now*. Matti?"

My son did not answer my call.

OMENS

The following dry season's deepest heat settled upon us like a scratchy wool cloak. Despite the weather, Razi insisted on baking fresh loaves every day. Age and hard work had deformed her hands, so I had taken to helping her with this task. Today my left arm felt stiff as I worked the dough, but eventually, we tucked the bread into the oven. I was massaging my forearm when, from the outside, I heard a sudden whoosh and then a thump. Through the window I saw the oak tree in the courtyard bounce, then settle itself onto the ground. Its leaves shivered.

"May we be spared!" Razi prayed. She clutched the small bronze charm tied around her neck, an amulet in the shape of a hand, closed her eyes, and prayed soundlessly.

"How strange!" I said. "Thanks to Adonai that no one was out in the courtyard!"

"The day is clear and windless and the ground is dry," Razi whispered solemnly. "Yet, an oak tree falls. It is an omen."

Her superstitions annoyed me. Nonetheless, my hand drifted to the small silver cylinder that hung from my own neck with its prayer inscribed on the tiny piece of parchment within it. *"The Lord bless you and keep you; the Lord make His face to shine upon you, and be gracious to you; the Lord lift up His countenance upon you, and give you peace."* "It must've been decayed," I pointed out. "It was getting too large for the courtyard anyway."

"An omen," Razi repeated. She held her talisman up, with the palm facing outward, to hold back the unknown malevolence on the other side of the wall. "Some evil will befall this house," she whispered.

The perspiration on my arms turned cold as spring water. I stood in front of the oven, hoping its heat would melt the chill of Razi's augury, and prayed. "I've followed Your commands, and You've sent me some peace. Please, please, do not take this contentment from me now, O Good and Gracious One."

The chill spread. It drained down through my skin, and I couldn't bake it out. I decided to inform Tobiah about the phenomenon of the fallen tree. He would have an explanation that would quell my unreasonable fear.

Tobiah was teaching in his library. I was reluctant to interrupt, so I stood outside the library's open door and waited for him to acknowledge me. Tobiah now had three students in addition to Matti. He had first begun tutoring Yochanen, the son of an acquaintance, in hopes that a fellow student would stimulate Mattityahu's interest in his studies. Yochanen's father wanted his son prepared for the Temple's beth-ha midrash and a life of scholarship in Jerusalem, such as Tobiah himself had enjoyed before coming to Sepphoris. Then Proclus's father, a Roman, asked Tobiah to tutor his son. Very few men in Sepphoris were as knowledgeable as Tobiah in languages, history, and law; and, since Proclus's parents couldn't bear to send their son away for his education, they paid Tobiah handsomely for schooling him. And when Miryam's son, Yeshua, outgrew the little beth ha-sefer and its hazzan in Nazareth, I convinced Tobiah to include him in his classroom without charge.

The students were seated at one long table strewn with tablets and scrolls, and Tobiah stood facing them. They were involved in a spirited discussion about theories of life after death. Proclus, the Roman, supported his belief in reincarnation with quotations from Plato. Yochanen was convinced that life existed only in this world. He mocked Yeshua's theory that the dead will someday be reunited with their bodies and live on in some form. "A peasant belief," said Yochanen with his arms crossed. "I'm not surprised that you would hold to it."

I hadn't noticed until then what an unattractive young man Yochanen was. Squat and self-important by nature, he would be paunchy and pompous in a few years, I imagined.

Yeshua ignored the insult. "Many peasants do believe in a resurrection, Yochanen. Wouldn't you hope for a better life in the next world if you suffered as they do in this one?" Yeshua's strong hand, hardened with manual labor, pointed to a scroll resting near Yochanen's fleshy arm. "However, the great prophet Isaiah, a nobleman, explicitly links the body as well as the soul to immortality. He writes that *'Your dead shall live, their corpses shall rise. O dwellers in the dust, awake and sing for joy! For your dew is a radiant dew, and the earth will give birth to those long dead.'*"

From the back of the room, where she had been quietly sitting by herself, Mariamme spoke up. "Scripture is full of references to life after death. *'But the souls of the righteous are in the hand of God, and no torment will ever touch them. In the eyes of the foolish they seemed to have died, and their departure was thought to be a disaster,'* just for one."

"Will you silence her, Rabbi?" complained Yochanen. "My father is not paying good money for me to sit in school and listen to a peasant preach and a girl recite."

Tobiah allowed Mariamme to observe in his schoolroom, over the objections of some of his students and their parents. She could recall, word for word, almost everything that was spoken or read aloud. Even though she couldn't participate, she learned everything the young men did. Occasionally, she couldn't contain her enthusiasm for some subject and spoke out as she did today.

I crossed Yochanen off my list of possible matches for Mariamme, even though he was from a good family and his father had praised our daughter publicly to some of our acquaintances. Mariamme's scholarship could intimidate a man. We would have to be very careful about the one we entrusted her to.

Tobiah struggled to conceal his amusement and pride in his daughter and turned to our son.

"What do you think about life after death, Mattityahu?"

Matti yawned. "I don't have a point of view on this subject. I thought we were going to work on mathematical proofs today."

Tobiah did not reprimand Matti. "Final thoughts, anyone?"

"What do you think, Rabbi?" asked Yeshua.

"That our earthly existence ends with the death of our bodies," Tobiah answered. "Though perhaps some part of us lives on in a Sheol-like region. But each of you needs to develop your own thinking on this matter."

Tobiah finally spotted me and smiled. "What brings you to our classroom, wife?"

My fears about the downed oak tree suddenly seemed childish compared to the issues they were considering here. "Nothing important. A tree fell in the courtyard this morning, but we can deal with the matter later. Gad and I will be going out soon."

Matti yawned again. "May I leave, Father? I'm expected at work." Chuza had arranged for Matti to apprentice with the architects and engineers building the theater in our city. This work had captured Matti's interest as nothing else had.

Tobiah excused Matti with one quick flick of his hand. Matti was fourteen years old now. Though it displeased Tobiah that Matti wasn't a scholar, he was beginning to accept the fact that his son had other interests and gifts.

Matti glanced at me on his way out. He looked relieved. Tobiah's admiring circle of young scholars drew in closer around him, filling the gap left by Matti's departure.

Gad found me in the classroom doorway and pulled on my hand. "Go now, Mama?" he asked. For months, I'd been taking Gad with me on my rounds to the shops. Though he was eight years old, he wasn't able to understand any reading or writing. The city of Sepphoris had become his classroom, and our walks through it his lessons. Each day, we encountered difficulties that Gad had to contend with. Spotting and getting around garbage and animal dung on the streets, keeping a safe distance from carts, and dealing with shopkeepers were all challenges for Gad. Though I was tempted to leave him at home where he was accepted and loved, I forced myself to take him out. He might outlive both me and Tobiah. Matti and Mariamme promised us they would take care of Gad, but, when that time came, no one could be certain that their circumstances would permit this. Gad had to learn to take care of himself.

I admired his courage. Though Sepphoris never felt like home to me, at least I understood the city. How much more complicated and confusing this place must be for Gad. Nevertheless, each day he took it on with great enthusiasm.

I had no coin today, which was often the case now, but there was still much to see and learn in the marketplace. We set out from our home near the eastern wall of the city and quickly reached the decumanus where we could stay in the shade of its covered sidewalks all the way to the agora. Gad identified the goods in the shops we passed: jewelry, linen, sandals, cabinets, perfume, lamp oil. Though some shopkeepers were kind, others were hostile, put off by Gad's appearance. They would mark his short, broad neck and flattened facial features and ask if he were a foreigner. One asked me if Gad had been stepped on at birth! But my son had to learn to deal with all of them, and so, taking a deep breath, I led him into a potter's shop. Even before the child had picked anything up, the shopkeeper barked at him, "Don't let that boy touch a thing!"

I picked up a pitcher, decorated with alternating red and brown stripes, and told Gad, "Run your finger along this. It's made of clay, dried and fired in a kiln."

But Gad was too frightened to touch it. The proprietor stood behind him and breathed heavily. The man's foul breath and ill manners repelled me. I returned the pitcher to the shelf where it teetered a bit before settling down. "We'll buy from the door-to-door peddler," I said to Gad. "His pots are properly weighted and rest squarely on their bases." We left that shop.

"Why man angry, Mama?" Gad asked.

My arm twitched involuntarily. I clutched it. I wanted to call the man a barbarian, but, for Gad's sake, I tried to demonstrate fairness if not kindness. "He's ignorant. And he has to sell poor quality merchandise. That makes him angry."

As I debated about entering the shop of a sign maker who was friendly to Gad when he had no other customers, but brusque when he did, a wasted, mangy dog bared his blackened teeth at us, then began barking wildly. Gad reached out to pat it, but I pulled him back.

"Do not touch strange dogs."

"But he's scared, Mama. And hungry. Can I feed him?"

"No, just leave him alone." I took his hand and maneuvered him around the starving beast, and we started walking again. But Gad kept looking back at the creature. It staggered into the street.

Gad yanked my arm. "No street! Help him, Mama," Gad shouted.

"Shhhhh," I said. "Stay here. I'll get the dog out of the street."

I hurried after the animal, but, feeling that I was losing my balance,

I had to slow my pace. While I was winding my way around a standing oxcart, the hooves of a fast moving horse crushed the poor dog's skull. Gad wailed. I rushed to him and stooped to hold him and pat his heaving back. Everyone passing by stared at us. Despite his years, Gad was small. Most people thought he was only four or five years old, but his crying in public was nonetheless embarrassing.

I concluded that we'd never make it all the way to the agora today. I decided to cut our walk short and ensure ourselves a pleasant experience by visiting Joanna and Naomi's shop. Fortunately, Naomi was there. And so was one of Joanna's dogs. Gad held the puppy until his sobs subsided.

"I was hoping I'd see you today, Gad," said Naomi. "Will you help me? I need to roll and tie some rugs in the back."

I stayed in front to watch the shop. Naomi displayed each of her tapestries with great care. I noted two new designs, a rosette and a meander of grape vines. Naomi had achieved wonders with her edging, trimming borders with borders and highlighting each row in a contrasting color. She employed accents of colored beads and fringes. But the most remarkable thing about these newly completed tapestries was their colors. Joanna's financing had allowed Naomi to send her wool to the dyers in Jerusalem who had access to the most expensive, luxurious dyes in the world: Tyrian purple, produced from the murex shellfish retrieved by divers off the coast of Phoenicia; yellow saffron from a type of crocus flower; and true reds from the bodies of a particular scaly insect.

The shop in Sepphoris had been Joanna's idea. "Naomi's gift is too great to be hidden away in Nazareth," she said. She'd sold some of her jewelry and invested in Naomi, forming a partnership that was a half year old and already enormously successful. Naomi knew how to make beautiful, rare goods, and Joanna knew how to sell them. Chuza had not yet taken a second wife, despite continual warnings that he would do so "any day now." Joanna still hoped her marriage to him would somehow be dissolved, and, when that day came, she intended to be able to support herself comfortably.

I was counting the shades of color in the tapestries when Joanna arrived carrying a bundle. "Good, you're here. I need your advice." She unrolled the item in her arms and shook out a scarlet tunic. She held the flawlessly woven, seamless cloth up to herself. "What do you think? I asked Naomi to experiment with clothing, and she made this for me."

"It's absolutely stunning. It looks like something a royal would wear."

"That's what I think, too. And there's a huge market in this city for a well-made tunic. When I'm forced to buy one in Sepphoris, I'm pleased if I find something with the bands meeting properly along the selvedge. Some women send all the way to Rome for theirs. But this is a masterpiece! You have to help me convince Naomi to expand our business into clothing as well as tapestries. She could start with belts, easy enough, and then work up to tunics and mantles."

"Joanna, there's only one Naomi."

"She could teach women in her village how to do this. I could run the shop alone. All Naomi would have to do is stay in Nazareth and design masterpieces for the weavers we'd hire."

"But then I'd never get to see my friends in Sepphoris," said Naomi as she and Gad returned from the backroom. "There's no end to Joanna's schemes, but that's her genius."

"Someday you'll get bored with tapestries," Joanna warned. "Then you'll come begging for my schemes."

Naomi laughed her old, fluttering, irrepressible giggle. "Maybe."

How good it was to hear that laughter once again. And how long had it been since I'd been carefree enough to laugh like a girl? I found myself envying Joanna and Naomi. They didn't have the burden of children. Why, they had the freedom to—no! I stopped myself. No childish jealousies.

When it was time for us to leave, Gad impulsively hugged Naomi. "I love you, Nomi," he said.

"I love you, too, Gad."

No childish jealousies. Gad was lavish in his affections with everyone.

Naomi pressed a silver coin into my hand and whispered. "For Tobiah's tutoring of Yeshua."

I pushed the coin back into her palm. "Tobiah tutors Yeshua for his own pleasure. He won't take this."

"But will you? For household expenses?"

Had my need become so obvious? I looked down at my clothing. My sandals needed replacing. But my tunic, though a bit worn, certainly wasn't shabby.

"I know that Tobiah has forgiven the debts of some of his tenants in Nazareth," said Naomi. "Such generosity doesn't come without someone paying a price."

I thanked her and took the coin. For my children's sake. They needed to be well dressed. Matti, to impress the men Chuza introduced him to; Mariamme, to attract proper suitors; and Gad, to deflect unfavorable attention. I always saw to it that Gad was handsomely clothed. When I could eliminate a reason for people to look down on him, I did.

Though I was tired and wanted to get home for a nap, we detoured on our way to view the construction of Sepphoris' long-awaited theater. I hoped to find Matti there and have him show us around. At breakfast last week, he'd tried to depict the theater's design for me. Grabbing a knife and a round of bread, he said, "You see, the structure is basically circular." He scored the bread into twelve segments and rendered a long, detailed explanation of its composition. But his bread loaf hadn't brought the theater to life for me. I needed to see the building for myself to understand it and the immense joy Matti took in it.

Laborers and artisans swarmed over the structure. We climbed some stairs, ascending a few rows into the seating area, and peered down towards the stage. A crew was laying wood flooring on it.

"Mother, Gad!" Matti called from high above us. "Come up!"

I leaned on Gad, and we climbed up what until recently had been the side of a steep hill. Now it was a smoothly polished limestone stairway providing access to some of the four thousand seats that had been chiseled out of the hill's bedrock. Matti met us at the top of the steps. "Isn't it magnificent?" He opened his arms as if he were embracing the entire structure. "I'm so happy you came. Now you can see for yourselves what a wonder it is."

After I caught my breath, I focused first on the stage building. It was more than ten cubits high, an elaborate stone block structure into which carvers had chiseled columns and pilasters and doorways. I pointed to one of them. "Is that where the actors enter and exit?" I asked.

"Yes, yes," Matti answered impatiently. "First look at the design of the whole, Mother." He took Gad's head and gently guided it left to right.

"See, the whole building is basically a circle, Gad. You know what a circle is. Its radius is equal to that of the orchestra—that area down there, see it Gad? See how the circumference is divided into twelve equal segments?"

Gad nodded and so did I, though neither of us saw what Matti did. He swept his finger from one imaginary point to another. "A line drawn here bisects the circle and determines the line separating the orchestra from the front of the stage, and the arc circumscribes—" Matti stopped and looked at our puzzled faces. "The proportions are perfect. Surely you can sense that much about it." Matti took my hand. "This is beauty, Mother. And I get to participate in creating it. Do you understand now?"

I did get a sense of order and balance that generated a feeling of peace in me. I kissed Matti on both cheeks. "Yes, I'm beginning to. I'm trying to."

I hadn't wanted my son involved in this. I thought a theater in Sepphoris was a needless expense. Antipas's palace, the basilica, a gymnasium, a pagan temple, and baths already littered the agora. All those buildings were funded by the many and used by a privileged few. Antipas levied a twenty percent tax on the yield from the threshing floors of every village, even though the peasants needed every kernel of grain they produced just to subsist. But at least this theater was beautiful, and all of us, even the poor, could attend it. In addition, it gave many men work and had opened Matti's eyes to a world Tobiah and I never could have shown him.

It was well into the afternoon by now, and we were overdue at home. After tutoring Matti and the other students, Tobiah usually spent an hour or two with Gad. When a son was incapable of learning his father's trade or profession, most men left that child's education to women or slaves. But Tobiah still believed it was a father's sacred duty to educate his male children, so, since Gad couldn't learn to read or recite Torah, Tobiah had decided to teach him how to garden. If Gad could acquire the skill of growing living things within the confines of our own garden, perhaps he could eventually work in the orchards and vineyards of the countryside.

Our garden plot lay outside the city walls, a short walk from our home. After Passover, Tobiah and Gad had tilled the soil and planted vegetables, herbs, and melons. For months, they watered, fertilized, and weeded. They harvested the lettuce, chicory, mint, and dill as it ripened. Soon the chickpeas, beans, lentils, cucumbers, onions, pepperwort, and melons would be ready to bring in. Gad's short, broad arms and legs seemed especially suited for the bending and stooping involved in garden work. He displayed remarkable endurance, continuing on even when Tobiah had to rest. Gad's patience with growing things and the care he took with each plant impressed and delighted his father. What Tobiah had undertaken as a grim but necessary chore had become a pleasant interlude in the day for him. He was disappointed when he had to miss it on the days he served in the courts.

Last week I saw the two of them, hand in hand, walking home from the garden. Their fingers had always looked so different: Tobiah's long, thin and expressive; Gad's short, thick, and awkward. Now a shade of deep copper burnished the backs of both of their hands, and the boy's rested companionably in the man's. *Loving kindly*, as Gad did naturally, had accomplished what all my arguing and anger and resentment had failed to do. The little clumsy-fingered boy, all on his own, mended the tear that his birth had rent in his father's heart. And in the process, he had stitched into mine the hope that Tobiah's healing heart would someday again bind itself to mine.

Today Tobiah and Gad stopped in the inner courtyard on their way to the garden. Superstitious Razi wouldn't allow so much as a stick of the mysterious oak tree to fire our oven. So Zohar had engaged the help of a woodsman who had been working on the forested slopes outside the city. For the contribution of his ax, saw, and muscle, this man could have the lumber from the tree. Tobiah took the opportunity to show Gad how to swing the ax and push the saw. They also helped Zohar and the woodsman load branches and logs onto the cart before they headed down to the garden.

I grabbed a goatskin water bag and caught up to them at the city's eastern gate. "Take this," I said. "You'll need plenty of water out there today."

Tobiah smiled. "Most thoughtful of you." He slung the water bag over his shoulder, drew me to him, and, in front of everyone on the crowded city street, kissed me on the lips.

My face warmed with embarrassment and pleasure. Gad giggled. I straightened my son's head covering that had slid back from his face and kissed him on the cheek. "Take good care of your Papa for me."

Savoring Tobiah's kiss, I sauntered back towards the cool of our house. Under this fierce sun, my own head covering offered me some protection, but it also trapped the heat. Sweat trickled down the back of my neck, and my braid stuck to it. When I was a girl working in the fields on days as hot as this one, we'd come in early from our outdoor work, pour cool well water over our heads, and take refuge in our little house until evening brought relief.

I napped for a long time. When I awoke, I discovered that Gad and Tobiah hadn't returned from their work. I decided to bring them another water bag and demand they get out of the sun. When I stepped from the door of the house, my vision blurred in the blazing sunlight, and the intense heat made me nauseous.

Gad was weeding the staked beans and wiping the perspiration from his face with his headcloth. "Shhh," he said when he spotted me approaching. "Papa taking nap."

Tobiah did not appear to be resting comfortably but was slumped down on the ground at an odd angle. His skin was hot to the touch and dry as parchment. His heart raced. He breathed, but he wasn't conscious. He was suffering from too much sun and perhaps other maladies. I loosened his clothing and poured water all over his head and neck. That didn't awaken him. "We've got to move Papa to the shade, Gad."

"But Papa want sleep. He said so."

"He's sick, Gad. He needs to sleep under that tree over there, in the shade." I grabbed Tobiah under the armpits. They were on fire. Gad lifted him by the ankles, and we dragged him out of the sun. I poured more water onto his headcloth and pressed it to his overheated head, neck, and chest. Still, he didn't rouse. He needed to be completely immersed. "Gad, stay with Papa. Put this cloth on his head and chest and keep it wet. I'm going to get people to help us lift Papa into the miqveh."

"Why miqveh? Is the Sabbath tonight?"

When I returned with Zohar, Razi, and Mariamme, Gad was sitting vigilantly next to his father, pressing the wet cloth to his lips. "I didn't wake him, Mama. Shhhhh."

Razi held up her amulet again in the futile hope that the bronze hand could keep misfortune from passing beyond its boundary. We immersed Tobiah in the miqveh, then wrapped him in wet sheets and placed him in bed. Still he did not awaken. Chuza and Joanna brought in the most skilled physicians to minister to him. The children and I prayed. When the cool night breezes finally swept in, we opened wide all the windows. In the courtyard below, all traces of the oak had been removed, creating an eerie void out there. A cold perspiration arose on my arms again as I sat by Tobiah's bed and listened to his short breaths weaken. Then, suddenly, they stopped. Tobiah's spirit left us.

SHEOL

We laid Tobiah's cleansed and shrouded body into a niche within the Kamith family tomb. Numbly, I chanted the prescribed prayers. When Chuza and Matti dragged a block of stone across the tomb's opening to seal it, an angry swirl of dust arose. I coughed and shielded my eyes from this literal reminder that my husband's body had already begun to decay. *"You are dust and to dust you shall return,"* Torah warns us.

Tobiah had believed that the dead inhabited a region called Sheol. Perhaps his soul was now consigned to such a place, as his body lay decomposing in this tomb. *"There is no work or thought or knowledge or wisdom in Sheol,"* according to the wisdom writings. What I did not know then, but learned in the days and weeks following my husband's death, was that the souls of the living could inhabit their own particular Sheol.

My Sheol was a place of separation where sight dimmed, sound faded away, and feeling numbed. I walked, talked, and cared for my children, but I performed these tasks of the living from somewhere within the gray mists of the land of the dead. When I worked with my hands, I couldn't stop myself from the senseless repetition of certain motions. I cracked nuts with a small wooden hammer until Razi had to pry the tool from my fingers. There was something inside one of them that I was supposed to find, wasn't there?

I thought writing might help me escape my Sheol's dull twilight, so I wrote about the trials that had beset Tobiah and me during the past six years, and how we were gradually overcoming them. The estates had struggled, but survived; all of our children lived and thrived; new buds of love had begun to form on the disease-battered tree of our marriage. But recounting these blessings only added to my grief. How would these estates, these children, and I survive without Tobiah? I put my scrolls aside.

In time, I learned to welcome my sojourns in Sheol. When I wandered outside its borders, memories stabbed at me. I might see Tobiah's cold, ashen body laid out on the long table in my workroom, Mariamme and I sitting by helplessly, like legless, armless beggars along the roadside, Joanna hemming the shroud, taking tiny stitches and setting them into perfect rows in tribute to the righteous man who would wear this garment. Or Razi cleansing her master's body with rosemary-scented water, a fragrance that had once so intoxicated Tobiah and me. Or Tobiah's lively, long-fingered hands caressing me or cradling our children at birth or grasping Gad's stubby fingers in loving acceptance. Or the two of us on our last night together, him sewn into his white linen shroud and me resting my head on his stilled heart until dawn came and separated us forever. My Sheol's shroud of gloom deadened the pains of my loss, so I visited there frequently.

Naomi, Chuza, and Joanna visited us every day. Miryam came often, until her husband, Yosef, suddenly took ill. Though I couldn't concentrate on what my friends and family were saying, their presence did console me. My brother's support was a particular comfort. He showed great kindness to each of my children. Only Chuza could make them laugh. Perhaps I had judged him too harshly in the past. Perhaps he was finally becoming the righteous man Father had taught him to be.

Gad's anguish worried all of us. "I should of waked him, I should of waked him," he repeated, day in and day out, despite our assurances that he bore no blame for his father's death. Gad needed distraction, but I was too tired to walk with him as I used to. Naomi took to bringing Gad to Nazareth with her, sometimes for several days at a time. In the village, he toted water, tended gardens, and fed the animals. When he was in Nazareth, he didn't cry.

Everyone assured me that grief caused my fatigue, and that it would gradually lessen. My energy would return in a few moons, they said. But my weariness deepened with each passing day. I rested more than I worked.

Since our laws didn't permit a wife to inherit her husband's property, Matti, at age fourteen, was Tobiah's heir. His obligations frequently drew him away from the house, so I didn't see much of him, but, from the brooding silences he maintained when he was at home, I knew he inhabited his own Sheol.

From the couch on which I spent much of my day, I could hear Mariamme reading aloud from the Scriptures. Her voice sounded shrill and urgent. She was seeking answers. Staying close to the father she had loved so dearly. Mariamme had lost her advocate and her protector, just as I had lost mine when I was her age. I knew that Tobiah's death would change my daughter's life forever, and this knowledge settled another layer onto my sledge of grief.

One morning I heard a crash from the library. Wresting myself from the narcotic of my Sheol, I went to investigate and found clay tablets shattered on the library's stone floor. Matti sat at Tobiah's desk, his head buried under his arms. At the sound of my sandals crunching chunks of broken tablet, he raised his head and said mournfully, "I can't make sense of it, Mother. Father should have accounted separately for rents, wages, taxes, and so on. But he mixed everything up. And he left so much out. I don't know what I own, what I owe, or what to do next." He pinched his nose to stop his tears.

I rubbed my son's sagging shoulders. "This is so much responsibility for you."

He sniffled and handed me a parchment. "This came yesterday." I unrolled a legal document, written in Greek, and tried to absorb its contents. "It summons me to appear in court for nonpayment of some tax," Matti explained. "I've been going through Father's accounts, but I can't find anything relating to this matter. There are other problems, too. I need Uncle Chuza's help."

A spider ambled over a shard of the smashed tablets and disappeared into a tiny hole in the wall. "Chuza is occupied with his own affairs," I pointed out. "I can help you."

"Mother, there will be legal battles. Women can't appear in court. I need an experienced, influential man to help me. I'm worried that we may lose our ancestral lands."

We heard the clink of coins dropping onto a table. Chuza had arrived for his daily visit. Since we'd been so suddenly deprived of the income from Tobiah's tutoring and magistrate duties, we had no ready source of coin for our everyday needs. Chuza had been supplying this without my even asking for it. He joined us in the library, and Matti showed him the document from the court, as well as several others: a foreclosure warning, a demand for a loan repayment, and a boundary dispute.

Chuza sighed. "Unfortunately, I'm not surprised. I've seen this before. When the unscrupulous see a young heir, they sense vulnerability and seize the opportunity."

We were only a woman and a young man now, no longer protected by a powerful leader of the city. Unprincipled, greedy men might conspire to steal our land. And, though Tobiah had ceased discussing financial matters with me long ago, the signs of deterioration were all around us. Tobiah had cut back on the household allowance and had taken up teaching for profit. He couldn't afford to buy slaves nor could he maintain them. Whether we were threatened by evildoers or by the effects of Tobiah's incompetence, we needed help.

Joanna arrived with a date sweet cake and found the three of us studying the document from the court. She frowned when I joined Matti in pressing Chuza for his intervention. "Assisting widows and orphans is a Jew's sacred duty," I reminded Chuza, not that performing mitzvoth had ever motivated my brother before.

Matti mounted a more convincing argument. "Uncle, you pledged to my father that you would assist me when I became steward of the family lands."

Chuza held up his hand to silence us. "I did and I will. But I have other duties as well, and now I must attend to those. We'll start in on all this tomorrow, Mattityahu."

In leaving, he passed by Joanna, and the corners of his mouth turned up in a suppressed smile. It could have been a gloat. Joanna ignored him and spoke up even before he was out of earshot. "This will give Chuza access to all your financial information and therefore enormous influence over the handling of all your other affairs as well. You're putting yourselves at risk."

The broken pieces of the tablets containing Tobiah's haphazard financial accountings littered the floor. Matti bent to pick them up. "I can't do this myself, Joanna. Chuza has supported and advocated for me for years. He has been kinder to me at times than my own father was."

"What choice do we have?" I observed.

Joanna groaned. "Don't you see? This is his pattern. It's how he traps people. He makes us think we have no other choice. But we do. We just have to keep searching for it."

"No. I trust Chuza," Matti insisted. "I'm pleased he's agreed to help us."

I was too tired to argue more about this and busied myself picking up the broken tablets.

"This will change everything," she warned.

"Everything has already changed," I said. Though this decision didn't feel completely right to me, nothing else did either. At least Chuza's assisting Matti would limit the interruptions of my sojourns in my Sheol.

For months, Chuza and Matti combed through the financial records of the estates, reorganizing and updating them. They rode out together to supervise the harvest and the plantings. They spoke with every worker about his wages and every tenant about his rent.

My brother had friends all over Sepphoris. Though his land holdings were small, certainly nothing like Tobiah's, he was considered a patron. His position within Herod Antipas's inner circle allowed him to influence appointments to official posts, negotiate tax relief, and manipulate legal proceedings. He had garnered many friends by granting such "favors." His clients reciprocated by providing him with information and performing a myriad of special tasks for him.

Through his connections, Chuza tracked down the holders and the amounts of Tobiah's outstanding loans and renegotiated repayment of these debts. In the courtrooms of the basilica, Chuza knew everyone by name, from the lowliest scribe to the most exalted judge. Time after time, Matti reported, his uncle argued brilliantly on our behalf. An order for payment of back taxes was rescinded. A lien on one of the estates was lifted. Foreclosure deadlines were extended. Matti believed that our family holdings would not have survived without his uncle's intervention. My son's spirits lifted, raising Gad's and Mariamme's, too. And even mine. Despite Tobiah's death, life swirled on all around me, drawing me into its whirlwind, demanding that I abandon my Sheol.

On a raw day in Tetbeth, the final legal matter was scheduled for disposal. I wanted to thank Chuza for his help in the courts in particular, so I decided to meet him and Matti at the courthouse to personally express my gratitude. By walking there myself, I would also prove to my brother that I was trying to regain my strength. He had joined the chorus of people who, concerned about my health, had been nagging me to get off my couch and venture from the house.

Heading into a chill wind all the way to the agora, I had to hold my mantle tightly under my chin. This rainy season had come early. The cold had lodged in my legs, and nothing could drive it out. My limbs stiffened and weakened. I'd become extremely clumsy since Tobiah's death, so much so that, when I got to the basilica, I didn't have the energy to ascend its high stone staircase to wait inside where it would be warmer.

I turned my back to the slash of the wind and waited for Matti and Chuza at the bottom of the stairway. Heads turned in passing. A woman alone always drew stares in this cold, critical city. But in my dark tunic and heavy veil, with my hair bound and covered, I was obviously not a prostitute, so I was left alone.

Chuza and Matti finally appeared on the wide porch of the basilica. Chuza had his arm around Matti. The two of them descended the stairway to my side, and Chuza said jovially, "Your troubles are over, sister. Mattityahu is now perfectly capable of managing his own estates."

I took my brother's hand. "My family is profoundly grateful to you."

Matti stared down at his boots, saying nothing. Though I knew he had thanked his uncle many times before, he didn't echo my formal expression of gratitude at this significant moment. I thought this uncharacteristically rude of him. "Mattityahu?" I prompted.

Matti cracked his knuckles, then he blurted out, "Mother, I don't want to manage the estates. I want to study engineering and architecture."

"In time you can return to your apprenticeship," I assured him. "They'll be building that theater for years to come."

"No. I've learned all that I can there." He lowered his head and mumbled. "I want to study somewhere else."

I hated to refuse him because I knew how much he loved his

mathematics and architecture studies. But my son going anywhere at this time, so soon after his father's death, was unthinkable. I rubbed the back of his hand to soften the blow I had to deliver. "Matti, we can't get along without you now. You're too important to all of us. Perhaps, in a few years, you could go to Jerusalem or Caesarea to study."

He pulled his hand away. "No, our cities don't have what I need." He pulled at the neck hole in his tunic, overheated even on this chilly day. "Mother, I must go to Rome."

To Rome! A child of mine go to Rome! My mouth turned dry as dust. I couldn't speak.

"Herod Antipas plans to build a new city on the western shore of the Sea of Galilee. Mother, this is my opportunity! I could become a great architect, a great Jewish architect, if I had the proper education. And the only place to get that education is Rome." He spoke in a mature, controlled tone. He must've been practicing this speech for some time. "I expect you will say that Father would never have permitted it."

I found my voice. "He never would have imagined a child of his abandoning his land and people to build palaces and baths!" But then I was suddenly so tired, I just wanted to lie down on the cold steps and go to sleep. To return to my Sheol where *there is no work or thought or knowledge or wisdom.* I gave in to my exhaustion and slumped down onto a step.

Matti sat next to me and pleaded. "I don't like managing farms and properties. I hate it! Chuza could act as my guardian while I'm in Rome. With his management, our lands will be in better hands than they've been in years. Look at how much he has done for us in just a few months."

I looked up at Chuza. "You wouldn't approve of this, would you?"

"It would be a burden for me." He crossed his arms. "Formal appointment of guardianship would be necessary were Mattityahu to leave the country."

"I need to leave, Mother. I want to do more with my life than . . . " he swallowed, then said boldly, "than steward a few rock-strewn hectares in a minor Roman province."

My energy suddenly returned. I spit out my hot, barbed words. "You call our sacred land 'a minor Roman province'? Shame on you!"

Chuza motioned to Matti to step away from us. Matti removed

himself and stood several paces away, tapping his foot anxiously. Chuza helped me up to my feet and spoke slowly, carefully choosing each word. "Mattityahu is a man now, sister. He doesn't want to follow the life his father chose for him. Neither did I. Neither did Lev. Think of Matti as Lev. His ideas of how to live his life are different from his father's. Not wrong. Different."

"Different—and wrong," I protested. "Look what happened to Lev! Now I understand Father's wisdom. Righteousness and holiness are attained by living a simple life in village communities, not by building cities for Imperial Rome."

"The Jews who built the Temple for Herod, a Roman-appointed king, weren't living a holy life? They weren't engaged in a sacred act?" Chuza challenged.

A prickle of annoyance rose on the back of my neck. "They were building the Temple, not a Roman stadium! This is all just a childish fantasy of Matti's. Antipas doesn't want Jewish architects for his imitation Roman city, anyway."

"He does if he hopes for any support from his people, and he will need Jewish architects for the synagogue he plans to build in Tiberius. It will be second to none in the land. Danya, everyone who has worked with your son says he could be the one to design it, if he receives the proper education."

"But Mattityahu can't be an architect. Life has made him a landholder. He has no choice, just as his father had none." I didn't dwell on how unhappy managing the family lands had made Tobiah.

"Tobiah could've returned to his scholarly life in Jerusalem," Chuza pointed out, "and he'd be alive today if he had. I offered to help him but he refused. Mattityahu, however, would accept my assistance."

My left arm twitched. I clutched it with my right hand. "You just said that would burden you."

"It would, but the truth is that I have no son and I love yours. I would do this for him."

I looked at Chuza and then at Matti. The two of them looked more like father and son than Tobiah and Matti ever had. A dust storm of confusion whipped up within me. Even without Joanna's warning, I knew I could never completely trust Chuza. Ever. He could find ways to take over the Kamith family lands and leave us all beggars in the road. On the other hand, Ezri's enslavement had forced Tobiah out of his scholarly pursuits and into management of the family's lands, which had become a form of slavery for Tobiah. Should Ezri and Tobiah's misfortune also hold our son captive?

"Danya, let Mattityahu have the choice. He can do this without your permission, as we both know. But he is a good son, and he won't do it without your blessing."

In my heart, I cried out to The Holy One, as I had so many times since Tobiah's death. "Where are You, Adonai? I beg You to make Your presence known to me. Tell me Your will." As always, a profound silence followed my plea.

"I'll think about it," I told Chuza. "Mattityahu, walk home with me."

The wind had let up. I didn't need to hold my mantle around me, so I leaned on my son with that hand. Matti said, "I hate the thought of leaving you and Mariamme and Gad, Mama. Especially now. So if you forbid it, I'll stay."

A thin crack of sunlight escaped the fortress of clouds above us. It threw itself down on the paving stones, painting a thin pathway across the agora. We stepped into the light, and the sun warmed the top of my head. I recalled the time I'd been allowed to choose the path I would follow. I had held our marriage contract in my hands, and Tobiah had invited me to tear it up. He had put his own desires aside, loving me enough to let me choose. And, just last Sukkot, as the two of us gazed out over the glowing city of Jerusalem, Tobiah had placed a pistachio nut into my hand. He had pressed the shell into my palm, curled my fingers around it, and enclosed my fist in his hands, squeezing until I felt the shell dig into my flesh. A shell of sin and guilt and duty had grown over it, but it was still there. The sweet, nourishing nutmeat of his love for me. The love I had been free to accept or reject. It was there even now.

Love had come from the choice Tobiah had given me. I must trust that love would come from Matti's. Everything would change again. It was time for me to abandon my Sheol. *"O dweller in the dust, awake . . ."*

ARRANGING A MARRIAGE

Mattityahu ben Tobiah to my dear Mother, greetings
I hope this letter reaches you by the second day of Elul so that you
know how I long to be with you and Mariamme and Gad on this
day marking the first anavirsari of Father's death. Uncle Chuza's
friends here in Rome have found me the finest teachers in the
world, but they cost a lot. Everything in Rome costs more than we
antissipaded, though I am living cheaply. Please ask Chuza to sell
ten more hectares to cover my added expenses. I will buy the land
back some day. I worry that my need for money will deprive you,
dear Mama. The death of Caesar Augustus also worries me. It is
said that his sucksesor, Tiberius, does not like Jews and may one
day expel us from this city. So I must study very hard and return
to you as soon as possible. I pray that your health improves. I am
lonely and I miss you all very much.
Farewell

Mother to my dear son Mattityahu, greetings
Your letter brought us joy. Though we miss you greatly, I'm pleased
that you have good instructors and are working hard at your stud-
ies. On the first anniversary of your father's death, we went to his
tomb to remember and honor him. We recited from Scripture and
the writings. We didn't transfer his bones to an ossuary. We'll wait
until you return to do that. Your father led a pious, righteous life,

and I believe his soul lives on, in peace, with The Holy One, even though he didn't believe in such a possibility.

Shortly after you set sail for Rome, Miryam's husband, Yosef, died. She now visits with me frequently. We share memories and sorrows, and Miryam's firm belief that The Holy One cares especially for the broken-hearted comforts me. Yeshua usually accompanies his mother on her visits to me. He and Mariamme study together. They sorely miss Tobiah's tutelage. Mariamme reads so much I worry about her eyesight. She rarely gets outdoors or engages in any physical activity. Perhaps it is time for her to marry. She spends too much time alone or taking care of me. Chuza continues to visit every day, and I appreciate his cheerful support. He tries to distract Mariamme, inviting her to banquets and ceremonies, but she usually declines. Gad, however, thrives by getting out and seeing people. Most days he works in Nazareth, supervised by Naomi. Chuza traded the horses and the carriage to Salvius Marcellus in exchange for the Roman's cancellation of a loan he'd made to your father. I showed Chuza your request that he sell more land and he's working on it. Don't worry that the cost of your education deprives us of anything other than your presence, dear Matti.

And now I send news that tickles me. Naomi and Joanna's business grows more and more successful. The wives of Chuza's Roman friends adorn their houses with Naomi's tapestries and lavish praise on Chuza for having a wife with such a clever business sense. This makes Chuza fume. The only thing more embarrassing for him than having a wife who works is having a wife who is so successful at it! Joanna is the pet of Sepphoris society women at the moment. She receives clients and admirers in the shop on the agora while Naomi weaves in Nazareth. Two village women help her with dyeing and weaving. One of these is Herma, a daughter-in-law of Samuel. It turns out that when she isn't trailing along behind her sour husband, Herma has a sense of humor. Naomi says she keeps them all laughing as they work. I wish I could join in their fun, but I'm still afflicted with this strange illness that saps my strength and weakens my legs. I've consulted with some physicians.

They, too, are puzzled. One suggested I drink porcupine blood, but the others say my heart is strong so that would be a waste of time. That was welcome news! I've begun to limp, so people worry that I'm in pain, but I'm not. My only real complaint is the lack of your company, dear son. But in time this illness will pass, you will be back in Galilee, and my discomforts forgotten. I long to embrace you on that happy day.

Farewell

Mariamme and I undressed in the subdued light of the miqveh chamber. My daughter knelt to remove my footwear. Instead of my own sandals, I now wore Tobiah's boots because they gave my ankles some support. Our tunics and underclothing shed, Mariamme slipped her arm under mine to help me climb down the stairway into the pool. A good thing after all, I thought, that Tobiah had built this second set of steps. How useful they were in a way we never could've foreseen. With Mariamme on the other stairway supporting me, I could still enter the pool to perform the ritual cleansing after my monthly menses.

"Aaahhh," we both said, as we descended, step by step into the miqveh. The bedrock containing these waters kept them delightfully cool even at the height of the dry season. A heat wave had descended on us two Sabbaths ago, and we'd been anticipating the pleasure of this purification rite since then. When we got to the bottom of the pool, though, we had to squat down to completely immerse ourselves.

"The water level's too low," said Mariamme. She pulled the plug from the pipe joining our pool to the storage pool. Water spurted in from the 'otsar. Mariamme giggled and placed her face in the little waterfall tumbling down from the pipe. Her dark hair fell in glistening rivulets down her back and breasts. She had begun menstruating and was maturing beautifully. Her hips were still a bit narrow, but they would soon be broad enough to bear children. My breasts, hips, and legs looked misshapen and withered compared to hers. But Mariamme smiled at me as if I were as beautiful as she. Smoothing back her hair, she said, "Don't you feel better already? We should come here every day during heat waves, Mama. For your health."

I leaned back against the stairway and stretched out one leg. It obeyed, floating like a rose petal. In the water, my leg lifted and turned gracefully with no reluctance or weakness. "This is lovely," I said. And, for a moment, I imagined myself dancing a lively circle dance at a wedding, maybe at my own daughter's nuptials. Then the leg twitched and, uncontrollably, dropped like a rock. "But stairs are becoming so difficult for me. Even with your help I might not be able to make it next month."

"Mama, don't say that. You'll get better. Someday you'll bring your granddaughter here."

"Oh, really? And whose daughter will that be?"

"Matti's, of course. This is his house, and soon enough he'll fill it with a wife and children."

"You, too, have a duty to fill a house with children," I reminded her.

Mariamme shoved the plug back into the pipe, shutting off the flow of fresh water. "I think that's enough for now," she said.

"Maybe not," I corrected her. "You're old enough to marry. We must start talking about this."

She fell backwards into a float. "Just because I'm old enough to marry doesn't mean that I should. It's little more than a year since Father's death."

"Yes, more than a year. Mariamme, this delay is my fault. I don't want to give you up. Tobiah didn't want to, either, but we both agreed that we had to—for your sake. It's time to betroth you to some good man. He'll have to agree to wait to wed until you feel truly ready, however. Tobiah waited for me, and I'll see that you are given the same consideration."

Mariamme paddled around on her back. She sighed. "What good man would want me?"

I splashed her. "What good man wouldn't?"

She laughed. "I won't marry anyone old or fat or stupid. And no one like Yochanen who would order me around like a slave. And no one who would forbid me to read or write. I won't live far away, either."

"Hmmmm. Not this one, not that one. You sound just like me at your age. Joanna should be here to listen to this! Thousands of men in Sepphoris and I bet not a one of them is suitable," I teased.

"True. The only man suitable for me is in Nazareth."

I waded closer to her to read the expression on her face. Surely she was joking. Mariamme was an aristocrat, not a village peasant. But she floated on her back with her eyes closed, as if she were dreaming.

"In Nazareth?" I asked.

"Oh, Mother, isn't it obvious that I'm in love with Yeshua?"

"In love with Yeshua!"

The only sound in the chamber for a long time was the drip, drip, drip from the imperfectly plugged pipe. So many times when Miryam came to visit me, Yeshua accompanied her. How nice for Mariamme, I thought, that she had another student to study with, the two of them reading while Miryam and I visited. I was so immersed in my own grief that I had failed to notice that my daughter was falling in love with someone completely inappropriate for her!

My arms and shoulders chilled, then stiffened. I stretched a towel around them. "Yeshua is a wonderful young man, Mariamme. Your father loved him, as do I. His mother is my dearest friend. But you know that Yeshua has no land. He's a peasant and therefore not a match for you. As the daughter of a priest and a member of a landed family, you have an obligation to bear sons who will dedicate themselves to preserving our sacred lands and being leaders of our people."

Mariamme rolled out of her float and stood. "Yeshua has no land, but he has vision, Mama, and great hopes for our people. He is powerful, though his power has nothing to do with owning land. He will be a leader of our people someday."

Of course I thought of Judah ben Hezekiah. Of his revolutionary hopes for our people. Then of the chaos and sorrow his movement had brought down upon everyone, including our own family. Was Galilee's fertile ground producing yet another revolutionary leader? During Mariamme's lifetime, Galilee had been uncharacteristically peaceful. She had no direct experience of the horrors of Roman vengeance, of the executions, massacres, and devastation that I had witnessed at her age. She had to understand the peril she might put herself in if she joined herself to Yeshua. I began calmly, "Mariamme, revolutionaries do not make good husbands."

She put her hands on her hips. "How would you know?"

"I just do."

Mariamme tilted her head and waited.

"Trust me, I know what I'm talking about." I pulled the towel tighter around me. "Now, let's go back to thinking about eligible young men from Sepphoris."

"No, Mama. How do you know revolutionaries make poor husbands?"

When Mariamme tilted her head that way and lowered her eyelids, she was imitating Gad. The two of them could be stubborn as donkeys. I knew she wouldn't let this go. But I would not tell her about Judah ben Hezekiah, partly out of pride. I didn't want my daughter to know that I'd almost followed Judah, even after I'd been married. But also because I was afraid that knowing about him and me might somehow give her permission to follow her rebel. I gave the pipe plug an extra punch and waited for the dripping to stop, and couched my arguments in generalities, trying to explain the difference between love and sexual attraction, and between loving a man and sharing a mutual love for a noble, righteous cause. But Mariamme was either too blinded by youthful desire or too willful to consider the distinctions I was trying to make.

She pushed her mouth into a pout. "Yeshua is not a typical revolutionary, Mother. He says love, not the sword, will transform and free us."

I pulled my towel tighter around my shoulders and found myself speaking as Tobiah would have. "Anyone who speaks of freedom for our people endangers himself and everyone associated with him. Rome doesn't care about the philosophies of the men who challenge its authority. It just eliminates them. Mariamme, I couldn't bear it if something happened to you!" The towel slipped from my hand and fell into the water as I hugged my precious daughter tightly.

She pushed herself away from me. Her lower lip quivered. "Marrying Yeshua is only a silly dream of mine, anyway. He says he can't marry me."

I relaxed. Good for Yeshua. At least he knows his place. I should've realized that and not gotten upset. I picked my towel out of the water and wrung it out. "We'll find you a good man, and you'll experience a happiness you can't even imagine now."

"No. I won't. You don't understand. I just know I'll always love Yeshua." Vigorously, she dried her beautiful, shining hair.

But I did understand. And I had made the sacrifice I was asking of her. If I hadn't, she wouldn't be here today! She should appreciate that. She should be grateful for all that I had done and wanted to continue to do for her. Mariamme was blessed with what I had always longed for: a mother, and a sympathetic one at that. But she refused to see this. Still, I tried to be patient. "Mariamme, some men are best admired and even loved, but not married. You'll just have to accept this as true."

From under the towel, her hair tumbled down in soft folds of black silk. Someday a husband would treasure the magnificent bounty of her hair. Someday she would treasure my wise advice. "Believe me. In time, you'll change your mind."

Mariamme suddenly ripped the towel from her head and looked at me, her eyes bright with renewed hope. "Yeshua could still change his mind," she said. "He isn't completely sure about his decision not to marry."

My scalp tingled. "Haven't you heard anything I just said? I'm not only trying to make you happy, I'm trying to keep you alive!" Suddenly, with no thought on my part, the twisted towel in my hand struck my daughter! We were both shocked. I had never hit my child before.

A scarlet stain flared across Mariamme's chest. She fled, naked, from the miqveh. I crawled out of the pool, untwisted the towel, and rubbed myself down with the wet, rough cloth. It was just to forbid her; unjust to strike her, I repeated to myself, scrubbing my skin raw in my attempt to assuage my guilt. Tobiah certainly wouldn't have been so patient. Not for one instant would he have countenanced the notion of his daughter marrying a peasant, no matter how gifted a one he might be.

Undried and unpurified, I fumbled with my clothing, as my heart ached for my daughter. If only she could understand that what might feel like cruelty was actually kindness, that broken hearts can mend, and that I loved her profoundly.

"Do not carry a sword," Judah had said. He should have added, "Or a wet towel."

It was more important than ever that I find a suitable husband for Mariamme, and soon. I invited Chuza for breakfast because he had a supper engagement and was leaving for Jerusalem the following day. I wanted him to be thinking of Mariamme's future when he met with his many important friends there. Razi set the table outside. She brought me a chair with arms to make rising from it easier. I settled myself down into it and set my walking stick under the table so Chuza wouldn't spot it and chide me for submitting to my weakness.

The door to the inner courtyard clicked open, and Chuza came through it bearing a basket of blackberries. He spotted only one other chair at the table and frowned. "Mariamme won't be joining us?"

"No. I sent her out with Gad. He loves to watch the construction of the new waterwheel."

"Old Zohar could've done that. What good are he and Razi anyway? They've become a needless expense."

"You know I couldn't get along without Razi and Zohar. I sent Mariamme out so that we could discuss a matter concerning her in private."

He grumbled about useless servants and household expenses while he settled himself into his chair. Though this was the largest chair we had, Chuza's haunches still hung over the sides of its seat. I set a bowl of hummus and a platter of melon slices in front of him and poured us each a cup of water, pausing to allow a cramp in my hands and forearms to loosen.

Chuza examined the contents of his cup. "No wine?"

"Not in the morning. At your suggestion, brother, I'm cutting household expenses."

"It was never intended that I should suffer from your economies, sister," he said sourly.

"Oh, Chuza, you're not the only one who can make a joke." I picked up the wine pitcher hidden beneath my chair and added some to his water cup.

"But I commend your thrift in other areas." He laughed. "And I apologize for my ill humor. I was disappointed when I didn't see my niece here. Now what's this matter concerning her?"

There were still moments when my longing for Tobiah caught me unawares and squeezed the breath from my chest. This was one of those times because I should have been having this conversation about our daughter with him. I added a few drops of wine to my own glass and drew a deep breath. "I think it's time for Mariamme to marry," I said slowly. "I would like your help in finding a suitable husband for her and in negotiating arrangements with his family."

"Hmmm. A suitable husband for Mariamme," he mused. He drained his cup and held it out for a refill. "She'll need a sizeable dowry because matching Mariamme well is important to this family's future prosperity." He took a handful of berries from the basket and dropped a few on my plate. They looked delicious, but I couldn't eat them because their seeds might stick in my throat. I'd been having difficulty swallowing some foods.

"I agree that a substantial dowry is essential. Should she ever be divorced or widowed, she needs proper endowment." I didn't mention, because I'd almost forgiven him, that Chuza had not dowered me when I'd married.

"Mariamme is the daughter and the granddaughter of priests on both sides of her lineage, a young woman of great value," he said. "If we're clever, we may get away without providing a dowry. We might even command a sizeable bridewealth from the husband's family."

Like you did from Tobiah's, I thought, but didn't say. "No, brother, that's an old-fashioned custom that no man would agree to today. My daughter must be dowered. She must have this protection. I think she'll need at least five hundred denarii. Most importantly, she must be matched to a man who will value her talents. I've promised her no one old or ignorant or living far away from us. And, it goes without saying, no one Roman, even if he happened to be Jewish." I had added the no Roman requirement. "So, given these considerations, let's discuss the possibilities." I picked an olive from the serving plate, removed the pit, and began to chew on it.

Chuza wiped his mouth with his sleeve. "Unfortunately, there's no money now to betroth her to an elite, educated, handsome young Jew from Sepphoris. Of course, that would be everyone's first choice. This harvest is the first in many years that will be profitable, though we can't be sure until all the accounts are tallied. In five years, more likely in ten, we'll have the dowry needed for such a match."

"Ten years? She'll be twenty-three years old! She can't wait that long to marry."

"What else can we do? Sell this valuable young woman to a farmer because the only dowry you can provide at this time is a herd of goats?"

Chuza could always find money when he wanted it. We both knew that. So, why was he holding back? I chewed on the olive, extracting the juice from its pulp as I reflected on how to gather the money for a suitable dowry.

"My bridewealth was five hundred denarii," I pointed out. Chuza had wheedled that sum from Tobiah at the time of our betrothal. Our marriage contract stipulated that this money be entrusted to my brother, as my oldest male relative. He was to hold this for me should I ever be widowed or divorced. I hadn't asked Chuza for it this year because I hadn't needed it. Now, I did. "I would be willing to use that for Mariamme's dowry."

Chuza shifted his weight in his chair, and it creaked. He ran his hand through his thinning hair. "Your mohar is gone," he said quietly.

"What do you mean, 'gone'?" I removed the olive pulp from my mouth.

"I lost it, years ago. Don't look at me that way. You didn't expect me to dig a hole and hide five hundred denarii in it, did you? I invested it for you, expecting to increase its value. By law I could've kept the profit from it for myself, but I wouldn't have done that. I would've given it all to you when you needed it."

"And so now I need it."

"Except that your mohar, along with some of my own money, cargo, and ten sailors are on the bottom of the Mediterranean Sea. I invested it in a trading ship that sank."

"Oh, Chuza, how could you have done such a thing?"

"Danya, I apologize. I'm truly sorry. But I was younger then, and sometimes unwise with money. I know I should've restored it, but I delayed in doing that, gambling that you might die before Tobiah and then I wouldn't have to. But since his death, I've set aside fifty denarii of my own money and will continue to do so every year until it is repaid."

"At that rate, it will take ten years! Ten years, again, is too long to wait to dower my daughter. We'll have to find the money somehow. Can we sell land?"

"If you sell any more land, the family's assets will be too depleted to recover. That much is certain." He rubbed his chin. "I could raise rents on your tenants."

"No. They're almost starving as it is."

"I could cut the wages of your workers."

"They're even hungrier than the tenants."

"I could dismiss your useless servants."

"They're family!"

Chuza drained another cup of watered wine. I worried a piece of cheese between my fingers, dropping it, crumb by crumb, onto my plate, and smothered an urge to further castigate Chuza for losing my bride-wealth. His financial expertise had been invaluable to the family during this last year, and we would continue to rely on it. Somehow, I knew he would find the dowry money we needed.

Mariamme called out to us from the kitchen window. "Uncle Chuza, Mama. Gad and I are back. Do you need anything out there?"

Chuza's face softened. "No thank you, my dear," he called back tenderly. He turned to me and said, "Mariamme looks just like her. Did anyone ever tell you that?"

"Looks like who?"

"Like your mother. Like Nahara."

"A few old women in the village said so, but they always say such things about grandchildren. They find something in the eyes or the nose or the crook of the forefinger that reminds them of one long deceased. I never paid them any mind."

"Well, she does. She has Nahara's complexion and her thoughtful eyes. That wave in her hair at the peak of her forehead is Nahara's; so are those expressive eyebrows that speak even when she is silent."

Though I was always hungry to hear about my mother, Chuza's remarks about my mother's appearance raised an uncomfortable prickle of heat on my neck. I fanned myself with a napkin. "My mother's hair? Are you certain?"

Almost timidly, Chuza set his empty cup upside down on the table. "I have a solution that I've been considering since Tobiah's death. You won't like it, Danya, but at least control your temper and consider it for a moment."

He stood up and lumbered back and forth like an ox. "I, too, have been thinking of Mariamme's future and fretting about the lack of a proper dowry for her. I also worry about how to support you since," he pointed to my poorly hidden walking stick, "your illness precludes your remarriage. I'm disturbed by the possible dilution of the family's resources, by my lack of an heir, and by Joanna's desire for a divorce."

He took a deep breath. "My solution is that I should take Mariamme as my wife."

A fit of coughing seized me as a piece of bread stuck in my throat. Chuza rapped me on the back, but I pushed him away. "Don't touch me!" I gasped, struggling to breathe.

Chuza waited for my coughing fit to subside. "The law permits an uncle to marry his niece," he argued.

I choked again. He handed me a cup of water and shot his arguments at me like arrows. "I need an heir. I'll divorce Joanna, granting her her fondest wish. I'm already in my forties, so Mariamme won't have to put up with me for long. When I die, she'll be able to marry again, probably while still young enough to bear more children. Your five hundred denarii will be restored to you in a few years. Finally, I pledge that, no matter how ill you become or what happens to the Kamith family lands, I will provide for you and Gad."

I drank more water and fought to control my breathing. Like a helpless insect, I saw too late the elaborate web that now ensnared me. Tobiah's sudden death had stripped us of a husband and father's protection, and Chuza had lulled us into trusting him by feigning sympathy and kindness. He had filled Matti's head with silly dreams, making him believe that he needed to be educated in Rome, and then tricked the boy into naming him his guardian. Chuza now controlled every drachma of our support, even to the very crumbs of bread I choked on. I was a widow whose son was too far away to help and whose fortunes were controlled by an avaricious, lustful, scheming half-brother.

"It is an abomination! It turns my stomach!"

He flushed. I hoped it was with shame, but I didn't care if it was with murderous rage. He would have to kill me before he could have my child. I stared into his little dark eyes, the flesh around them so bloated with excess that they looked like shrunken raisins dropped into bread dough. "Why are you so evil?"

He blinked rapidly as if holding back tears. "Evil? Me, evil? But I love Mariamme!"

I howled. "You don't know what love is. You only know desire. I would never give my daughter to someone as depraved as you. Furthermore, Mariamme would never—ever—want you!"

His eyes narrowed. His lips tightened. His face looked hard as a grinding stone. "If I don't get her, no one will. I'll see to it that there will never be money enough to dower her."

"She will be properly dowered, and I will find a husband for her myself. The courts will require you to restore my mohar to me, even if it means selling all you own. You owe me my bridewealth of five hundred denarii. It is so written in the ketubbah."

"What ketubbah?"

"The marriage contract of Danya of Nazareth and Tobiah ben Mattityahu of the Kamith family. The document witnessed in Jerusalem and stored in the courthouse in Sepphoris."

He snickered. "The copy of your ketubbah in the courthouse makes no mention of a bridewealth. I've seen to that already. And those who witnessed the signing of the original document have long since died, except Joanna whose testimony would be suspect, if it were even allowed. If you press your case, it will come down to your word against mine. What magistrate would believe that Tobiah ben Mattityahu, a prudent man, a doctor of the law himself, would be so foolish as to have agreed to a marriage granting your family a bridewealth of five hundred denarii and his receiving no dowry in return? I will remind you that I have many friends in the courts of Sepphoris and Jerusalem. You wanted my help in arranging a marriage for your daughter. I have done just that. You have no choice."

RETURN TO NAZARETH

The next morning, Chuza and Herod Antipas's retinue set out for Rosh Hashanah in Jerusalem. They would stay through the Sukkot festival. He left this message for me: "While I am away, I expect you to make preparations for the nuptial."

Joanna had once given me advice about submitting to Chuza's schemes that I had ignored at the time. "He makes us think we have no other choice. But we do."

I sold jewelry to a pawnbroker. A pair of gold earrings and a silver brooch garnered enough coin for me to hire a private messenger to carry this letter to my son in Rome.

Mother to my dear son Mattityahu, greetings
You must return to Sepphoris. Chuza has betrayed us. He is trying
to force your sister into marrying him. I suspect he is also scheming
to take over your patrimony for himself. He is not the kindly uncle
you think he is. We need you. Come immediately.
Farewell

I gathered my family and fled to Nazareth. Though I was loath to put Mariamme anywhere near Yeshua, Nazareth was the only place in the world I had ever felt safe. Gad, Mariamme, Razi, and Zohar traveled on foot. I rode on the donkey because I wasn't strong enough to walk that short a distance. We took only what we could carry and strap onto the other donkey: changes of clothing, some bedding, and food for a few days. Naomi took us in, questioning neither the inconvenience nor the danger this posed for her.

In the courtyard Naomi shared with Miryam's family, I set out the cheese, bread, and figs we had brought as a supper for everyone. The men sat at one long table, the women at another, but the subject at both tables was how to protect Mariamme. Where could we seek refuge? Was there a village, a city, or even a country that lay beyond Chuza's reach? If one existed, how could my family support itself there?

All this would take time to investigate. In the meantime, it was decided that my servant, Zohar, with help from Miryam's sons, should build a house in this village for me, Mariamme, and Gad. We might have to stay here for quite some time, at least until Matti returned from Rome. Even under the best of circumstances, that would be several months. After the house was built, Zohar and Razi would return to Sepphoris and maintain the Kamith family home until it was safe for us to return to it.

"We get to live in Naz-ret?" Gad said, clapping his hands. He didn't understand that defying Chuza carried the danger of retribution, and that this was the reason we would cluster around the protection of the courtyard of our friends.

Yaakov, the oldest son in Miryam's family and its head since Yosef's death, propped his toddler on his knee. "We'll need a third new house. Marriage is Mariamme's best protection, so she should wed immediately. Yeshua should take her as his wife."

Joses, Yeshua's elder by two years, said, "Yes, when Chuza returns from Jerusalem, Mariamme will already be the wife of another man."

Mariamme, sitting between Yeshua's sisters, blushed. They embraced her and Assia said, "We would love to have Mariamme as our sister."

I had not removed my daughter from Chuza's clutches only to have her fall into Yeshua's, but I kept silent.

"I know you're in love with her," said Shimon, giving Yeshua a shove. "You're always making excuses to get yourself over to her house."

Yeshua looked at Mariamme. His forehead crumpled as if struck by a blow of Shimon's fist. Mariamme said quietly, "Perhaps Yeshua does not wish to marry."

"Not marry? Nonsense," said Yaakov. He slapped Yeshua on the back.

"Yeshua is seventeen years old. I took a wife when I was his age. Marriage is the best thing for a man. What do you say, brother?"

Yeshua stood and faced my daughter. "It's no secret that I love Mariamme. I long to take her as my wife, but . . . "

"But she's too good for the likes of you!" Shimon shouted.

"But," Yeshua continued, "I can't marry. I think I must join the Essenes at Qumran. An all-male community. I've prayed about this for a long time. I believe it is The Holy One's will for me."

Mariamme covered her face with her hands. Assia and Lydia tightened their arms around her. Joses laughed scornfully. "The Holy One's will? That makes no sense. Since you're so religious, Yeshua, we shouldn't have to remind you that it is a sacred duty to marry and procreate."

"Yes, O pious one!" said Yaakov. "Why would Adonai give you and those at Qumran your own Law?"

I couldn't restrain myself any longer. "I can't allow a marriage between my daughter and Yeshua. Chuza could be vengeful. He could hurt your family in all kinds of ways. At the very least, he could unleash his tax collecting friends on you and others in this village."

Everyone dreaded tax collectors. Some of them were extortionists, and peasants who refused to meet their unjust demands were subject to land seizure. Also, Yeshua now supervised a crew of hired men working in Sepphoris. His construction skills and facility with Greek had become valuable assets. Since Yosef's death, Yeshua's work supplied his family with some much needed coin. I pointed out that Chuza was capable of using his influence to force the termination of Yeshua's employment.

These arguments seemed to sway Yeshua's brothers. I didn't need to voice my unwavering opposition to a marriage between my daughter and their landless, possibly revolutionary, brother.

But I had opened a door with my fears about Chuza taking revenge on them.

"Chuza might punish us for giving refuge to Mariamme even if Yeshua doesn't marry her," Yaakov grumbled to his brothers. "Maybe Danya and her family should move on and leave us out of their family squabbles. I have my own wife and children to protect."

Miryam rose and collected her sons' dinner plates, clacking them one by one onto a stack. "There will be no more such talk," she said. "Our friends stay with us as long as they need to."

Supper broke up disagreeably, but in the morning, the men began to gather the wood and stone needed to build our houses, and I began Mariamme's instruction in village living. We would have to do our share of the communal chores, so that we didn't become too great a burden on our friends. Also, experiencing the hardships of village living for herself would help Mariamme appreciate another reason why I did not want her to be a peasant's wife.

Though grinding grain had been a regular chore of mine at her age, Mariamme had never performed this task. In Sepphoris our wheat was ground at the storage silos and conveyed in sacks to our house. I poured some barley kernels into the trough in the mill. Because of my illness, I didn't have the strength to help Mariamme rotate the handle of the top-stone that crushed the kernels into a coarse meal. So, from a bench in the shade outside Naomi's door, I directed her efforts. She plodded around and around the dusty circuit, pushing the stone's long handle until blisters bubbled up on her fingers. Then she bruised her shoulder trying to shove with it instead of with her sore hands. Once, she stepped on the soiled hem of her tunic, stumbled, and let go of her end of the topstone's handle. She caught herself before falling all the way down to the ground, but not before the handle clipped her from behind.

"Owwww," she whined, rubbing the back of her head.

I was tempted to help her, even though I wouldn't have been of much use, but I kept to my bench. These were all lessons my daughter had to learn, just as I had. When the grinding was done, I sent her to the well. I stayed in the shade and brooded over Joanna and the difficult position she was in. My sister-in-law had probably known nothing about Chuza's machinations to entrap Mariamme. Of course, she would be furious with Chuza when she found out. But wouldn't she harbor at least a tiny hope that he be successful? Finally, Joanna could be rid of him. She could marry someone else and have the children she had always wanted. I could imagine her giving into the temptation to accept Chuza's scheme because I might do so if I were in her position.

Joanna's abrupt arrival in a hired carriage interrupted my dark thoughts. She helped herself down from the carriage and directed the driver to wait at a distance. "Naomi told me," she said. "Chuza's really done it this time, hasn't he?"

Strands of her beautiful honey-colored hair sprang from the captivity of her combs. She looked as disheveled as she had that day on the Temple Mount during Sukkot except then her disarray had been intentional, a ploy to goad Chuza into divorcing her. On that day, I had pledged that, if a way presented itself, I would help her win her release from Chuza. But I never dreamed that her rescue might require the sacrifice of my own child. I prayed that Joanna had not come to hold me to my promise.

I spoke up before she could kiss me in greeting and before she dared to ask it. "Joanna, I'm very sorry, but your freedom can't be gained at Mariamme's expense."

Joanna blew at a strand of hair that had dropped in front of her red-rimmed eyes. "Of course it can't," she snapped. "After all these years, Danya, don't you know me better than that? Why do you always think you're more virtuous than I am?"

Her remark stung. It might be true. I did think I was better than Joanna, didn't I? Because I valued learning and studied Torah and she, I assumed, valued only pleasure and pretty things. Because she socialized with Romans and even liked some of them. Because my husband had been a good man whereas hers had proven to be evil. My name, Danya, means "God is my judge." God judges. Not Danya. All this time I'd been judging Joanna when I should have just been loving her. God is my judge and hers. I'd been so wrong.

"Joanna, forgive me. You've never been anything but kind and loving to me and to my children. How unjust of me to think you would harm us now. I beg you to pardon me."

"I do. Because you must be out of your mind with worry. I know you must first protect your daughter, and that is also my intention. That's why I'm here. I have a plan. Where is she?"

"At the well. She'll be back soon."

"Where can the three of us talk privately?"

"In the orchard. There's a bench where I can sit." I could only stand for short periods now and sitting down on the ground had become impossible.

We moved to the bench under an almond tree and waved Mariamme over to us as she returned with the water jars. Joanna got right down to business. "I have a solution to our dilemma, Mariamme, but I need your help and your mother's."

"Of course," said Mariamme. I said nothing.

Joanna smoothed back her hair again and then covered it with her mantle. She looked around to confirm that no one else was in the orchard. Nevertheless, she whispered. "Find me a lover. Conceal the arrangement from Chuza."

Mariamme dropped one of the water jugs and it emptied quickly into the thirsty ground. "What?" we both exclaimed.

"Shhh," said Joanna. "I've decided to take the advice that my Roman women friends have been giving me for years. Since I believe I'm fertile, I should take a lover, get pregnant, and tell Chuza the child is his. That way, I'll have the child I've longed for, and Chuza will have his heir. He'll give up this nonsense of another wife."

Mariamme laid the other jar on the ground. "You can't just take a lover."

Joanna kept talking, faster and faster. "I dare not attempt such a liaison in Sepphoris. Danya, you must find me someone discreet. I'll pay him well. All I ask is that he be healthy. And transient. I don't want him around once I'm pregnant. Mariamme, you must help by stringing Chuza along, making him think you'll marry him, but delaying the wedding until I can prove I'm with child. No one, except the three of us, can know about this. What do you say?"

I was too shocked to say anything, but Mariamme didn't hesitate. "I say no. You can't debase yourself like this for my sake, Aunt."

"Debase myself? Pooh! I should've done this years ago. Many other women have, over many thousands of years."

"But what if Chuza suspects the child isn't his?" Mariamme said.

"He won't object. He'll be saving face because people will think he's virile enough to father a child. And he'll have his heir."

I found my voice. "Joanna, you would be risking your life! If you were exposed as an adulteress, you could be stoned!" I put my arms around her. "I see what an extraordinary person you are and how much you love Mariamme, sister. But this defilement of yourself isn't you. Besides, it won't work. Even if you became pregnant today, Chuza won't be strung along for nine months. You know that."

She slumped onto the bench beside me and let her head drop to my shoulder. "What will stop him? If I had a drachma for every tear that man has wrung from me! It was bad enough when it was just me, but now he's preying on this dear child. What else can I do?"

"As you pointed out, Joanna, he makes us think we have no choice, but that's not true. We just need to keep searching for a way around Chuza's schemes. Oh, he is so evil!"

"Not evil. Sick," said Mariamme. "Understanding him better may help us find the solution to this problem. There are things you should know about Uncle Chuza."

"Tell us, then, though I'm not going to change my mind about him," I said, taking Joanna's hand.

Mariamme snapped a leaf off a branch and slowly peeled it apart as she spoke. "Several times since Father died, Chuza has told me that I remind him of my grandmother, Nahara. When he said this, I would ask him to tell me about Nahara, and he did, little by little. It's a long story."

"It's time we heard it," said Joanna.

Mariamme sat on the ground and crossed her legs. She kept peeling leaves as she spoke. "Chuza and Grandfather moved to Nazareth when he was thirteen years old. One of the first people they encountered here was Nahara, another outsider, who had recently arrived in Nazareth from Nabatea. She was hiding in the village to avoid an arranged marriage with a Gentile member of Nabatea's ruling clan. Only Chuza, Grandfather, and an elderly male relative who brought Nahara to Nazareth knew her reason for living here."

"Most of this we already know," I said.

"Yes, but what you don't know is that Chuza fell in love with Nahara."

"Chuza was in love with my mother? Impossible!"

"Remember that she was only a few years older than Chuza. As I said, he loved her but he kept his love a secret from everyone, including Nahara. He said he would crouch under her window at night just to listen to the sound of her breathing while she slept. He ran to the tops of the hills and shouted 'Nahara, Nahara, Nahara, I love you' into the wind so that he could hear himself confess his love out loud."

"Chuza lied to you," I said. "He's never loved anyone but himself." I stomped on a spider idling near Mariamme's knee.

Mariamme continued, "Chuza was shocked when Nahara married Grandfather and moved into their house. That only made his love for her stronger. Inhaling the fragrance of her hair in that small space and feeling the warmth of her fingertips on every object in it drove him wild with desire and jealousy. So he moved to his own house at the edge of the village."

I swallowed the lump in my throat because I had to ask my question. "Did my mother . . . did Nahara . . . love him?"

"Chuza said no. That she treated him playfully, like a pet. But that she didn't love him as he did her. And that brought him more suffering. However, when Grandfather came to understand what Chuza's true feelings for Nahara were, he insisted that Chuza leave Nazareth."

"Another lie," I said. "Chuza hated village living. I heard him say so, many times. He left Nazareth to fulfill his own base ambitions. Against Father's wishes, he returned to Jerusalem to make money and gain power."

But, as I said this, a tiny doubt crept into my mind. If Father had been angry at Chuza for leaving Nazareth, why had he given his son his house in Jerusalem? Had Chuza, smarting with the pain of banishment, taken up with the Romans as a kind of revenge against Father?

Mariamme shrugged off my remark. "Chuza wanted to stay in Nazareth to be near Nahara, but Grandfather threatened to tell her and everyone else about his love for her. Chuza feared that the whole village, including Nahara, would laugh at him, so he agreed to leave. The reason he gave for leaving was the one you know, but he made that up to keep his passion for Nahara a secret. Exposure of it would have humiliated him."

So Chuza had been in love with my mother. My head spun. "May I have some water?"

Mariamme held the jug up for me, and I drank straight from it. Water dribbled onto my chin; I spread it around my face to cool it. If there was a speck of truth in Chuza's story, it might explain the terrible fights he and Father had during my childhood and the longstanding alienation between them.

"This may be true," Joanna mused. "He did have a romantic strain in him, years ago. And sometimes, when he gets very drunk and feels sorry for himself, he mumbles about a lost love."

"This is why I say he's sick, not evil," said Mariamme as she swept her pile of shredded leaves off her lap. "If he's sick, maybe he can be cured. I feel a little sorry for him."

I remembered witnessing that strange, tender encounter between Father and Chuza the night before Father was killed. Father disapproved of Chuza working for the Roman-appointed Herod Archelaus. But he also acknowledged that he might have driven Chuza to it. "What a stupid, jealous fool I was," Father had said. And the two of them had embraced. This memory and Mariamme's story annoyed me because it upset my convictions about my brother. I didn't want that. I was comfortable just hating him. "Why didn't you tell me about all of this before?" I barked at Mariamme.

"Chuza asked me not to. He thought you would think he was a fool for loving Nahara. He hates being ridiculed."

"Yes, he'll go to great lengths to avoid it!" said Joanna.

"Though he delights in ridiculing others," I pointed out. "Wait. Ridicule. That's it!" I actually stood up without assistance. "Why didn't I see it sooner? Chuza's dread of public ridicule: we can use this to our advantage."

Mariamme and Joanna stared blankly at me. I explained, "The Law may *permit* a man to marry his niece, but do people actually *approve* of this?"

They continued to stare. Joanna said, "It happens so rarely, I don't know."

"I know what one person thinks of it," I said. "This morning I over-heard Naomi tell her helper Herma about Chuza's designs on Mariamme. Herma said, 'My father-in-law is a greedy lecher, too, and he's the village joke these days.'"

Joanna roared with laughter. "Yes! People need to see Chuza as a silly, old lecher. As a buffoon to be laughed at."

Joanna and I crafted a simple but brilliant plan. She would inform her customers, the wives of Sepphoris's wealthiest, most influential Roman men, that Chuza wanted to marry his young niece. She would portray him as ludicrously lustful and as losing his faculties due to his advancing age. She wouldn't let these women sympathize with her, but rather get them to laugh with her and interpret Chuza's treachery as a preposterous antic. After all, though Roman men would sympathize with an older man lusting after a young woman, there were prostitutes and mistresses to satisfy that urge. They would wonder what was wrong with this Jew. Why would a man, unless he were an unsophisticated provincial who was losing his mind, divorce his well-endowed, beautiful wife—and have to repay her dowry—in order to marry an undowered young woman who would soon make a cuckold of him? Joanna's Roman friends would pass this delicious gossip and their derision of Chuza onto their husbands. Chuza would become the target of every coarse wit in Sepphoris.

"But wait," Mariamme cautioned. "If Chuza learns that you initiated this, Joanna, he could beat you. He could even kill you!"

"With luck, he'll divorce me, but he won't harm me," she said confidently. "Because just as I have the power to spread the story, I also have the power to suppress it."

"How?"

"When he promises to drop his pursuit of Mariamme, I'll stop the ridicule. I'll confess to these same gossips that Chuza had never intended to marry his niece and that I had made up the whole thing to get back at him after a marital spat over his taking a new mistress. They'll feast upon this new tidbit and spread it around the whole town. Chuza's reputation will be restored, Sepphoris will enjoy the titillation, and Mariamme will be safe."

"But won't you then become a subject of scorn yourself? You may lose the very friends who helped you," I said.

Mariamme added, "And you'll be right back where you were, Joanna, still married to Chuza, except that he'll treat you even worse."

"Compared to protecting Mariamme, my reputation among the Romans is insignificant, as is Chuza's opinion of me," said Joanna. "And in time, Chuza will be grateful that I spared him an expensive misstep. You know, his secret about Nahara explains things about him that I'd never understood before. It stirs up a little sympathy in me."

"But you know we can't trust what he says," I reminded them.

"I still feel sorry for him," said Mariamme. "An unrequited first love, his father driving him away. That must've been very painful for a young man."

"And now he's an old man," I said. "These heartaches don't justify his preying on his niece. He should've put his disappointments behind him a long time ago." I kept my grief for Nahara locked into one small corner of my heart where I would occasionally visit with it for comfort. Chuza should do the same, not let it out and exploit my daughter.

When Chuza returned from Jerusalem a few weeks later, he found the whole city sniggering at him. A story circulated that Herod Antipas had ridiculed him by pointing out that marriages had been arranged between uncles and nieces in his family, but their purpose was to form alliances with other kingdoms! And Salvius Marcellus, a respected Roman of the Stoic school of philosophy, donated one of his own female slaves to Chuza, noting that an aristocrat with a penchant for young girls should have the dignity to satisfy his cravings in this way. Mortified, Chuza returned the girl to Marcellus with appropriate expressions of gratitude.

Though I hated to admit it, it was the Romans of Sepphoris who were our strongest allies in this matter. Ultimately, their influence liberated my daughter.

Shortly after this scandal had died down, Chuza sent a messenger with some coin, the original copy of my ketubbah with its bridewealth amount properly noted, and this letter.

> **Chuza to my dearest sister Danya, greetings**
> *I withdraw my offer to help you find a suitable match for your daughter. Please come home to Sepphoris with Mariamme and Gad. If you do not return soon, people will say that you are extending your family's stay in that village to hide from me.*
> **Farewell**

This self-serving plea was not enough to lure me back. I was determined that we would remain in Nazareth until Mattityahu returned from Rome and revoked Chuza's guardianship over all matters pertaining to our family.

There were other reasons to stay, as well. Gad began to sing. In the orchard and garden and along the dusty village road, he sang snatches of psalms and made up his own little chants. "Gad means happy/Gad is glad/He in Naz-ret/Never sad." Naomi and Herma sang his compositions and created their own as they wove. Miryam and her daughters hummed as they washed and sewed. Gad's playful music made music bubble up in all of us.

I also thought that Mariamme would benefit from further experiences of village living. Physical necessity, not intellectual pursuits, now consumed most of her day. She battled with the rodents over our food. Dust wafting up from the dirt floor, soiling the furniture and utensils, required her constant attention. She burned her hand baking loaves on the charcoal grate and wrenched her back dragging water from the well. Insects nesting in the roof's bundled reeds made a habit of dropping down into her hair and the cooking pots. She shrieked more in those first months in Nazareth than she had in all her life. A straw mat curtained her sleeping space from mine and from Gad's, affording her very little privacy. However, all these disadvantages seemed offset by her proximity to Yeshua. She never mentioned leaving.

One more reason to stay, in addition to my abiding suspicion of Chuza, was my health. I'd begun to drop things. Though I wouldn't feel my grip loosen, the crash of a pot or the sensation of water soaking through my tunic alerted me to the fact that some object had slipped or tipped from my hand. Walking became increasingly difficult. My stick didn't prevent me from stumbling. At mealtimes, maneuvering from my house to the courtyard table wearied me. I labored to swallow food and, sometimes, even my own saliva. I felt as if a thief had crept into my body and was pilfering pieces of my physical abilities, the gold I had once been so proud of. I was no longer the girl who could run and wrestle and throw a sling as well as any boy. Would the thief stay until I had nothing left, or would he leave soon, chased off by the sudden return of my good health? I had no way of knowing, but the loving care I received here stifled my terror of the looter.

Naomi's daily massages temporarily released the stiffness from my limbs and back. Miryam concocted new ways to prepare foods, making them easier for me to swallow. Despite our differences about Yeshua, Mariamme helped me, tenderly, with the simple tasks that had become difficult for me, like walking, reaching, and lifting. She prayed with me, plucking from her vast memory the psalms that she thought would bolster my courage.

My disabilities shrank the size of the world I inhabited, but I found beauty in small things I hadn't noticed before. I would run my hand back and forth across the surface of the perfectly planed, splinter-free table in my house, and admire the marvel of human craftsmanship. My tiny house was so well built that heat, rain, and cold did not penetrate its walls. I appreciated the skill and kindness it had taken to carefully lay each stone and pack it tightly around with mud. I sat in Miryam's garden for long periods of time. Sometimes I watched Gad at work there and recalled Tobiah's delight in his son as he gardened. Other times I just enjoyed the sun on my face, the calls of the birds, the play of the clouds and sun, and the smell of growing things. Miryam often joined me there. We talked about all kinds of things, meandering freely from topic to topic. Tobiah and I used to converse with such ease early in our marriage, but it had been years since I'd had this pleasure.

Of course we shared our worries and joys about our children. Miryam also had daughters who would need to marry in a few years, so finding husbands for them as well as for Mariamme concerned us both. Miryam also fretted that Shimon used his fists too freely, and that Yaakov was too strongly opinionated. Neither Matti in my family nor Yaakov in hers had yet developed the wisdom to be good heads of their families. Miryam was not above boasting about her children, either, though perhaps I encouraged it by bragging about mine.

One day as we lounged in the garden, Miryam pointed to a row of endive. "Look at the lovely webbing that spider is winding through the lettuce."

I recalled the horrid orange spider I had watched when I was a girl. Hapless insects twisted and struggled and met their deaths in the snare the murderer created. I extended my walking stick to sweep away the hideous net, but Miryam said, "Don't. That web will protect the vegetables from predators. Spiders, too, have their place."

Reluctantly, I withdrew my stick. It was her garden after all. The sun shone brightly on the dew-covered web. Miryam turned her head as she looked at it. She took a step sideways. "Danya, come and see this."

She helped me to my feet and we both examined the slender threads closely. In the sunlight, a gorgeous shimmer of blues, greens, yellows, and reds radiated in the spider's silk. Even I could appreciate the loveliness in the web. "Are the colors in the threads?" I wondered. "How could such beauty come from a spider?"

"I think the colors are in the sunlight," said Miryam. "But we need the web to reveal the beauty contained in the light, like we need the rain to see the rainbow."

Miryam was comparing a spider's web to a rainbow. But we believed that the rainbow was a link between the heavens and the earth, a sign of the covenant between The Holy One and His people. Surely a spider's web wasn't that. I hobbled back to my chair. When I tilted my head one way, I could still see the dazzling colors in the sun-drenched webs. When I held it another way, I saw only dark, murderous snares.

One deprivation of life in Nazareth, the lack of reading and writing materials, did disturb Mariamme. In the few moments of the day when she wasn't doing chores or caring for me, she paced, not knowing what to do with herself. When our stay in the village had extended into its third month, Yeshua stopped at our house one morning before setting out to work in Sepphoris. Mariamme was washing my feet since I couldn't bend over to do this for myself.

Standing in the doorway, Yeshua said, "Today I'm going to call on Chuza and ask his permission to bring a scroll from Tobiah's library to Mariamme. Which one would you prefer?"

"He won't admit you to the house," I warned.

"Then I'll find him at his work."

"Nor there."

"On the street, then."

"He'll detour into the baths."

"In time, he'll have to speak with me."

"You'll only make him angrier than he already is."

"We'll see."

I shrugged. "Yes, you will see."

Mariamme grinned at me as she dried my feet. "I told you Yeshua was different."

The young man pursued my brother, day after day, until Chuza finally decided to give him a hearing, probably to dismiss the pest, once and for all. On that day, as I had predicted, Yeshua returned to Nazareth empty-handed. "But Chuza and I had an interesting conversation," Yeshua reported to us as Mariamme folded the clothes she had washed that day. "I'm going to talk with him again tomorrow."

Mariamme gave me her I-told-you-so look. Most evenings after that, Yeshua stopped by to tell us that he had spoken with Chuza during the day, yet he never produced the promised scroll. I concluded that all of this was just an excuse for Mariamme and Yeshua to see each other. Or that Chuza was using Yeshua in some way the guileless young man did not realize.

Late in the month of Marchesvan after a communal Sabbath dinner, Naomi, my family and Miryam's lounged around in the courtyard. A horse and cart bounced up the rutted village road. The driver's head covering obscured his identity, but no good Jew would drive a cart on the Sabbath, so this man could be an enemy. Miryam's sons drifted over towards the woodworking shed to be close to the tools if they needed weapons.

Shimon crouched into a wrestling stance when the driver got closer, and we saw that it was Chuza. Yaakov, Joses, and Shimon, armed with carpentry tools, formed a circle around Mariamme. *Yeshua's meddling has raised Chuza's ire,* I thought.

Chuza reined in his horse and held his arms in the air. "I've not come to take her, boys. If I'd wanted to do that, I would've hired an army."

"Show him your weapons," I ordered the young men.

Gad waved and called out to Chuza. "Are you here for Sabbat, Uncle?"

"No, I see that I'm not welcome." He stayed in the carriage. "Mariamme, I've brought you some of your father's scrolls. Where shall I put them?"

Mariamme raised her arms in elation. "Really? Oh, thank you so much, uncle."

Chuza smiled like a boy who had delighted his mother with the gift of a wild lily. "You're welcome. I hope this will make your visit here more comfortable."

"It's the only thing I've been lacking."

I stayed slumped in my chair. I must've changed a great deal since Chuza had last seen me because he paled when his eyes settled on me. "Sister, I've brought writing materials for you. And letters you should see." His voice dropped. "Danya, I was told that you were sicker, but now I see for myself how you've declined. Please, come home. No tricks. Allow Joanna and me and your servants to care for you."

"No. I'm well cared for here. Leave me and mine alone."

He hung his head while Yaakov and Shimon unloaded the precious cargo and Mariamme fluttered around it. Yeshua whispered to Chuza. My brother nodded and said to me, "I'll leave you in peace, then, Danya. But I ask you to forgive me. I've been a fool. I'd like to make amends for the suffering I've caused."

"The only amends you can make are to leave my family and me alone. Go away!"

"As you wish." He picked up the reins and drove away slowly. His back stooped. He wore a wig. He must've lost a lot of hair lately. And some of his vitality as well. Perhaps the thief stole from him, too. Of course in his case, this was his own fault, and the wig was probably just another of his Roman vanities.

Mariamme ran into the house and came back out with two of the scrolls. She danced around the courtyard with them and said to Yeshua, "You've made more trouble for yourself than you may have realized. Now you'll have to build some storage shelves for these manuscripts."

"Yaakov has already done that," said Yeshua. "They're hidden behind his house."

"Yaakov?" wondered Mariamme.

Tentatively, Yaakov put his big, callused carpenter's hand on one of the scrolls. "Mariamme, I was wrong for saying you shouldn't stay here. I'm so sorry. But I've always wanted to learn to read. Will you teach me?"

Mariamme smiled. "It would be my joy to teach you to read," she said without hesitation.

My daughter's instantaneous forgiveness of Yaakov showed a generosity of spirit I didn't share. But I was proud of her.

While Yaakov and his brothers fetched and positioned the shelves in our house, I unbundled the letters that Chuza had labeled, "For Danya." I fervently hoped they contained some word from or about Matti.

Chuza had always been a meticulous record-keeper. These letters turned out to be copies of ones that Chuza had written and sent to places all over the world. The top one said:

> **To the Mighty Phraates, Ruler of the Great City of Sidon, greetings**
> *I seek my brother, Lev ben Micah, of the village of Nazareth in Galilee, in the land of Judah. He disappeared in the twenty-fourth year of the reign of Augustus. He is clever, literate, and well-born enough to command a substantial ransom. I will reward you for any information you can supply about him. His sister weeps for him, and I long to have my brother at my side.*
> **Farewell from Chuza ben Micah, Chief Steward of Herod Antipas, Tetrarch of Galilee and Perea. Dated this third day of Julius in the thirty-second year of the reign of Augustus.**

I inspected letter after letter. **To the Mighty Ruler of the Great City of Heliopolis. To the Mighty Ruler of the Great City of Palmyra. To the Mighty Ruler of the Great City of Petra.** Several were dated as recently as this year, the first year of the reign of Tiberius, but most were written long ago. Could these copies be recently composed fakes? No, the faded ink and discolored paper confirmed the age of the older ones. Chuza had been searching for Lev by letter for many, many years.

On the back of the bottom sheaf, Chuza had added a note to me. "Danya, Tobiah's locating Ezri gave me renewed hope in my efforts to find Lev. The agent I had hired to find our brother just after his disappearance found out nothing about him in four years, so I turned to letter writing. I had always hoped to surprise you by returning your beloved brother to you, but I have failed. Lev was my brother also, and, though you won't believe this, I loved him, too."

The salty spittle of regret pooled in my mouth as I reread the letters. All these years I had mourned alone. Needlessly. Chuza and I could have consoled each other, but I had judged him as too hard-hearted to grieve for our brother as I did. Another unjust judgment. And another loss. This one was my own fault.

While the renowned Roman physician, Celsus Manlius, stood outside our door, Mariamme set her jaw tightly and whispered to me. "I spend my days taking care of you, Mother, yet you only get sicker. How do you think that makes me feel? Here is someone who may be able to help you, and you want me to turn him away?"

"Yes. Because Chuza sent him. He's bribed the man to harm me or to fabricate some reason to require my return to Sepphoris."

"You're being stubborn, Mother. Celsus Manlius is the most distinguished practitioner of the medical arts in the world. For my sake, you must at least allow him to examine you."

"All right, all right," I said to appease her and my own conscience. My miscalculation of Chuza's affection for Lev still smarted. But I took pains to speak loudly so that the physician could hear me. "I won't take any medicine he prescribes. It could be poison. Nor will I follow any treatment regimen he prescribes. It could injure me further. And I won't be left alone with him."

Mariamme pushed aside the mat and admitted a surprisingly young, nearsighted Roman. He rolled back the folds of his toga, freeing thin, boyish arms. "Your brother thought that I wouldn't get through the door, so I'm already more successful than he predicted," Celsus joked.

"What is my brother paying you?" I demanded.

"An exorbitant sum just to examine you. And more if I cure you." He had an open, honest face.

Celsus Manlius placed a bench only a span away from me, sat upon it, and peered at me. His eyes were enormous, but gentle, like a deer's. But I wouldn't be fooled. He smelled strange. "This man smells of nard," I said to Mariamme.

"The oil used to anoint the dead?" she said. "Mother, how rude of you!"

Celsus held the forefinger of his small hand to his nose. "Your mother is correct. Yesterday we buried my Jewish uncle, whose illness had brought me to Caesarea, which is where your brother found me, by the way. In my haste to come here, I must not have washed thoroughly enough. Please bring me a basin."

This Roman had a Jewish uncle. Well, at least that explained his kind eyes. And he'd traveled all the way from Rome to tend to the man. I'd answer his questions, but nothing more.

"Are you in pain?"

"Some cramping in my limbs, but no pain."

How long had I experienced this weakness? When did I first feel the stiffness? When did the clumsiness start? Was it difficult for me to swallow? Did anything relieve the symptoms?

He took a tiny mallet from his sack. "I'll demonstrate first on your daughter, so you don't think I'm attacking you." He tapped the little hammer on Mariamme's shoulder, elbow, wrist, and knee. Each time, the tapped body part jumped slightly and then settled down. When he did the same to me, each joint leapt up, as if it were straining to reach something high above it. It would twitch and keep twitching, until I restrained it with my hand.

He asked me to put my foot on the floor, and, leaving the heel down, to lift my toes. I couldn't do this. He held my wrist. His hand was as gentle as his eyes. He asked me to open my fist. I couldn't do this either. "Try again," he urged. "Can you stretch out one finger, just a little?"

No. I couldn't. A deep rift settled between his eyes. He sighed then shook his head solemnly. "I wish I could help you, but I cannot. One other time I saw an illness such as yours. I tried everything I knew, but I only added to that man's suffering. I won't harm you with any experiments." He turned away from me and put his hammer back into his sack.

"You can't do anything?" Mariamme said. "I was told that Celsus Manlius was the most accomplished physician in the world." She crossed her arms and blocked his departure.

"I'm sorry. The medicine I know cannot cure your mother. But some people have been cured by priests or religious healers," Celsus said calmly. "Exorcism has its place, if you believe in demons. You can look to those kinds of cures." He touched my shoulder. "May your God protect you."

"Wait," Mariamme said. "The man like my mother. What happened to him?"

Celsus cast his large eyes down and rubbed his forehead. "He died in a few months. I am very sorry."

"No!" Mariamme shrieked.

Celsus left quickly. I opened my arms to my daughter and she fell into them. "Shhhh. It's all right. This is just another trick of Chuza's," I assured her. "If Chuza can make me believe I'm dying, he thinks we'll hurry back to Sepphoris. The man Celsus was talking about was probably twice my age. I have many more years to live."

But I knew that even Chuza couldn't have bribed that good, gentle man. Celsus had shined a light on what had been lurking in the shadows and disquieting my soul for months. The thief's work was almost done. I was dying. Only thirty-three years old and I was dying.

I lay awake for hours that night, as rain rattled the reeds on the roof and questions rattled my soul. What would happen to my children? What if Matti did not return from Rome to take his rightful place as head of the Kamith family? Perhaps he never got my letter or chose to ignore my demand and stay in Rome. Maybe he died on the dangerous journey back to Galilee. It could be months or years or never before we received news of him. Mariamme and Gad would be the ones left waiting and wondering now, as Chuza and I had waited all those years for Lev.

And what about Mariamme? If she were not properly married before my death, what would become of her? She could end up back in Chuza's hands. Even if Matti lived and acted as her legal guardian, Mariamme might continue to reject the rightful place assigned to her. By never marrying or by joining herself to Yeshua or some other peasant, she would squander the blessings The Holy One had bestowed on her.

And who would care for Gad? What if Matti and Mariamme had spouses who wouldn't tolerate Gad's peculiarities? He could die a beggar, rejected by his own people. It was too early in the season for the rains to begin and too early for my life to end!

When, finally, I fell into a light sleep, I dreamt again of the shore of the Sea of Galilee. In this version of the dream, I boarded a boat while my children clustered on a dock and waved to me. Suddenly, a storm blew in and the mooring line snapped. I was cast adrift. The wind howled and huge waves pitched my tiny craft about. Even though my children were close by and threw me a rope, the line did not stretch all the way out me.

The next morning I sent Mariamme and Gad to the village center. They could occupy themselves with the festivities associated with the late olive oil pressing. I had much to think about and needed time by myself.

Celsus Manlius had said that the man with my symptoms died in a few months. Died. In a few months. Not much time. And yet, if I became completely helpless and was in great pain, a few months would be too much time. Now I envied Father and Tobiah their sudden, unexpected deaths. One moment living and the next moment not. How fortunate for them. They didn't have to attend a long, agonizing procession to their own tombs.

My fright-filled night had left me feeling exhausted and battered. I could go to my bed and stay there. I could bid the fog of my Sheol to roll in. It would hear my screams for help, pull me in from the storm, and numb me in its embrace. The idea of spending my last weeks shrouded within its gray mists sorely tempted me.

But no, I must not go there again. I must flee from this temptation. I pulled back the doorway mat and spotted Shimon stacking wood by the outdoor oven. "Could you help me get to the festival?" I asked.

My walking stick supported my stronger side. I put my other arm around Shimon's shoulders, and he lifted and dragged my right side, nudging me through the crowds that mingled around the food stalls and trading booths.

"I wish they'd stop staring," I said.

"No one's staring. Well, maybe a few are." He laughed. "But you must admit, the two of us are a strange sight."

I was the woman with a peculiar-looking son, a daughter who could read but not weave, and a son who had gone to Rome to collaborate with the enemy. I suddenly preferred being alone rather than joining the village festivities, and pointed to the top of the ridge above the village. "Would you take me up there instead, Shimon?"

He frowned. It was a long way and a steep climb.

"I know it's far. But you're the only one strong enough."

"I can try," he said. Shimon grunted with the effort of hoisting me up the hill path. Once he tripped on a tree root, and we both almost fell, but he managed to get me to the top.

As I had hoped, the hilltop was deserted. The rest of the village was eating, drinking, playing, arguing, bartering, criticizing, laughing, and creating a raucous din down below. They would continue to do this, very competently, without me. For generations to come.

Shimon settled me down between the two large rocks on the edge of the ridge overlooking the valley below. "Thank you. You can go now," I said.

"But how will you get down?"

"Tell Mariamme to come with a donkey."

"But should you stay here by yourself?"

"I'll be fine. Please, leave me alone now."

"I don't think my mother would want me to."

"Go."

Alone on my memory-laden mount, I waited motionless, expectant, sitting erect as Father used to do when working on his writings. Waiting for inspiration. Waiting for enlightenment. Waiting for Adonai to speak to me. Waiting, waiting, waiting.

But a dust cloud did not rise from the valley below. A light did not break through the clouds across the valley. The scent of balm did not fill the air. "Where are You, Adonai?" I whispered. "I am so frightened. I'm so small and so alone. Where are You?"

Silence. Only silence.

I gazed out at the vista most beautiful to me in all the world. How I loved this sight! How I would miss it. The vineyards layered down into the olive groves that spilled out into the vast, fertile grain fields of the plain. The trellised vines rested in weary splendor from the rigors of producing their cherished fruits. The branches on the olive trees that had dragged low with their ripening treasures now danced high above the ground, as if in celebration of their accomplishments. These plants had yielded magnificent harvests this year.

But my garden would not. Blight infected it. My desire to serve the people of Israel had been pinched back and had never bloomed. The family that Tobiah and I had created and carefully cultivated was withering and might die out completely. I had allowed Matti a choice, and he had chosen to leave his family and his patrimony. Mariamme tossed aside her gifts to pursue a foolish dreamer, and yet I couldn't bring myself to force her into a marriage she didn't want. Gad would never have a wife and children. No matter how good his heart was, no one would give his daughter to a man who thought like a child. The Kamith family might vanish from the earth, and this would be my fault. I would have failed my husband and my people. I had sinned. I needed time to atone, to mend this breach between me and The Holy One and me and my children. More time! Please, please, more time!

I looked down upon the grain fields, plowed and poised to accept the sowing before the rainy season set in, and an angry flame ignited in me. These fields would be granted the time they needed to complete their mission. But I would not. A wheat seed would complete its cycle of life and be harvested in the autumn, but the scythe would cut me down, unripened, in the summertime of mine.

The fire inside me enlivened my limbs. I struggled to my feet and teetered on the edge of the precipice. I lifted my arms in anger. "Why now, Adonai?" I shouted. "Why do you take me now? I am trying to do Your work. You must give me time to finish it!" With great difficulty, I curled my fingers into fists. My outstretched arms heaved like branches in a windstorm. I almost lost my balance and tumbled down the hill below me. "Answer me! Why now?"

Hands gripped my shoulders. "Step back a little," said Naomi. "You're scaring me."

"And me, too," said Miryam.

"Shimon should have told you I wanted to be left alone."

"Come back with us," said Naomi. "We brought a donkey."

"No. I'm not ready to."

"Then we can sit here together, as we did when we were girls," said Miryam.

They settled themselves and me down on the ground. We wedged between the two tall rocks, as we had done so long ago before our first separation from each other. The two of them smelled like baking bread. They must have left their ovens to chase after me. Miryam took one of my hands and Naomi took the other; we looked out over our beloved valley together.

"Mariamme told us what the physician said," said Miryam. "It's a shock. No wonder you wanted time to yourself."

"I can't die yet. My work isn't done," I said.

"Good," said Naomi. "You want to live. Let's go back to the village now, and we'll help you do that."

"No."

"What work of yours isn't done?" Miryam asked.

"I have to provide for the continuation of the Kamith family," I said.

"Fine, fine," said Naomi. "We'll help you with that. I have a wealthy Jewish customer from Jerusalem with a handsome son who would be just perfect for Mariamme. Now, no more talk about dying." She grabbed my arm and tried to pull me up. I stayed in place.

"Are you certain that the Kamith family's continuation is The Holy One's will?" asked Miryam.

I dropped her hand. "Certain? Of course not! Who knows what The Holy One really wants? I've never been certain, as much as I've searched. Maybe I've done everything wrong and I'm being punished for it now." A knot arose in my throat. I pushed my fist against it. "Maybe He did want me to join a revolt after all, and by marrying Tobiah and raising impious children, I rejected His plan for me. Perhaps I've misused His gifts and angered Him."

Naomi said quietly, "If you hadn't persuaded Efron to ransom me, I would be dead. That doesn't sound like a misuse of your gifts."

Miryam rubbed my back. "We never could have survived in Nazareth without your help when we first returned from Egypt. The food, the live-stock, the seeds, the household goods. And you convinced your husband to educate Yeshua. You've made good and generous use of your gifts as far as I'm concerned."

"But those were small kindnesses," I said. "This may sound foolish to you both, but I thought I might have been especially called, like Judith or Esther, to undertake some holy mission for our people." I kicked at a rock near my foot and watched it bump down the hill, bouncing off a vine, slamming against a larger rock, and crashing into another vine before coming to rest. "I feel like that rock, pushed and bumped by people and circumstances beyond my control. Now here I am at the end of my life and I don't yet know what The Holy One wanted of me."

They were silent, trying to understand. Then quietly, Miryam said, "We're all called to holy work, Danya, whether we are a queen, a peasant, or a prophet."

I picked up another rock and threw it. It landed with a thump and stuck, going nowhere. "Still, now that my life is coming to an end, I'm deeply disappointed that it has turned out to be so insignificant. I haven't even managed to raise righteous children, much less help restore God's kingdom to Israel. What a fool I am!"

Naomi sniffed. "There you go again, Danya, feeling sorry for yourself. I would take your insignificant life. Along with the faithful husband, the children, and the big house in Sepphoris."

I glared at her. My fingers itched with the urge to rip at the shrubbery of her hair like I used to do when she annoyed me as a child.

Miryam laughed. "If there were a prize for the smallest, most insignificant life, I would win it."

Miryam's sense of humor could still sweeten my foul temper. Naomi put her head on my shoulder. "I'm sorry, Danya. I know I'm being hard on you, but I want you to fight back. I don't want to lose you!"

I sighed. "I'm so tired of fighting. I just want to understand before my life ends."

Miryam tilted her head and stood up. "Do you remember how I brought you both here and told you about the light that enclosed me?"

"Of course," I said. "You were specially chosen, like I wanted to be but wasn't."

"No," said Miryam. "I wasn't alone in the light. Remember that I told you that I had company, the company of magnificent sounds, of people and animals, of the sea and the wind. We were all wrapped up in the light together, all part of something vast and intelligent and beneficent. To me, it meant that all of creation is favored, that we are all loved, and all called to perform sacred works every day of our lives."

"Hmmmm. That's a nice idea," said Naomi. "But how is lugging water from the well and weaving a few threads, as I do, 'sacred'"?

Miryam knelt in front of us. She was smiling. "Most of us never know what tasks Adonai has assigned specifically to us, but when we act with love and compassion and justice, we carry out His plan. Don't you see? Taken together, our seemingly small acts of goodness to each other and to the rest of creation are great. They outnumber the stars!" Despite the long shadows cast by the late afternoon sun, Miryam's face glowed as she spoke. "It is our collective goodness that will restore God's peace on this earth, not the armies of kings and revolutionaries."

She wound her arms around me, and Naomi did the same. I lifted my own clumsy arms onto theirs. The pressure of their embrace melted down deep into me, all the way through to my raw, angry heart. We stayed silently encircled like this until my trembling stopped.

Then Miryam slipped her hand under my elbow. "Come now. You do have more time. You have today, at least. Let's go home."

I allowed my two friends to help me up and onto the donkey. The scent of baking bread lingered on their hands. Naomi had once said that angels smelled like baking bread.

A week later I was dozing on the garden bench. I was awakened by an embrace I had feared I would never again experience.

"I'm home, Mama," said Matti.

I'd never been happier to see anyone in my life! I held my son until my arms drooped, though my heart wanted to hold him all the day. "Oh, look at you, Matti: you're a man now!" During the year of his absence, he'd grown as tall and lean as Tobiah. And he was handsome, too, with Lev's intense dark brown eyes and wild black curls.

"I thought that my letter hadn't reached you," I said.

"What letter?"

"The one demanding that you come home, the one saying that Chuza had betrayed us."

"I never received that, Mama. I'm here because Uncle Chuza sent me this letter. Here, read it for yourself."

Chuza ben Micah to Mattityahu ben Tobiah, greetings
It is imperative that you return to Sepphoris immediately. Your mother is very ill. Your sister needs your protection. You will find

them in Nazareth. I am not a suitable guardian for them. You must come home and take up your rightful place as the head of your family.

Farewell

"Chuza's letter frightened me so that I left Rome the very day I received it. Mama, what has happened here?"

"You're sure Chuza sent this? It doesn't sound like him."

"He did. He's here with me now. But he says you'll have to tell me what's happened. He says he's too ashamed to."

A remorseful Chuza. A miraculous work of The Mighty One? Or a new scheme? "Find Mariamme and bring her and Chuza here. We have much to talk about with each other. And hurry. There isn't much time. . . . "

JOURNEY'S COMPLETION

Danya of Nazareth to The Holy One, greetings

This is my last letter to You. It will be full of splotches because I often drop the pen. However, I pray you will accept this blemished offering of my imperfect hand. I thank You for granting me thirty-three years of life, though I respectfully wish I could have had more time. Thank you for so many blessings. My family, my husband, my children, my friends, my people, the sacred land of Judah, Your Word to us in Scripture. So many, many generous gifts. I beg forgiveness for my sins, which are many. Often I failed to follow the directives that You in Your goodness allowed Judah ben Hezekiah to convey to me. Though my husband for a time acted unjustly towards me, I confess that I treated him unfairly as well. I tried to change him into the man I wanted him to be; he was trying to be the man he thought You wanted him to be. I've been unjust to other people as well: Yeshua, Naomi, and Joanna in particular in years past, but I've tried to correct that. I've also failed to love kindly: Romans, almost always, and often my brother Chuza, though many times he deserved it. Adonai, I now walk humbly and what a joy it is! Until now my pride had kept me from understanding this directive of Yours. But walking humbly, as a child does, trusting in Your love and care for me, is the only way I can walk now. I am completely dependent on other people. I am clothed and bathed like a child and soon I will need to be fed like one. "Walk humbly," Judah told me, "and you will see Him." I do see You now. The people who walk and clothe and bathe me, You are there in them, aren't You? Mariamme, Razi, Naomi, and Miryam: their arms are Your arms, aren't they? You are so clearly enfleshed in them that—Miryam smiles when I say this to her—sometimes I wonder if You are a woman. I wouldn't have known this if I hadn't been forced to walk humbly, as I do now. Joanna wants to summon more physicians, exorcists, and even magi to find a cure for me. Mariamme believes that Yeshua could restore my health if I asked for his assistance. But I say "no" to them because I am already healed. My soul is healed. In my dependence, I feel the intensity of Your love for me. Now that I walk humbly I understand that You have been here all along, at every moment of my whole life. It was easy to see You in my blessings: in the births of my healthy children, in the threads of Naomi's artistry, in the bounty of Galilee's rich harvests, in the love Tobiah and I shared, in Matti's safe return to us. But now I see Your Light everywhere. The dust cloud has finally settled; the once obscure is now manifest. You were in the whirlwind and in the rainstorms; in the heat of my fever and in the chill of my desolation. You were there with me in the deaths of my mother, father, brother, and husband, in my Sheol, in my children's rebelliousness, and even in Chuza's schemes. The colors of Your Light show themselves to me not only in the rainbow, but, as Miryam once showed me, in the spider's web as well. Glimmers of Your Divine Self flash all around me, illuminating Your tender care for me and for all You have created. One final gift I thank You for is the blessing of writing. I have written the story I know best, that of my own life, which I now understand is the story of my journey to You. In doing this, I was reminded that ink is a liquid, too, and like drops of rain and the threads of a spider, it has disclosed colors I never knew were there. Of all my treasures, writing is the one I am most pleased to bestow upon my daughter. I pray that the ink flowing from her pen will reveal the colors in which, always and forever, You make Yourself known to us. When I am afraid, a lump forms in my throat. The lump is often there now. I fear that my death will be very painful. What dulls my dread of suffocation is knowing that You have been with me in every breath I have taken. So I trust that You will be there with me in that awful moment when I cannot take another. And when I cannot take another humble step, You will lift me gently into Your loving arms.

Farewell from Danya of Nazareth

This is the year 3776 since the creation of the world.

EPILOGUE

I am Mariamme. My mother's father was Micah who was born and educated in Jerusalem and whose writings provide direction and consolation to spiritual seekers. My father was Tobiah ben Mattityahu, of the Kamith family of Sepphoris. My mother preferred to be called Danya of Nazareth. Shortly before her death, she disclosed that she had been writing an account of her life from the time she was a young woman. After she died, I retrieved her writings from the places where she had hidden them for me. They have proven to be an inheritance of inestimable riches.

Tomorrow is the tenth anniversary of her death, an appropriate day for me to set out on the great journey of my life. Tonight I feel the imprint of my mother's fingertips on the back of my hand, guiding my pen to the inkwell, dipping it, and putting it down on this sheaf of papyrus. Though her dying wish was for me to write, until this moment I have not attempted to fulfill it. My language lacks her coloration; I did not have an important subject. But tonight the ink flows like stormwater coursing through a wadi.

After many years, Yeshua has returned from the Essenes. In the morning, I will join him and a few others to travel around Galilee, carrying a message of hope and deliverance to our people. Joanna will accompany us. She says Yeshua's teachings "intrigue" her, but I believe they will soon take root deep in her heart, as they have in mine.

I am grateful to my friends and family who, by assuming my responsibilities, free me to join this holy adventure. Gad will live under Naomi's care in Nazareth, an arrangement pleasing to both of them. He will grow food for their table and collect plants for her dyes. Miryam's grandchildren have befriended him, so he will have the playful company he needs.

Yaakov has agreed to take over my tutoring in the village. He has custody of my wax tablets, my grandfather's scrolls, and other materials. During the rainy season and in stolen moments of the busier times, he will teach boys how to form their letters and read from the Torah, as I taught him and them. He promises he will allow girls to continue looking on.

My brother Mattityahu happily occupies himself with his wife, their five children, and the family estates. He designed a beautiful synagogue for Tiberius, Herod Antipas's new capital, but built nothing else there. An ancient necropolis was unearthed beneath the city, rendering it unclean for Jewish habitation. Matti seems to have adopted Mama's disdain for all things Roman, with the exception of its architecture and engineering. He has accepted his position within the hereditary priesthood and serves his turn at the Temple with the rest of his course. He has converted my uncle to a stricter observance of Jewish Law. Well, a little bit, anyway. Chuza teases Matti, calling him "a Pharisee," but they are close friends, and Chuza delights in being a grandfather to Matti's children. The Kamith family estates recovered and now flourish, thanks to Chuza's sound advice and supervision in the early years of my brother's stewardship of them.

Matti permits me to use my mother's mohar, which Chuza restored to her before her death, for my own support and that of my friends. He has never required me to marry. It was Matti who finally told Joanna and Chuza and all of Nazareth to cease their matchmaking efforts on my behalf since I prefer to remain unmarried.

Since my mother's death, her written words have counseled, consoled, and inspired me. I know her well enough through them to imagine her face tonight as she learns I will follow Yeshua. Her eyebrows touch in a thunderous frown. She calls Yeshua "a landless, revolutionary peasant." But I know now that she, too, was once a young woman who listened for a call and longed to perform a great service for The Holy One. So I see her frown ease into a smile of acceptance when she recognizes that I have been called to a great and holy mission, something that she had so fervently desired. "Yes," she whispers to me, "turn to the light."

For it is a light, a bonfire, that draws me to Yeshua. I burn with the desire to share his prophetic message, wise teachings, and healing works. This fire frightens me, but it transports me with joy. I am anxious; I am at peace. I am burdened; I am freed.

And so, as my mother wished, I will use the treasure that she, my father, and my grandfather have passed on to me, the gift of the written word. The ink that flows onto these pages will record the sayings and stories that Yeshua employs in his teachings. I will write in Greek, as well as in Aramaic, so that Yeshua's teachings can be read by people of other lands as well as our own. My hope is that all peoples will come to know this spirit-filled, compassionate man, and like me, be changed forever.

But the task ahead awes me! I fear I am unworthy. I may fail. What if I do not remember correctly? What if I make mistakes as I translate from spoken Aramaic to written Greek? What woman has ever dared undertake such a work?

There they are again. My mother's fingertips on the back of my hand, guiding me, emboldening me, commissioning me. . . . I dip my pen into the inkwell and begin to write.

SAYINGS OF YESHUA OF NAZARETH

Be merciful even as your Father is merciful.

Do not judge, and you will not be judged;
do not condemn, and you will not be condemned.
Forgive, and you will be forgiven.

I am telling you, love your enemies, bless those who curse you, pray for those who mistreat you.

So do not worry, thinking 'What will we eat,' or 'What will we drink,' or 'What will we wear?' For everyone in the whole world does that, and Your Father knows that you need these things. Instead, strive for His Kingdom, and all these things will be yours as well.

AUTHOR'S NOTE:

Most scripture scholars theorize that a collection of the sayings of Jesus existed and predated the gospels, and that Matthew and Luke independently used this source in composing their gospels. This hypothetical collection of the sayings of Jesus is referred to as "Q," from the German word *Quelle,* "source."

The "Sayings Q Gospel," also called "The Lost Gospel Q," is believed to have been distributed among the earliest followers of Jesus. Then it was lost and, to date, no copy of it has ever been recovered. Its author is unknown.

ACKNOWLEDGMENTS

I am very grateful to the following readers of earlier versions of my manuscript whose insights and enthusiasm kept my fingers on the keys: Margery Rieff, Joan Meskill, Janet McGivern, Mary Miller, Marilee Matthews, Peggy MacNamara, Terry Broccolo, Francie Byrne, Ede Snyder, Alice Byrne, Nancy Deneen, Rev. Steve Ryan, OSM, Joan Naper, Rosemary Naphin, Elaine Miller, Lisa Nagel, Marge Braband, and Joe Durepos. My proofreaders, Katie Byrne and Joan Naper, generously shared their professional talents with me. I appreciate Luis Calzada Zubiria's help with my author photo. Special thanks to Ede and Aaron Snyder for introducing me to the name Danya when they bestowed it on their lovely daughter.

My deepest appreciation goes to my family members: husband, Art, daughters Brigid, Martha, and Mary Kate, and son, Art. Each supported me, in his or her own way, throughout the book's many drafts and revisions. My late brother, Rev. Richard Byrne, priest, monk, and scholar, first sparked my interest in the study of the historical Jesus. His enthusiasm for the subject eventually led me to the writing of this book. I only wish he were here to share my joy in Danya's coming to life.

The scholarship of many historians, archaeologists, anthropologists, theologians, and Scripture scholars was essential to my understanding of ancient Palestine. I relied most heavily on the research of the following: Rami Arav and John J. Rousseau, Richard Batey, Marcus Borg, K. C. Hanson and Douglas E. Oakman, Richard Horsley, Tal Ilan, Elizabeth A. Johnson, Jonathan Reed, E. P. Sanders, and James F. Strange.

Finally, I owe a boundless debt of gratitude to the members of my writing group: Cecelia Burokas, Shelley Hamilton, Linda Schneider, and Jan Tubergen. There simply would not have been a Danya without their intelligent criticisms, unfailing encouragement, and generous sharing of their talents. And laughter. Lots and lots of laughter.

www.ingramcontent.com/pod-product-compliance
Lightning Source LLC
Chambersburg PA
CBHW070215030726
47505CB00006B/1692